NOT QUITE ROOMMATES

AMY LARK

berry lark

CHAPTER 1

THREE MONTHS. Jonah Sinclair tried to focus on that fact instead of the fine ass swaying before him. He walked down the hallway to the apartment he'd agreed to sublet for three months. The longest he'd been in any one place since college. New city, big enough to get lost in. Northeast coast in autumn. New job, only one office. No travel. At twenty-eight years old, it was time for no more fucking hotel rooms.

The petite blonde leading him was legit hot. Any man would willingly follow that ass showcased in denim anywhere she led. But he wasn't following her to fuck her. He didn't plan on doing anything with his new roommates, let alone fuck either of them. This one definitely qualified as completely fuckable. If the other one was as gorgeous, he'd have to make arrangements to get laid on the regular to stop himself from making a mess of his living situation.

If things went south, he couldn't leave. He'd keep his hands to himself. This had to work out. The last few years of constant travel had worn on him. He wanted something less nomadic.

"Did Brenda tell you much about the apartment?" Sophie,

the hot blonde, turned toward him for a second. Her big, blue eyes tracked up his entire body before meeting his gaze. Interest lay in those eyes, but no heat.

She liked what she saw. Hopefully she had a man and it wouldn't become an issue. He didn't need to deal with a roommate who decided he would be her next snack.

"Don't need much." He kept his tone gruff and his eyes blank.

He wasn't here to make friends. Maybe at work, but not in this apartment. These roommates were temporary. Three months and he'd figure out if he needed to find his own place. He hadn't wanted to commit to a year-long lease when his new job might not work out, but he couldn't imagine living out of another goddamn hotel room. Thus the sublet.

She stopped at the door and glanced at him again. Her lips pinched and her eyes narrowed. Her mouth opened but then she closed it again with a small shake of her head.

He stood still and let her evaluate him however she needed to. He wasn't a threat. He didn't plan to interact. He just needed a place to lay his head at night and occasionally fuck.

Blowing out a breath, she opened the door. He followed her through.

"I'm in love with Logan O'Connell and we're going to live happily ever after," someone in the room professed.

Sounds like this other roommate wouldn't be an issue.

Sophie moved to the side and his gaze landed on the woman sitting on the couch with her back to them against the arm of the couch and her iPhone facing them. The couch sat in the center of the open kitchen/living room, with the back toward the kitchen but in line with the TV sitting on a low stand. The woman reclined against the arm with her bare feet up on the cushions in front of her. The woman on the other end of the iPhone pointed at him and Sophie.

"Wha—?" The roommate on the couch glanced to the side without turning around.

"And this would be your other roommate, Lacy." Sophie stepped slightly behind him.

"Call me back." The woman on the screen winked and disconnected.

His new roommate, Lacy, took a deep breath and set her phone on the coffee table as she stood. She brushed popcorn crumbs from her kitten pajamas while she turned. Her brown hair was pulled up in a messy bun. Her pink-painted toes peeked out from beneath the oversized pajama pants draped over them. He'd never been a foot guy, but something about those toes. . . .

When she straightened, she barely reached his chin.

Her brown eyes started on Sophie, but as soon as they landed on him, they widened. Where Sophie's gaze had been assessing, Lacy's seemed intense and innocent. As a good-looking man, Jonah was used to attention, but Lacy took her time raking her gaze over him. While she was distracted, he took in more of her small frame. Her smooth, golden skin peeked out where the bottom button of her cotton pajama top had come undone. As she took a deep breath, her chest rose and fell, drawing his attention to her decent-sized breasts. She stood with confidence as her eyes caught his.

She had a pretty face, with a dimpled chin, button nose, and large eyes. As he studied her, her pink lips slightly parted. Her brown eyes were wide and unassuming. *Soft and sweet* floated through his mind, but that didn't stop his thoughts from wandering down naughtier pathways.

Not a woman he would normally look twice at, but also not someone he'd kick out of bed. That hint of innocence drew him, begging him to corrupt her.

"Lacy Hatcher, Jonah Sinclair. He's subletting Brenda's room." Sophie's voice broke the stare-off. Lacy's gaze jerked to Sophie. For a second, he wanted Lacy to return those eyes to him. She wasn't sex on a stick like Sophie, but he couldn't deny she tempted him.

Shit, this situation had gone from bad to worse.

Lacy smiled and held out her hand. "Nice to meet you."

Her voice was bright and welcoming. His fingers ached to touch her, but he flexed them. Touching her was not a good idea. He glanced at her hand and gave her a brief nod of acknowledgement before turning to Sophie. The less he interacted with either of these women the better.

"Where's the room?" The sooner this tour was over, the sooner he could crash for the night. He'd have to put out some feelers for tomorrow night though. He needed to get this urge out of his system. Obviously, it'd been too long if pink toenails fascinated him. He knew a few women in this city who were usually good to go whenever he came to town.

"Um, right this way." Sophie led him down the hall. "This is our shared bathroom. Your room is here. Lacy's and mine is over here. Since I travel a lot for work, it'll mostly just be you and Lacy here unless you travel too."

He glanced Lacy's way without a smile and no comment. At least Sophie would be out of sight and out of mind, but that left him alone with Miss Fuck-me-toes. His gaze ran over her. He couldn't resist. Her frolicking kitten pajamas consisted of loose pants and a button-down shirt. Tilting her chin up, she crossed her arms and tightened her lips. She might have been trying for fierce, but those pajamas and her bare toes ruined the effect. When his gaze finally met hers, the corner of his lips crept up slightly before he managed to go blank again.

She had a guy and he didn't mess around with taken women. Besides, being here was temporary, like everything in his life. And she didn't seem like the type of woman that did temporary. Like she said, she wanted happily ever after. A fairytale. True love and all that bullshit.

Sophie opened the door to his room and he stepped inside. She hung back for a second before coming to stand in the doorway. The room had red walls. Huge loft style windows. A king-sized bed, closet, a decent armchair, nightstands. Better than the same hotel room in different cities.

Sophie backed out of the room and into the common area as he headed her way. "It'll work for you?"

The kitchen seemed a little small, but it would do. A bathroom was a bathroom. As long as it had a toilet, sink and shower, he'd be fine.

"It'll do." He didn't look Lacy's way. He could feel the weight of her eyes on him though.

He didn't need to look to remember the way the fabric of her pajamas draped over her in a way to suggest the slender curves beneath. Those hints of golden skin peeking out made him want to explore. Would her skin be as hot to the touch as it looked?

Fuck. No, he needed to get his head on straight and find someone not living with him to take the edge off. He refused to skim over Sophie in her tight jeans cradling that ass and the T-shirt hugging her breasts. He didn't know who tempted him more at the moment, but it shouldn't matter. Both were off-limits, at least for the next three months.

"Here's the key and the code for the door downstairs." Sophie grabbed them from the kitchen counter peninsula and handed them to him. "When will you move in?"

He pocketed the key and code in his low hung jeans. "I've got my things downstairs."

"Great." Sophie went over to stand next to Lacy.

He nodded, not really looking at either of them and headed out the door. Fuck, maybe before he moved out he'd see if they'd be interested in a threesome. The angel and the temptress.

~

Holy crap crackers! A gorgeous beast had just wandered through Lacy's living room. His voice, dark and gravelly, sent shivers down her spine. He'd looked her over and then dismissed her.

No one had told Lacy they'd be getting a guy for a roommate. Especially a hot one with an attitude. Fortunately, her type was hot guys who were *nice* and not interested in her. She'd given up on guys with attitudes after college.

As soon as the door shut, Lacy turned to Sophie. "Him?"

Sophie blew out a breath with her hands on her hips. "Apparently he's some friend of Brenda's who got a new job in town and needed a place for a while. That's about the extent of what I know. He's not much of a talker."

"Ha, that's an understatement."

He'd left her hand hanging in the air instead of shaking it. Who did that kind of stuff? It was polite to shake someone's hand when offered. Not look at it like she offered him rabies with a side of syphilis.

"At least he'll be a quiet roommate, maybe." Sophie pushed her hair from her face. "But nice eye candy."

Eye candy or not, it didn't matter. After all, Lacy had been in love with Logan O'Connell ever since they first met six months ago at Taylor and King. She had been the new copywriter and he'd been the new marketing guy. Perfect didn't begin to describe it. The best meet-cute ever. They'd met in the coffee room and he'd offered her a mug from a high shelf. Then they'd both sipped their coffee together as if they were totally in sync. Coffee and Logan. Heaven.

Lacy sank onto the couch and cringed, remembering the

conversation Sophie and Jonah walked in on. Even though she and Beth were both twenty-six and gainfully employed adults, they had been best friends since grade school. Talking to Beth always made Lacy feel like a teenager again. Especially when the topic focused on guys. Which it usually did. Well, one guy on her end.

Not knowing when Sophie and Jonah came in, Lacy had brazened it out, hoping they'd heard nothing at all, and especially not her spouting her hopeless infatuation with her crush. "How much did you guys hear?"

"You mean about your blazing love for Logan?" Sophie laughed as she sat next to Lacy. "Mostly just your undying love. I'm sure he would have overheard it eventually anyway."

"Yeah, well." Lacy sighed. Sophie was right. If he lived here, he'd hear it eventually. Most people knew Lacy's business. Secrets weren't exactly her specialty. She only hoped the people at work hadn't guessed yet. "That was supposed to be a private conversation."

"Which is why we have bedrooms. For privacy." Sophie rolled her eyes and turned the TV on.

"Better reception in the living room." Lacy yanked the afghan off the back of the couch and pulled it over her legs.

"You didn't sound at all stalkerish," Sophie reassured her as she patted Lacy's knee.

"Well that's good. I'm not a stalker, you know. I work with him."

It wasn't like she stole his underwear or stood outside his apartment and took pictures. She didn't even know where he lived. She just liked him and wanted to be more than coworkers.

Lacy pulled her phone up to text Beth about the new roommate. Beth had moved halfway across the country after they graduated college. "I really like Logan and maybe someday he'll feel the same. It happens that way sometimes. You know, friends to lovers."

Sophie snorted. "I think you at least need to be friends first for that to happen."

The door opened to the apartment and Lacy thought she'd been prepared to see Jonah again.

Nothing could prepare her for the giant that would be sleeping across the hall from her. He had to be well over six feet tall. His black T-shirt and jeans clung to his lean, solid build. His dark blonde hair was buzzcut except on the top where it was long and fell over his blue eyes. He had a well trimmed beard, a few shades darker than his hair with just a hint of red in it.

She accidentally made eye contact with Jonah again. Little sparks lit along her spine. She dropped her gaze and noticed he carried a suitcase and a guitar case. Guitar? Maybe he had a hobby or maybe he was a musician? Was that why he was subletting?

"Do you play?" The words were out of Lacy's mouth before she could even think to stop them. She couldn't help herself. He would be living with them, after all. They should get to know each other a little bit. Right?

He glanced over at her as he passed behind the couch. His eyes narrowed as if her question vexed him but she shrugged. He looked away.

She wasn't surprised. Most men didn't give her a second glance. Overall, she was unremarkable, especially when next to her roommates. It really didn't bother her anymore. Guys like Jonah were definitely after a hot chick. She didn't have the bra size to attract a guy like him. Not that she wanted to attract him.

Besides, she didn't do attitude. And she had Logan.

Gah, she needed to focus.

"What? Just trying to be friendly," Lacy said with a forced smile.

Sophie snickered next to her.

He gave Lacy a brief nod before heading into the bedroom across from hers. Whether that nod was an acknowledgement of just trying to be friendly or affirmation of playing the guitar, Lacy wasn't sure she'd ever find out.

"This is going to be fun," Lacy muttered as the door shut behind him.

Jonah didn't make an appearance for the rest of the evening. After an hour, Lacy had finally relaxed when Sophie bid her goodnight before slipping off to bed. Lacy remained on the couch, vegging out to *High School Musical* while texting with Beth.

Sweet uncomplicated high school romance. Her favorite drug of choice.

You really should give up on Logan, Beth texted. She'd filled Beth in on the new roommate. Beth had been interested, but Lacy knew it would only be a matter of time before Beth circled back to the Logan conversation. The same song and dance Lacy had heard for the past ten years.

Beth had Lacy's best interests at heart and just didn't want her to get hurt. After all, when the crush either exploded or fizzled it was Beth who helped Lacy pick up the pieces.

Lacy leaned back, stretching her spine. Always a different guy, but the same argument. It started Freshman year of high school when Lacy had been in love with the star quarterback, Jack. Who, by the way, had been seriously hot, but only went out with cheerleaders. However, one time in the hallway between classes, Lacy had dropped a pen and he'd picked it up and handed it to her. He'd even smiled at her. Gah, that smile. She'd been a goner after that. She'd spent two years being hopelessly in love with the guy until he went off to college. She'd even tried out for cheerleading, so she'd be perfect for him. She didn't make the team but she'd tried, for him.

This time, though, she might actually have a shot. *Why should I give up? It's only been six months. He's gorgeous and nice. We work together. There's potential.*

Overall, she didn't have the best track record with guys. Every guy she'd wanted hadn't exactly been banging down her door, so she really hadn't had a relationship. She'd never even had a guy friend before. Wanting to remain and appear available for her crushes, she hadn't really looked at other guys.

Her overprotective brothers, of whom she had too many, hadn't even given her any real-world knowledge about guys. Besides to stay away from guys. She had no idea how to attract or keep men.

Her phone dinged with Beth's text. *Because it's not going to happen. It never does. You pin all your hopes and dreams to a guy who is totally unattainable.*

Beth sent another. *Okay, you don't want to give up. Fine. Stop waiting and make it happen!*

Lacy's heart raced. Like ask him out? She couldn't just ask him out. The air stuck in her lungs. What if he wasn't attracted to her? How awkward would that make the office? Every day having to see him after he rejected her. No, thank you. Besides she wanted him to make the first move. She'd been bold once and it had backfired horribly.

She shook her head. She texted, *I can't just ask him out.*
Why not?
I want to make sure he wants to want me.

The three little dots appeared on her screen and then went away. Lacy slouched down farther into the couch. A whole musical number later, Beth finally responded.

Fine. Make a plan then. Talk to the man and see if you guys even have anything in common besides the fact he's hot and you think he's nice.

Flirt. Make actual eye contact and smile. Dress in a way that he'll notice you.

Find a way to spend time with him outside of work, even if it's not a date.

Lacy swallowed and looked around the empty room. If she wanted Logan, she had to do this. She didn't want to settle for any guy, but who cared if dreaming about a guy took her off the playing field for a while. Offers weren't exactly pouring in for her. The last date she'd been on had been almost two years ago and had been a complete disaster. The guy thought she'd sleep with him on the first date. As if. She didn't do random hookups.

If she wanted Logan to be it for her, she had to go all in. She could do this.

Okay, Lacy replied. *I will. I'll go all in and make him ask me out.*

Good. If he's who you think he is, he'll be yours. If it doesn't work out, promise you'll give up on crushes for a while.

I love you and don't want you to get hurt. Someone will love you for you even if it isn't Logan. Beth's text made her heart swell.

Got an early morning tomorrow. Night.

Love you too. Night. Lacy set her phone down.

This wasn't like cheerleading tryouts. It wouldn't require her to know how to do a cartwheel. Just a few small tweaks and actually talking to Logan. Okay, the talking part might be hard, but she was determined.

This weekend, she'd do research on flirting. By the time Monday morning rolled around, she'd be all over it!

Lacy turned the TV off and started her nightly checks. Most nights she ended up alone in their three-bedroom apartment. Sophie travelled and Brenda usually stayed at some guy's place.

Lacy glanced at Jonah's door. Would he be around? Would he even come out of his bedroom? Did she want to engage with him? After all, this was only temporary. Brenda would return eventually. Thankfully.

Lacy shook her head while she checked the locks on the door. She proceeded to the kitchen and made sure the window was closed and locked. After, she checked the windows in the living room, even though none of them had been open today. All the while, she could hear her mother's voice reminding her that she lived in the big city now and who knew what kind of weirdos were out there.

It seemed like a good enough habit she just went with it. Better safe than sorry.

She shut off the light and moved into the hallway. After a quick trip to the bathroom, she started out and stopped as she came face-to-face with Jonah. Okay, not face-to-face. But face to very naked, very toned chest. Holy crap, he had actual six pack abs and those muscles that made a V leading into his jeans, hanging low on his hips. Any lower and she'd be able to see his. . . .

She swallowed as she tipped her head back to meet his eyes. They reminded her of the Caribbean waters near the beaches of Jamaica. This close with the bathroom light, she could see flecks of green in the blue. Guys shouldn't be allowed to have eyes that pretty.

"I'm sorry," she said but couldn't exactly leave the bathroom with him right there, blocking her in.

His eyebrow rose over one eye before he took a step to the side to let her pass to her room. She inhaled a breath and caught a whiff of his cologne. He even smelled like the Caribbean, standing on a beach on a sunny day with the scent of the ocean on the breeze. A pulse of energy went through her, keying her up. Probably just remembering all the rum Beth had made her drink while they'd been in Jamaica two years ago.

He moved farther out of the way.

That chest though. . . . She'd seen pictures of guys like that and she imagined Logan was similarly shaped, but seeing it, right there, in her face had been. . . unexpected? Her fingers twitched as she wondered what those muscles felt like. Warm, firm, maybe soft. He cleared his throat and she lifted her gaze to his eyes again. A hint of amusement danced in them.

Oh, hell. She'd been caught checking him out when he was letting her pass.

She should have taken the out, but she couldn't help her curiosity. She crossed her arms under her breasts. "Do you know Brenda well?"

He leaned against his doorframe and slid his hands into his pockets, pulling the jeans down a little farther and showing off more of his solid frame and the black waistband of his boxer briefs. She almost wiped at her chin to see if she actually drooled. A body like his would draw anyone's atten-tion. It didn't mean anything.

However, she couldn't seem to stop dropping her gaze to take in more of his golden skin stretched taut over so many muscles. So many dips and curves, her fingertips tingled. He gave a curt nod, pulling her attention back up.

What had she asked? Oh, Brenda.

"You don't talk much, do you?" When she was nervous, words just tumbled out of her mouth. And a half naked giant in her hallway while she stood barefoot in her kitten covered pajamas made her nervous.

"I'm not looking for friends." The low gravel of his voice hit her oddly. Warmth flowed through her and her stomach flooded with butterflies. Must be her nerves. He was a stranger. A stranger who would sleep across the hall from her tonight and for the foreseeable future.

"We don't have to be friends." She put one barefoot on top of the other and pulled her shoulders back. "But if you're going to live here, we're going to cross paths. Especially with one bathroom."

Trying to play tough, she gestured with a jerk of her chin over her shoulder at the bathroom.

His gaze dropped to her feet and her toes curled under. She nearly squirmed from the intensity of his eyes. Her breath caught in her chest. Gah, he was gorgeous and the way he looked at her made her feel weird.

"I'll try to stay out of your way if you stay out of mine." His gaze met hers and she could see the determination in his as well as a coldness. Okay, not a nice guy.

She dropped her arms to her sides, trying to be less confrontational. He may not be nice, but she was. "Brenda and I would try to consolidate grocery shopping. To make it easier. There's a list on the fridge for when we need to replace something. You're welcome to add to the list. . . if you are going to be around? Or do you travel for work?"

Please say you travel for work. Being around him day in and day out would be difficult if he didn't talk much and continued to be as standoffish as he was now. It would be awkward, and she didn't handle awkward well. Ergo, the talking.

"I start work on Monday," he finally said.

She inhaled and huffed out her exhale. Well, this was going splendidly. "Do we need to figure out a bathroom schedule for the workweek? Or do you work second or third shift?"

He shrugged. "It'll work out."

She narrowed her eyes at him. Time to give him the girl reality trip. "I take really long showers in the mornings. Then

I have to do my hair and makeup which takes forever. I also get up as late as possible to get as much sleep as possible. Brenda always went in later than me, so it wasn't an issue. But if you want to be late for your first day, we can 'wing it.'"

The corner of his lip curved slightly before the hint of a smile disappeared. He pushed off the doorframe and shifted closer again. The heat of his body engulfed hers. Lord, he was warm. And tall. And smelled ridiculously good. She swallowed and tilted her chin up to meet his eyes again.

Was he trying to intimidate her? Was it working? She swore her body temperature increased from the heat in his eyes.

His slight smile drew her attention to his full lips as he said, "Guess we'll just have to learn to share the shower. You can wash my back and I can wash yours."

CHAPTER 2

BRENDA HADN'T MENTIONED her skittish roommate when she offered Jonah her place.

He'd never been in one place long enough for a year lease. Thankfully, Brenda had needed someone to sublet for a few months, that way she wouldn't lose her room in the shared apartment. It would give him time to see if this staying in one place could really work.

Last night, the poor nervous roommate's mouth had dropped open at his innuendo and then she'd fled. If he thought for a moment she'd take him up on the offer, he never would have said anything. But she was more fluff than bite. She reminded him of a little wren who puffed up to appear fiercer than it actually was, but when it came down to it was still just a scared little bird.

She'd had her light brown hair pulled into a messy bun. Her huge brown eyes had travelled over him repeatedly as if she were memorizing him. That hint of a blush on her delicate features made her seem fragile. And her sun-kissed skin almost glowed in the light from the bathroom.

A button had slipped open on her pink kitten pajama top,

revealing a hint of cleavage, especially when she crossed her arms under her breasts, which she probably hadn't intended for him to see. She hadn't been flirtatious. Just like a little bird she'd tried to appear fierce, but as soon as he made a move, she'd fluttered away.

But he'd counted on that. Relationships weren't something he put much thought into and that woman had *relationship* written all over her. His whole life had been spent going from place to place. He'd never stayed anywhere long enough to become attached to anything or anyone.

His watch read almost nine o'clock on Saturday morning and the little bird hadn't made an appearance yet.

Jonah had left earlier for his workout and returned to the apartment with some fresh fruit and stuff for his morning smoothie.

He stood in the kitchen, chopping off the stems when Sophie came out of her bedroom wheeling a bag. She rapped on Lacy's door and hollered, "See you next weekend. Text if you need anything."

A faint grunting noise came from the room which seemed to satisfy Sophie. Sophie reminded him of his little sister. A tough petite woman who would smack down anyone who messed with her or hers. She also didn't look at him like she wanted to consume him as a snack like some women did, which helped. Sure, she'd checked him out, but her eyes hadn't shown any heat.

He'd been concerned when Brenda mentioned two female roommates. He couldn't afford to have any distractions right now. But he'd deal with it.

Sophie stopped in the living room and turned to look at him in the kitchen. Her lips tightened and she released her suitcase before approaching the counter and taking a seat on the stool opposite him. She studied him.

Jonah lifted his gaze to hers and she didn't drop her eyes.

"Brenda vouched for you," she said.

He didn't blink, not sure where she wanted to go with this.

"I don't know you, but I know Lacy. We've been friends since college." She snatched a piece of strawberry from the cutting board and popped it in her mouth.

He wasn't sure what she wanted from him, but she seemed to have an agenda in mind. He lifted handfuls of fruit and added it to the yogurt and ice in the blender, but he waited to turn it on.

"Lacy's not a normal girl."

He lifted his eyebrow at that. Who called a woman in her twenties a girl?

Sophie fluttered a hand in the air. "Just be nice or don't, but she's one of the nice ones so don't fuck with her."

What the hell did that mean? He had no intentions of doing anything with either of his new roommates. Not fuck them. Not even split a pizza with them and definitely not braiding each other's hair. He didn't get close to people. Made it easier when he had to leave.

Sophie seemed to be waiting for a response.

"I won't," he assured her.

Her lips tightened and she narrowed her eyes at him before she nodded. She slid off the stool and walked over to her suitcase. "I'll be back in a week. Our list of numbers is on the fridge if you need anything. Lacy normally calls the maintenance guys. They think she's sweet. They fix things faster if she calls."

He glanced up at her.

Sophie held up her hands. "Yeah, I know, you'd think the hot girls would get things done faster, but turns out they think of Lacy like a daughter who needs taking care of." Sophie smiled and shook her head. "She's like our little sister. It's probably why we're protective of her too."

Everyone wanted to protect the little bird. Not surprising. He wondered if anyone treated her like a woman. Then shook that thought out of his head. He didn't care about his new roommates. A new job would be stressful enough. He needed to focus on work and figuring out how to live out of a room rather than a suitcase.

Sophie headed out the door. "Enjoy your week."

He gave her a nod before the door closed behind her. He turned on the blender to finish his smoothie. The thing ran so loud he couldn't hear anything. He was surprised when a hand touched his side, sending sparks of awareness across his skin.

He stopped the blender and looked down. The little bird was definitely ruffled today. Her messy brown hair covered her eyes which didn't appear to even be open. Her arms stretched out in front of her, briefly touching everything. Her pajama top had slipped off her slender shoulder. Without thinking, he reached down and put it right.

His fingers brushed over her warm skin and the warmth lingered as he took them away. A tiny shiver raced over her.

She lifted her hair from her eyes and squinted at him. "Too noisy."

He smiled. Dammit. He dropped the smile the next instant, but he couldn't be sure if she'd seen it and would think they were friends now. Sure, he kept up with a few people, but he didn't need to add to the list. She put her palms on the counter next to his cutting board.

"Coffee."

He raised his eyebrow at her, but she didn't seem to notice. It wasn't a question, more like a demand.

She glared up at him and said, more emphatically, "Coffee."

This was the sweet girl everyone loved? He almost laughed, but he seriously worried she would shiv him with the knife from the cutting board if he did. A pot of coffee sat on the warm setting next to him. Sophie must have made it earlier.

He reached up and grabbed a mug off the open shelf and handed it to Lacy, but she had him blocked in and pushed the cup against his side. "Coffee."

Shaking his head in amusement, he grabbed the pot and poured some into her cup.

She lifted it to her lips and took a sip. Her lips curved into a calmer smile and she said, "Thank you."

She retreated and went to the couch, huddling into the corner and sipping her coffee. Her bare feet tucked beneath her.

He poured his smoothie into a glass and went to sit on the other end of the couch. It wasn't his initial intention. If she hadn't emerged, he probably would have just drunk it in his room. He probably should have drunk it in his room anyway, but he was a little curious if the "nice girl" would reappear after enough coffee was in her. Would she be at all embarrassed about how she had behaved pre-caffeine?

The more she drank, the more she uncurled from her position until she released a heavy sigh. Her hair sat in a tangled mess on top of her head, very different from the "messy" bun last night. She had a pretty face without makeup on. Honestly, she didn't look like she needed makeup at all.

"What?" Her brown eyes were wide open and met his. Just a hint of attitude behind that one word made him shrug at her. Still more homicidal than sweet right now.

She drank a little more, like the fierce little bird she was. She set the mug on the coffee table and gave a full body stretch. Her top inched up revealing the curve of her tiny waist and her flat stomach. His mouth went dry, and he took a drink.

He could imagine slipping his hands beneath those loose

pajamas and finding ways to make her at least have a more pleasant morning. He shook that thought out of his head as she finally spoke.

"Let me guess, you are one of those people that pops out of bed looking just as hot as when they went to bed and requires no drug to make you jump out of bed and start exercising. Minimal effort." She glared at him, but it was a little softer now, like she was actually almost awake.

His athletic shorts and his tank spoke for themselves. That and he hadn't showered yet, he probably didn't smell the greatest covered in dried sweat.

"Some of us require beauty sleep." She latched onto her mug again and drank some more. "Blenders and sleep don't mix."

He grunted to let her know he heard her. Not that he'd change anything, but. . . . "Sophie left."

Her hand went to her hair to try to pat it down. Failing horribly. "She does that."

"You worried?" He finished his smoothie and set the glass on the coffee table.

She raised her eyebrows as she looked at him over the rim of her coffee cup. "Should I be?"

He shrugged. He didn't want her to worry about him. After all, he just needed a place to sleep and that was what he had here.

She shrugged back and her pajama top slipped down her shoulder again. "I'm sure we'll do great. You learn to get your smoothies on the way to the apartment and we won't have to have conversations before I've had my first cup of coffee."

His fingers itched to move her top back in place, which made no sense to him. Usually with women, he wanted to take clothes off, not straighten them. He shook his head. "I make my own smoothies."

Another eyebrow raised. "Hmph."

"Shower?" He leaned forward to get ready to stand.

"Thanks, I'm good." She looked at him over the coffee rim with a little smug smile on her lips.

He fought the smile that tugged at his own lips and nodded instead. "Next time?"

Her cheeks flushed red and he couldn't stop his smile as he walked past her to get to the bathroom. Fuck, he might actually like her.

SATURDAY WAS LAUNDRY DAY. Lacy didn't see Jonah again that morning. Drinking her second cup of coffee, she waited until she heard the shower go off and the click of his bedroom door before she took a quick shower and changed into a pair of jeans and a soft blue long sleeve shirt for the day. She pulled her hair up into a bun and decided just to ignore the elephant in his room.

Fortunately, their apartment had a washer and dryer. A very small washer and dryer, but it worked. As her clothes washed, she pulled up Netflix on the TV and scrolled to *To All the Boys I've Loved Before*. She now had three movies to watch since the sequel and the final movie were out. She let out a happy sigh. Perfect Saturday afternoon.

By midafternoon, she'd just finished the second movie as she heard Jonah's door open. A wave of his ocean scent hit her as he walked past the couch. It smelled like someone had poured sunshine in a bottle and applied it liberally. Not obnoxiously, just soft and inviting. She tried to ignore him as he went into the kitchen and grabbed a drink from the fridge. But then she figured she should at least offer to make things work.

"I go grocery shopping tomorrow. If you want me to pick anything up for you, just add it to the list." She didn't turn to see if he did it or not. He probably wouldn't even answer her. But she would be polite. She grabbed her phone to check for messages.

"Going out tonight?" he said from behind her.

She set her phone on her lap and stared straight ahead. It sounded like a question, but it had been a long time since anyone had asked her that. Certainly, he wasn't asking her to go out with him? Her chest squeezed at the thought. Right?

"Is that a question or a statement?"

"It's Saturday. Don't you go out?" The low growl that undercut his words sent a shiver down her spine like he was the big bad wolf and she was little red riding hood. That was one fantasy she'd never considered. She might keep it in mind for the next time they needed a perfume ad idea for a client. At least then she'd have something more than cute to contribute.

"Not particularly." She got up and pulled her last load from the dryer.

"Boyfriend?"

"What?" She lifted her gaze to his. He leaned against the counter in the kitchen like he had nothing better to do in his black button-down shirt and low-slung jeans. He wore work-style black leather boots that could kick serious butt if he wanted. The guy was hot. When she dragged her gaze back up to his face, it was blank.

"Never mind." He walked into the bathroom. "What the fuck?!"

He came out with one of her pink bras dangling from his finger. "What is this?"

"It's called a bra." She jumped up and snatched it from his finger. Her face flushed with heat. She took it in the bathroom to hang it back up to dry with the others on the shower curtain bar.

"Why?" He followed her. Standing in the doorway, he

grabbed the upper trim and almost leaned into the bathroom.

"Typically they are used to hold up breasts." She did not want to have this conversation. If he'd been a woman, they wouldn't have this conversation. But her brothers were just like that. They hated anything girly hanging around the bathroom at home.

He growled as if her answer wasn't good enough. He growled? Who growls?

She swung around to face him, knowing her cheeks were almost as pink as the bra at this point. "If you are referring to what they are doing currently? They are drying. When things are wet, you hang them to dry so they won't be wet when you wear them next."

His blue eyes held hers, entranced, like staring at the ocean during a storm as wave after wave crashed in. Each one threatening to pull you under. Hypnotic. A shiver coursed down her spine.

"Why don't you hang them in your room?"

"It'd damage the floors." She gestured to the bathroom floor, pointing like he was an idiot. "Tile." Then she pointed to the doorway. "Wood. Water bad."

He didn't release her from the bathroom or his gaze. She crossed her arms over her chest and straightened. If he was trying to intimidate her, it wouldn't work. She had three older brothers. Sweet would only get her so far with them. Sometimes she just had to be plain ornery.

His eyes softened a little before he smacked the trim and began to retreat. She took the out as soon as it was available.

"How long?" he said, right as she ducked under his arm.

She paused, feeling the heat of his body. "Sometimes overnight, but usually before bed."

"Fine."

She smiled up at him and practically skipped into the

living room away from him. Score one for Hatcher. Welcome to girl world, Sinclair.

❧

THE BATHROOM HAD LOOKED like a fucking lingerie store. Jonah closed his bedroom door and took a deep breath.

Lacy's bright eyes had tracked him from the bathroom to the bedroom with mild interest before returning to her show.

He hadn't shared a bathroom with anyone for years. He figured he'd see floral scented shampoos and purple poofs with softly perfumed shower gel in the shower, but he hadn't been prepared for underwear.

Women's undergarments had covered the bathroom. Bras *and* panties. Not sweet grandma undergarments either. Lace-covered, soft-colored bras and lace-edged matching silky underwear. It might as well have been a declaration from Lacy she was a woman who wore sexy panties.

And his brain had melted with images of Lacy last night and this morning in those pajamas that should have been the furthest thing from sexy, but on her body. . . . Shit. Add silky panties that begged to be touched and. . . .

Fuck.

He wasn't supposed to think about his roommate like that. She should be a non-sexual being who happened to share the same space. Instead, she curled up on the couch, watching some movie, looking sweet and wholesome, but now he knew her taste in naughty underwear.

Add to the silky skin she'd flashed him this morning and he needed to get the fuck out of there and get laid before his dick made him do something truly stupid.

He glanced at the clock and cursed. It was still too early to go out. He walked over to the chair and picked up his copy of *American Gods* by Neil Gaiman. He hoped it would distract him for a while before he could reasonably go out.

As the light outside the window faded, he set down the book. Still a little early but fuck it. He could grab a bite to eat and drink at a bar before heading to the club.

He stepped out of his room and closed the door. Lacy looked up at him with wide eyes. The book had helped, but his gaze dipped down to her breasts. Her shirt clung to her curves. He needed to leave. He crossed behind the couch on his way to the door, catching her peaches and cream scent.

At the door, he stopped. Maybe he should ask her to join him for dinner at least. To be nice. Silence filled the room as the sound cut off. He lifted his gaze to find her curious eyes.

What the hell was wrong with him. No sharing of food. No taking out the roommate. No being nice and making her believe he was someone she should get to know.

He wasn't.

He shook his head and strode out the door. Tugging it closed, he locked the door from the outside. He knew exactly who to find tonight to get the little bird out of his mind.

CHAPTER 3

Without opening her eyes, Lacy became aware of a woman's voice and a dim light. She blinked the sleep from her eyes and tried to figure out what the hell was going on. She dug herself out from under the blanket.

Darkness still surrounded her, but a soft glow of light came from over the back of the couch. She had apparently fallen asleep while watching Netflix. Not an uncommon occurrence. The TV had auto shut off at some point, so it had to be well after midnight.

"Jonah," a woman's voice sighed from behind her.

Lacy froze. The light came from the kitchen and apparently Jonah hadn't come home alone.

The woman gasped and moaned, followed by the rustle of clothing. What the hell were they doing? Lacy's cheeks heated. Okay, she knew what they were doing, but where in the process were they?

Maybe they were only making out and would head to the bedroom shortly. The sounds seemed a little more involved than kissing though. Was that a zipper? If Lacy peeked over the back of the couch, would she be getting a PG, PG-13, R, or NC-17 show?

Guess Sophie didn't have the chance to have the "your bedroom is your privacy" talk with him. Of course, Lacy having a private conversation in the common area and Jonah being inside someone were completely different and shouldn't have been up for the same level of discussion. It should have been a given.

She could only assume they hadn't seen her under the blanket on the couch. . . or had they? Was that a kink? Doing it with your roommate in the room? She didn't know if she wanted to know if it was a kink. Or his kink.

A soft moan filled the room, followed by a feminine gasp.

Jonah probably should have mentioned that particular fetish. Or at least discussed whether she wanted to take part in his twisted sex game. Not that he talked enough for that to actually come out.

"Jonah," the woman's breathy voice exclaimed. Apparently, she really liked whatever he was doing. The sounds really didn't help Lacy much though.

Lacy could wait here. With the blanket over her head. They hadn't seen her, hopefully, and would eventually move to the bedroom, right? She just had to remain quiet.

Suddenly the wine she drank prior to falling asleep pressed on her bladder with a sense of urgency. Great.

"Do you like that?" the woman whispered. Jonah moaned soft and dark. The sound made Lacy press her thighs together.

Maybe Lacy could sneak away before they noticed her; after all, they were occupied. It made sense, but to figure out the best time and to find out if they could see her, she'd have to look. She cringed and heat flooded her cheeks again.

Would they think this was her kink? Watching? She was pretty sure that was an actual kink.

The noises, rough and deep, were definitely pointing toward the NC-17 rating. Which in her vast experience—yeah, right, she mentally chuckled—couldn't possibly last long once they got to those noises. But then again, the romance books she read seemed to indicate some men cared if a woman came and could go all night. Talking with her friends, though, she knew that was mostly fantasy. Beth even claimed to have a ten-second man. In and then quickly done, but that also didn't seem to be common.

Lacy had read an article claiming five minutes was average, but the range was crazy from seconds to almost an hour. Her bladder might make it five minutes but much longer than that and she'd be out of options.

Her thoughts distracted her from the sex noises for all of a few minutes.

"Do you have protection?" The woman's husky voice filled the silence.

Crap. Well, apparently Lacy misjudged the progress. She should just run for the bathroom. They'd know she was up anyway as soon as she closed the door. Maybe they'd think she came from her bedroom. Maybe they wouldn't see her and think she hadn't seen them. Maybe they'd figure out to use his bedroom rather than the common area for sex.

The wrapper tore. After a moment, the woman cried out in pleasure and seemed to really be enjoying herself if her noises were anything to go by. Well done, Jonah, but that didn't help Lacy's time crunch problem.

Of course, Lacy's own experience with sex hadn't sounded like this. There had been no talking and not a lot of noises. . . from her at least. Besides, she was fairly certain she would have heard these two even in her bedroom if she weren't such a heavy sleeper. Which Jonah didn't know what type of sleeper she was. There he went being rude again.

Her bladder made her aware time was of the essence.

The noises the woman made escalated. How long was this going to take?

Curiosity would always be the bane of her existence. Now she wanted to see what they were doing because the woman sounded really into it. Maybe the woman was faking it. Would Lacy be able to tell if the woman were faking it?

Lacy held her breath. She needed to go to the bathroom and soon. The longer she stayed here the worse it would be when she emerged. If they even saw her. Maybe they were too occupied to notice her. She moved slowly and planned on peeking over the back of the couch as quickly as possible to verify their location and determine whether they would see her leave the couch.

That was the plan.

As quietly as possible, she positioned herself and slowly raised her head. The kitchen counter peninsula came into her view and so did the side torso of the woman. Huh? Her shirt hung open, unbuttoned, as she pressed her breasts down onto the counter. Her face was turned away from the couch.

Lacy's cheeks burned hot. Was the woman comfortable like that? By her moans and words of encouragement, she seemed to be enjoying herself. Lacy shook her head.

The woman wouldn't see Lacy when she made her mad dash for the bathroom. The woman's skirt gathered around her waist. Her ass and legs were bare and pointed into the kitchen so Lacy only saw her bare hip with the angle of the couch. The woman wore really tall heels, which seemed to help her lean over the peninsula, braced on it.

Okay, seeing this should embarrass Lacy, but she couldn't help her curiosity. After all, the nudity was discreet. She tried to stay purely clinical—just to satisfy her curiosity, but then her gaze shifted.

Jonah stood behind the woman. His shirt from earlier

hung open, revealing his sculpted chest and abs. His hands gripped the woman's hips. His pelvis pistoned into her as she pushed back against him.

Lacy's breath caught and her bathroom emergency skittered to the far reaches of her brain. Analytical flew out the door when Jonah entered the equation. Sure, the woman had been sexy, but she'd seen enough ads like that to make her almost immune to it.

But Jonah. She had never seen anything this erotic before. Maybe it was the live motion. Her sex pulsed, startling her. Her initial purpose temporarily forgotten as she watched Jonah. The couple of X-rated films Beth had tried to show her when they were teens she'd only seen through the cracks between her fingers as they laughed. She couldn't have mustered a chuckle if she tried in this moment. She didn't want to look away.

It was more like a really steamy romance novel brought to life in front of her than porn since she couldn't see much of the actual goings-on. The woman's head remained turned away as she made encouraging noises. One of Jonah's hands slipped around the woman's hip, capturing Lacy's attention as it disappeared between the woman's legs. Another throb went through Lacy and her heart ricocheted in her chest. Almost as if Jonah had touched her there instead of the woman.

The woman cried out and tensed against him, but he didn't stop his hips. His movements became faster and harder, chasing after something Lacy couldn't understand. Her heart pounded and her breath shortened. Her insides clenched.

Oh my God.

Lacy lifted her gaze to Jonah's face. His eyes were opened and focused on hers.

Oh my God!

She froze. He saw her. Watching them. Oh, hell. His expression didn't change and he didn't stop pumping into the woman. Lacy's chest rose and fell in time with his thrusts. Heat coursed through her body. He didn't look away and his eyes held her captive, pinning her in place, watching him in this intimate moment she shouldn't even be aware of.

A tug low in her belly startled her. Her breath caught and her body felt heavy. His eyes never left hers and she couldn't seem to look away either. His lip curled up on the side in a small smile and her insides trembled. The woman cried out in pleasure again and he thrust a few more times. His groan rippled through her. His face tightened as he gave himself over to his pleasure but his gaze never left Lacy's. Finally he collapsed on the woman's back. His body covering hers as he pressed a kiss to the woman's nape.

The connection broken, Lacy slid down on the couch and threw the blanket over her head. Her chest rose and fell hard. Her face burned and her whole body felt like a raw nerve waiting to be found. He'd watched her watching them. Her pulse ran riot throughout her body. What would she say? What would she do?

The sound of clothes rustling made her wonder if they were putting them in place or becoming more stripped down. Surely, they'd go into his room or leave now, right?

Her body trembled. She couldn't get his eyes out of her mind and that hint of a smile. Her insides whipped around like a hurricane and the throbbing had become relentless. She clamped her thighs together against the incessant heartbeat between her legs. Crap. Crap. Crap.

What was she supposed to do now?

A door opened.

"Are you coming in?" The woman's voice was low and coaxing.

"Give me a minute." His voice rubbed at Lacy in a way

that wasn't natural and did nothing to disrupt the hurricane within her.

The door shut and she jumped, but she gripped the blanket tighter around her. What did a guy do to a girl who watched him have sex? She had no freaking clue and didn't want to find out. She definitely never expected to be in this position. She didn't even like sex.

For her, when she reflected on it after the fact, sex had been messy and left her feeling empty.

His footsteps drew closer. The heat of him reached through the blanket, scorching her, as he stopped beside her. The coffee table groaned slightly when he sat on it.

"Little bird?" He released his breath.

She squeaked. *Little bird?* She could just pretend to be asleep. Sleep watching, that was what she'd done. She tried to slow down her breathing, but her heart pounded harder, mocking her attempt.

The blanket started slipping off her. She clutched at it harder until it uncovered her head and she saw it gathered onto Jonah's lap. His shirt was closed again, but untucked. She stared at one of the buttons because she definitely could not look him in the eyes. Not again. Not after... that.

"I was asleep?" Her voice sounded too high for hers. She thought for a second about saying she didn't see anything, but the lie would have been way too obvious.

He didn't say a word, but he tossed the blanket down toward her feet. She didn't want to see his face because she didn't want to know how he felt about what just happened. She just needed to pretend it didn't happen. That her body wasn't keyed up in a weird way.

She swung her feet to the floor, next to his booted feet. He hadn't even taken off his boots. Her skin buzzed, waiting to be touched, which he wouldn't be doing, but it didn't stop the craziness within her. "You have company you should really return to and I have to use the bathroom."

He exhaled again. "I didn't think you'd be out here."

"I fell asleep." She tried to take a breath to calm down the racing of her heart. She glanced up at his concerned face and instantly regretted it, dropping her gaze back to the button. She couldn't look him in his eyes and talk to him about this. She never wanted to talk about what happened. Her face burned. "I was watching TV and apparently it didn't hold my interest so I fell asleep. Or maybe it was the glass of wine. The cable box automatically turns off if no one changes the channel and then the TV shuts off. I didn't know you'd be bringing someone home."

"It's not your fault." His hand rose and she automatically flinched, worried he'd touch her and she didn't know how it would feel. Did she want him to touch her? Would it feel different? Would she like it? Her brain couldn't stop spinning. But then he stroked his hand down his beard. "I wouldn't hurt you."

"Habit. My older brothers picked on me. I always got the two for flinching." She grabbed the afghan and balled it up on her lap. "Honestly, I'm not afraid of you."

Frankly she was terrified, but not of him, by whatever her insides were currently doing. Did she want him to do that to her? Bend her over the counter and. . . . Her cheeks flushed with heat and that small pulse between her legs ached.

Even though she wasn't watching his eyes, she felt his gaze roam over her like a physical caress. Her chest kept rising and falling and she couldn't get her heart to calm down. This was physical attraction, right? He was gorgeous and well-built; it made sense for her to primally want him. Surely, this was a temporary attraction and it would go away by the morning.

"Good." He stood.

She couldn't stop herself from looking up at him. He seemed distracted and confused. His blue eyes met hers and once again his gaze pinned her in place. The moment stretched and she swore she could hear her heart thundering in her ears as his gaze dropped to her lips. A breath escaped her as she thought about his lips pressed against hers. Did she want him to?

"Jonah," called the woman from his room, breaking the spell.

He closed his eyes and when he opened them, the heat in them had vanished. He was just Jonah again. "Good night."

He turned and walked toward his bedroom. Lacy stood and hurried toward the bathroom. He paused and she accidentally clipped her side with his elbow. She almost fell into the wall, but he grabbed hold of her arms at the last minute and steadied her. Her mouth dropped open as she gasped at the heat of the contact. His hands tightened on her arms. Her heart stopped.

Just as quickly as he'd grabbed her, he released her. He disappeared into his room with his woman, shutting the door softly.

She closed her mouth and shook off the weirdness flowing through her. Her arms still burned from his touch. She had no idea who got the point for that interaction. Neither of them seemed to win.

WHAT IN THE holy hell was the racket this morning? Lacy struggled to untangle herself from her blankets. Eyes still closed and hair doing its normal morning bird's nest, she found her doorknob and headed toward the sound. Arms stretched out to stop her from running into the counter.

Her fingers rammed into solid flesh. She patted the warm

skin a couple of times to try to determine what it was. The noise stopped.

"Too loud," she said, still not one hundred percent with it. She tapped the solid skin in front of her. Part of her wanted to press into the warmth. "Coffee."

A dark, low chuckle preceded a hot cup of coffee pressed into her hand.

"Thank you."

She wandered away, opening her eyes to follow the floor to her spot on the couch, and nursed her coffee addiction.

"Does she do that every morning?" a woman's voice asked.

"So far." Even through the gravel of his voice, his amusement registered somewhere in her brain.

"She's a feral little kitten, isn't she?" The woman sounded amused as well.

Good, be amused. Coffee was life. In the morning, it was the only thing that mattered.

Jonah didn't respond, vocally at least. Lacy felt like hell in the mornings and her brain didn't function properly before at least one cup was down her gullet. A habit she'd developed in high school, because her second crush worked at a Starbucks. She cuddled into the corner of the couch and continued to take sips of her life-giving drug of choice.

When she had enough to open her eyes, Lacy pushed the hair out of her face. She looked over the back of the couch and met the curious gaze of the brunette sitting across from Jonah at the counter. Her brain still wasn't firing on all cylinders. Something niggled in a corner of her mind, but when she turned to Jonah, her brain short circuited again.

Athletic pants hung off Jonah's hips. His chest was bare and Lacy swallowed before she returned her gaze to the woman. Her fingers tingled remembering his warm skin beneath them.

"Well, good morning." The woman smiled and Lacy resisted the urge to hiss at her like the feral cat the woman thought she was. "I'm Candy."

Of course, she was. Tall, leggy, beautiful Candy. Just the type of girl who would get someone like Jonah. Not even offering a nod to the lady, Lacy drank more coffee. Jonah leaned against the kitchen sink, drinking his smoothie. She glared at the smoothie.

For a second, she thought his lips tipped into a smile at her, but then it vanished.

"I don't think you'll get much from her this morning," Jonah said. He winked at Lacy. "She had a late night."

Lacy straightened, suddenly alert. Why would he wink at her? Late night? Her eyes widened and her heart raced as images of last night flooded her mind. Jonah pounding into Candy over the counter. Locking eyes with Jonah as the couple both came. Her face flushed with heat. Oh God, did Candy know too?

Jonah gave her a knowing smile as she met his gaze. Her skin felt like she would combust into flames.

"Don't tease the girl, Jonah. She obviously hasn't had enough coffee to deal with your shit." Candy popped a piece of fruit in her mouth. "I've got to get going. I work this afternoon. I had fun last night. A pleasure as always."

She stood up and sauntered toward the couch. Her eyes were a light green and kind. Lacy hadn't seen her face last night. "Sorry I can't stick around to see if your new kitty has claws. But it was a pleasure to meet you, kitty."

Lacy nodded and sipped more coffee. The woman slipped out the door and it closed with a finality. Leaving her and a half naked Jonah all alone. *Oh, my God.*

Lacy wasn't ready to deal with Jonah this morning and whatever the hell last night had been. Maybe if she didn't bring it up, he'd forget about it, and they'd pretend she hadn't seen him pounding into a woman and watched both of them orgasm.

Under her embarrassment, frankly, she couldn't help being a little jealous. She closed her eyes and savored her coffee. It had looked like they both enjoyed the encounter. Sex wasn't a big part of her life. Her one time in college had been an eye-opening experience, but not in a good way. The only enjoyable part about it had been because her crush had finally seen her, but she definitely hadn't enjoyed it as much as Candy did.

Her friends seemed to enjoy even the idea of sex. Not Lacy. Maybe Lacy was just built wrong.

She opened her eyes. At some point, Jonah had crossed the room to sit in the chair near her. His bare feet rested on the coffee table and his gaze stared straight ahead instead of at her. Small favors.

"What were you thinking about?" He drank his smoothie like he really didn't care what her answer would be.

She narrowed her eyes at him and drank more of her coffee. She seriously wanted to hiss at him too this morning. Not only had she not been tired at all when she climbed into bed last night, the dreams she did have may have been more vivid than usual. Like *way* more vivid. It wasn't every day she caught a sex show before bed, and it had leaked into her dreams. *Jonah* had leaked into her dreams. Not Logan. It would have been okay if it had been Logan. But it had been gravelly-voiced Jonah and it hadn't been Candy leaning over the counter. Heat flooded her cheeks.

Not going to think about that.

Plus the damn blender woke her up again.

"You going to make me do all the talking today?" His gaze swung to her and she raised her eyebrow at him, daring him.

He set his drink on the coffee table and leaned forward with his elbows on his knees. He held her gaze. "I promise not to have sex in the kitchen again. I thoroughly bleached the counter this morning. Are we good?"

Her heart clattered in her chest. That was it? No talk about her watching? No, "what the hell was that" when she watched him come and he kept her pinned in place like she'd been part of the experience? Not to mention how her body reacted during the whole thing, which she really hadn't wanted to discuss. So instead, she just released the breath she'd been holding.

She finished her coffee and put her bare feet on the cold wood floor. She snatched her feet back under her. Too cold to get more coffee.

He chuckled low and stood, took her mug from her and went into the kitchen. He filled it with coffee and brought it to her. She carefully took it from him and murmured, "Thank you."

Returning to his seat, he didn't break her gaze. "Is this an every morning thing?"

She took a sip and looked in her cup. Sophie wasn't here. Had Candy been drinking the coffee too or had he made the coffee knowing she'd come out? Warmth spread through her, but she refused to smile at this man. "If you insist on using the blender, yes."

He nodded and finished his smoothie. "Noted."

Maybe they could just pretend the whole sex thing had never happened.

CHAPTER 4

"IF YOU DON'T FINISH your shower in two minutes, I'm breaking down the door and joining you." Jonah hadn't taken her threat of monopolizing the bathroom serious. But now on Monday morning, he needed to at least take a shower before he left. His first fucking day of work.

"You wouldn't dare." Her voice was strong like Saturday night never happened. The shy little bird had vanished.

He leaned against his doorframe and closed his eyes. He hadn't known she was on the couch. He'd had an itch which Candy had always been willing to scratch for him when he was in town on business. It hadn't occurred to him he had roommates now. It'd also been almost two in the morning.

When he'd opened his eyes in the middle of it, there Lacy was. Eyes wide, pupils blown, cheeks flushed, and chest rising and falling fast. He figured she'd look away when she realized he saw her, but she hadn't. Her eyes had felt more intimate than what he'd been doing with Candy.

He should have stopped and taken Candy to the bedroom as soon as he realized Lacy was there, but Lacy's gaze had kept him locked in that moment. He wasn't into being watched, but something about Lacy fired him up.

Candy had been upset about not getting a second round, but he couldn't get Lacy out of his head the rest of the night. And even though Candy and him were just a sex thing, he didn't want to fuck her while thinking about Lacy. Wondering if Lacy would have the same look on her face as he buried his cock deep inside her.

He shook his head. He needed to forget that. Particularly right now as he had to get to work. "One minute, little bird."

"Oh, I'm shaking," was her sarcastic reply. Mornings with her were a trip. Coffee mellowed her into the likeable girl everyone else adored. He preferred this feisty little bird, though, with just a hint of deviousness.

Fuck. Picturing her in the shower made him harder. The smooth skin of her shoulders. Her eyes latched onto his. Her lips parted. The water would make her body slick as he drew his hand—

Fuck. He closed his eyes and took a breath. She fascinated him in a way he didn't really understand. Maybe it was that weird mix of her curiosity and naivety.

The shower stopped and he held his breath, bracing himself.

The door opened and she stood in the doorway wrapped in a towel with another towel wrapped around her hair. Her skin glistened, still slightly damp. He held himself still because if he moved right now, it would be to sweep her into his arms and ruin his first-day-on-the-job good impression by being hours late. Not to mention, ruin his housing situation.

"All yours." She swept a hand into the bathroom as she went to her bedroom and slammed the door.

"Fuck," he breathed out as he entered the bathroom and closed the door. Her peaches and cream scent clung in the air, and seeing her dripping wet, with a towel barely covering her hadn't helped diminish his erection.

She opened her bedroom door and yelled, "You have five minutes."

He shook his head as he stepped into the shower and quickly washed the sweat from his workout off. He wouldn't have time to trim up his beard. Dammit. He'd even made Lacy coffee this morning, but she was still a fierce little bird. She'd taken the cup into the bathroom with her.

A curt knock on the bathroom door made him turn the shower off and grab his towel to throw around his waist before he opened the door.

"What?" His patience was completely shattered by this woman.

Her eyes went wide as she took in his wet physique. She inhaled sharply and wet her lips. She dressed in business casual. Gray slacks with a black sleeveless top that looked like satin. Would her skin feel like satin beneath his touch? Her bare feet peeked out from below her pants. Toes had never been his thing, but hers weakened his resolve to stay away from her.

"I. . . . " Her brown eyes flitted all over his body. Her lips practically begged to be taken.

He was pretty sure she wouldn't be happy if he dragged her into the bathroom, stripped her naked and had his way with her. Maybe she would, but that wasn't on the agenda today. Or any day. Instead, he grunted and went around her to his bedroom and slammed the door. Work would be the break he needed from her.

～

HOLY CRAP, *this morning was intense.* Lacy quickly texted Beth before slipping her phone in her purse as she rode the elevator up to work. She hadn't even filled Beth in on Saturday night yet. How would she ever communicate effectively what had happened? Live porn show? Unintentional interactive sexual experience?

But this morning. . . . Holy crap. Jonah's blue eyes had damn near scorched her. Her whole body had burned from the look in in his eyes. Was he angry at her? Which if she hadn't been so busy trying to get ready for work, she would have asked what the hell was going on. She'd given him fair warning about the amount of time it took for her to get ready. Including long showers. She hadn't exaggerated.

When she had finished getting ready, she wasn't sure if he was still home. Not running into him again had been a relief. She wasn't sure if he'd been serious about barging in to share the shower, but she hadn't wanted to press the issue either. After all, she had been a participant in his sex on Saturday. Not a willing one, but she hadn't exactly looked away either.

Would he take that as an invitation? That she wanted him to join her in the shower because she'd watched him? Just the thought of him completely naked and wet in the shower with her had her stomach doing crazy flips and not necessarily in a bad way. The image wasn't hard to imagine when he'd opened the door, still dripping wet in only a towel.

After only a weekend, she needed a break from Jonah.

Fortunately, at work she wouldn't have to deal with him. . . until she got home tonight. Depending on how long he stayed at work, she might not see him at all during the week. It was his first week, so good impressions and all that. Fingers crossed.

Please let Jonah be a workaholic. She worked with two workaholic bosses, but fortunately they didn't expect all of their staff to be like them. Only when a project had a tight deadline or needed a quick turnaround.

The small boutique advertising firm, Taylor and King,

had just celebrated their first client a few months ago. More clients had filled out their portfolio, and the owners Morgan Taylor and Drew King decided to expand their office staff from eight to ten. They'd discussed it at the meeting last week and the new people should be starting within the next few months.

Lacy pushed open the door and the first face she saw was Emily's, the receptionist.

"How was your weekend?" Emily smiled. Blond, brown eyes, and beautiful, she was practically perfect. Emily had to be the nicest person Lacy knew. Seriously, she was sunshine packaged in a pretty person. Her outfits flowed and swirled around her as she walked. And the things she remembered about everyone. . . just little stuff, but it made Lacy feel like she was part of a family at work. "Did your roommate finally sublet her room?"

"New roommate moved in Friday. A dude." Lacy made a wincing face, knowing Emily would commiserate. "How about you?"

"Spent the weekend at Grandma's beach house. Quiet but nice." Emily smiled softly. The phone rang and she reached to pick it up. Emily's love life resembled Lacy's. Non-existent.

Lacy knew why her own love life sucked. Someone like Emily shouldn't be single. She should have a steady guy ready to put a ring on her finger.

They'd talked about it at one Happy Hour when Emily had been able to attend. Usually, she spent her weekends at her grandma's and left a little early on Fridays to beat the traffic rush to the beach. Taking care of her grandma didn't leave her with a lot of time to date or even find a guy.

Lacy waved to Emily and continued past the reception area. They had an open office. Desks in the center so as they worked, they could throw out ideas. The bosses shared an office, but the door typically remained open. A couple of small offices were available if someone needed to make a phone call or have a small meeting. A large conference table sat along one wall of the area for meetings with the whole team. Ben Clarke, the accountant, had the other office. His door was typically closed. He never joined the team at Happy Hour. He didn't really talk much at all.

Unlike the normal divisions, like in larger advertising firms, the bosses encouraged everyone to be a part of the team and contribute to whatever proposal or ad campaign they could. Even though Lacy had a couple of years of experience in copy writing and Claire's experience was in the art department, they all worked together, dividing things when necessary.

Dropping her purse in her desk drawer, Lacy headed into the kitchen for more coffee. As she opened the door, Logan and Claire stepped away from each other. They were best friends and always had their heads together. But there didn't seem to be an actual sexual relationship there.

Claire was the type of girl who was one of the guys. Otherwise, her beauty would have intimidated Lacy and she wouldn't even have thought of having a crush on Logan. Because if Claire decided she wanted Logan, Lacy wouldn't stand a chance.

Claire smiled and tucked her dark hair behind her ear. "Hey, Lacy, good weekend?"

"Yeah, you?" Lacy met Claire's eyes before glancing over at Logan. His dark crew cut hair and dark eyes made her internally sigh. In the afternoons, his strong chiseled jaw would be speckled with dark hairs, making her want to rub against it like a cat. Gah, she loved him so much.

She brought her gaze to Claire as she started talking.

"We went to the bar and watched the game on Sunday." Claire smiled at Logan, who smiled back. "Good game."

"You need a cup, Lace?" Logan asked. See, he even had a pet name for her. Lace. Man, he was the real deal no matter what Beth thought. Beth just couldn't imagine it because she hadn't seen them together. Maybe she should have Beth come and visit and introduce her to Logan to get a general read on the situation.

"Thanks," Lacy smiled and made eye contact with Logan, but not in a creepy way. That's what the flirting articles on Sunday all said to do. At least the ones she read before she'd given up and put on *The Kissing Booth*. Time to incorporate the new interactions with Logan.

He handed her the cup and smiled. "Know you need coffee to keep that huge brain of yours running on all cylinders."

See, he liked her. He thought of her. Beth was insane. He wasn't like all those other guys who had been out of her league and didn't even know her name. Okay, maybe he was a touch out of her league.

And he had no problem going after what he wanted. But maybe when it was real for him, he just took things slow, which she appreciated. He just needed to get some things out of his system first.

Who needed hot and fast?

A flash of Candy and Jonah in the kitchen hit her mind. Definitely hot. And that look this morning from Jonah. She poured her coffee and ignored whatever the hell that was because she wouldn't think of Jonah while at work. And definitely didn't need to think of what she'd witnessed or the way his eyes had burned into hers this morning, stirring up that hurricane to devastate her insides again.

He hadn't made her nervous, per se, but had made her feel warm all over and achy.

"Did you see the new guy?" Claire asked Logan, pulling Lacy out of her thoughts.

"Nah, is he in with Drew and Morgan?" Logan leaned against the refrigerator like a GQ model. Lacy was proud of herself. She didn't drool or sigh happily; instead she just drank her coffee like a normal person. Beth would be so proud.

"He's some hot shot from L.A." Claire sank into one of the chairs around the break table. "Apparently he used to travel a lot for work, he decided to come here so he could stay in one place. From what I saw, he's a hottie."

"You're saying I have competition for sexiest male in the office." Logan's eyes lit up and he grinned.

Claire laughed. "Calm the fuck down. Nobody thinks you're hot. Besides, what about Drew? Just because he and Morgan are basically hitched doesn't mean he's not smoking. Guess you didn't get laid this weekend after all?"

Lacy almost choked on her coffee and made it a point to not look at either of them. She usually was at her desk by this time, but she'd gotten caught up thinking about Jonah and they'd clearly forgotten about her.

"That chick was too much work." Logan sank into the chair across from Claire. "She was hot, but definitely looking for more than I was willing to give."

"You mean a relationship?" Claire covered her mock shocked expression with her hand and winked at Lacy. Apparently *she* hadn't forgotten about Lacy. "God forbid Logan O'Connell settle for one woman for longer than a weekend."

The heat crept up Lacy's cheeks. Okay, she knew that wasn't a plus in the Logan column, but love could make a man want to change. It wasn't like he was a cheater since he didn't commit to anyone.

If he fell in love with Lacy, then he'd only be with her. Right? Love could make a man want to settle down. At least they did in the movies and books.

Logan laughed. "My parents have been married for thirty-five years. Commitment is bred into us O'Connells. Sue me if I want to spend my bachelor years experimenting."

Claire laughed. "Experimenting is the new word for random hookups?"

Lacy's heart lurched at him talking about commitment. She hadn't been wrong about him giving up his ways for the right woman. However, a pit formed in Lacy's stomach. Experimenting? What the hell did he mean? And what would that mean for that special lady he could finally settle down with? And how could she be that lady for him?

"I think you broke Hatcher," Claire stated, drinking her coffee.

"Too early for sex talk, Lace?" Logan lifted his eyebrow at her.

She blinked at them, feeling the heat rising to her cheeks, and shook her head. "Not enough coffee. Still in zombie mode."

Logan shook his head with a soft smile on his lips. "She's so cute when she's in zombie mode."

"When they finally make injections of caffeine, Lacy will be first in line." Claire nodded.

They laughed, and Lacy chuckled with them, even knowing she was the butt of the joke. When they started talking about the stats of some player on some sports ball team, Lacy slipped out and went to her desk.

Cute was good, right? She wanted to latch onto that, but Logan was still experimenting. By hooking up.

How long would that last? A few months, a year, two, five? Could she wait that long to start her life? Could she wait for Logan? Of course she could, but maybe she could find a way to hurry things along.

Maybe if she could convince him to experiment with her, he would figure out she was the one for him and skip to the happily ever after. She cringed. Only if he wanted a failed experiment. If she didn't want what happened in college to repeat, she needed to figure out what was wrong with her.

What if she plain just sucked at sex? That would be a problem, especially if she only had a weekend to prove herself to Logan. But she didn't want to be a weekend fling, she wanted to be the one for the long haul. That meant figuring out how to get him to ask her out and figuring out how to have sex that didn't make him never want to talk to her again.

"We already have a handful of clients and a few potentials we need to prepare proposals for," Drew's voice filled the open area.

Lacy still had her head in her cup of coffee when she remembered Claire saying the new guy started today. Easier to focus on the new guy than trying to decode her lack of a romantic entanglement and inability to keep a guy with sex.

Curiosity latched onto her as she waited to see the hot shot from L.A. Would he look like a surfer dude or some smarmy Hollywood guy? Maybe he was older and sophisticated. Wait, Claire had called him a hottie, but older guys could be hot. She settled on the imaginary surfer dude. Long blond hair, sun-kissed skin and loads of "dudes" and "whatevers." Maybe a Heath Ledger type. That would be some nice office eye candy.

She needed to make a note to do a Heath Ledger marathon this weekend. *10 Things I Hate about You. A Knight's Tale. Casanova.*

She lifted her gaze to where Drew stood in the doorway of his and Morgan's office. Drew always dressed in a suit and tie, even if he left his jacket in his office all day. Curly dark hair and stunning blue eyes completed the package. He was handsome and super friendly.

Lacy sipped her coffee as Morgan came out. Morgan's

blond hair was pulled into a bun and she always dressed in pencil skirts and blouses. So professional. Lacy wished she could get away with that look but didn't have the attitude or confidence to pull it off.

Drew gave Morgan a soft look that made Lacy want to happy sigh. Drew and Morgan were #relationshipgoals.

"Most of us work the standard eight to five, but we don't discourage people from working late or arriving early or shifting their time by an hour or so. We try to be flexible for personal time as well." Morgan glanced over and nodded at Lacy. "We're trying to build a team here. We don't have a lot of the rules larger corporations have."

"That's why I decided to come here."

Lacy froze mid-sip. No. It couldn't be. That voice. Dark and gravelly. Nope. There's no way *he* was the new guy.

"Fantastic," Drew said. "Let's get you acquainted with the team."

Jonah stepped out of the office and his eyes connected with hers. She swallowed her coffee hard and started choking and coughing. Great, this was how she'd die. Fitting. Death by coffee.

CHAPTER 5

JONAH STARTED FORWARD, but Drew stood closer to Lacy and got there first.

"Are you okay?" Drew patted her softly on the back as she nodded and waved him away.

"I'm good," she choked out and lifted her gaze to Jonah's again. Her brown eyes were huge.

Jonah smiled. How could he not? Little bird was here too. Of course she was. Brenda had mentioned she worked in advertising, but at the time, he hadn't thought anything of it. The city had its fair share of advertising firms, after all. Honestly, he hadn't given any real thought to his two new roommates-to-be, because they would all go about their own business and not interact. That plan had gone up in smoke.

Morgan moved to stand next to Drew, asking Lacy, "Are you sure you're okay? Do you want a water or something?"

Lacy shook her head. "Just went down the wrong pipe is all."

Morgan smiled and held out a hand to Jonah. "Jonah Sinclair. Lacy Hatcher. She's an experienced copywriter, but she's been doing a lot more since she started working with us."

"Lacy." Jonah held out his hand and raised an eyebrow at her, wondering if she'd take his hand after he'd made it a point of ignoring hers when she first offered.

Her lips thinned and her eyes narrowed on his hand. "You know they see our employment forms. They'll know we're roommates and realize we've probably met before today."

He withdrew his hand and stroked it down his beard. He shrugged. "Haven't filled out any HR forms yet."

Drew and Morgan watched them for a moment before Drew laughed. "Well then, you don't need introductions. Lacy, would you be able to show Jonah around and introduce him to the rest of the team? We've got a call in five minutes."

Lacy stood and ran her hands over her slacks. "No problem."

Jonah wondered if he made her nervous. Or was she remembering their weekend together?

Morgan smiled at them before following Drew into the office, leaving them alone.

"Where is everyone?" Jonah looked around the office, surprised to see only the two of them in it.

"Phoebe comes in later. The others are around." Lacy sighed and closed her eyes for a second. When she opened them, she seemed determined. "Okay, so you probably met Emily on the way in."

He nodded. Focus on work, definitely a good plan.

"Your desk is there."

His sat directly across from hers and she'd be in his sightline all day long. "Great."

"Don't sound so enthusiastic." She rolled her eyes.

"Got enough coffee in your system now?"

Her eyes narrowed at him. She seemed less than thrilled he was here, but it didn't matter. This was work. He'd be able to put his head down and ignore her for the majority of the day.

A couple came out of a room laughing. The brunette paused and waited, while the guy figured out what was going on.

Lacy motioned for Jonah to follow her. "Jonah Sinclair. Claire Lake."

Claire shook his hand, very perfunctory. Her dark eyes swept over him though and he could detect a hint of interest there. She was all curves and long dark hair. Her heels brought her almost to eye level with him.

He kept his smile strictly friendly. Most corporations were okay with employees being friends, but usually not good with dating amongst coworkers. It happened sometimes, but in an office this small, it would only amount to trouble.

"Logan O'Connell," Lacy said.

That was a name he remembered. "You must be Lacy's—"

"Nope. We don't have work partners here." Lacy interrupted and smiled huge, but Jonah could tell she gritted her teeth. "We work as one team instead of in divisions. So we're all in the trenches together."

"Nice to meet you, man." Logan's handshake was firm and brief. "It'll be nice to have another guy around."

Jonah glanced between the two. Lacy was tense, but Logan didn't have a care in the world. Not even a hint of a spark between them. This was the guy she claimed to be *in love* with? If so, the guy didn't have a clue.

"Let me show you the breakroom." Lacy led the way into the room the other two just left.

Jonah went through and grabbed a cup from the shelf. Lacy closed the door.

"Wolverine isn't your boyfriend?" He poured himself

some coffee and turned around to see Lacy holding the door shut as if someone would bust in any moment.

"What?" She glared at him confused.

"Logan." He gestured toward the office.

"No. He's not my boyfriend," Lacy whispered, harshly.

He raised an eyebrow. "But you were telling your friend—"

She charged him and put her hand over his mouth. "Shhh. How the hell was I supposed to know you'd be working here? We can talk about this at home."

To reach his mouth, she had pressed her body against his for a second. All soft curves and heat. He grinned against her palm. She snatched her hand away, giving him a chastising look, and stepped away.

"Promise?"

She probably hoped he'd never mention it again. Kind of like not bringing up her watching him fuck Candy. That was a lot more complicated than the Logan situation. She'd would possibly ask why Jonah hadn't acknowledged her and moved the proceedings elsewhere. Which he didn't have a good answer for.

After all, what could he say? *Seeing you watching me fuck Candy got me off harder than fucking Candy did?*

But Wolverine was all her and her awkwardness. She'd proclaimed she loved him, and the guy clearly had no idea how Lacy felt about him. Jonah almost rubbed his hands in anticipation of the ruffled feathers.

"Fine." She tugged the bottom of her shirt in an effort to straighten it, but it hadn't been crooked. Straightening her shoulders, she held out a hand, his official tour guide again. "Breakroom."

Right, time to win over the coworkers. He'd focus on Lacy later.

~

Today had been hell. Gone was sullen, man of few words Jonah. This Jonah smiled and teased and came up with witty catch phrases and charmed the pants off everyone he met. Lacy knew a few times she'd stared at him with her mouth hanging open, because when he'd caught her, his eyes would drop to her mouth meaningfully.

His laughter was infectious. Unlike the dark chuckles he'd given her before that echoed throughout her body, he had a good, rich laugh. Emily seemed half in love with him already. Even tomboy Claire had a soft spot for the Jonah who came to work.

What a crock of shit. . . er crap. Dammit, he even made her cuss in her head now.

Lacy had been elected the person to show him the computer system so he'd sat beside her the rest of the morning. His breath caressed her cheek. The heat of him was almost overwhelming. She'd scooted away multiple times, but somehow his hand would always manage to brush her bare arm, leaving goosebumps in its wake, or she'd inhale his ocean scent as a reminder he was right there.

When over-the-top Phoebe Butler had strolled in, she and Jonah had become the best of pals. Between Logan and Claire, and Phoebe and Jonah riffing off each other, the whole office could barely breathe from laughing. They did manage to get some work done though. The time flew by until the end of the day finally arrived.

The time Lacy had been dreading.

"See you tomorrow," Logan said warmly to Lacy.

See, he cared. She smiled brightly at him. "See you tomorrow."

She'd completely forgotten about the plan to flirt with Logan. Logan turned to Jonah.

"Can't wait until Friday happy hour." Logan held up his hand for a high five from Jonah.

Jonah slapped Logan's hand. "Definitely."

"I'll give you the deets on all the ladies." Though Logan had lowered his voice, Lacy still heard it. She wondered what "deets" Logan would have to say about her. What "deets" would Jonah feel compelled to share?

She narrowed her eyes at Jonah who just flashed her a smile. He was like an entirely different person.

The office had almost emptied out. Morgan and Drew were still in their office with the door closed. They were the only true workaholics at the company, but they seemed to like it that way. Most everyone put in extra hours as well. But typically not on Mondays. The company was still growing. The extra work to build up the business would pay off.

Lacy grabbed her coffee mug and took it into the break-room to rinse it and to start the dishwasher.

"One more." Jonah stopped next to her at the sink and rinsed his cup quickly. He placed it in the dishwasher and Lacy closed it. He leaned against the counter next to her while she finished setting it. "Want to carpool?"

She glanced up at his smiling expression. He'd barely smiled this whole weekend. Now it was like he couldn't stop smiling. "Doesn't that make your face hurt?"

He didn't even blink at her question. "Come on. I've got a Lyft waiting."

"You're paying." She shrugged. She had to get home and they were heading to the same place. Stopping at her desk, she grabbed her purse.

He chuckled, but it was lower and darker than it had been during the day, sending shivers racing down her spine. "You want me to buy you dinner too?"

"My god, don't you ever shut up?" She raised her eyebrow at him.

"Touché." He gestured toward the doors.

She inhaled and made her way out into the lobby with him hot on her trail. This day had been never-ending. By some miracle, she hoped Jonah had forgotten their earlier conversation about Logan. She really didn't want to discuss her love life or lack thereof with her new roommate and coworker. The elevator opened and they got in and moved to the back. For a second, they were the only ones on it, until the doors opened a floor down and more people crowded on.

Jonah moved closer to her to make room for the people. His ocean scent flowed over her and his shirtsleeve brushed her bare arm. A flutter started low in her abdomen. Her breath caught in her throat as an image of him coming out of the bathroom this morning, water coursing down his muscles, flooded her senses. She tried to shift away from him, but there was nowhere to go.

His head tipped toward her like he wanted to start a conversation, but she refused to lift her gaze to his and instead stared at the numbers above the elevator doors. The back of his hand brushed the back of hers and a flurry of butterflies swept through her. His gaze was still on her. Even though she didn't look, she could feel it like an itch underneath her skin.

The elevator stopped on the ground floor and people pouring out. She hurried to follow but knew she couldn't get too far away from Jonah. They were headed home together. He just made her feel weird inside. It wasn't normal.

His hand grasped her elbow and guided her toward a different exit than the one she had headed for. His fingers were warm on her bare skin. She allowed him to lead her out the doors and to the car. Too aware of his touch on her to feel truly sane. He opened the car door for her. When he released her arm, she exhaled, not realizing she'd been holding her breath. She slid in and kept sliding across the seat so he had room. Her skin burned from where he'd held her and she rubbed it, hoping to erase the feeling.

The ride was silent and tense. When they got home, he would ask about Logan, but what could she say? She had a huge crush on a guy who was so far out of her league it might never happen? He was kind of a player and she didn't hit any of his requirements for his type of woman. Not new news, but the next bit had hit hard this morning. He was in an experimental phase which could last who knows how long. And worse, her own experience was miniscule compared to his and she had no idea what he would even like or if she was even qualified to try with a guy like him.

She'd been called sweet and caring, but no one in their right mind would call her sexy. She was more likely the one you wanted to cuddle on the couch with during a movie, not bend over the kitchen counter. Her face flushed at the memory.

Not going there.

What if she was bad at sex? In college it had been over almost as soon as it started and the whole experience had left her feeling less than. He'd been her crush of the moment and had used that to get her to sleep with him. He'd dropped her immediately after. Maybe it was because she'd been bad at sex and he hadn't wanted to repeat it.

What if she finally got the man of her dreams but she couldn't live up to his standards and lost him. Of course, she'd have to get him first, which meant actually sticking to "the plan."

She followed distractedly as Jonah led the way up to their apartment and unlocked the door. She stepped in and put her purse on the table, still lost in her thoughts.

The door closed with a finality and she jumped. Her breath caught and she waited.

"I'm ordering a pizza. You want some?" Jonah brushed past her and sat in a living room chair.

"What?" Lacy lifted her head and stared at Jonah for a second. His gaze remained on his phone. She walked around the couch and sank down on it. She stared at her hands. "Pizza. Yeah, sure."

"Veggie, okay?"

She glanced at him. "Yeah."

"Done." He slid his phone into his pocket. "What's going on in that head of yours?"

"Nothing." She slid her eyes shut, trying to block out all the thoughts of being bad at sex and Logan only being a fantasy. Maybe she should just get on one of those apps and find a guy. Someone who thought cuddling was the best way to spend Saturday night.

Jonah leaned forward with his elbows on his knees and nudged her leg with his.

She reluctantly lifted her gaze and his blue eyes held her in place, like he could see past her bull.

"Tell me." His gravelly voice was soft and gentle. So different from office Jonah. More like grrr angry, off-putting Jonah, who she might actually like more. Which was a shock to her. Office Jonah and Logan seemed to have a lot more in common than grrr Jonah.

She sighed and closed her eyes. "You're going to ask me about Logan, but I don't know what to tell you. We haven't ever gone out. I've had a major crush on him for months. He doesn't know, or at least I haven't told him. But it's not likely to happen, which is what my friends keep telling me. Over and over again."

"Why couldn't it happen?"

She opened her eyes expecting to see him mocking her, but his eyes were sincere. He legit wanted to know why it couldn't happen. Besides her track record with her infatuations, she could probably list off a dozen other reasons why it wouldn't happen.

But if Jonah thought it was a possibility. . . and Logan *had* called her cute today. . . . But the reality of the situation was. . . .

"I'm not his type." She looked down at her hands. It hurt to admit it, but she couldn't deny it.

"What's his type?" Jonah's voice was soft and not accusatory.

She sighed and reclined on the couch, covering her eyes with her hands. "Sexy, experienced, cool. Someone like your girlfriend probably."

"Girlfriend?"

"Candy." She dropped her hands and looked at him. "Candy would be Logan's type and obviously I'm no Candy."

CHAPTER 6

Jonah didn't dare react. No smiling or laughing. Lacy was serious about this, and he'd take her seriously. First thing. "Candy's not my girlfriend."

"Oh." She looked down at her hands again. She'd been nervous since they left the office, so he'd waited to let her bring up Logan.

Sexy, cool, experienced. Jonah leaned back in his chair. She'd chosen those words intentionally, but what did they mean to her? He wouldn't disagree with her about her not being Logan's type. From today, he could tell Logan was shallow when it came to the women he dated. Jonah had talked to him a little in the breakroom when it was just the two of them and Logan had talked about the best spots to find a hookup.

No one in their right mind would think of Lacy as hookup material. She wore kitten pajamas, and from what he'd observed over the weekend, watched teenage chick flicks. He wanted to rile up her inner fierce little bird, but he also knew it'd been a long day for both of them.

For work, Jonah had to put on a show. Prove he could be

a part of the team. Lacy had been giving him confused looks all day because of it.

He'd also seen the looks she gave Logan when Logan wasn't looking at her. Hopeful, soft looks which had made Jonah want to punch someone though he didn't understand why.

"Logan is an ass." The words slipped out before he could think.

Lacy lifted her gaze to him, those brown eyes of hers questioning. "You barely know him. He's actually a pretty nice guy."

Jonah grunted. He knew plenty of guys like Logan, but he'd give him the benefit of doubt since Lacy seemed to like him. He wondered why she thought she wasn't sexy. Even in her pajamas with her hair tangled over her eyes, she'd had a weird mixture of innocence and sexy going on that Jonah wasn't one hundred percent immune to.

He wasn't immune to her at all, which frustrated him on a whole other level. And now they'd be together all day and in the evenings and the mornings for the foreseeable future. He wondered if this job would be worth staying in one place.

The buzzer for the apartment rang, and Jonah moved to let the pizza delivery up. Lacy continued to stew on the couch while Jonah got the pizza and took it over to the table.

"Are you going to join me?" Jonah grabbed a bottle of wine and two glasses from the kitchen. He sat at the table and kicked out the chair next to him.

Lacy sighed and crossed over to drop into the kitchen chair. He handed her a glass of wine and she immediately drank half of it. He tried not to smile, but knew he'd failed when she glanced over at him and her eyes widened.

He slid a plate in front of her and opened the pizza box. She grabbed a slice. He took a couple of slices and closed the box. Like the weird little bird she was, Lacy picked off the veggies and ate them one by one, before she finally lifted the remains of her pizza to take a bite, by the time he'd finished his first piece.

"Can we not talk about Logan anymore? It's a crush and it's so embarrassing." She tore up the crust on her plate into little bird bites. She put her bare foot onto the edge of the chair seat and reached around her knee for her wine.

He nodded but didn't offer a topic. She let out a breath and straightened a little. Was she relieved he let it drop?

"You're weird at work." She tilted her head at him like he was an abstract painting she couldn't understand.

He raised an eyebrow at her. She was one to talk about someone being weird.

She munched on a piece of crust. A little glint lit her eyes. "You talked. Sometimes without being asked something and absolutely no grunting. And the smiles. . . all those smiles, I swear I thought you'd turned into the Joker. I was worried you'd been taken over by aliens or something."

"Aliens?" He tried to keep a straight face, but he knew she noted the tug at the corner of his lips.

"Or something." She leaned forward, getting close to his face and searched his eyes. "You sure you're not actually Jekyll and Hyde? I mean, it would explain so much."

He filled her wine glass again. "Maybe."

A grin lit up her face. "See that's what I'm talking about. You're grumpy and growly. Not nice and helpful."

"Want to ride together tomorrow?" He took another slice of pizza.

She flushed pink as she drank more. "Well, we are living together and you did pay for my dinner so. . . ."

He held up the bottle of wine to offer her more, but she shook her head.

"What was L.A. like?"

He didn't answer, but she kept going, "Do you know any

actors? Did you date any? Did you travel like Sophie does? Did you even have an apartment there?" The questions rattled out of Lacy and she didn't wait for him to answer. Maybe she just didn't expect him to answer.

He leaned back in his chair, stretching his leg out until it rested near her one foot on the ground. She kept throwing out questions and he just watched her. He didn't know about her experience or even what she thought cool meant, but sexy....

Fuck. He still couldn't forget the sight of her wide eyes darkened with desire while watching him, or the hints of perfect golden skin he'd caught glimpses of. Especially this morning in only a towel. Lacy might not be overtly sexy like Candy, but there was definitely something about her he almost couldn't resist.

Almost. Because he knew better. Lacy wasn't the kind of woman you hooked up with. She was the kind you kept, and he wasn't the keeping kind.

She was sweet and a little sassy. The more time he spent with her, the more he wanted to, but he couldn't make a habit of spending time with her. He already thought about her spread out on his bed with only those skimpy panties on. Her eyes dark with desire for him. Best to back off and keep to his plan.

THE WEEK HAD DEFINITELY BEEN odd for Lacy. Tuesday to Thursday had been like any week, just with the addition of Jonah. Thankfully they'd figured out mornings, and that first morning traffic jam in the bathroom never happened again. Evenings, Jonah retreated to his bedroom.

But they rode to work and home together because it made sense. Lacy entered the breakroom on Friday morning not even a little frazzled from sitting next to Jonah on the way to work. That weird feeling when she was close to him hardly even registered now. Finally, she could fall into a routine.

Except this weekend meant he might go out and she might be subjected to more free live porn. Her cheeks flushed.

"Hey there." Logan's voice woke her up and she glanced around the breakroom to find they were the only ones in it. "Looking a little dazed and confused this morning."

"Morning." She managed to get out. She hadn't even been able to start flirting with Logan because of Jonah. Jonah working here had distracted her from her goal. She glanced at the coffee mugs. She almost asked where Claire was, but that would be weird, right? Just because she was usually there didn't mean she should always be there.

He pulled a coffee mug down and held it out to her. "Just waiting on the coffee to finish brewing."

She took the mug and nodded, tucking a stray hair behind her ear. This was her chance. Oh, crap, what did she talk to him about? How did she flirt with him? What even did they have to talk about? She'd only heard him talk about sports with Claire, and Lacy knew nothing about sports. Find common ground, that had been advice on all the websites, but how did one find common ground? What if they didn't have any common ground? What if they had nothing to talk about?

"Ready for the weekend?" Logan asked. His lips curved into a soft smile.

Lacy nodded and watched the coffee drip, trying to come up with actual words to have in a conversation. "You?"

"Definitely. I can't wait for happy hour tonight. Might try to convince Jonah to join me on Saturday night. There's this new club downtown I've been wanting to scope out. You guys are roommates, right?"

Her heart beat in her chest so hard she thought he might actually be able to see it. This definitely qualified as an actual conversation. Not work-related. "Yup."

"You should both come." He turned to the coffee as it finished brewing, which was a good thing because he would have seen the shock on her face before she hid it. Going to a club would definitely be outside of work. She just had to keep her cool and not freak out. Because she was totally freaking out.

"Maybe." She managed to get past her internal squeeing. She'd practically turned into grrr Jonah with one-word answers.

Logan held the coffee pot to fill her cup. "Claire and I usually go to this bar to watch the game, but I could see if she wants to come to the club too. I know he's not technically new to town. Jonah's been here before, but it's not like he stayed here long enough to make friends."

Unless Candy counted as a friend. Lacy took a sip of her coffee and just nodded. Maybe Candy was a friend. Would Candy be considered a fuck buddy? Maybe she should ask Jonah. He'd been distant the past few days. But that was the grrr Jonah way. A smile tugged at her lips.

The door opened behind her.

"Hey, I was just telling Lacy you two should come to the club with me and Claire on Saturday." When he said it that way, it almost sounded like a really awkward double date. Maybe she should clarify to Logan that Jonah and she weren't together together. Just temporary roommates.

Lacy turned to face Jonah who had on one of his fake smiles. That was the other thing Lacy had been occupied with all week: figuring out Jonah. Instead of flirting with Logan, she'd deciphered that Jonah had real smiles and fake ones, and this one was so fake. She started to smile, but then realized he planned to tell Logan no.

This was her shot with Logan or at least a shot at getting him to notice her. He had to say yes. No way would Logan invite Lacy without Jonah.

"I don't—" Jonah had gotten down his coffee mug and looked at her. His smile fell a little. She probably looked a little desperate, but she didn't care. She was desperate. This was going out with the guy she liked. To a club. Together. Yes, with other people, but still. . . .

"It's okay if you can't, man." Logan started toward the door.

Lacy mouthed "please" to Jonah.

Jonah closed his eyes and said, "That sounds great. We can talk logistics at happy hour."

"Fantastic," Logan said. "I'll check with Claire."

The door shut.

"Thank you." Lacy grinned and went up on her tippy toes. "I can't wait to tell Beth about this."

"It's not a date." Jonah filled his mug and gave her a serious look.

"I know, but it's the first time he's asked to do something outside of work." Lacy took a drink. Still riding the high. "It's not a date; it's an opportunity."

Jonah shook his head and his lips tipped into a real smile this time. "Watch your expectations. Don't feel bad when he goes home with someone else."

Lacy straightened. She hadn't thought this through. Logan always hooked up on the weekends. Well, usually, according to Claire. That also meant Jonah could potentially hookup this weekend too. She and Jonah had been polite but distant most of the week, but there'd been moments where he'd whip up a storm in her.

They hadn't discussed the sex show or her unrequited

feelings for Logan or anything significant. But it'd been sitting there festering. And every now and then, she'd seen a heat in Jonah's eyes when he looked at her. Like now.

Her breath caught in her throat and the storm started in the center of her. His blue eyes were locked on hers. Her pulse raced and a tremor worked down her spine. Clutching her coffee mug with both hands, she couldn't stop herself from asking, "What about you?"

He stepped closer, surrounding her with his heat, and asked in his low, gravelly voice, "What about me?"

"Planning on bringing someone home?" Her heart thundered within her as she chastised herself for even asking the question. It wasn't any of her business.

He leaned down until their faces were eye level. His blue eyes searched hers. His lips kicked into a grin. "Hoping for another show?"

She squeaked as her face burst with heat.

The door opened behind her. He'd already moved away as Claire walked in. Lacy spun on her heel and was out the door before it shut.

"Morning, Lacy?" Claire's voice trailed out after her.

Lacy couldn't slow the racing of her heart. They weren't supposed to talk about it. His eyes from that night. . . . She couldn't get them out of her head. She sat in her chair and drank her coffee while her computer booted and she tried not to think about Jonah.

CHAPTER 7

LACY FOUND a spot next to Phoebe for happy hour. Phoebe had been the first official employee at Taylor and King. She and Morgan were besties. Phoebe would talk to everyone and include Lacy in the conversation. It made sense to sit here.

And even though another seat remained open across the table, Jonah claimed the chair next to her. His thigh settled against her thigh, but he didn't comment about it. Those weird feelings swirled through her again. They did anytime he drew close to her.

Unless she wanted to sit in Phoebe's lap, she would be stuck mostly pressed up against him. As it was, the tendrils of Phoebe's red hair brushed against Lacy's shoulder a little as Phoebe turned to talk to Claire.

Fortunately, Logan sat across from Lacy so she'd be able to focus on him instead of Jonah and his warmth. She still couldn't believe they were going out tomorrow. Yes, it was a group thing, but it was more progress than in the past few months. And yes, it was because of Jonah, but she wasn't one to turn down an opportunity.

"I'm getting shots for the table." Phoebe slid out of her seat. She had a few years on Lacy and a ton more experience when it came to men and wasn't afraid to share details. She also could drink a lot without getting falling-down drunk, unlike Lacy.

Lacy tried to get her attention to say no shot for her, but Phoebe had already left. Oh well, one shot wouldn't be the death of her. It would also prove to Logan she could hang out with the big kids at the popular table. One drink was usually her limit or sticking to wine, but she wanted to show Logan she could be fun.

"How was your first week?" Claire asked. She sat next to Logan but unlike Jonah, Logan actually gave her space.

"Good." Jonah leaned forward and his thigh pressed more into Lacy's.

Manspread much? She should press back to reclaim her space, but she didn't want to engage in a petty battle with Jonah either. They seemed to have reached a truce in their relationship. Instead, she waited until Logan's gaze collided with hers and she gave him a shy smile before dropping her gaze, then she lifted her gaze back to his. Flirting. Supposedly, according to the internet.

"You used to travel a lot for your old job, right?" Claire's smile seemed pleasant, but there was a hint of interest there. Maybe? Did Claire have a thing for Jonah? Maybe tomorrow's night out was for Claire to get to know Jonah better, which would leave Logan for Lacy. She couldn't stop the smile on her face, even as a rock settled inside her chest.

"Eighty percent of the job was travel. I barely had a place to call home. Parker Anderson was a global advertising firm. We went where the work was." Jonah leaned his elbows on the table. "Figured it was time to try to find myself some roots."

"This is the city to do it in. Everything you need is here."

Logan stretched his feet out under the table and accidentally bumped one of Lacy's.

Was it on purpose? She didn't think so, but she couldn't help the little lift in her chest. The little thrill she got when he was near. Was he flirting with her?

"I'm back, bitches." Phoebe set the shot glasses in the middle of the table. She grabbed hers and held it up. Only the five of them had been able to come out tonight so they had a smaller table than usual. The bar, however, was packed.

Phoebe waited until everyone lifted their shot glass before saying, "Everyone has a way to get home, right?"

Everyone nodded, so Lacy did too.

Phoebe grinned. "Let's get shitfaced. To the fucking weekend. Cheers!"

After tapping everyone's glass, Lacy took a deep breath and held it before downing the shot. It burned through her chest. When it hit in her stomach, she gasped.

Jonah turned. His mouth pressed against her ear. His hot breath made tingles shoot through her. "I'll make sure you get home okay."

A shiver passed over her, but she just smiled at Logan. All her energy needed to be focused on Logan and not Jonah. She'd wasted all week watching Jonah. But not tonight.

Apparently, everyone thought it was a good idea to do shots because another shot appeared. Lacy usually wasn't a big drinker, but with Phoebe and Claire, she at least needed to try to keep up. After all, Jonah would make sure she got home.

"So, how do you like the office?" Claire leaned against the table and Lacy got a good view of Claire's cleavage pointed at Jonah.

"It seems like a good fit for me." Jonah's thigh bumped into Lacy.

She'd only had two shots so far, leaving her rather gushy

inside. Otherwise, she was doing just fine. Better than fine. Superb.

"How long were your assignments at the other company?" Claire played with the straw in her water.

Lacy should be taking notes because this was real life flirting happening in front of her. Of course, if she stroked a straw, she'd probably look ridiculous and not sexy. And while Lacy had some cleavage, it wasn't as impressive as Claire's.

"Usually changed locations about every two to three weeks. I'd be ready to move on if it lasted a month."

"That's crazy." Claire flicked her hair over her shoulder. She had gorgeous dark hair that kept a soft curl all day. "How often were you at the home office?"

"Not much." Jonah's hand went to Lacy's thigh and she sucked in a breath. His warmth spread up her thigh. "I didn't even keep an apartment in L.A. It wasn't worth the expense."

At that statement, Lacy looked up at Jonah and wanted to wrap her arms around him. He needed a hug. She couldn't imagine not having a place of her own. Somewhere to call home.

Jonah's gaze collided with hers. If she were drunker, she'd probably hug him and not think twice about it. He gently squeezed her thigh like saying it was okay. He got pulled into a conversation with Logan. Phoebe tapped on her shoulder, drawing her attention away.

Everyone talked over everyone else. They talked about the week and what to do around the city for fun. Jonah told a story about a travel delay overnight in an airport with sixty other passengers that had everyone laughing. That was before the third shot appeared. Lacy didn't even feel the liquor go down that time and everything had a hazy glow around it. Some things went quicker and some slowed down.

A few appetizers showed up and again Jonah's lips touched her ear. "Eat or I'll be carrying you home."

Shivers went down her spine and settled into a warmth in her gut. Her insides glowed. She turned to look at him and got caught in his blue eyes for a moment before he smiled and returned to the conversation.

The chatter went on around her and Lacy knew she participated, but she couldn't recall what they talked about or even what she said. A glass of water appeared before her and she looked up to see Jonah smiling at her.

She smiled back and leaned into his warmth. Everything felt different tonight, likely because of the booze, but she wasn't worried. Everyone was laughing and having a good time.

Claire gave her an odd look once, but it was there and gone so quick Lacy was pretty sure she imagined it. Another shot appeared. Lacy drank it without even a thought.

Logan leaned across the table to Jonah when Claire and Phoebe disappeared. Where had they gone? Was she supposed to go too? When she started to rise, Jonah's hand pressed down on her thigh. She glanced at him, but his attention was directed on Logan. Maybe Jonah had a crush on Logan too.

"Claire is awesome. I don't normally have friends that are girls, but she's the best. When we go out tomorrow, you'll see." Logan lifted a glass of beer to his lips. Man, he had nice lips.

"The whole office seems like good people." Jonah's hand remained on her thigh. His thumb stroked back and forth lightly. Tingles danced along her veins from his touch. His hand seemed really warm. Lacy placed her hand over his to see if it was really that warm.

"Claire is one of the guys. Emily is friendly. Phoebe is

awesome and knows the best places to find a hookup." Logan stopped.

"What about Lacy?" Jonah asked.

"Yeah, what about me?" Lacy swore there were two of Logan across from her now. She squeezed her eyes shut and then opened them, but they stayed as two. So weird. Maybe she only liked one of them. That would be awkward. She giggled.

"I've never seen Lacy drunk before." Logan smiled that soft smile of his. "She'll probably forget I said this, but Lacy is cute. She's like the office puppy or kitten. Everyone wants to take care of her. Just like a little sister."

That was sweet. Jonah squeezed her thigh and her goofy grin dropped as she turned to him. His beard looked weird. Like it was all tangled up together like wires. She reached out and touched it. Huh, it was softer than she thought it would be. His lips looked soft too. Maybe she'd touch those too.

"Yup, Lacy's drunk." Phoebe returned to her seat. "She's officially cut off."

Lacy kept her fingers in Jonah's beard and turned to Phoebe. The room spun just a little around her. "I'm not drunk."

Phoebe smiled at her and patted Lacy's hand on the table. "Of course not, dear."

JONAH SWALLOWED as Lacy's fingers started stroking his beard. Yeah, she was gone.

"Logan and I are heading out. Are you going to be able to get her home?" Claire didn't look worried for Lacy at all. They all said they wanted to protect her, but not from him. If he wasn't a stand-up guy, he could totally take advantage of

Lacy. He wouldn't, but how could they know that? They've known him all of a week.

"I've got her." Jonah definitely wouldn't be leaving her in the care of someone like Logan. Turns out, Lacy was a handsy drunk. Her finger lightly brushed the corner of his mouth, sending warmth pulsing through his system. Sensations he would definitely be ignoring or at least attempting to ignore.

"We'll see you tomorrow night. I'll text you the deets." Logan stood and headed with Claire to the door.

"What about you?" Jonah looked at Phoebe. "Are you going to be okay to get home or do you want to catch a ride with us?"

"I'm waiting for the bartender to get off in an hour, so we can both get off." She winked and smiled at Lacy, who still seemed enthralled with his beard. "You good to get this one home?"

"We live together," Lacy said and smiled at Phoebe.

Jonah chuckled. "Yeah, I'll make sure she makes it to her bed before passing out."

Phoebe laughed and headed toward the bar, leaving just the two of them.

Jonah looked down at Lacy who still seemed enthralled with his beard.

"Lacy?"

She lifted her eyes to his. "Your beard is soft."

He captured her hand in his to stop the teasing touch. "You ready to go home?"

Her eyes went in and out of focus before she nodded. "I'm sleepy."

"I know, little bird, but we need to make it to the apartment before you pass out." He stood and helped her up with him.

"I've never passed out before." She leaned heavily into him as they made their way to the door. "Am I drunk?"

"Yes." Jonah opened the door and never released her arm as they stepped to the curb to find a ride. He pulled out his phone to open the app.

Lacy leaned into him with her nose pressed to his shirt. "You smell nice."

"Thanks, you do too." Peaches. He rested one arm around her waist to keep her close. She kept listing to one side and if he didn't hold her, she'd end up on the ground. He also liked the way she felt pressed against him, but she was way too drunk for anything more than leaning on him tonight. Thankfully.

"Ocean air," she sighed. Her fingers grasped his belt loops.

The driver was only two minutes away. Jonah put his phone in his pocket and draped his arms around Lacy's waist while she leaned against him.

"Did you have fun?" he asked, trying to keep her focusing on words rather than their closeness. He didn't want her to feel self-conscious, but she also needed him to hold her up. Not that he minded holding her.

"I don't think I should do shots again." Lacy looked up at him. Her hands pressed lightly against his chest.

"Why not?"

"Because I feel woozy and— Your chest is really solid, like rock hard." Her eyes drifted down to his chest where her fingers pressed into his pecs. "Have you felt your chest?"

"You can lay down when we get home."

"Both of us?" She glanced up at him with a sly look in her eyes.

He raised an eyebrow at her and she giggled. The sound tugged at his heart.

The car pulled up. At last.

"This is us." He managed to get drunk Lacy into the car and seat belted with no problems.

"That your girlfriend?" the driver asked, looking over Lacy in the rearview mirror.

Jonah nodded. Not liking the way this guy looked at her. Jonah had stopped taking shots long before Lacy did, knowing it would be on him to get her home safely. He was completely sober.

"Cool." The driver pulled away from the curb. Maybe the guy was just looking out for the drunk girl. Maybe he had hoped to hit on the drunk girl.

Lacy didn't seem to notice the exchange and stared out the window on the ride home. When they pulled up to the apartment building, Jonah helped Lacy out of the seatbelt and onto the curb.

"Thanks," he said as he closed the door on the guy and watched him take off.

"Did you tell him I was your girlfriend?"

Jonah looked down at Lacy's wide eyes. "You are a girl and my friend. . . ."

"I'm your friend." She got this aww look on her face. She started to reach for his beard again, but he captured her hand. She shook his hand with hers. "You said I'm your friend. You like me."

He shook his head. "Come on, let's get you into bed."

"Mr. Sinclair, I'm not that kind of girl." Her goofy grin and chuckle spoiled the insulted look. "Though you are that kind of guy. Logan's that kind of guy too. Maybe I should be that kind of girl. What do you think?"

"I think we should get into the building." Jonah got her through the front door and into the elevator. She slumped against the elevator wall and her eyes started to close.

"Nope, not time to sleep yet, little bird." He tugged her against him and rubbed her arms to try to keep her awake.

"Little bird," she chuckled. "You are so weird. You make me feel weird too."

"How so?" He glanced down at her. She drew a circle on his chest with her fingertip.

"Like a storm inside. Like sexually," she whispered loudly. She glanced up at him, her pretty brown eyes blank. "What are we talking about?"

Fuck, this woman would kill him. He couldn't go there with her. He shook his head. "I have no idea."

"Good. Me either." Her grin was sloppy as she leaned into him again.

The elevator arrived on their floor and he shuffled her down to their door. Finally, they walked into their apartment.

"I'm home," she yelled and stumbled toward the couch.

Jonah locked up and got a couple of bottles of water from the refrigerator. "You hungry?"

"Yes, I am," she replied in a low voice.

"Are you mocking me?"

She tipped over on the couch, laughing. "You growl words. How does someone growl words?"

Stifling a grin, he shook his head and grabbed some crackers and cheese before heading to the couch. He sat next to her and gave her a bottle of water after removing the lid. She'd kicked off her shoes beside the chair. Her forehead crinkled like she was thinking hard about something. He wanted to reach over and smooth the lines.

"Do you think I'm cute?" She drank some of the water and reached for a cracker.

"I'd say more annoying than cute, currently." He grinned as she started to tip to one side. He reached out to steady her and her gaze fell on his hand.

"It's like you're on fire. I like it too much." Her words

were soft. But then she pouted at him and said, "You don't think I'm cute. Logan thinks I'm cute."

"Yes, you are cute and a little funny when you are drunk." Jonah didn't really want to talk about Logan. Her mind wasn't exactly firing on all cylinders at the moment, hopping from topic to topic.

"Am I sexy?" Her wide brown eyes lifted to his, her hand landed on his chest, and he forgot to breathe.

"What do you think?" He pushed out around the sudden frog in his throat. Hell yeah, she was, but she was too drunk right now. He couldn't admit to her what he wanted to do to her. Even if he didn't think Logan was the right guy for her, somewhere out there was a guy who would be everything a woman like Lacy needed. Stable, loving, invested. And that wasn't Jonah.

"I think everyone thinks I'm cute, but no one thinks I'm sexy. I need to flirt more." She set down the water. She pushed her hair from her face, gathering it in a ponytail before letting it fall down. "Logan isn't my first crush to call me cute."

"Oh?" Again with Logan. The guy barely gave her the time of day. Jonah didn't understand what she saw in him. He needed her to eat or she'd end up sick. Jonah handed her another cracker. She took it and used it as a prop for her speech.

"In college, I met Chet. He was in a fraternity, and holy crap was he gorgeous. Like so gorgeous." She waved the cracker in his face and sighed. "I could see us together after just meeting him once. He picked up my ID card that fell in the quad. Like destiny, you know?"

"You don't have to tell me this." Jonah really didn't want to know. He already wanted to deck Logan at times. Now he'd have it in for guys named Chet. Chet was a douchebag name anyway.

"I want to tell you." She straightened, saw the cracker in her hand, and ate it. "I was at one of the frat's parties. He called me cute. See, Chet liked me back. Which was a first for me. My crushes never liked me back and my friends always told me that, but Chet liked me back. He started hanging out with me a lot. He kissed me. Me!"

"Okay." Hopefully she would lose her train of thought.

She sighed and looked off. "Chet said we had something real and so we slept together. I mean sex. We had sex. But then it hadn't been real at all. The sex was, but he just wanted to sleep with me. Another notch for him. So I'm okay with going slow with Logan to really figure out if he likes me, but I can't figure out if he likes me. Do you know what I mean?"

Jonah nodded. He really wanted to find that Chet guy and kick his ass.

"Are you mad at me?" She frowned up at him.

"No."

She reached out and used her fingers to try to smooth his forehead before he pulled her hands away.

"I'm supposed to flirt and smile and make eye contact and connect. You know?" Lacy's eyebrows pulled together. "There's more."

"To what?" Jonah couldn't quite figure out what she was talking about.

"To get Logan to ask me out. Duh." She booped him on the nose. Or at least attempted to but her finger landed on his lips. "Whoops."

She pulled her hand back and looked at it like it had done something wrong. Jonah exhaled. Surely she'd had enough water and crackers to make it to bed without getting sick by now. He started to open his mouth, but then she sighed.

"Thank you." Her hand softly touched his.

"For what?" He lifted his gaze to hers. She really had incredible eyes, dark and vulnerable.

"For making sure I made it home and taking care of me when I drank too much." She smiled and leaned back against the couch. Her head rolled toward him. "It's not every day a guy calls me his girlfriend and then gives me water and crackers with cheese."

Jonah relaxed into the couch. "You're not every girl."

She chuckled and he wanted to kiss her. It wasn't the first time he'd had the urge, and it wouldn't be the last time. He wouldn't kiss her, but the urge lingered. He just wanted to feel if her lips were as soft as they looked. His desire for her hadn't lessened over the week. He tried to ignore it. Tried to avoid situations where it would be obvious.

But he always felt like he was seconds from leaning in to kiss her.

He cleared his throat. "When does Sophie return?"

A buffer for when they were home alone seemed essential and Sophie would provide that.

Lacy lifted her hand as if to say I don't know, but then held up a finger. "Wait."

No one had said anything. She looked like she was receiving a message from the other side.

"I think. . . yes, she texted. Something about not being home for a week. Work something or other. I don't know. It was before that second shot. Why did I do shots? I never do shots." Her hands went to her stomach. "I don't think the crackers were a good idea."

Jonah sat up, alert. "You do look a little greenish."

She covered her mouth and started for the bathroom. He was right behind her as she knelt next to the toilet. He held her hair and rubbed her back as she vomited. He'd worried this would be the ending to her night when she hadn't passed on the shots. Her poor body shook beneath his palm.

When she finally stopped, he wet a washcloth and filled a glass with water.

He settled on the floor and leaned against the tub before drawing her between his legs to rest her back against his chest. Her body went limp against his, but she was still awake. He wiped her face with the washcloth including the tears. He helped her sip some of the water and then she sagged against him, turning into him. He gathered her against him as she sat on his lap.

"Drinking isn't fun." She buried her face into his shirt and he continued to rub her back.

He rested his chin on top of her head. "Not always."

"Did you have fun tonight?" Her voice was small and fading.

"I did. Did you?"

"Hmmm." Was the only response. She had curled into him and fallen asleep.

He brushed her hair off her forehead and placed a kiss there. She snuggled into him and sighed softly. Maybe Sophie had been right; everyone seemed to want to fix things for Lacy. To take care of her. Even him.

He held her for a little while on the bathroom floor just in case she got sick again. He grudgingly admitted he liked how she felt in his arms and didn't want to let her go.

Lacy would be mortified if she remembered tonight. Telling him about Chet. Letting Jonah hold her. Feeling his beard. He couldn't help his gentle smile at the thought of her pinkened cheeks and bursts of words to cover for what she'd done. He could stay like this all night, but she wasn't his to hold and never could be.

Finally, he lifted her into his arms and carried her into her room without turning on the light. She still wore her clothes from work, but he tucked her in anyway, dragging the blankets from the center of the bed to cover her.

She snuggled into her blankets with a slight tremor, like

she was cold. Her hand closed around his and dragged it to her chest, curling herself around his arm.

"Lacy, I need to go." He sat on the edge of the bed. This was a bad idea.

"Stay please," she whispered. "Just for a minute."

She probably didn't even realize who she was talking to. Using his other hand, he brushed her hair from her face. "I'll stay until you go to sleep."

She let out a sigh and relaxed. "Good."

The temptation to lie down with her and offer his warmth tugged at him, but he knew he shouldn't. She tempted him beyond reason even when he just wanted to hold her. Instead, he pressed his lips against her forehead again. Her breath had evened out and he gently pulled his arm away. She exhaled softly and he left the room.

THE BLENDER! Always the blender. Lacy sat up in bed and shoved her blankets off. Her head ached and her throat was dry. She didn't have to open her eyes to realize she still wore yesterday's clothes. It didn't matter. Coffee was the answer. Always.

She stumbled out of her room and, using her hands, felt her way into the kitchen. Her fingers crashed into Jonah's skin. Not his shirt. A surge of warmth spread through her, almost like a shot of coffee. But without the caffeine, it wasn't the same. Her fingers lingered on his hard muscles as a memory tried to rear forward.

Her head pulsed in protest. One of her hands left Jonah to clutch at the pounding in her brain.

Jonah's hands caught around her waist and lifted her to sit on the counter. He grabbed her hand with one of his and with the other, pressed a warm mug into it.

"Drink, little bird." Jonah. She relaxed. He stayed close to her. His heat comforted her, and his presence kept her from falling off the counter as she drank.

His fingers tucked her hair out of her face, but she still didn't want to open her eyes. "Noisy."

"Sorry."

She could almost hear the smile in that word. He wasn't sorry at all. She sighed.

"Head hurts."

"Not surprised."

She cracked open an eye as she drank more coffee. "You?"

"Me?" Jonah leaned against the corner of the kitchen counters, close enough to catch her if she fell. She appreciated that since she didn't go sitting on the counter usually and never before her coffee.

"Your head?" She gestured vaguely toward him.

"I stopped drinking after shot number two."

She groaned and closed her eyes. "Why didn't I?"

He chuckled. The cabinet opened and the rattle of a pill bottle sounded. "Here."

She opened her eyes and looked at the pills in his hand. She took them and swallowed them with her coffee. "Thanks."

"Anytime." He picked up his smoothie and drank.

Even after drinking over half her coffee, last night was really fuzzy. The shots had kept coming and she'd wanted to keep up with the other ladies, who must be professional drinkers. "Did I do anything embarrassing last night?"

"Would you consider dancing on the table embarrassing?" His eyebrow rose.

Her mouth fell open.

"I didn't." She would have remembered that, right? "Did I?"

He chuckled again. "You didn't. Stop worrying."

She rubbed at her temple, trying to remember. "After the third shot, things got really funky."

"How so?"

She caught the little tilt of his lips. "I remember your beard. . . why do I remember your beard?"

"You might have been feeling it up." He smirked as he took a drink.

"Oh my God, I did." Her hand covered her lips and warmth flooded her cheeks. If feeling up Jonah's beard was the worst thing she did, she'd be happy. She sipped a little more before saying, "You asked Logan about me."

He nodded. "We discussed the woman at work."

Something teased at her brain. Something Logan said. "Did he. . . ." What was it? "He said I was cute."

"Like a puppy." Jonah's voice deepened a little and she shot him a look.

She felt the burn of anger before she realized, "Did he say I was like a little sister?"

Jonah nodded, watching her intently.

She finished her coffee and held out her mug for more. Of course Logan would think of her as a little sister. That explained those stupid soft smiles. She wasn't even on his radar. And why would she be?

Jonah filled her cup. She glanced down at her wrinkled clothes. Even they were a disappointment. Flattering and comfortable, but they didn't scream hot or sexy like Claire's high heels or Morgan's pencil skirts or anything Phoebe wore. Hell, even Emily's flowing clothes were romantic. Lacy was utilitarian.

Another memory drifted in. Lacy remembered sitting on the couch and telling Jonah about Chet. "Oh, crap."

"What?" Jonah's eyes weren't filled with pity thankfully. Just the same old Jonah stood there, watching her.

"Did I tell you about Chet?" She winced as if saying his name out loud would summon the jerk.

A flash of anger went through his eyes, but then it vanished. "Yeah."

Well, shit.

"Can you help me down?" She glanced at Jonah. With her up here, they were practically the same height. She didn't trust her legs to catch her if she jumped down.

He didn't say anything, just put his glass beside the sink and lifted her from the counter and set her on her feet. His bare chest was directly in front of her. Her fingertips tingled to trace over the ridges of muscles. Being this close to him felt familiar before he backed away.

"Did you hold me?" The memory was blurred but she swore she'd felt his arms around her and not just once. She had this urge to lean against him, like he would keep her safe.

"It was either hold you or watch you wipe out on the sidewalk in front of the bar." Jonah leaned in his spot, watching her warily.

"There's something else." What was it? She couldn't put her finger on it. "Did I get sick?"

"Yes." He seemed more closed off suddenly. Weird.

A bit of a memory crept into her mind of kneeling on the bathroom floor and a warm hand rubbing her back. Then being held again. She glanced up at Jonah. He was the only one here. Had he held her or was that a dream?

"How did I get to bed?" She barely remembered being in the apartment. She was thankful she didn't remember much about getting sick, but she had no idea how she made it to her bed. For all she knew, she stumbled in and crashed.

"I carried you."

Heat flooded her face. She definitely didn't remember that.

"Okay." Well, one mystery solved, but why was he stand-offish again? "Did I hit on you?"

A slight tilt to his mouth, almost the illusion of a smile. "No."

"Huh."

He had taken her to her bedroom and put her fully clothed in bed. Sleeping would have been more comfortable in pajamas, but at least she didn't have to blush every time she looked at him, knowing he had undressed her. "Thank you for *not* helping me undress."

"Of course." He nodded with a faint lift to his lips.

Okay back to the thought that kept spinning around in her head like a noisy gnat. "Logan said little sister. That I was like a little sister?"

Jonah nodded. His expression gave nothing away.

"Is that how everyone sees me?" she said it mostly to herself, but Jonah nodded again.

"Well, crap." She set down her almost empty second cup of coffee with a little more force than necessary. "Nobody *wants* their little sister as a girlfriend."

Something about that last word triggered something, but she couldn't hold onto it. A feeling of being cherished and safe floated through her memory. But it came with a slight pounding again.

Hangover from hell. "Remind me to not drink like that again."

"I will." The sincerity in his voice calmed her. He was a good guy.

She glanced up at Jonah and felt that whirlwind whip through her. He held so still, but his eyes almost burned her with heat. He stood there with no shirt on and his athletic pants hanging low on his hips. He had carried her to bed. He had held her to keep her from falling. He'd kept her safe after she'd drank too much. He'd taken care of her when she'd gotten sick. Something pinched in her chest as a thought occurred to her.

"Do you see me as a little sister?" She lifted her eyes to his and mentally chastised herself. She didn't want to know. It would hurt if he did, but what did it mean if he didn't. "Never mind, that's stupid."

"No."

His word made her freeze.

She searched his blue eyes hoping for something to tell her what she should do. What she could do with what he stirred up in her. Because it made her frightened. Not of him. Never of him. But the cravings he sparked. The desire to press a little further than she normally would and that would lead to trouble for her.

Just like with Chet.

Except she wasn't a virgin teenager now.

"Good." She broke the eye contact because her heart pounded so loud she swore he could hear it. "We're meeting them out tonight?"

He nodded and turned to rinse his cup. The muscles in his back rippled with his movement. Lacy swallowed at the prickling down her spine and reminded herself to focus on Logan.

Somehow, she needed Logan to see she wasn't a little sister. She wished Sophie was here or Beth. They always had great clothes to wear out and loved to give her makeovers. Even Brenda would do in a pinch, and she definitely knew what guys liked. As his friend, maybe Brenda knew what Jonah liked. Not Jonah, ugh. Lacy shook that thought out of her head.

She didn't have her friends to help her this time.

Plan B.

"You're a guy." Surely he could help. He knew what guys liked women to wear. What Logan would like.

It was like Jonah turned to stone at the sink. "What?"

"Beth and Sophie are gone and they usually would help me become better than cute for a night out, but you're a guy and know what looks sexy on women, right?"

He made a non-committal grunt.

"You could help me get ready for tonight." She bounced on her toes. "I need something new and I suck at shopping. Please say you'll come shopping with me. I want tonight to change things with Logan and they won't if plain Lacy shows up."

His shoulders tensed and she worried he would say no. If he said no, she'd need a female of some sorts. Asking Claire would be beyond embarrassing. Emily left for the weekend. She didn't feel close enough to ask Phoebe or Morgan. Candy's outfit had been awesome last weekend. . . .

"I mean. I guess I could just ask you for Candy's number. She seemed nice and would probably help me find an outfit to make the boys drool. So there you go. You are off the hook. Do you think she'd be available? Just give me Candy's number and you'll be free to do whatever you like and won't have to be burdened with taking me shopping." She smiled up at him, satisfied to find a good answer to her problem. Sure, she didn't know Candy, but that could be beneficial. Because Candy wouldn't put Lacy into the same box everyone else did.

He still didn't move or look at her. Maybe he'd stopped listening to her. She did have a tendency to ramble around him.

"Jonah?"

"I'll do it." The tension in his back released.

"What? Candy's number?" Lacy stepped away not sure what she'd gotten herself into.

He turned and his eyes pinned her in place. "You and me. Shopping. In an hour."

∾

WITH HIS ARMS crossed over his chest, Jonah stood inside the boutique next to the door, while Lacy wandered through the rows of clothing. Her fingers trailed over everything, but she didn't pick anything to try on. He didn't tell her earlier that she didn't need to try to be sexy, but apparently that was only obvious to him. And Candy was an okay person, but she didn't need to fill Lacy's head with more doubt. Or tart up Lacy too much, until she was uncomfortable the whole night. Lacy had to be Lacy to be sexy.

She lifted her gaze to him and then it skittered away again. The jeans she had on fit over her curves and showcased those long legs of hers. Her shirt was one of those fluttery numbers that just hinted at the curves underneath. He wanted to slide his hand under it and absorb the heat of her skin as he pressed her against him.

Jonah uncrossed his arms. They needed to get this over with before he did something he'd regret. He walked over to the rack she was browsing.

"Maybe some skinny jeans and a cute top." Lacy stopped and flinched. "Not cute. Sexy. Definitely sexy."

He gave her a noise to let her know he heard her. He didn't shop a lot, but he had a sister. He also paid attention. "You need to try on clothes."

She turned and stepped in close to him before lifting her gaze to his. "I don't know what to pick." She glanced over her shoulder as if people were trying to listen to their conversation. No one stood anywhere near them, but she leaned even closer and fake whispered, "Obviously I don't know what's sexy."

"We're in advertising. We tell people what's sexy." Jonah did his best to keep his eyes from falling to her lips. She had on the lightest touch of makeup, including a swipe of gloss over her lips. They practically begged to be kissed.

It wasn't the makeup though. She just had to be around

him and he wanted to kiss her. He wanted to do more than kiss her. But for the sake of his current living and work situation, he wouldn't be doing anything with her, except be her friend. Which also hadn't been part of his plan, but he could adapt.

"I'm not good at that part of our job. I'm great at the cute part though." She smiled up at him and turned on her heel to the rack of clothes.

"All right. How about we make this a challenge?" Jonah waited for her to look at him.

Her eyebrow rose. "What kind of challenge?"

"Let's see who can pick out the sexiest outfit for you."

"What does the winner get?" Both of her eyebrows raised with curiosity.

"Lunch. I'd say drinks tonight, but something tells me you won't be drinking a lot." He couldn't help the quick flash of a grin on his lips.

She groaned and pressed a finger against her temple. "Not drinking for a long time."

"Do we have a wager?" He held out his hand.

She eyed it and looked up at him with a smirk on her lips. "I thought we didn't shake hands."

"We could kiss on it." The words slipped out of his mouth. He wanted her to say yes. He wanted her to laugh it off. He wanted to kiss her until she knew how sexy she was to him.

Instead, she grabbed his hand with hers. "Fine. We'll shake on it. Lunch."

His hand engulfed hers and he smiled. There was his fierce little bird.

She gave him her sizes and then they spread out. He'd shopped with his sister before and he knew what he liked on a woman, but shopping for Lacy was different. He'd seen her work style, even her casual weekend clothes, and her pajamas, but she'd never worn anything that screamed sexy. To him, even her kitten pajamas were sexy because she wore them. They tantalized with brief glimpses rather than giving everything away, and they were loose on her, making for easy access.

Soon they stood in the changing room area with a decent selection of clothes for her to try on.

"No wimping out. You have to come out and show me." He held onto the clothes when she went to take them from him.

She smiled, obviously placating him. "Of course."

"If you don't, I'll have to come in." He gave her a wicked grin.

She flushed pink and dropped her gaze for a second. "Noted."

He released the clothes. As she slipped into the room, he sat on the bench, still in the changing room area away from the other customers. The light piped-in music covered any sign of anyone else's existence. The rustle of clothing behind the curtain seemed amplified. Taking out his phone, he answered a few texts from Logan about tonight. Where to meet. When. That kind of thing. Anything to distract him from Lacy undressing. Some nightclub named Fire and after dinner around eight.

"This is definitely a no," came her distasteful tone from behind the curtain.

"You still have to show me." He grinned at her groan of displeasure. "A deal has been made. I'm more than willing to com—"

"Fine." Her voice was curt. She came out in a chunky dress that looked like it belonged on a doll and not a woman. It was sleeveless and the shape was almost like a bell. It didn't show any of her curves, but it stopped at the top of her thighs. She made a face. "See I told you."

He dropped his smile. "Yeah, that's not it."

"Why did you even pick this?" She held up the hem and he saw more of her thigh or more precisely her hip.

The dress was actually quite short. Her long legs were completely exposed and her legs were amazing, which was one of the reasons he'd picked it.

She narrowed her eyes at him and then followed where his gaze had settled. "Oh my God, you can almost see my underwear."

She escaped behind the curtains.

"Underwear is sexy." Jonah chuckled as he leaned against the wall. Suddenly aware that she stood behind a flimsy curtain in only her underwear. He'd seen her in only a towel. He'd also seen her panties hanging to dry. But he hadn't seen Lacy in just her panties.

"I need something to go over my underwear and still be sexy." Lacy's voice was muffled and he wondered if she was putting something on or taking it off.

The store hadn't been busy and everyone else was somewhere up front, not near the changing rooms. No one would know if he slipped in there with her. What would she do? Fluff up indignant and force him out or would she bite that lush bottom lip of hers with those eyes darkened with longing. . . .

He shook off his lustful thoughts. He should have never agreed to this. Keeping his distance had kept his desire for her banked during the week, but holding her last night and spending time with her today had stoked the fire into a burning flame. Tonight would be a trial by fire and he would get burned.

Lacy needed someone to be here for her. Not a guy who felt untethered and lost. Not a guy who grabbed onto an opportunity to find something to hold him and make him feel a part of something. Not a broken man like him.

The fire adequately banked again. He managed to

distance himself a little from her as she continued to try on outfits. The next few outfits were all no's from either him or her or both. They either didn't fit right or just didn't do Lacy justice.

She came out again. A pair of tight jeans hugged her curves. The top was a high-necked crop top in a soft green color. Between the low cut of the jeans and the crop top, her stomach was bared. Trim waist, slight curve to her belly. If she were his, he'd have a tough time keeping his hands off her exposed skin in this outfit. He flexed his hands. Her hands tried to cover her stomach from his eyes.

"What do you think?" he asked her. She seemed horribly uncomfortable and it was obvious.

"Skin is sexy, right?" She glanced down at her belly button and winced before crossing her arms over her stomach. Her cheeks flushed pink and she wouldn't meet his gaze. She had nothing to be ashamed of.

He stood and crossed over to her. He turned her around to face the mirror and drew her hands away from her stomach, holding them out to her sides. He met her gaze in the mirror. "Is this a sexy look on you? Fuck yes. But if you aren't comfortable, you won't be confident."

"But I'll be sexy?" Her arms remained out to the side because he hadn't dropped them. He ran his gaze over her in the mirror because he could and he wanted to. He wished he could run his hands over her, but that wouldn't be smart.

"Let me tell you a secret." He released her hands and stepped closer until a breath separated his front from her back. Heat radiated from her body, stirring his desire hotter.

She gazed up at him in the mirror with her huge brown eyes wide. Her arms wrapped around her middle, but she leaned into him a little, listening.

"Confidence is sexy, and if you aren't one hundred percent confident, you won't be sexy even in your underwear." He stepped away, more for his own mental health than anything else. He gave her a thorough once-over. "But you are sexy no matter what you wear."

"You're just being nice." She tried to head into the changing room.

"I'm rarely nice, little bird." His words stopped her. "I don't believe in handing out compliments so someone will feel better about themselves. When I say you are sexy, I mean it. I'm not sure why no one else sees it, but I do. In your weird little pajamas or your work clothes, you are sexy to me. Every. Fucking. Day."

She bit her lip and held her breath.

He didn't know if she believed him or not, but he'd said his piece. Not that he'd do anything about it. She needed to find a nice guy to settle down with, not someone who would leave. "Go find something you like to try on next."

CHAPTER 9

LETTING HER ARMS HANG DOWN, Lacy stayed in front of the three-way mirror and really looked at herself. She could see Jonah's reflection in the mirror as he returned to the bench. His eyes still had heat in them that made her want to melt.

Focus. She took her time to assess what he said. This outfit was sexy which made her uncomfortable. It showed her curves which weren't like Claire's or Morgan's. She didn't have a classic hourglass shape. But her waist was small and the outfit helped emphasize it without revealing every-thing, but it also showed a lot of skin.

She met Jonah's gaze in the mirror and sucked in a breath. He liked what he saw and didn't hide that fact. Heat rose to her cheeks and she broke the eye contact to go hide in the changing room. She didn't know what to do with the words Jonah had put out there, but she could keep trying on clothes.

The clothes they'd picked out weren't necessarily what she would normally buy, but she sorted through them to find something to spark joy in her. Too many of them were similar to the crop top. But a pleated plaid skirt that fell to mid-thigh and a black halter top caught her attention. Jonah had picked it out. It would show off a little more leg than she usually did and her shoulders would be bare, but she liked it.

After changing into it, she turned to look at herself in the mirror. She didn't feel the need to cover herself, which was a good start. She tried to look at it the way Jonah might.

Or rather Logan might. After all, she was doing this so Logan might actually see her as more than his little sister to protect from the big bad wolves of the world.

"Do I need to come in?" Jonah's low gravelly voice ricocheted through her insides like lightning. Speaking of big bad wolves. What would happen if she let him in? Would he help her undress? Would he back her up against the wall and kiss her?

Kiss her? Where the hell had that come from?

"Coming out." She opened the curtain and stepped out, looking at the ground, trying to figure out what was going on in her brain. Sure, she was attracted to Jonah, but it was most likely because of his little sex show. It should pass.

A low whistle came out of Jonah, drawing her attention. His gaze blazed a trail of fire across her as he took her outfit in. Her knees almost gave out and her bare toes curled under his scrutiny.

If she hadn't felt sexy before, his look told her she was, and that went straight to her head like the shots from last night. Not to mention the sparks it ignited across her skin.

To avoid his eyes and the whirlwind starting within her, she turned to the mirror. Her shoulders were completely bare. The black shirt tied around her neck and the ends of the string teased the middle of her back. Her back was exposed but no more than when wearing a swimsuit. A hint of skin showed between the shirt and skirt, but not nearly as much as the crop top.

"I don't think I can wear a bra with this," she mumbled more to herself as she looked at how low the back was.

"Would that make you uncomfortable?" He hadn't moved, but his voice felt like he was right at her ear, like last night when his lips had brushed her ear when he'd leaned in to talk to her. Her whole body lit like a sparkler at the memory. She wanted his warmth to engulf her, to sink into his heat.

"Probably not, but I could always wear a strapless bra." She met his heated gaze in the mirror. She wanted him to look at her like that. The memory of him and Candy came crashing down over her. Candy bent over the counter, skirt around her waist, and Lacy had met Jonah's eyes. . . . Damn, Jonah's eyes had the same look in them now as that night.

A pulse hit her between her legs. Her whole body stood at attention, waiting for him to make a move. Wanting him to make a move. To come over and show her exactly how Candy felt with him behind her, thrusting in and out. Her breath caught.

What the hell had gotten into her? Jonah didn't want her like that. No one did. She forced her eyes closed to break the connection and took a deep breath.

"You okay?" His low growl only fanned the flames trying to engulf her.

She heard Jonah stand and she wanted to put out a hand to stop him from coming any closer, but she couldn't. She'd never felt this way about any guy before. Like every inch of her longed for his touch.

And that was so freaking dangerous.

She didn't need Beth to remind her of Chet and her horrible first time where she thought they'd been in love. He hadn't cared about her at all. Her attraction to Chet was barely a candle compared to the inferno Jonah sparked within her.

This thing with Jonah would pass. It had to. She didn't love him. He definitely didn't love her.

Logan was the guy for her. It had been him for the past few months. She couldn't just let what she felt go. He would be the real deal for her. He had to be. She knew it. She had to focus on Logan.

Logan's smile warmed her heart. He always talked to her, not like the guys in her past who had ignored her. He did sweet things like making sure she had a coffee mug when they were out of reach. He included her on projects when he and Claire had a handle on it. He wasn't just some guy who once picked up her pen in the hallway. He was part of her work life. Logan would be it for her.

She took another deep breath and opened her eyes. Jonah remained next to the bench. Concern lingered in his eyes. Her heart couldn't stop pounding.

Forcing a smile, she said, "I'm good. I think this is it. So I owe you lunch."

Stepping away from the mirror, she returned to the dressing room.

"Just give me a minute to change and we can go." She tugged the curtain closed and pressed her hands over her pounding heart.

"I'll wait out there for you."

She released her breath and looked up at the ceiling. What the hell was that? Jonah was a hot guy, but he was also her roommate and coworker. They'd brushed aside the incident she'd witnessed and had actually done well this week. But last night, his lips to her ear, his hand on her thigh, his body holding hers. She sank into that decadent warm feeling for a second.

All these thoughts didn't help her tame this longing swirling around her insides. She straightened up and got busy.

Quickly she put on her own clothes and felt a small hint of relief at seeing she really hadn't changed. The mirror showed the same plain Lacy. Even though her cheeks had extra color in them. She shook her head at her reflection and grabbed the outfit.

Tonight, she would focus on Logan and see if she could break through his perception of her being the office puppy. She'd try to push Jonah on Claire. That way she wouldn't feel guilty about ignoring him and his words that turned her inside out.

She paid for the clothes as Jonah leaned against the wall next to the door. Resolved to just be friends with Jonah, she walked up to him and smiled. "Ready for lunch?"

LACY SPENT the afternoon texting with Beth and hiding in her room. She sent Beth a pic of the outfit and they discussed jewelry, hairstyle, and makeup to go with it.

Are you ready to go all in? Beth texted. *You've got the look. Flirt with him. See if he responds positively to your flirting. Pay him compliments.*

Lacy took a deep breath. She could do this. She was a sexy woman, not a child or a pet. She glanced at her closed bedroom door. Jonah thought she was sexy. He said he wasn't just being nice, but what if he was? It didn't matter. She couldn't afford to have more than a passing attraction for him. He lived with her and had become her actual friend. A friend who made her weak in the knees when he looked at her, but still...

Something has to change. I'm going to get Logan to ask me out tonight, Lacy texted. She could only hope that would happen. Obviously, she was hardwired to want guys who wouldn't want her. It didn't make sense, but eventually one of them had to want her the same way, and unlike Chet, actually want to keep her, not just use her.

Logan wouldn't use her that way.

He'll be eating out of your hand before you can turn into a pumpkin, Beth texted.

Suddenly Lacy had another thought and didn't want to type it out. She pressed the call button.

Beth picked up immediately. "What's up?"

Lacy bit her lip and looked at the door. She didn't want to say the words and make it real, but she had to. "What if I'm broken?"

"What do you mean?" Beth's voice was steady but concerned.

"What if I'm doomed to repeat the same pattern over and over again? What if I never find a guy who wants me and who I want in return?" She squeezed her eyes shut and took a deep breath before revealing, "What if the reason Chet didn't want me anymore was because I'm no good at sex?"

"Fuck Chet." Anger edged Beth's voice. "I never liked him. He was a pervy frat boy and after what he did to you, he's lucky I didn't come there and castrate him."

"Sophie spread a rumor he had a micropenis." Lacy smiled and laid back on her bed.

"I love Sophie."

"Me too." Lacy stared up at her ceiling as her smile slipped.

"You're not broken, Lacy. Chet wanted to score and he took advantage of you." Beth sounded so confident, but Lacy wasn't sure.

"I've never been in a real relationship. The one time I had sex, the guy wouldn't give me the time of day afterwards. I'm pretty sure that means I'm broken."

"Listen to me. You are not broken. When you fall for someone, you don't do it by half measures. You don't just think maybe this is the one. You commit to him with your whole heart and soul. If a guy doesn't see that, that's on him. Not you."

Beth blew out a breath. "Lacy, someone's going to see you and he is going to love you so hard he'll never let you go. I just hope you are open to it when it happens and not so strung up on some other guy who will never give you anything but nice words that you miss the real guy."

Lacy inhaled a deep breath and absorbed Beth's words. She had to focus on her goal. "I'm going to make Logan see me as a woman tonight."

"Yeah, that's the spirit." Beth's grin could be heard in her words.

"I'm going to flirt so hard he won't know what hit him." Lacy smiled wide.

"That's my girl," Beth said. "Whatever happens, have fun tonight. You deserve a night out even if it's not with me."

"It would be better with you." Lacy wanted to hug her friend through the phone. "We need to set up a visit. Not an emergency intervention visit, but just you and me hanging out and eating ridiculous amounts of carbs."

"Send me your schedule and I'll work something in. Love you."

"Love you." Lacy let the phone fall to the bed beside her and sighed. Getting the guy was only part of the issue. The problem was she'd barely even kissed guys. She could count the number of guys she'd kissed on less than one hand. Yes, she'd slept with a guy, but it had meant more to her than to him obviously.

Assuming the guy was the right guy, her sexual inexperience shouldn't matter. She could learn to be better by being with that guy. Right? He'd give her time to learn what she needed to do. He'd find her sexy no matter what.

Jonah's blue eyes flashed in her mind. Nope. Focus on Logan. Dark hair, dark eyes. Gorgeous.

She sat up on her bed and scooted to the edge. It had gotten late. She needed to grab a bite to eat and then start getting ready for tonight.

Barefoot, she walked to her door and listened to figure out if Jonah was anywhere near. Not that she was avoiding him, but honestly. . . she was avoiding him. Lunch had been nice and the conversation light, but her stomach had been doing flip flops the entire time.

Not hearing anything, she opened her door and released her breath on finding the hallway empty. She rolled her eyes at herself. Because Jonah always stood in the hallway waiting to trap her. She really was going crazy. Maybe she should have a mental evaluation done. Was Chronic Love Sickness a valid diagnosis?

She shook her head as she went into the living room. The coast was clear. Jonah had either left the building or was in his bedroom. Acting like a complete loon, Lacy crept into the kitchen and pulled open the refrigerator door. She could probably get away with drinking a little tonight if she ate a decent dinner. She'd just milk each drink for all it was worth.

Everyone else would be drinking so having a drink in hand would be nice to fit in. Besides it would also help settle her nerves a little.

But she definitely needed food. She'd barely touched lunch. Her nerves had been so frazzled. She didn't know how to act around Jonah. And time definitely hadn't helped yet. He was nice and sometimes even sweet to her, but he pushed buttons that hadn't been pressed before. He turned her insides into liquid and put the blender on high speed.

"Dinner?"

"Holy crap!" She spun around.

Jonah smiled. "Gotcha, huh?"

Lacy let out a small laugh, but her heart didn't slow down. "Are you out of shirts?"

Once again Jonah strolled around without a shirt on.

Jonah glanced down at his chest. "Spilled something on it. Thought about putting on another, but need to take a shower before tonight."

That seemed logical enough, but they should seriously have a roommate meeting about appropriate dress for common areas when Sophie returned. Not that Sophie would mind. She enjoyed a little man candy and Jonah was a really fine specimen. Sophie might make a rule for topless Tuesday.

"Dinner?" He raised an eyebrow at her. She cleared her throat of the lump lodged in it.

"I was just looking for something." Lacy gestured at the open fridge behind her.

"Want to order with me? I know this Chinese place that's awesome." He held up his phone. "We can get ready for tonight while we wait."

He was so reasonable and helpful. Ignoring him and how he made her feel would be easier if he was a total asshole. Instead, she found herself nodding and closing the fridge door. "Sure. Do you have a menu?"

He held out his phone to her and she scrolled through the online menu before picking out a dish. She handed it back to him, careful to keep contact to a minimum.

"Do you want to use the shower first?" he asked.

She swallowed and looked up at him. His beard looked soft and her thumb tingled as she remembered his lips were soft too. Her breath caught. She'd been feeling his beard last night at the bar when her thumb had stroked the corner of his lips. Her eyes widened.

"I should take my shower." She stepped around him and scurried into her room. She grabbed her towel and some lacy underwear for courage (because no one else but her would see them) before sneaking into the bathroom. Okay she didn't really sneak, but she tried not to be noticeable.

Her shower steamed up the bathroom entirely. She may have taken an extra long shower, but she felt good and settled when she got out. With one towel wrapped around her hair and another around her body, Lacy stepped into the hallway.

Jonah stood in his doorway holding his towel. "Did you leave me any hot water?"

Lacy shrugged. "Probably."

His lips tipped into a smile and he said, "Had I known, I would have joined you. Food will be here in ten minutes."

"Sounds good." She nodded and went to her bedroom, holding her towel tight around her.

His deep chuckle followed her and she thought about what she said. Of course he knew she meant the food sounded good and not the shower together, right?

As she closed the door, she glanced at her outfit for tonight. She didn't want to mess it up with dinner, so she pulled out a pair of pajamas to slip on. This one had frogs kissing on it.

When the buzzer sounded, she went into the living room to let the delivery person up. Her hair still wrapped in a towel, she thanked the delivery person and took the food to the table.

The bathroom door opened and steam billowed out preceding Jonah. With a towel hanging on his hips, he held up his free hand. Her gaze lingered on his muscles and that towel. "I'll be just a minute."

With a dry mouth, she nodded and went to grab a couple of bottles of water. When she returned to the table, Jonah walked out of his room wearing a pair of jeans and again no shirt. His damp hair was slicked back. Her heart skipped a beat or two.

She pursed her lips and put her hands on her hips. "How would you like it if I walked around topless?"

"I'm all for that." He gave her a cheeky wink.

She realized what she said and chuckled even as flames licked her cheeks. She dropped into the chair and put one foot up on the seat.

"Besides I already ruined one shirt today." His hand stroked over his chest. "This is much easier to clean."

Lacy swallowed and focused on opening her water bottle. "That's why I put on my pajamas."

He smiled and joined her at the table. He leaned close and his ocean scent washed over her. His fingers touched the hem of her pant leg that rested on the chair. "Frogs?"

As he straightened, she released her breath. "Frogs."

"Have you been to Fire before?" Jonah grabbed a box and opened it.

"The nightclub? No." Lacy found her noodles and grabbed one of the forks. "I don't know if you know this about me, but I don't go out much."

Jonah chuckled. "I had a feeling."

"Have you ever been?" Was that where he went last weekend and brought home Candy?

"No." Jonah drank his water. "Do you ever go out?"

"When we all first moved into the apartment." Lacy took a bite and chewed thoughtfully. "Do you know what it's like to go out with someone like Sophie or Brenda?"

He shook his head and kept his eyes locked on hers. It was a little too intense, but he seemed interested.

She started to tear her napkin into little pieces. "They are beautiful and well put together. Guys would flock to them and every now and then one of the guys would notice me, but not because of me. They thought if they were nice to me, Sophie or Brenda would want to date them."

She tried to smile it off, but she knew from Jonah's look she didn't quite pull it off. "It didn't matter. I stopped going out with them. I stopped trying to date guys who would never be who I wanted them to be and let my fantasy life have free rein. Ergo, Logan."

Jonah put his hand over hers, stopping her from mutilating a second napkin. Blushing, she pulled her hands away from his warmth.

"I know Logan isn't perfect. I know it's a long shot he would want someone like me. But. . . ." She shrugged. "I can try, right?"

Jonah didn't say anything as he took another drink.

"Enough about me. Do you think you'll bring someone home tonight?" She looked down into her noodles when she asked. She didn't even know why she asked. It wasn't any of her business and he'd likely keep it in his room this time. She just couldn't handle him looking at her with almost pity.

Crap. She remembered she'd asked him before at the office. Heat flooded her cheeks. What if he got the wrong idea?

"Hoping to bring you home tonight."

Her gaze shot up to his. He had a teasing smile on his lips. Not a hint of pity.

"Well, thank you. I appreciate it, but if you want to. . . you know. . . . I can make myself scarce. . . at least when we get here." She waved her fork around like it was a magic wand when she spoke, killing all the awkwardness. She set it down and grabbed her water to drink.

"I'll let you know as the night progresses."

She sputtered a little on her water before giving him a thumbs up.

"Lacy?"

She took a breath and met his eyes.

"I'm not looking for a hookup tonight. My main concern is getting to know our coworkers and making sure you make it home. Though how anyone gets to know someone in a loud nightclub is beyond me." He took a bite.

She relaxed, not even realizing she'd been tense. She wanted to see if things went somewhere with Logan tonight, but she still wanted to take things slow. She had no intention of going home with Logan and becoming one of his notches. She wanted more than that. Besides, she wasn't even sure what to do once she got to his bed. Maybe she should do some research like she had on flirting.

It helped Jonah wouldn't be trying to score tonight either. "Okay."

Jonah gave her a slight smile while he continued to eat. It warmed her and she found herself enjoying just being here with him.

CHAPTER 10

JONAH FINISHED GETTING ready and then stepped out of his bedroom. The minute his door clicked shut, Lacy's door opened. She had her hand pressed against her halter top with the strings dangling down her back.

"Can you help me?" Lacy turned her back to him and tipped her head to the side. Her hair was pulled up into a messy bun. "I untied the knot from the store and can't get it to hold now. I don't want to go around flashing everyone in the club. Not my idea of fun. You know?"

"Probably not." He cleared his throat. "You want me to tie your top?"

She nodded. "Tight. Like Superman will have to help me out of it tonight."

He chuckled but caught a whiff of her peaches and cream scent as he reached out to grab the strings. The skin on her shoulders and back was smooth and the same tan as her legs. No sign of a bikini line lingered on her shoulders. Maybe the golden glow was natural, but the sudden urge to search for tan lines had him inhaling to calm the fuck down.

He cleared his throat and concentrated on tying her shirt and not on the smooth silky skin beneath his fingers.

"I don't normally pick difficult outfits." A tremor went through her as his thumb brushed across her nape. "But it's such a good top and goes so well with the skirt. I really think Logan is going to like it."

Mentioning Logan helped Jonah get himself under control. Lacy didn't want him. She wanted Logan, and if Logan weren't a complete idiot, he'd want her too. Not that he deserved her. She was definitely too good for either of them.

Jonah tied the knot and then tied it again. The backs of his fingers brushed along the nape of her neck a final time. "There you go."

Lacy turned with those wide eyes of hers. Her lips were slightly parted. She wasn't immune to him. He'd known that from the start, but he wasn't the one she wanted to want. Besides it would complicate everything if he gave into the temptation she presented. They were too entangled. She was looking for forever, not just right now.

And he was an asshole who only took what was offered and then left.

He glanced down and her toes as always were bare and she still had on her frog kissing pajama bottoms. He couldn't stop his smile.

"What? This isn't sexy?" She grinned and twirled. "Honestly I'm tempted to wear these pants to the club. I'll definitely be the only one wearing them. They are super comfy and when I get home, I'd just have to change tops to go to bed."

"I already told you how I feel about your pajamas. You don't need to dress to impress me, little bird."

Her grin slipped a little and her cheeks flushed with

color. "But I did buy a really nice skirt. It'd be a shame not to wear the whole outfit."

He retreated and leaned against his doorframe. "Don't let me stop you."

"I. . . ." She looked down at her toes and then peeked up at him as she smiled tentatively. "I'll be ready soon."

OKAY, soon wasn't really possible. Lacy took several minutes to finish getting her hair and makeup just right. Then she had to pick shoes which was a hassle in and of itself. If she wore heels, they'd be off within seconds of being in the nightclub, but they looked really good with her outfit. If she wore flats, she'd be comfortable, but they really didn't scream sexy.

She grabbed both and walked into the living room. "Need a man's opinion."

"You're in luck. I happen to be a man." Jonah sat on the couch with his cell phone in hand. He had on the jeans from before and a soft blue button-down shirt that made his eyes stand out even more. And those shit-kicking boots. Her insides squeezed. Definitely, a man.

"Heels or flats?" She tried on the flats and held out her hands to her sides. Then slipped on the heels and struck the same pose.

He stood and walked over pausing about a foot from her. The heels raised her up to his chin height. "We're going for sexy over comfort?"

She nodded and bit her lip. She knew the answer for sexy but she had a small hope he'd say the flats. Flats could be sexy, right? Besides, would a pair of shoes really win over Logan? Jonah didn't seem to care what she wore, but Logan only saw her as the company pet.

"Can you walk in those?" He put his hand on his chin thoughtfully.

She inched a few steps forward, closing the distance between them. She forgot how they pinched her toes, but she bet it looked sexy. And that was all that mattered.

She glanced up at Jonah's face, but he had covered his lips with his fingers and his eyes were definitely more amused than impressed.

She frowned. "What?"

"The flats." He dropped his hand from his lips, but still had a slight smirk. "Definitely."

"Is it that bad?" She winced as she looked down at the pretty shoes on her feet.

He chuckled. "Little bird, it looks like you are walking on broken glass. It doesn't matter how sexy the shoes look if you walk like each step might be your last."

"Oh, thank God." She released her breath. Grabbing his shoulder for support, she slipped them off and toed on her flats. "I was willing to make a sacrifice to the fashion gods, but if they don't look good."

He cleared his throat and stepped back. Her hand fell to her side. She hadn't even realized she'd touched him. Okay, that was a lie. She always knew when she touched him and when he touched her. That whirlwind swirled almost at a constant when she was even near him or just thinking about him. Which happened way too often.

She carefully dropped to pick up the heels. The skirt wasn't as short as that one dress she'd tried on, but she would definitely flash someone if she bent over.

"I'll just put these away." Why were things suddenly awkward with Jonah again? Maybe he was worried she'd start crushing on him if Logan didn't want her. That had to be it. She tossed her shoes in her room before returning to the living room.

Jonah had called a car for them, so they went downstairs to wait. On the elevator ride down, Jonah leaned close to her and said, "You look very sexy tonight."

A flush hit her cheeks and she couldn't help but smile. "Thank you. You do too."

He gave her a small smile as the elevator stopped in the lobby. Her insides lit up at his smile. He held open the door for her as they went out into the night. Lacy wasn't used to going anywhere on a Saturday night, and usually she would be asleep by ten. That wouldn't be happening tonight. Jonah's hand brushed the small of her back as they walked to the waiting car. Her breath caught and held at the surge of electricity flooding her from the touch.

If he kept touching her, she doubted she'd ever be able to fall sleep tonight.

As the car started off toward the club, she turned to Jonah. "Can we just say tomorrow morning, no blender?"

He leaned closer to her, eye to eye, and said, "Oh, there will be a blender, but it might be later than normal."

She glared at him for a second. "Fine, but there better be coffee."

"Always." He looked out the window as the city sped past them.

Lacy had to admit a restless energy flowed through her. After all, she'd only gone out a few times with Sophie and Brenda before she figured it would be easier not to. Those two stayed out so late she usually started fading before the party even began. She wasn't familiar with the club scene. But tonight, she'd be going out with Jonah, Logan, and Claire.

Three beautiful, tall people and her. Not that she was short, but around them. . . and especially in flats. Her stomach twisted. Maybe she should have worn the heels.

Maybe her skirt was too prim and proper to be sexy. Maybe this was a mistake.

The car stopped in front of the nightclub. "Fire" in big red neon lights bathed the sidewalk in red. People lingered around the front of the building, obscuring the entrance.

Jonah stepped out before she could tell him she changed her mind. She wanted to hide in her apartment in her kissing frog pajamas with her Disney Plus subscription. She didn't "club." She sighed and followed him out. After all, this had been her idea.

"Now what?" she said as the car left. A line stretched around the building to get in. When the door opened, bass boomed out in the street.

Jonah's hand slipped into hers. "Come on."

He dragged her toward the scary looking bouncers and gatekeepers. Keeping her hand in his, he leaned in to one of the bouncers and said something. The guy glanced at her and nodded.

Jonah led her inside. The music overwhelmed everything. If one wanted a quiet place to get to know someone, this wouldn't be that place. The music filled her head so no thoughts could exist at all. Black and red covered every surface. The dance floor pulsed with the music and lights. Bodies writhed as one in rhythm. A living mural of color.

Her hand tightened on Jonah's, not wanting to lose him in the crowd. Wrapping her other hand around Jonah's arm, she scooted closer as he led the way though all the people. His hand squeezed and never left hers.

After a while, he tugged her into a corner and braced himself over her, hiding her from the rest of the club. Her whole being went on high alert as his scent and heat wrapped around her. The space, or lack thereof, had him almost pressed against her. His rolled-up shirtsleeve brushed her bare arm, causing goosebumps. His forearms flexed as he pressed his hands against the wall beside her head. Her skin practically trembled for his touch, as his head dipped near hers until his lips brushed her ear. Her knees weakened and she grabbed onto the front of his shirt to hold herself up.

"I'm going to text Logan to see where they are." He pulled away a little until she could see his eyes. The heat in them stirred something restless within her. That heat couldn't possibly be for her though. The overstimulation of the area probably caused it. Just like the sparks dancing along her veins. His breath caressed her lips. Her eyes widened. Were his lips as soft as they looked? She wanted to press up and find out.

What the hell was happening to her?

Releasing his shirt, she nodded and let the wall hold her up. He took out his phone and texted. A second later his phone lit up. He reached down and grabbed her hand before he nodded toward something. She wrapped around his arm again, hugging it to her like a teddy bear. It didn't matter where he led her. She'd follow him. Even with her heightened emotions around him, after last night, she trusted him to keep her safe.

This time he led her behind the DJ stand into a section with tables and chairs. The music wasn't as intrusive in this area. It still blared into the space, but she could almost hear her own thoughts. She spotted Logan and Claire in a booth. Logan wore jeans and a black button-down shirt. Claire wore a short black dress that hugged her curves and high heels which made Lacy's feet ache just looking at them.

Lacy fell behind Jonah and released her grip on him as they stopped at the table. Claire stood up and hugged Jonah before she saw Lacy hiding behind him.

"Oh my God, Lacy, you look phenomenal. You clean up good, girl," Claire said as she gave Lacy a hug.

"Thanks, you always look amazing." Lacy fought against the blush creeping up her cheeks.

She glanced over at Jonah who greeted Logan. She took a deep breath and almost reached for Jonah's hand again. Instead she edged near him and let his heat comfort her. Big moment. This was for the win. Would Logan act any differently to her new outfit?

Logan stepped to the side and his dark eyes found her. "Shit, Lace. You look fine tonight."

He added extra emphasis to the word fine. Not cute. The heat in her cheeks amplified.

"Thanks." She managed to get out.

"We should all hang out more outside of the office." Logan returned to the booth and Claire slid in beside him, leaving the other side open for Jonah and Lacy. "We clean up good."

Okay. She could do this. Jonah helped her up the slight step of the booth and she scooted in, careful of her skirt. Jonah moved in beside her and his thigh brushed hers. She inhaled at the rush of electricity that shot through her from the contact.

"I don't know about anyone else, but I think I'm tapped out on shots after last night," Claire said loudly to be heard over the music. "How about some margaritas instead, Lacy?"

Lacy smiled. She could nurse a margarita all night. "Strawberry sounds good."

"How about it, handsome?" Claire turned to Jonah and gave him a smile that made Lacy's stomach clench. "Want to help me get the drinks?"

Jonah glanced at Lacy. Maybe he wanted to check to see if she'd be okay. Maybe he just remembered she was still there. After all, he might think she was sexy, but Lacy had nothing on Claire.

Claire's dark hair cascaded over her shoulder in a partial

updo. Her strapless black dress hugged her curves and her breasts looked magnificent in it. If Lacy were into girls, Claire would definitely be crush worthy. She wore these dangling earrings that teased at her shoulders. She was anything but plain.

Lacy finally met Jonah's eyes and found heat in them that stirred her up like crazy. Was it for her or for Claire? She needed to get her head on straight. Tonight was about Logan, not Jonah. Jonah's finger touched her hand. She nodded to let him know she'd be okay.

He gave her a slight smile before he turned to leave with Claire.

She straightened in the booth seat and smiled at Logan. Holy crap, she was actually alone at a club with Logan O'Connell. At least for as long as it took to get drinks. Something she could definitely brag about to Beth. Lacy was lucky she wasn't grinning like the village idiot right now.

"You and Jonah seem tight." Logan spread his arm over the back of the booth.

She nodded and swallowed the complicated feelings Jonah sparked within her. "We're friends."

"That's cool. Probably makes it easier being friends when you live and work together." Logan's gaze strayed down to Lacy's breasts. Not that they were as impressive as Claire's. But his gaze did linger there for a moment.

Okay, that was definitely a first. She crossed her legs and glanced toward the bar where Claire stood close to Jonah as they talked while waiting for the drinks. Maybe Claire did have a thing for Jonah. What if Jonah decided to bring Claire home tonight? That would be so awkward.

"I have to say I definitely didn't expect you to show up looking like a snack." Logan's voice drew Lacy's attention to him as he leaned forward and nodded toward her. "You've been holding out on us, Lace."

His frank appraisal made heat flood her face. Thank God she went with the outfit she felt more comfortable in. She would be dying in the crop top right now. She didn't have big enough hands to cover all the skin that outfit revealed. With her hair down and around her shoulders, she didn't feel as exposed in this one.

"We should definitely hit the dance floor after we get a few drinks in us." Logan smiled.

"Sounds like fun." Okay, flirting. She could do this. Dancing she couldn't do, but she'd have to wing it.

Logan glanced over at Claire and Jonah. Claire's hand rested on Jonah's chest.

Lacy felt a sinking feeling inside of her which didn't make sense. Claire wouldn't touch Jonah like that if she didn't like him, right? Lacy should be happy for her friend Jonah. Shaking her head, Lacy tried to settle that weird feeling inside. Getting Logan to consider her an option for dating was her purpose tonight. Not worrying about who Jonah might decide to bring home. But as she looked at Logan, his gaze stayed on Claire and Jonah still. A muscle ticked in his jaw.

"So you and Claire hang out a lot?" she asked. Maybe she underestimated their "friendship."

"She's my best friend and I do *not* have girls as friends." He smiled and played with the coaster on the table. "She's easy to hang out with. Sometimes, I forget she's a woman."

"That seems impossible." Lacy shook her head. Claire might be "one of the guys," but no way would anyone not consider her a woman, especially in that dress.

"You haven't seen her on a game day. I don't know Jonah, but Claire seems to like him." Logan shrugged. "And it'd be nice to have another guy to hang out with."

Lacy recrossed her legs. "You think something might happen between the two of them?"

She glanced over, but they still hadn't gotten the drinks. Jonah had leaned down to say something, but when he didn't put his mouth to Claire's ear, something settled inside of Lacy and she could breathe easily again.

"I don't see why not." Logan's words pulled her attention. He gave her a smile. "After all, he's hot. She's hot. They're both single. They could probably do worse."

"What about you?" The question was out, but Lacy had no idea how he'd interpret it. She should have been more specific. Or maybe not asked the question at all.

"Oh, I'm hot too." Logan winked at her and a little surge went through her heart. Those crush tingles scattered through her as he leaned forward with his arms on the table. "We're all young and hot."

Was he calling her hot? That was definitely a step up from cute. His gaze swept over her a little too intensely. She shifted uncomfortably. But she held his gaze and smiled.

"We never get a chance to talk, Lace." Logan's dark eyes slipped down to her lips before returning to her eyes. "Do you go out a lot?"

This was a good sign, right? He wanted to know more about her. Lacy shook her head as she leaned in too. "I prefer to snuggle on the couch and watch movies."

"Netflix and chill." Logan grinned. "I can dig that."

She opened her mouth to refute the "and chill" part but stopped. She needed to find common ground with him. Not argue the difference between snuggling and sex. "What kind of movies do you watch?"

"Action or heist movies, mostly." Logan smirked. "When I'm not watching football or basketball."

Ah, sports ball. Not her best subject. "Do you follow a particular team?"

"Grew up on the Bears and the Bulls. But I have to admit

I've been a fair-weather fan since moving here." Logan glanced toward the bar.

She only had so much time. "I wish I knew more about sports. My three older brothers played in high school, but I never paid enough attention."

"I played basketball in high school. Mom didn't want me to damage my noggin, so football was off the table." Logan grinned at her. "You know, I might be able to teach you more about the game. Claire and I go to the bar for games. You could come with."

It wasn't a date, but it was something. Hanging out outside of the office was on the list. "That would be cool."

Logan reclined, stretching his arms over the back of the booth again.

Glasses arrived at the table as Jonah passed her a strawberry margarita. Claire slid into the booth and Logan left his arm behind her.

Jonah moved in next to Lacy. He gave her a questioning look and she just smiled. Yes, she'd gotten some alone time with Logan. And an offer to hangout outside of the office, this time without Jonah. Things were definitely looking up.

CHAPTER 11

Lacy hadn't been completely quiet since Jonah returned with the drinks, but she definitely seemed reserved as she nursed her margarita. A smile graced her lips. Apparently, alone time with Logan had gone well. Every time someone mentioned getting more drinks, Lacy gestured to her half full glass. Jonah couldn't help the smile that nudged his lips when she did.

"Oh, it's my song." Claire turned to Lacy and reached across the table. "Come on. Let's dance."

Color flooded Lacy's cheeks. "I'm not really much of a dancer."

"Finish that margarita and I bet you will be. You've been nursing that drink too long. Drink it." Claire winked at her before turning to Logan. "Logan, as my best friend, you are required by law to go shake it on the dance floor with me when my favorite song comes on."

Logan gave her a skeptical look. "By law?"

Claire snagged his hand and pulled him from the booth. "Come on, you two. We didn't come to a dance club to sit around and drink."

Jonah slid out of the booth and held out his hand to Lacy. She finished her drink, which by now must be mostly water, and took his hand. Keeping his eye on Logan and Claire, he drew Lacy out onto the dance floor. The music pounded into his ears. The press of bodies on the floor was almost too much. Not to mention the heat.

Lacy practically plastered herself to his back, sending a rush through him. They finally managed to find the small chunk of dance floor Claire and Logan had staked out for them.

Lacy tugged on his shirt sleeve when they stopped in the middle of the people. He leaned down so her lips almost touched his ear.

"I don't know how to dance."

He lifted his head and met her eyes. A slight edge of panic lingered in them. She knew all day they were coming to a club and she just now mentioned this. He bent down to her ear and said, "Just move your hips and do what everyone else is doing."

Claire leaned closer to Jonah and yelled over the music, "Everything okay?"

He nodded and dragged Lacy in front of him. Logan and Claire had started to dance in beat with the music. Lacy started moving side to side, stiffly. She seemed as uncoordinated as she'd been in the high heels.

He said in her ear, "Just relax and go with the music."

She nodded and bit her lip as she concentrated on trying to move. She was all awkward elbows and hips, jerking. While he thought she was cute, she definitely wasn't hitting the sexy vibe she'd been hoping for. Fortunately Claire and Logan seemed off in their own little worlds as they danced and didn't notice Lacy's chaotic moves.

He dropped his hands on her bare shoulders, and she stopped and looked over her shoulder at him.

"We'll be back," Jonah yelled at Claire and Logan. Claire gave him a thumbs up.

Taking Lacy's hand, he dragged her to the bar where it was a little more quiet. He leaned over the bar. "Two shots of tequila."

"Are those for you?" Lacy asked, warily.

"No, we're going to do a shot and then we are going to return to the dance floor. You desperately need to loosen up." He brought his head down until he was at her eye level. "This is just a faster margarita. Between the dancing and water, you'll be sober by the time we head home. Promise."

The bartender put the shots down and a small plate of limes with a saltshaker. Jonah handed her a shot.

"Have you done a tequila shot before?"

She shook her head, still looking wary, as she lifted the shot to her nose. She recoiled at the smell. "I think I like margaritas better."

"If you drink a margarita, you'll just have to use the restroom more."

She glanced at the dance floor and took a deep breath before meeting his eyes. She gave him a quick nod.

"Lick, shoot, suck." Jonah grabbed the saltshaker. Her eyes widened. "Hold out your hand."

Jonah licked the back of his hand and put salt on it. Lacy followed his example.

"Okay, we're going to lick the salt, shoot the shot, and then suck the lime. You ready?"

Her brown eyes met his and they were full of trust. She nodded.

"Lick."

Her pink tongue flicked out and licked the salt. She would be the death of him.

"Shoot."

They took the shots together. Her face scrunched up at

the taste and she shook her hands in the air.

He held out the lime to her. "Suck."

She didn't even take the lime but grabbed his hand, brought it to her lips, and bit into the lime. Her gaze flew up to his as he sucked his own lime. A shudder coursed through her body. Her hands held his with her lips wrapped around the lime and her eyes looking up at him. It didn't take much for his mind to slip into the gutter. His cock hardened, but he ignored it.

She released his hand and he put the used limes down. "Now what?"

"You should be loose enough to dance soon." Jonah steered her to where Logan and Claire danced.

Lacy's smile was a little looser as they carved out a space on the dance floor. Claire shimmied forward and grabbed Lacy's hips to get her moving. Lacy laughed. Before long, Lacy found a rhythm and danced on her own. The music changed slightly.

A group of people danced across the dance floor, separating Claire and Logan from Jonah and Lacy. Lacy seemed oblivious as she continued to move with her eyes closed.

Jonah pulled Lacy away by her hips to stop her from getting trampled. She backed up into him, but still kept swaying her hips against him. He couldn't help the erection she stirred more with her movements. Hoping she wouldn't notice, he wrapped an arm around her waist and drew her farther away until they found an open area again.

He released her and she turned to look up at him. Lips parted. Eyes wide, dark and bottomless. Her tongue darted out to wet her lips. What he wouldn't do to kiss those lips. Lick them, taste them, suck them. He could spend an hour doing nothing but kiss Lacy.

～

LACY's whole body pulsed in time with the music, and when Jonah had pulled her against him, her skin had gotten tight and needy. She didn't need to be a sexual expert to notice the hardness he packed in his jeans. Especially when it had been pressed into her bottom.

She wanted him. It should have startled her to realize that, especially when Logan danced a few feet away, but it didn't.

Jonah's eyes were hungry as he returned her look. She wanted to kiss him. Maybe it was the tequila talking, but damn, she wanted his lips on hers. She lifted her hand to touch his lips, and he grabbed her hand before she could touch them. He gave a little warning growl that rumbled through her chest more than she heard it. She stepped forward to close the space between them.

"There you guys are," Logan yelled over the music. "Should we get another drink? The dance floor has gotten crowded."

Lacy didn't look away from Jonah. His thumb grazed her wrist in his hand, sending tingles rippling down her spine. His gaze held hers for a heated second.

"Lead the way," Jonah finally said. He squeezed her hand before linking their fingers together.

They followed Claire and Logan to the bar. Lacy stumbled a little as they stopped behind Logan and Claire. Jonah settled her against him again. She rested into his warmth as she watched the bartender make their drinks.

So much stimuli surrounded her. Lights. Music. People were everywhere. But right here, as she leaned against Jonah, a calm settled over her. She wanted to sink into his warmth and stay there forever. Safe. She glanced at Logan. She really should have protested the earlier shot more because it messed with her brain.

Logan turned with another margarita and handed it to

her. His eyebrow cocked up at her and Jonah. She should care, right? She held his eye contact though and smiled. Because that was flirting. Beth would be proud.

"Thank you." Lacy took the strawberry margarita and licked the sugar on the rim before drinking some.

"Why don't we find a table to nurse these drinks before Claire decides her favorite song is on again?" Logan reached out his hand to Lacy. Her eyebrows shot up. That was new.

She stepped away from Jonah's warmth and slid her hand into Logan's, letting him lead her to the same booth. Her eyes were drawn to Jonah who gave her a supportive smile.

Logan's hand was cold from the drinks. She should be feeling something more. Like the rush she got when Jonah touched her, but instead she kind of felt something settle in her chest. Not fireworks, just something like she'd feel for a guy in grade school who held her hand. Must be the tequila.

He helped her into the booth and then scooted in on her side. Unlike Jonah, Logan's thigh didn't settle next to hers. Ah, Logan wasn't a booth hog. But still, progress! Well, damn, she wanted to take a picture and send it to Beth. She'd caption it with, "see it worked."

Jonah and Claire sat across from them. Jonah sat directly across from Lacy. His legs went on either side of hers under the table, so his calves brushed against hers. Booth hog. A pulse of heat flowed through her from the contact. Jonah flashed her a smile and her face flushed. He knew what he did to her. Did everyone?

Lacy took a drink to avoid looking at him. She glanced over at Claire and Logan to see if they'd noticed but they seemed content to drink.

"How about a game?" Claire set down her drink.

"Not a drinking game." Logan smiled. "After those shots last night. I wouldn't want to have to drag your drunk ass home again."

"I wasn't drunk." Claire stuck her tongue out at Logan. "I was happily buzzed."

"I'd like to avoid another hangover," Lacy said. Her gaze collided with Jonah's smiling eyes. That feeling of being safe and held filled her with warmth and she pulled her gaze away. Jonah was her friend. Logan was the real deal. She looked at Logan, who smiled at her.

Nothing, not even a skip in her heart. What the hell was wrong with her?

"Okay, not a drinking game." Claire tapped her finger to her red lips. "I've got two."

She turned in her seat toward Jonah. "As the new guy, you get to choose."

"Okay," Jonah said, warily.

"Would you rather, or kiss, marry, fuck?" Claire winked at Lacy.

"Wait, isn't it kiss, marry, kill?" Lacy asked.

"Where's the fun in killing someone?" Claire shrugged. "There are plenty of celebrities I would much rather fuck than kiss or marry."

"Fine." Jonah wrapped his hands around his drink. "Kiss, marry, fuck, it is."

"Excellent." Logan rubbed his hands together. "I'll start. For the ladies, though, I can assume we are comfortable enough in our manhood to play both sides. . . ."

Logan met Jonah's eyes with a questioning look. Jonah nodded and gestured for Logan to continue.

"All right." Claire relaxed into the booth. "Bring it on."

"Let's start with the Chrises. Chris Evans, Chris Hemsworth, Chris Pratt?" Logan raised his eyebrow.

"Which Chris Pratt?" Claire leaned forward, resting her elbows on the table and putting her head on her hands. "Early "Parks and Rec" or *Guardians of the Galaxy*?"

"Guardians of the Galaxy." Logan mimicked her stance with a smirk.

"Hmmm. Kiss Chris Evans, obviously. Marry Chris Hemsworth, because come on, who wouldn't want to wake up to that every morning. And fuck Chris Pratt." Claire rested back in her seat. Her eyes sparkled as she looked at Logan. "What about you?"

"Kiss Pratt, marry Evans, fuck Hemsworth." Logan smiled and took a drink before turning his gaze on Lacy.

She gulped. What the hell did she know about fucking?

"I agree with Claire," Jonah said. "After all, Evans would be fine for a kiss, but he seems to be all talk. Hemsworth is not only funny, but the dude is ripped and has a good accent. Pratt, well, he's a giant dick, but funny, therefore, fuck would be the right answer."

"Sounds good to me." Lacy smiled at Claire, who seemed fine with her non-answer. Thankfully.

"Okay, one for the guys. Michelle Pfeiffer, Michelle Williams, and Michelle Obama," Claire rattled off. For a while they came up with more celebrities for the list. Lacy was happy to listen to the others and their reasoning, but she nearly squirmed when everyone turned their eyes to her. Of course, the tequila in her margarita helped to make it less of an issue.

"How about we make this a little more personal?" A wicked glint sparked in Claire's eyes. "For the guys, kiss, marry, fuck. Me, Lacy, and Phoebe."

Lacy's eyes went wide. What the what? That wasn't the game.

"I don't—" Jonah started.

"It's just a game." Logan laughed. "All right. Hmmm. Only for the game obviously. Phoebe's the non-wild card here. Obviously I'd fuck Phoebe. Lacy and Claire, though, are a little harder. Claire is my best friend, and they say you should marry your best friend so. . . . Why not? Marry Claire and kiss Lacy."

Not exactly where Lacy hoped to be on the list, but it wasn't awful. Marriage would have been preferable. At least they weren't playing kiss, marry, kill. He could have killed her, which would have been much worse.

"How about you, Jonah?" Claire smiled at him.

Jonah took a swig from his drink and set the glass down. He glanced Lacy's way once, making her heart stop. "Marry Phoebe, kiss Claire, fuck Lacy."

And her breathing stopped along with her heart. Suddenly her brain recalled not Candy sex but dream sex with Jonah. She crossed her legs under the table.

Claire laughed. "Not where I thought you were going."

"Okay, ladies' turn." Logan's voice still sounded distant to her, like she was in a tunnel. Lacy took another drink.

Lacy wasn't the type of girl to land on any fuck list. Kiss or marry, yes. Logan had been right, obviously fuck Phoebe. That woman had to know tricks. Or even Claire, she definitely had the body, but Lacy. . . come on. She barely qualified next to those two. She was lucky to be on the kiss list for Logan.

"Lacy?" Logan's voice brought her out of her stupor.

"Yeah?" She glanced down into the empty glass. Oh, that was not good. The equivalent of three shots of tequila? She lifted her gaze to Jonah. His leg brushed her and a shudder coursed through her. Was his hair as soft as the silk it looked like?

"Kiss, marry, fuck." Claire gained her attention. "We took Drew out because Morgan would kick our asses. So that leaves us with Jonah, Logan, and Ben."

Oh, shit, she should have known it would come to this.

"It's just a game, Lace," Logan said and winked at her. "Man, if I had to choose, it would be marry Ben, the guy is an accountant and that's gotta be good for something. And kiss—"

"I don't want to know if you'd fuck or kiss yourself. That's just weird, man. The answer is totally obvious," Claire straightened, gathering everyone's attention. "Marry Ben, kiss Jonah, fuck Logan. You've got to pick the fuckboy to fuck."

"Aw. Thanks, Claire." Logan shook his head and held his hands over his heart. "My mother would be so proud."

"You're welcome." Claire turned to Lacy. "So, what will it be?"

Anyway she sliced it, she'd have to put the two men at the table in one of the categories. With Ben not here, shouldn't she put him in fuck? That would definitely be easier. But then would they just tease her on Monday that she wanted to fuck Ben? When in reality, she really didn't. Maybe she was reading too much into this. It was just a silly game. But Jonah had said he would fuck her. Was that true?

Claire snapped her fingers. "Go with your impulse, Lacy. We all know you are a little sloshed at the moment and will completely forgive you tomorrow. So, marry?"

Logan would normally be her answer, but she wanted him to actually consider her for that position eventually. Saying it now would totally scare him away. "Ben."

Oh, shit. Now she had to do what was necessary to keep from being a hook up which meant she couldn't put Logan in the fuck column. She lifted her gaze to Jonah. Those heated eyes tugged at something low inside her.

"Kiss?" Claire asked. "Logan or Jonah?"

Was this game supposed to make people hyperventilate? "Logan."

"Interesting choice." Claire shot a look at Jonah. "Even though there's only one choice left, fuck?"

"Jonah." His name sounded way too breathless coming out of her mouth.

Claire made a tsking noise. "Sounds like you two are on the same page."

"It's just a game," Jonah said, his voice gruff, sending a tingle racing down Lacy's spine.

"Yeah, Claire, it's not like I really want to marry you." Logan stood and reached his hand to Lacy. "Drinks are gone. Time to dance."

Lacy slipped her hand into Logan's and wished for a rush of something but got nothing from the contact. Maybe she did want to fuck Jonah. Wouldn't that be a trip?

"Come on, Jonah. Maybe if you're lucky, you'll get that kiss tonight." Claire's voice carried to Lacy.

Her chest tightened. She couldn't hear if Jonah answered. Why did he pick her to fuck when Phoebe would have been easier? Of course, she should have just said marry Jonah, but that would be weird too, right? This was the worst game ever.

Logan swung her around in a circle when they reached the dance floor. As they settled in to dance, the area left by the moving bodies wasn't that big. Lacy kept bumping into one of her coworkers every few beats.

Logan tried to dance with Lacy a few times, but Lacy couldn't get with the beat and ended up laughing instead. Eventually Logan's attention got pulled away by a woman wearing a mini skirt and crop top. Lacy never could have worn anything like that outside of the dressing room. Jonah would have had to barge in to even see it.

She looked over her shoulder at Jonah. He always danced nearby and guided her out of the way whenever people came crashing through.

"Looks like we may have lost Logan for the night," Claire said with a sigh.

Lacy followed her gaze to where Logan danced with the mini skirt woman while talking in her ear. He practically wrapped himself around the woman. She should feel someway about that. After all, she loved the guy and he was all over another woman.

"I'm actually surprised he lasted that long before straying." Claire shrugged her shoulders. "It's what the weekend is for. Hooking up, am I right?"

Lacy smiled and nodded like she knew what Claire meant. For Lacy, weekends meant laundry, grocery shopping, and movies, maybe even a new book by her favorite author. Perhaps she really was broken. For a second there, she'd started to feel like she belonged as part of the group. Silly her.

Claire leaned in to yell in Lacy's ear. "I hope you don't mind me ditching you with Jonah, but there's this guy that's been giving me *that* look. You know?"

Lacy nodded even though she didn't actually know.

"If you guys don't hang around, I'll see you Monday at work. It's been a lot of fun." Claire took Lacy's hand and squeezed it. Then she turned to Jonah and said something to him. He gave a nod.

Claire finger waved goodbye as she skirted around the dance floor to a tall guy on the sidelines. Lacy couldn't help watching as Claire smiled up at the guy and pressed against him to talk to him. It looked so effortless. Before long they were dancing together.

Jonah's heat engulfed her back. He leaned down to her ear. "Do you want to stay or go?"

Shivers worked through her again. Lacy looked over at Logan with his new dance partner. She should feel jealousy or something but all she felt was apathy. Must be the tequila. She turned her face toward Jonah's.

"Let's go."

CHAPTER 12

"I'm not normal." Lacy's words were so soft Jonah almost didn't hear them. She'd been a little wobbly and quiet as they made their way out of the club and back to their apartment building. Currently they rode in the elevator and she leaned into his side against the backwall.

Lifting his arm, he slid it around her shoulders and pulled her tighter against his side. "Normal is highly overrated."

"I wouldn't even know how to hook up." She tilted her face up to his. "Forget hooking up. I don't even date. I just sit back and dream about dating. I'm thinking normal would at least be dating."

He stroked his finger over her shoulder and upper arm, lost in his thoughts, enjoying the warm, smooth feel of her skin. Was Lacy normal? No, and thank God for that. If she'd been normal, he never would have left his room after meeting her. He would have avoided her like she carried the plague.

She shivered against him and he met her gaze. Her pupils were dilated and her lips parted. Her cheeks heated. Her lips were so near he could easily close the distance between them. His lips would be against hers and. . . .

Everything would be over. He wasn't the right man for her. Neither was Logan but definitely not Jonah. Jonah would ruin her worse than the asshole frat boy had. Because he would leave. He always did. It was all he knew how to do. He'd never stayed anywhere long enough to be someone's. He was untethered.

Sure, he wanted to stay and had even committed to stay this time, but things could change. He hadn't even been able to commit to an apartment for a year. Which was why he sublet instead of leasing.

"If you want to date, then date." Lord knows it would help Jonah to stop obsessing over her if she was some other guy's girl.

"That's easy for you to say."

The elevator stopped and they got off and walked to the door.

"I'm not like you guys." Lacy slipped her shoes off inside the door and headed to the refrigerator. "I can't just go up to a guy and flirt. I can't just start a conversation with someone. I have these ridiculous crushes on guys who would never actually want me."

She pulled out a bottle of water and downed about half of it. "I didn't learn how to flirt with guys in a normal way. You want to know what I did last weekend?"

Jonah moved to the table and took a seat. She didn't need him to answer. He just waited.

"I stayed at home and googled how to flirt with a guy. All because my best friend who has put up with my weird-ass obsessions told me to shit or get off the pot. Finally do something to get Logan to notice me as not his fucking little sister but as a grown-ass woman."

She drank more of the water. His little bird had her

feathers ruffled and needed to let everything out. It had to be hard to watch the guy she liked go off with another woman when she'd done everything to make herself available to him.

"You know what was so hilarious tonight?" She didn't look like she was about to laugh or even allow him time to answer. "Kiss, marry, fuck."

She started pacing.

He leaned back in his chair. Logan had pissed him off during the game. But Jonah hadn't misstepped or lied. Honestly he didn't want Claire or Phoebe. The only woman he wanted to kiss and fuck stood in front of him, ranting about another man. Saying he wanted to fuck her hadn't been just about helping her out. Even though he hoped it would help Lacy's case to be seen as someone desirable to that fuckwad Logan. In the end, it was all Jonah could think about when she was near.

Of course, he'd been only partially surprised when Lacy had put him in the fuck category, but he could follow her logic. One didn't tell a fuckboy they would want to fuck him if that wasn't what she wanted from him.

Lacy had been occupied drinking more water. "Sure, there are guys I'd want to marry or kiss, but how should I know about fucking?"

Not where he thought she was going with this. He leaned forward and listened.

"I've never even had a boyfriend. In high school, my brothers scared everyone away. Not that many were looking. Chet went from zero to sixty so I didn't even get to do the whole courtship rituals with the one guy I slept with. I thought it was great because it finally meant this one must love me, right? In my messed-up brain, sex equaled love. And all that other stuff would come afterwards because he would want to be with me."

She stopped and finished the rest of the water, throwing the bottle in the recycle bin.

"Instead I'm left wondering what I did wrong. That maybe somehow I'm defective because the one guy in my history of crushes only wanted me one time. I don't even know if I did it right. There's obviously a right way to do it right. Right?"

She swung around until her gaze landed on him. His breath caught at the determination in her eyes. Fuck, he wanted her.

"You." She pointed and started toward him.

He took a breath. "Me."

"You obviously know what the hell you're doing. I mean, I wasn't even involved when you had sex and felt something, which is more than I can say about that bastard Chet."

Fuck. He shouldn't be getting turned on by Lacy at this particular moment, but even before she said she "felt something," his dick had hardened. Her skirt swung with every dramatic turn. Her hair was off her shoulders, falling down her back, and he couldn't help himself from wondering how responsive she would be to his touch. She had shivered when his leg brushed against hers. What would happen if he kissed her?

Lacy's innocence shouldn't make him want her more. What was he thinking? He wanted to give in, but what happened to Lacy when he disappeared from her life? Did she end up hiding forever? What if he stayed and it didn't work out? What if he broke her far worse than any Chet could?

Or could he find a way to set her free without hurting her?

"Would you please let me in on the secret everyone else knows?" She sank into the chair next to his and grabbed his hand on the table with both of hers. "Why would I ever just want to fuck someone?"

"You can be attracted to someone but not want to have a relationship with them."

She released his hand and eased back in her chair. "Is that the way you feel about Candy?"

"Candy and I have an arrangement. If I'm in town and she's free, we get together for the night because the sex is good." Jonah swallowed. He shouldn't be having this conversation with Lacy. But he also couldn't resist.

LACY PICKED at the hem of her skirt absently. "So, if you wanted to have sex right now, you could call up Candy and she'd be your hookup? And she wouldn't expect anything more from the relationship?"

"If I wanted to have sex with Candy, yes." His blue eyes had darkened and his hungry gaze dropped to her hem. His intensity had her warring between jumping him and running away to take a cold shower.

Inhaling, Lacy had to ask. "Why did you pick me for fuck?"

"Why did you pick me?" He didn't move an inch, but he seemed closer somehow. Sparks lit under her skin.

"I didn't want them to tease me at work about Ben so I picked marry for him. I also couldn't pick Logan for marry because I didn't want to tip my hand and scare him away. But then I couldn't pick Logan for fuck because I want to date him, not be a hookup for the night." Her heart fluttered in her chest. It might be the simplest explanation, but it wasn't the whole explanation. Desire, hot and heavy, poured through her every time Jonah was close. He'd invaded her dreams more than just that one night.

"But you would hook up with me?" Jonah's voice was deep and gravelly and stroked across her skin. Damn, his voice was potent.

She lifted her eyes to his. His blue eyes captured hers and held her in place. She couldn't answer his question. He thought she was sexy and chose her over Phoebe and Claire to fuck. She didn't understand him at all.

"Why did you choose me to fuck? Because it was the only category left?" She didn't dare drop her gaze. She wanted to see if he flinched. To see the truth that if there had been a kill column, he might have put her in it. She was just what was left over.

He leaned forward slowly as if he feared she'd run away. He probably wasn't too far off. Her heart raced and she couldn't quite catch her breath. Him being this close put her on edge, but she didn't want to be farther away. She wanted to be closer, pressed against him fully. His hand reached out and tucked a strand of hair behind her ear. Her whole body shook from the electricity flooding her system from his touch. Her breath caught at the look in his eyes.

Closing the distance, he stopped when his nose was a breath away from hers. She couldn't move or breathe, stuck in anticipation.

"Little bird, if I'd had the choice" —his gaze dropped to her lips and he swallowed— "I'd have put you in every category. I'm not looking to get married though. If you weren't my roommate and coworker, I'd have fucked you every day since we met. And kiss you? Fuck. The worst part is I haven't stopped thinking about wanting to kiss you."

She inhaled and her lungs filled with his scent. He tilted his head slightly and leaned a little more forward. Her heart beat out a crazy rhythm in her chest. Would he kiss her now? God, she hoped so. She couldn't take her eyes from his. She could lose herself in the blue depths, like slipping under the warm waves of the Caribbean and never surfacing again. Let his current drag her under.

"What secrets do you want to know, little bird?" His words were soft and his warm breath caressed her lips. She had asked him. "I'll tell you everything."

She swore her panties melted from the fire he ignited within her. She should back away. She should do what she always did and retreat. She couldn't even blame her buzz on this. This was all her.

To hell with it.

She swallowed hard and even though everything within her screamed not to ask, she had to know. "Do you want me?"

"Yes." The word was soft, brushing against her lips, making her insides burn brighter.

"Show me." The words were barely a whisper, but his eyes darkened at them. She wet her lips.

His hands slipped behind her knees and tugged her towards him. She gasped at the contact. His knees settled between hers. She bit her lip as his thumbs rubbed the insides of her thighs, taking away any thoughts of running away.

"I don't do relationships." He was so close but still separate. Each word caressed her lips. "I've never settled in one place long enough in my life to have anything steady. I had women I visited to help scratch the itch whenever I needed it. If we have sex, I'm not going to change. But I will promise to only be with you while we do this."

She swallowed.

Did she really want to do this?

Could she do this?

Just sex?

With Jonah.

"More than once? More than just tonight?" She had to know.

"Definitely."

"I don't know what this is between us." She closed her eyes for a second and couldn't slow the frantic beat of her heart. She opened them to continue. "But I can't keep pretending I don't feel it. I want you. Show me everything. No promises. No flowers. Not even a potential future. I just want you now."

She searched his eyes even as she held her breath. She wasn't a virgin, and she never thought she could have sex without love. But Jonah was different. She leaned in and pressed her lips against his. This was what she wanted. His lips against hers. Her heartbeat heavy in her ears.

His lips moved tentatively at first, letting her lead. But what did she know about kissing? Maybe she did it wrong. She sucked at this. How would she get better if she sucked at kissing? She started to pull away.

That was when he took control. His mouth claimed hers like she'd never been kissed before in her life. At least never like this. He consumed her. The storm within her spread like lightning flowing through her veins. His hands slid up her thighs, beneath her skirt, to her panty-covered ass and lifted her onto his lap, pulling her tight against him.

She straddled his lap. Her sex tingled as his hardness press against her intimately. If someone asked her if she'd been kissed before Jonah, she would assert she had not. Before this kiss had been a tragic wasteland of pecks and sloppy mouths. His lips parted over hers and his tongue slid across her lips. She gasped at the touch and he didn't hesitate to deepen the kiss.

This was more than a kiss. It was an awakening. Since she met Jonah, she'd been slowly stirring, but now she was wide awake. Her whole body enflamed by his touch.

He didn't feel close enough. Aching for more, she wrapped herself around him. Her hands slid into his hair, keeping him there with her. He fit perfectly against her. Everything within her screamed this was right. Logically she knew it'd only been a week since she met him, but she trusted him with her body.

The heat of his hands caressed her ass cheeks through the thin satin of her panties. His thumb skimmed over her sex and the fire in her turned into an inferno. She moaned against his mouth and his lips curved slightly into a smile. He urged her hips into his again as he tasted her tongue.

He released her mouth and rested his forehead against hers.

"I want you," she whispered the secret she'd barely admitted to herself. She panted in his arms, trying to regain her breath. The world had tipped on its axis and she no longer knew which way was up. And she didn't care as long as Jonah continued to touch her. He'd keep her grounded to Earth.

"You aren't defective, little bird." His low gravelly voice slipped like a caress against her lips. "You've just never flown before."

She opened her eyes and looked into the same dark stormy eyes she'd seen the night she'd watched him. Her sex pulsed with the memory. Would he do that to her? God, she wanted him to. She'd dreamed about it often enough. Every scene she'd ever read in a romance, she wanted to try with him. She didn't want to overthink this. She wanted his lips on hers, leaving no room for any thoughts. She'd never catch her breath again and that would be awesome.

"Tell me," he said, trailing his finger over her bottom lip, sending shivers down her spine. His eyes held her prisoner. "Did you orgasm when you had sex, little bird?"

Her face flamed with heat. She shook her head, afraid to say the words out loud and break this wonderful spell.

"What about by touching yourself?"

His words should not turn her on, but they did. She should be mortified, but honesty between them was important. She'd never had the urge to touch herself before last weekend, before Jonah, and even then she hadn't. She'd never had a compelling need to quench. She shook her head again.

"Fuck." The word was whispered and not harsh. As he settled onto the chair, he rocked his hips under hers and she gasped at the burst of sparks flooding through her. His lips turned down slightly. "You've had three drinks tonight."

"Hours ago," she whispered, tightening her arms around his neck, tangling her fingers in his hair. *Please don't stop.*

He pulled his head away from her a little. "This isn't going to happen tonight."

She opened her mouth to protest and he kissed her before he continued.

"Two reasons. One, alcohol. Two, Logan."

She started to protest again and his lips closed over hers. This kiss lasted longer and made her wonder what they were even talking about.

Sex, that was what they'd been talking about. Tonight. She wanted what Candy had. What Logan probably found with the miniskirt woman tonight. What everyone else in the world felt when they had sex. Jonah made her want more. She wanted to be normal.

Jonah raised his head and smiled at her, pressing his thumb against her lower lip. "I won't have you regret anything we do together. A little kissing is one thing, but sex is a major step. Especially for you."

Okay, that made sense, but even kissing was kind of a big deal to her. She'd never just made out with anyone before. She still felt the need to point out, "I'm really barely buzzed."

He chuckled darkly and the vibrations flowed through her. He ran his hands over her spine up to where her shirt tie hung and her back was exposed. His hot hand rested against her bare skin between her shoulder blades. Shivers trickled down her spine to pool liquid warmth between her thighs. If these simple touches made her weak, what would sex with him feel like? She never wanted him to stop touching her. He made her come to life.

"Reason two, you just saw the guy you like go off with another girl." His face was serious.

She frowned at that one. What did that have to do with anything? Logan did that every weekend. It wasn't like she expected him to take her home tonight. She didn't work that way. Normally.

She hadn't expected to be making out with Jonah at this point. Or considering having sex with Jonah tonight. Jonah wasn't normal for her. Maybe her normal needed to be shaken up.

"You may not think it has anything to do with your decision, but add that to the drinking and all I can see is a whole lot of regret in the morning." Jonah's fingers teased the knot of her shirt. "I'm more than happy to make out with you though."

She laughed at his sly look. "I thought Claire was your kiss."

He leaned in until his lips hovered over hers, a breath away. Butterflies launched in her stomach as she held her breath in anticipation. "I already told you I would have chosen you for everything."

Her heart swelled as he captured her lips. He took his time exploring her mouth and she tried to follow his lead. He was patient with her. She'd never been kissed like this before. The few quick kisses over the years hadn't been a full-on make out session, and even Chet hadn't just settled in to kiss her without trying to grab her breast or ass.

Jonah's full attention stayed on her mouth and lips. His hands remained on her back, but she could feel his hardness under his jeans pressed against her underwear. Barely anything separated them. Instead of being embarrassed, she wanted those layers gone.

He didn't rush the kiss, just gentle touches of his tongue and the movement of his lips over hers. But the urge to grind against him, to get some friction, almost overwhelmed her. Then his hands slid into her hair, gently massaging her scalp.

Maybe she would be horrified in the morning when she thought about the moans that came from her throat when he sucked on her tongue. Maybe she'd regret sucking his tongue to see if she could get the same response. She got a moan and a thrust of his hips against hers.

But right now, she wanted more. She wanted his hands to wander over her. She wanted to feel his hot skin beneath her fingertips.

She ached with need she was just beginning to understand when he lifted his mouth from hers.

His thumb traced over her swollen lip. "Beautiful."

Her heart ricocheted inside her chest as his lips descended to hers again. His hands slid down to her bottom and she squeaked in surprise when he stood with her still attached. Her legs wrapped around his waist, drawing him closer to where she needed him most. She throbbed at the contact.

He lifted his lips and his eyes captured hers. He rested his forehead to hers. "I want to fuck you so bad."

Her sex clenched in response. She almost nodded. She would totally be okay with that.

He looked over her shoulder at their bedroom doors and then at the counter.

She would be game for either one right now. Instead, he walked over to the couch. The couch could work.

"But not tonight." He sat with her still straddling him. Her fingers still tangled in his hair. His hands still cupped her ass.

His breathing was heavy, but so was hers. She didn't want to think anymore. Not about what she had in the past. Not about drinking. Not about Logan. She just wanted to feel what Jonah made her feel through her whole body.

"Please," she whispered.

He groaned and pulled her in tight against him again. "Little bird, if you wake up and still want this, I will be more than willing to take you as high as you want to go."

"I don't want to stop." She couldn't help the words from falling out of her mouth. She never wanted this to end. As if he dangled something shiny in front of her for the first time in her life, she wanted to grab it and hold onto it forever. Keep feeling this exquisite sensation pouring through her body.

He slid his lips against hers. "Neither do I."

"So don't," she whispered against his lips. Her insides were caught in the hurricane. "I don't want to sleep tonight."

"Fuck, Lacy." His lips took charge of the kiss. His hands skimmed up her sides, finding the bare skin of her back. Except for brief contact, he hadn't really touched her anywhere that would provide her any relief.

"Jonah," she whispered against his lips, feeling his control hanging by a thread. Wanting to snap that thread and have him take her.

He growled as his hand gently cupped her breast. His thumb trailed over her covered nipple, just enough to send pleasure spiraling through her. Was this why someone would want to just fuck someone else? These intense feelings of longing and desire flowing through her?

She wasn't in love with Jonah. She liked him and found

him attractive, but love? That wasn't part of this. Besides, he didn't want love from her and she didn't need it from him. But this fire between them had slowly started to consume her. Earlier she'd wanted his kiss and now she couldn't even think about separating from his lips. She wanted more.

Maybe some day she'd be able to love and be loved by someone. Until then, Jonah could unlock her passion and show her how it was supposed to feel as opposed to her experience. Right now, she wanted this. More kissing. More touching. More Jonah.

Rocking her hips against him, Lacy lost herself in the feel of his hands and lips on her. He broke off their kiss.

"It's too much, little bird." His thumb traced her jawline.

It wasn't nearly enough. She tried to lean in to capture his lips; instead he flipped her around. Her back to his chest. Her legs dangled on the outside of his thighs. He brought her head down to rest on his chest. He pressed a kiss against her temple before he grabbed the remote and pressed it into her hand.

"Put on a movie," he growled.

She wanted to protest, but feared he'd reject her entirely if she pressed him. Send her to bed all hot and needy. Squirming to get comfortable, she found something on her watch list and tossed the remote onto the coffee table.

The movie began and she could barely pay attention. Her body still keyed up. Everywhere Jonah had touched her tingled, waiting for more. Her sex throbbed with need. She took a deep breath to steady herself and tried to relax against Jonah. His erection pressed against her ass.

Jonah tugged down the blanket and covered them.

He brushed the hair away from the nape and his lips caressed her neck. She gasped at the fresh surge of need coursing through her.

"Jon—"

"Shhh." His hot breath teased her skin. "I'll make it all better. Watch your show."

She shivered in his arms. His lips remained on her neck, but his hands stroked up the insides of her thighs under the blanket. Her eyes glazed over and the images on the screen blurred into colors. His knees parted and spread her legs open farther. Her breath caught in her throat as her skirt rose higher and higher. He paused at her underwear. His fingertips slid along the lace at her legs beside where she throbbed for him. She wondered if that was all. Just another tease.

But then his hand trailed over the front of her panties before it slid beneath them. She froze, waiting. His first touch was soft, almost non-existent as the heat of his hand paused over her. She ached for his touch.

"Jonah?" She wondered if he'd actually do it. She lifted her arms to thread her fingers into his hair behind her. She hoped he would touch her, but she was terrified he wouldn't. The anticipation was killing her.

When his hand cupped the heat of her, her fingers tightened into his hair to hold on. Books told about it and movies sometimes alluded to it, but she'd never been touched like this before. It was so much more than anything she'd experienced. Jonah was so much more.

His fingers slid between her folds intimately while his lips continued their slow torture of her neck. Her breathing grew erratic. He rubbed his fingers against her, erasing any thoughts. Pressure built within her, winding her tighter and tighter. When his finger slipped inside her, she hissed at the sensation.

"Okay?" His rough voice was next to her ear.

She gasped as he began a steady, slow rhythm. In and out. She forced herself to nod because she couldn't think. Let alone vocalize whatever the hell was happening to her. If this was making out, sign her up. Her hips moved on their own accord, finding a rhythm with him as he took her higher.

Something was bearing down on her. The more he touched her, the closer it got. His thumb slid against her right where she needed it most. Her eyes slid shut as she focused on Jonah's hands and his lips against her neck. Her breath fell in sharp pants as she let her instincts take control, following his wicked lead.

His breath was heavy in her ear and the noise from the movie floated in the background. He slipped in another finger, stretching her, filling her, stroking her. Arching against him, she clung to his hair like an anchor that would keep her here with him as the storm within her threatened to tear her apart.

"Let go, Lacy." His voice took her over the edge. It slammed into her like the wall of a hurricane, lifted her, tearing her free from the Earth. He continued to whisper things in her ear as she rode the edge of storm, clinging to him. She spun into pleasure she couldn't even fathom before she came down to the Earth. Down to Jonah.

Her anchor. She released a hiss of breath as his fingers slowed within her. Her sex squeezed against his fingers in an aftershock.

He removed his hand from her panties and turned her around on his lap. She was a rag doll in his grasp. He could do anything with her and she would gladly follow him.

His lips captured hers gently. She'd never known it could be like this for her. The stories she read seemed like fantasy. A fantasy she'd never been able to explore. When he lifted his lips from hers, he guided her head to his shoulder and she released a breath. His hand stroked her back, softly, slowly. She sighed against him, knowing he'd keep her safe. Her eyes fluttered closed.

CHAPTER 13

Sunlight streamed in through the window onto Jonah's closed eyes. Jonah woke to Lacy sprawled over him with one of his legs dangling off the couch. Her head rested over his heart. Her fingers clenched into his shirt. Something soft slipped within him like a puzzle piece sliding into place. He took a deep breath and shook off the feeling.

The TV had long ago turned itself off. He didn't even know what movie she'd put on. Mostly because he'd been too occupied with Lacy. His cock jerked as he remembered her expression as she came. That hint of surprise mixed in with pleasure. He wanted to see that expression over and over again.

That might not happen. This morning, she might regret kissing him and letting him touch her.

He stroked his hand down her back and settled her more firmly on top of him. The couch wasn't very comfortable for two people, but he didn't want to move an inch. If he had moved them to a bed, he didn't think he would have been strong enough to resist sinking into her. He hadn't meant to touch her like that, to go that far, but he also couldn't resist seeing her fly. She'd been responsive to every touch and so wet. . . . If that ended up being all she'd let him do, he'd move on a happy man, knowing he'd given Lacy her first orgasm.

Today was Sunday and he had nowhere he needed to run off to. He usually worked out, but he didn't need to today. He hoped last night hadn't been a drunken mistake on Lacy's part. If not, they would have the whole day to explore each other.

Lacy twitched and almost fell off him, but he shifted her onto him. She let out a huge sigh and he wondered what she dreamt about. He brushed her hair away from her face and smiled at her pursed lips as the sunlight hit her eyes.

She turned her face into his chest and tried to burrow into it. He couldn't stop the laugh that slipped out of him. Lacy froze and lifted her head, eyes still closed. She blinked open her brown eyes and focused on his face.

"Morning," he said.

Her nose crinkled and she glanced at the window as if the sun offended her. She dropped her head to his chest with her head turned away from the light. "What time is it?"

"No idea."

Her fingers clenched into his shirt and he tried to remain unmoved, but he'd woken up to her soft warm body over him and his cock hadn't gotten the message it needed to wait until she decided whether to take this further. But she hadn't scrambled off him immediately, there was that.

"How do you feel this morning?" His hand settled over her lower back and the soft material of her shirt. They had slept in the clothes they went out in.

She breathed in a deep breath. "Not hungover."

"That's good." He wanted to ask her more but she didn't usually wake up alert and ready to talk. He could be patient.

Her fingers flexed into his shirt.

"I don't suppose you made coffee?" The hopeful tone of her voice made him chuckle.

"No, little bird. I didn't want to move from where I am." That wouldn't reveal too much. Besides she knew he wanted her. He didn't have to hide it, not that he'd really tried to hide it from her before.

She brought her hands under her chin and propped her head up to look at him. He couldn't stop himself from reaching out and tucking her hair behind her ear, but otherwise, he remained motionless. She needed to lead this conversation. She would determine where they went next.

He wouldn't apologize for what happened last night, but he would respect any decision she made on it. Except now that he'd kissed her, he wanted to do it again and again. Not just that either. He wanted to slip his hand between her thighs and show her heaven again. So much of her he hadn't tasted or touched. Yet. Those thoughts definitely didn't help his erection.

"Are you having regrets?" she asked and winced like she wished she hadn't.

"Never." He couldn't resist trailing his thumb over her bottom lip. "You?"

Her eyes darkened and she shook her head. "No."

"Good." He cupped her cheek and she leaned into his hand. He never wanted to leave this couch again. He could stay in this moment with Lacy forever. Later he'd think about what that meant, but right now, he just wanted to stay.

"Can we. . . ." Lacy trailed off and her eyes wandered away from his.

"Can we?" he prompted. He didn't want to assume she meant what he hoped she meant.

She buried her face into his chest again. She muttered into his chest, "This was easier when I was angry and a little buzzed."

He played with the string on her top, lightly brushing her nape with his fingers. She inhaled swiftly but didn't lift her head.

"Do you think coffee would help?" He trailed his fingers over the exposed skin on her back.

She peeked up at him. "Maybe?"

Jonah pushed up to sitting with one arm tight around Lacy so she wouldn't scramble off him. When he sat up, he arranged her legs until she once again straddled him on the couch. Her cheeks flushed with color when he tipped her chin up.

Her eyes widened as he leaned in and pressed his lips to hers. Her whole body softened against his and her fingers threaded through his hair. She closed the distance between their bodies as he wrapped his arms around her. For a moment, it was bliss.

She pulled away with her eyes wide and covered her lips. "Morning breath."

"Fuck morning breath." He growled low in his chest and lifted her hand away before reclaiming her lips. This time he didn't hold back. He slipped his hand under her shirt and cupped her lace-covered breast. She gasped and he seized the opportunity, parting his lips. He discovered the contours of her breast with his fingers as he explored her mouth with his tongue. She groaned and tugged his hair to pull him closer.

If someone had told Jonah when he moved into the apartment, his fierce little bird of a roommate would be making him want to forget everything and just spend the day showing her all the ways fucking could be a good thing, he would have laughed in that person's face. Right now, he just wanted to figure out if this was really what she wanted. Her body responded to his as if it had been starving and he was more than willing to feed it, but he needed Lacy's brain to be up to speed too.

He reluctantly removed his hand from her breast and lifted his head. She sighed. Her lips were full and red from his kiss. Her nipples hardened beneath her shirt. Her cheeks flushed with color. And when her eyes opened, they were blown with desire. He almost leaned in to reclaim her lips; instead he lifted her to her feet.

She swayed slightly but he held her hips until she steadied herself. When he stood, she stared up at him. Her eyes wide and open and so fucking vulnerable. He kissed her forehead.

"Go freshen up and I'll start the coffee."

LACY hurried off to the bathroom and after she closed the door, she took a deep breath and leaned against it. She wasn't sure she needed coffee this morning. That kiss had been fucking spectacular and her body had hollered a "hell yes" when he pulled her to straddle him. Even now her sex pulsed with longing. Finally she understood what everyone else craved.

It felt like she'd stepped on a freight train that was about to go off the rails. But she most definitely didn't want to get off the train. She quickly used the toilet, brushed her teeth, and tried to detangle some of her hair. She scrubbed off what makeup remained from last night.

Her hands went to the sink to hold herself upright. Last night. Dancing. Tequila. That shot with Jonah. She'd wanted to lick the salt from his skin. Just being near him made her feel drunk.

Meanwhile, Logan had been more attentive than he'd ever been before he went off with another girl. That girl had been a sure thing and Lacy definitely wasn't.

Except when she and Jonah had gotten home. The kisses. Yes, please. And what he did with his hands. Her sex clenched just thinking about it. She had no idea how to broach the subject with him this morning. He'd said if she still wanted to, he would be down for it. And that morning kiss. . . .

Something caught her attention in the mirror. She brushed her hair over her shoulder and noted the trailed of red marks on her neck. Her face flushed. Hickeys?

She smiled as her fingers traced over them. Jonah had given her hickeys. She'd never had a hickey in her life. Fortunately, her hair would cover them for work tomorrow. She took a bracing breath and met her eyes in the mirror. She was a healthy adult and so was he. She wasn't a virgin. Neither of them were in a relationship. They would use protection. So why not?

She opened the bathroom door and Jonah leaned against his bedroom door opposite her. His eyes were guarded, but he smiled at her. As he closed the distance between them, her heart clamored in her chest.

"You gave me hickeys." The words popped out of her mouth and she quickly covered her lips with her hands.

His gaze dropped to her neck. He lifted his hand and his fingers traced down the line of love bites. Heat burst within her. She couldn't stop the gasp that fell out of her mouth. At the possessive look in his eyes, her knees almost gave way.

His blue eyes met hers. "Coffee is almost ready. I'll be out in a second."

He ducked into the bathroom as she wandered into the kitchen. When she sank into the kitchen chair, memories of last night flooded her. The storm had already started whipping through her and the longing followed. She wanted to know it all. Experience it all. With Jonah.

To calm herself, she quickly walked over to stare at the coffee machine as it didn't have any memories of kissing associated with it like the chair did.

She tensed but didn't turn around when she heard the bathroom door open and Jonah's feet padded across the floor. His arms wrapped around her waist from behind and pulled her against him. She squeaked when his lips found the back of her neck. Then she tipped her neck to the side, eager to feel the sparks igniting from his every touch. His erection pressed against her, giving her a good idea of where he was on the whole "fucking" thing.

Heat flooded through her and her sex pulsed hot and heavy.

His hands went to her waist and turned her around before lifting her and setting her on the counter. He stepped in between her legs and reached up for a coffee cup. Her skirt rode up her thighs. She wished it wasn't there at all. His heat flowed over her. She couldn't decide which she was more eager for, his lips on hers or coffee. Definitely his lips.

"We should probably have a talk." Jonah filled the mug with coffee and handed it to her before getting another cup down for himself.

"Talk?" She took a sip of coffee and arched her eyebrow at him. Consent? He was the one who had initiated everything this morning. But she most definitely had been a willing participant.

"About sex." He took a sip, deliberately arching his eyebrow like she had.

She smiled at him before taking a few more sips of coffee. "We haven't even changed clothes since last night."

He made a sound of acknowledgement. Tracing her finger around the rim of her coffee mug, she raised her eyes to meet his.

"You want to fuck me?" She managed not to wince at the curse word and not to look away. See, she could be mature.

His lips lifted on one side. "Always."

Panty melting. The coffee wasn't the only thing making her hot. "What about work and living together?"

"Convenient." He shrugged.

She couldn't help the smile that came to her lips. "I'm just convenient?"

"The situation is convenient, but I'd want to fuck you even if we didn't live together or work together." Jonah's blue eyes held her entranced. His words made her feel drunk. Her insides were already swirling. If what happened last night was any indication, she wanted to go forward with this. Explore her lack of sexuality with Jonah. He made her feel safe.

"So what's there to discuss?" She cocked an eyebrow at him and sipped her coffee.

"What do you want?" His hand settled above her knee at the hem of her skirt. "Sex no strings yes, but. . . ."

Holy crap. Sex no strings. She never thought she'd be someone who could do that, but then she'd met Jonah. She sipped at her coffee, trying to look thoughtful and not panicked. She could do this. Have a talk about sex. "But?"

"What limits do you want to have in place? Time? What do you want to explore?" Jonah's hand moved up her thigh slightly.

She inhaled a quick breath and would have pressed her thighs together against the ache, but Jonah's body blocked her. "Should we set a time limit?"

"It can be helpful. That way we both know when it will be over."

Her heart dropped at the *over* part. It hadn't even begun and he was saying it would be over. But of course that was how no stings attached worked. "How long do these things normally go?"

Jonah chuckled and his thumb soothed the skin of her inner thigh. "Days, weeks, depends on the participants."

She nodded like she knew what he was talking about. She didn't want to make him commit to longer if he decided she wasn't worth the trouble.

"Can we circle back to that one? I mean what if either of us decides it just isn't going to work out. What if it's not good?" She ducked her head, not wanting to see his expression.

His coffee cup hit the counter with a thud and his fingers tipped her chin up until she looked in his eyes.

"It *will* be good."

"You can't know that," she whispered.

He took her coffee cup from her and set it down, before taking her chin in his fingers. "I know."

"I don't want to disappoint you," she barely got out. His eyes held her motionless.

"You won't." His lips covered hers in a gentle touch. He rested his forehead against hers and when she opened her eyes, he watched her. "If something doesn't feel right or if you want to change anything or stop anything, tell me. If something is too fast or not enough, tell me. I'm doing this for you."

She swallowed.

"Only me?" The words came out hollow. She thought he wanted her, but what if he just wanted a body and like he said she was convenient.

"Fuck, Lacy." He grabbed her hand and pressed it against his erection. "I thought we already went over this part. I want you. You letting me have you is a fucking miracle. You need forever and I'm not that guy, but I'm more than happy to show you just how passionate you really are."

She tightened her hand around him through his jeans. He was solid and hot beneath her palm. She'd never actually touched a guy before. At least not like this. "Can I . . . ."

She bit her lip and glanced up at his eyes. He watched her

struggle with her words, patiently. She needed to get over her hang ups.

"Can I see. . . it?"

His eyes widened, but his lips curved into a smirk. "I'm hoping we'll be doing more than seeing."

She didn't think she could blush any harder, but damn if her cheeks didn't feel hotter by the minute.

His lips captured hers and his hands left her. Her attention focused on the movement of his lips against hers, but she could tell he was working on his shirt buttons. The fabric brushed her hand still on his cock. She started to move her hand away, but his hand captured hers and held it there. Her breath caught.

His tongue sought entrance at her lips. She parted hers willingly and his unique taste combined with the coffee they'd shared made her groan. As if Jonah's kisses weren't addictive enough, adding coffee just made her want to spend all day with his lips fused to hers. His hand left hers and he shrugged out of his shirt, not releasing her mouth.

Her free hand went to his bare chest, running over the dips and curves of his muscles. His hand went to the front of his jeans. She didn't remove her hand as he undid the buttons holding them together. As soon as his jeans opened, she slid her hand into the opening against his cotton boxers and the solid heat of him.

He sucked in a breath against her lips. Biting her lip, she wanted him. He reached into his pocket and removed something before sliding his jeans down his hips. They hit the floor with a quiet thud. He lifted his lips from hers but didn't move away.

She opened her eyes to look into his. Desire stripped bare in his eyes.

"We can talk later, right?" His eyebrow went up and all she could do was nod. His hands went to his underwear.

Propping herself on her hands, she leaned back on the counter slightly so she could watch him. Somewhere in her mind, she thought maybe she should act more shy, but she was way too curious. Her first time had been quick and forgettable. Everything she'd done so far with Jonah was permanently etched in her brain. She didn't need to feign shyness with him or look away when she really wanted to see the beauty of all of him. All of Jonah.

His cock strained against the cotton boxer briefs. She bit her lip.

He removed his underwear, quickly stepping out of it. He stood between her legs completely naked in front of her. In her kitchen. And she couldn't stop her eyes from taking everything in even if she'd wanted to. She knew he worked out, but damn, he was cut from marble with an artist's loving touch. Everything about him was perfect.

It should make her nervous about him seeing her body, because she most definitely did not work out. But instead, she just felt very overdressed in this moment. She followed the lines of his muscles down to his cock. It stood upright and proud. The skin looked ridiculously smooth and she tentatively reached out a hand to touch it.

Her eyes flicked up to Jonah's face. His eyes stayed on her hand. When she made contact with his hot, smooth skin, his eyes closed. Her gaze dropped to his cock pulsing against her hand. She wrapped her hand around him and traced her fingers over his length.

Her own sex throbbed like when he'd touched her.

"Jonah?" Her voice was lower. She didn't know what she was asking for, but she knew he'd be able to give it to her.

His eyes opened, and his mouth claimed hers. His hands went to her hips and pulled her flush against his cock. Only her damp underwear kept them from touching skin to skin. It fueled the ache between her legs.

Trailing up his body, her hands found their way into his hair again.

His hand slid beneath her shirt to just beneath her breast. His fingers traced the band of her bra to the clasp. Her breath caught and held in anticipation. Every whisper of touch he'd given her before made his hands on her now feel like so much more. When he released it, he pulled the strapless bra out from under her shirt before his hand found its way to her skin. He cupped her breast and dragged his thumb over her nipple.

She gasped against his lips. Sensations flooded her from everywhere his skin touched her. He rocked against her, sliding his cock along her slit against her panties, sending ripples of desire in his wake. His hands pulled hers down to the counter slightly behind her as he broke off their kiss.

"Lean back," his gravelly voice said in her ear.

A part of her wanted to run before things went too far. The other part of her knew that point had already been breached. She wouldn't leave, not for anything. His kiss last night had opened her eyes to what she'd been missing. It had probably been too late when he first stepped in the door a week ago. She leaned back on the counter for him, trusting him with her body. She propped herself on her elbows to watch him.

His eyes were the color of the ocean at night, dark and forbidding as he watched her face. His hand trailed up inside her halter top until his fingertips brushed her bare nipple. Her lips parted and she almost closed her eyes, but she couldn't stop gazing into his. The same look lurked in his eyes as when he caught her watching him have sex. It pulled at her deep inside.

He leaned over her and trailed his lips down her neck. His hands lifted her shirt. She should be mortified, but she couldn't take her eyes off Jonah as he exposed her breasts.

His mouth closed over her nipple. Her eyes shut at the overwhelming sensation. His other hand trailed up her thigh until his thumb rubbed against her center through her satin panties. When he shifted backward, she tightened her thighs on Jonah's hips.

She started to protest, but then his hands dragged her underwear down her legs. His tongue flicked over her nipple as he stepped back between her knees. Desire overwhelmed her. His finger slid along her bare slit and she moaned, longing for the release he'd provide. He peppered kisses across her chest to take her other nipple into his mouth. Her elbows shook from the effort to hold herself up as his finger slid inside her core and out. Over and over.

The pressure built within her as he stoked the fire within her higher and higher with every touch. She practically panted when he lifted his head from her breast and tugged her shirt into place. His hands left her for a moment and she opened her eyes to meet his dark hypnotic blue ones.

A wrapper ripped and for a moment she tensed and winced. This had been the part that hurt last time.

Jonah leaned forward until his lips brushed over hers. He touched her forehead with his.

"It won't be the same as your first time, little bird."

She took a deep breath, still worried. "How do you know?"

"You might feel a stretch, but if there's pain, we'll stop. Okay?" Jonah searched her eyes.

She trusted him. She did, but she still worried. Theoretically she knew the first time hurt and it shouldn't hurt now, but her only experience had been bad all around. But Jonah wasn't that guy. Everything he'd done had been to protect her. To make sure she was ready for him. Breathing in, she nodded.

He lowered his mouth to hers. This kiss was tender and

sweet. Her heart filled her chest and she started to relax. His hand skimmed up her inner thigh and stroked her gently, slowly. Reminding her of last night and the pleasure he gave her.

She relaxed as he deepened the kiss and his fingers moved within her. Before long, her hips moved with him, seeking that release.

He lifted his head slightly until they could see each other. His fingers moved steadily in her and she bit her lip as she got closer and closer to the edge. His eyes pinned her in place and she wanted to slip over the edge. It was so close she could feel it bearing down on her. He removed his hand and she felt the head of his cock against her. But she was beyond caring. She wanted more. She craved more.

He pulled her hips closer to the edge of the counter as he slid into her. She didn't have any time to register what was happening as he filled her completely, except the pleasure. Her eyes widened, but she didn't have any pain, just fullness.

"Good?" His gaze never left hers.

She nodded. It felt strange but so much better than good.

He pulled her body up against his, supporting her weight. Her arms shook slightly as she wrapped them around his shoulders. This feeling of being closer to Jonah than anyone else in her life filled her. He propped her knees against his hips.

"Pain?"

Heat rushed to her cheeks. How she could still feel embarrassed at this point, she had no idea. He was being so considerate of her. Her heart wanted to burst from her chest.

She shook her head and whispered, "No."

He pressed his forehead to hers. "Good."

She searched his eyes while he watched her. Nothing had been more erotic to her than Jonah's eyes. She experimentally moved her hips against him gently and moaned at the sensation. So much better than his fingers.

He gave her a crooked grin and began to stroke in and out of her slowly. Her legs wrapped around him to hold on. She tried to bite her lip to stop from moaning again. Then Jonah's lips found hers and he held her to him as they continued to thrust together.

Lifting his mouth from hers, his gravelly voice said, "Lacy, open your eyes."

She opened them and his eyes were the same as that night he'd caught her watching him, but there was something more in them. It pushed her even closer to that edge. She would never forget his blue eyes in this moment.

She cupped his cheek and whispered, "Jonah."

Giving him a piece of her she'd never shared with anyone else. She arched into him as her body exploded into fireworks. He let out a satisfied groan and his face tightened as he found his own release. Time stood still for a second as they stayed connected. Eye to eye. Chest to chest. Him buried deep inside her. She wanted to hold onto it forever. This image. This moment.

Then the world rushed backed in. She dropped her head to his shoulder, exhausted and energized at the same time. She never wanted to move again while they waited for their breathing to return to normal.

CHAPTER 14

STILL PROPPED ON THE COUNTER, Lacy remained half draped over Jonah. He didn't want to move an inch. He rubbed his hand over her back. He hadn't meant to fuck her on the counter, but her touch on him had been too much. They were supposed to talk through everything first. And then he'd take her to his bed and make her come multiple times before taking things slow. He threw the condom in the kitchen trash and lifted Lacy against him. He'd make it up to her.

"Shower time," he announced as he headed to the bathroom.

Lacy tucked her head into his shoulder. "Together?"

"Yes." Jonah didn't know how long this would last between them but he would take advantage of every opportunity he had with her.

He set her on the counter in the bathroom while he turned on the water. Her eyes followed him. Her cheeks were pink by the time he returned to her, but she didn't drop her gaze. He stood fully naked while she had way too many clothes on.

He helped her down to her feet and turned her around to face the sink. He brushed all her hair over her shoulder so he could see the knot he tied. She shivered. He met her dark fathomless eyes in the mirror.

"Was that okay?" Lacy dropped her eyes at the end of her question.

"Perfect."

Her eyes shot up to his in the mirror.

"In fact, I'm hoping to continue to show you how good sex can be for the rest of the day and into the night." He loosened the knot and kissed the nape of her neck.

She shivered and turned in his arms. "Really?"

If she wanted the answer to that, all she needed to do was look down. His cock was hard and ready. Fortunately he had a few condoms in here he'd stashed earlier, just in case.

He grabbed the bottom of her shirt and pulled it off over her head. Her hair spilled around her shoulders. He lowered his head to hers until their mouths almost touched. "Really."

His lips touched hers as his fingers released the zipper on her skirt, letting it flutter to the ground. Anxious to feel her soft skin pressed against his, he pulled her naked body against him and she moaned against his lips. That was what he wanted. Her complete and utter surrender. No more worrying about her body or if she was doing things right.

When he lifted her in his arms again, she wrapped her arms and legs around him. His hands supported her bottom, as he brought them both into the shower and pulled the curtain closed. Every morning he had fantasized about this while her peaches and cream scent surrounded him, and now she was here in his arms. He dipped his head to hers and kissed her like it was killing him not to.

Her legs slid down until she stood against him. The warm water trailed over her and he took a step away from her until he could see all of her. He'd been right: no tan lines, all smooth golden skin. From her pert breasts to her small waist to the dark curls between her legs to those amazing long legs, she was perfection.

She wrapped her arms around her breasts to hide them from his view.

"Don't hide, little bird." He tugged her into his arms and turned her around into the water. He dropped his head beside hers and said in her ear, "You're perfect."

"You don't have to lie to me." She glanced at him over her shoulder. "I'm not anything special."

"Fuck that." He wrapped his arm around her waist to pull her flush against his hard body.

She gasped at the contact and probably at his erection against her ass. She dropped her hands to his arm.

His other hand went to her neck. "You have a gorgeous neck I can't help but want to kiss every time I see you. I want to mark it every fucking day. That way everyone knows how fuckable you are."

Her breath shuddered in and out of her. So fucking responsive. He trailed his fingers over her wet breasts, cupping them and making her nipples harden. "Your breasts are the perfect size. Enough to hold, and the feel of your nipple against my tongue is my new favorite thing. I want to devote a day to exploring just your breasts."

Her head fell back against his chest and her eyes slid shut as he continued to touch her breasts. He slid his hand to her waist and rested both of them right on top of her hips. The perfect fucking handful.

"I've had fantasies about your waist and hips. When you stretch in the morning, you display your small waist and the curves of your hips. It makes me want to follow you into this shower and worship every inch of you." He kissed behind her ear and pulled her hips into his cock. "Your ass is fucking delectable. Your legs make me want to drop to my knees and worship them."

He slid his hand between her legs and her wetness had very little do to with the shower. Lacy was built for sex and he seemed to be the only man who saw it. He didn't know if he'd ever tire of her.

"And this." He stroked his fingers between her folds, teasing her opening, until she panted for him. "So many things to be done here. With my hands. With my mouth. With my cock."

"Jonah," she breathed. Her body melted into his. Every inch of skin touching. "Please."

"It's not just your body, little bird. You are kind and thoughtful. Intelligent and even funny sometimes. Stubborn as hell and feisty when you get riled up. And you're so fucking sexy." He grabbed a condom and sheathed himself. "Perfect."

He placed her hands against the shower wall, bending her over. She spread her legs and hung her head as he massaged her slit with his fingers before he slid his cock all the way in. He didn't go slow this time, but he reached around and rubbed her clit as he thrust steadily into her.

She cried out as her orgasm took her over the edge. He continued to piston in her, and when she shattered around him a second time, he couldn't hold back anymore. Her cry and his moan combined to make sweet music as he tumbled after her over the edge. He sagged against her as the water poured over them.

He took care of the condom and then pulled Lacy into his arms and just hugged her to him. Her arms wrapped around his waist and her head rested on his chest. She was addictive.

"Thank you," she mumbled against his skin.

He chuckled. "No need to thank me, little bird."

He gave her a final squeeze and released her to grab her

mesh sponge and her body soap. The scent of peaches filled the humid air. If he hadn't just come, he'd have a hard on just from the powerful scent.

"I will never be able to smell peaches and not think of you," he said as he smoothed the sponge over her body.

"Your scent reminds me of the ocean. Sunshine and waves, crisp air." She grabbed his scrubby and his body soap. She held her arms up as he moved down her body with the sponge.

He knelt before her and washed her leg and foot, before doing the same to the other. "We should probably figure out breakfast or lunch."

When he stood, she started to rub his body with his soap. By the time she finished his back and moved to his front, he was fully hard again. She rinsed his scrubby and set it to the side. She put some soap in her hands and rubbed her hands together. Her eyebrow cocked up as she met his gaze.

"Will you tell me if I do something wrong?" She watched his face as her hands touched his cock. She spread the soap up and down and even down to his balls.

"If need be." He wanted to assure her anything would be fine, but with her hands on him, he could barely form words.

"I've never touched a. . . ." Her eyes drifted down.

"Cock, dick, penis. You can call it Fred if you really want to." He leaned his forehead against the top of her head, trying to focus on her words.

"Cock." She tested the word and he swore he got harder. "Penis, too clinical. Dick sounds like a bad thing. I've never touched a cock before, but I've read romances and always wondered."

She leaned forward and pressed her lips against his chest, all while her wicked hands worked him up and down. "Is this good?"

He moaned as she quickened her strokes. He nodded his

head against hers. Fuck, he wasn't going to last long, which was surprising after he'd already come twice this morning.

"About breakfast." Her voice was slightly breathless. Did this turn his little bird on too? If he touched her, would she already be wet again?

"We could make some eggs," she said.

Her hands continued their torture, while his mind tormented him about her own arousal. Fuck, he wanted to touch her, but he also wanted her to explore at her own leisure. Even if it drove him insane.

"Eggs sound good," he groaned out. If he hadn't already taken her twice, he would have grabbed a condom and taken her again, but he didn't want to make her too sore. He appreciated she needed a rest, but only for breakfast. Besides, he was confident she could get him there with her hands.

She flattened her tongue against his nipple and he knew he'd come soon.

"Faster, love," he whispered. So close.

She raised her head to look up at him. Her eyes were dark with desire and he couldn't resist those full lips. He took her mouth with his and she opened to him, deepening the kiss. He didn't know how he'd resisted kissing her before last night. She took over the kiss, giving back everything he'd given to her. He let go as he tipped over the edge.

The shower washed away everything as she continued to kiss him. He cradled the back of her head as he plundered her mouth. When he finally lifted his head, she had a hard time catching her breath.

He looked down into her eyes and smiled. "Perfect."

THE SHOWER ENDED QUICKLY after that, because they were turning into prunes. Not that Lacy cared. Her insides felt all warm and fuzzy. When they broke apart to grab fresh clothes from their rooms, she put on her kissing frog pajamas and braided her wet hair.

If they decided to leave the apartment, she'd change then. Not that there was any reason to leave the apartment. Soreness lingered between her legs, but the shower definitely helped ease it. She came out to the kitchen and picked up her underwear and bra Jonah had stacked on the chair. Heat coursed through her. She didn't say anything as she passed Jonah on the way to her bedroom.

"Eggs?" he yelled after her. He had on athletic pants and a tank top. Everything looked good on him.

"Eggs sound good." Her body pulsed thinking about his cock in her hands. She hadn't known it would turn her on that much, and if they hadn't been turning into prunes, she would have begged for some relief. She shook her head at her thoughts.

She walked to the kitchen table and sat to watch Jonah cut onions and peppers for the eggs. She propped up one leg and wrapped her arms around it while resting her head on her knee to watch him.

"What do you want to do today? It's only eleven." She couldn't get enough of watching him.

Jonah had really great arms. She sighed as they flexed while he worked.

He looked over at her and gave her a look even she knew meant sexy times. Her insides whipped around, ready for another round.

"All day?" What a stupid question. She should have her woman card revoked. This beyond sexy man wanted to do things to her body all day long. She should be screaming yes, please, not questioning him.

He shrugged and winked at her. Her heart fluttered. She was such a girl.

"How about a movie marathon?" she said.

"How about a sex marathon?" He pulled out a skillet and then grabbed the eggs.

"How about both?" She scrunched her nose at him. She wasn't sure she had the stamina to go "all day."

He chuckled as he cracked the eggs and beat them before adding the veggies. "Sex while watching movies?"

"Maybe more interspersed?" She smiled at his look of disbelief before he turned to the stove. "Do you really want to spend all day having sex?"

"With you. Is that even a question?"

"Why did we even bother getting dressed then?" She arched her eyebrow at him when he turned back to her for a moment.

"Because hot eggs on skin hurts." He gestured to the coffee machine. "Want fresh coffee?"

She stood and dumped out the coffee from this morning before making a fresh pot. Going to the fridge, she pulled out some fruit to go with their eggs. "Do you want toast?"

"No thanks."

She shrugged and dropped in two pieces for herself. She leaned against the sink and watched him work the omelets. He seemed at home in the kitchen.

"Did you cook a lot as a kid?" She couldn't even begin to imagine Jonah as a little kid. Surely he'd popped out of the womb his perfect, ornery self. That thought made her smile.

He plated the omelets. "Sometimes. I got away from it when I got older. Travelling meant eating out a lot. I found if I wanted to eat healthier, I needed to make my own food."

She buttered her toast and placed it on one of the plates. "I've never been great at cooking. Living in the city, there's always so many places to try. Why bother making my own?"

She grabbed their mugs of coffee and the fruit, and he

took the plates to the table. Just as she set down everything, Jonah tugged her onto his lap.

"Back to sex all day." Jonah's lips touched the nape of her neck, sending a pulse of desire to pool between her legs and awakening her unfulfilled desire from the shower.

"We definitely need breakfast if we're going to do that." She started to get up from his lap, but he tugged her back down.

"Breakfast first." He moved her plate from her space to in front of him too.

She laughed but gave up trying to change seats. After she took a bite, she said, "This is good."

She'd never sat on someone's lap to eat that she could remember. It was a different experience having his thigh pressing between her legs, knowing what he wanted to do after breakfast.

"Am I going to be able to keep up with you?" she asked halfway through the meal.

"What do you mean?" His plate was almost empty.

"I. . . ." How did she explain this? "I've had sex once before you. I just don't know how I'm going to keep up."

"We can go at your pace." His hand slipped under her pajama top at her waist.

Sparks flew through her body. Did she need him to slow down? His warm lips kissed along her neck. If he kept doing that, she'd be on him in a second.

"I don't have a pace. What's your pace?" She glanced at him over her shoulder.

His eyebrow lifted and he smirked. "Normally or with you?"

Heat pooled low in her belly. She kept it together for a second before she slid off his lap and onto her own chair, dragging her omelet with her. "I need energy to keep up."

He chuckled and took care of the dishes while she

finished eating. When she brought her dish to wash it, he took it from her and gave her a quick kiss.

If she lingered next to him, things would definitely progress. So she went over to the couch and scrolled through the menus to find something to watch. She put on *A Cinderella Story* and it had just started when Jonah came and sat next to her on the couch.

"Let me guess," he said, "movie marathon is all teen rom coms?"

She smirked at him. "Of course."

He lifted her onto his lap with her back against his front and her legs on either side of his. Her body definitely remembered this position from last night. Her breath quickened and her skin tingled in anticipation of his touch.

She nearly came when he whispered in her ear, "Watch your movie."

His hands slid under her top. One moved up to torment her breasts and the other slipped beneath her pants and panties over her sex. This definitely wasn't appropriate for movie watching. She tried her hardest to focus on the TV while he sucked on her neck.

When he spread his knees to open her legs farther, his fingers stroked through her wetness, drawing lazy circles around her core. She bit her lip, refusing to give him the satisfaction of a sigh or a moan. She made it through the first fifteen minutes of the movie. His finger slipped inside her and she couldn't stop the groan from leaving her lips.

"Can we—" The words got caught in her throat as he added another finger inside her and pumped them in and out, while his thumb found her clit. Her hips followed the motion. His other hand tweaked her nipple, shooting sparks straight to her sex. "Jonah."

She grabbed his wrist to make him stop for a moment.

"Yes, Lacy?" His voice sounded way too smug, but she was too far gone to care.

"Bed," she finally forced out. "Can we try a bed?"

The movie was forgotten. Jonah set her on her feet before dragging her to his room.

He opened his door and led her in. When he closed the door, the lock snicked in place. Not that anyone else was there.

It wasn't much different than her room. The room itself was big and Brenda had painted the walls a dark red. The wall with windows was exposed brick. Even though it was daylight, it still felt dark in the room. Close and intimate. A chair sat near the windows and a large king size bed with a brown leather headboard dominated the rest of the space. Her pulse pounded as he walked over to the nightstand and flicked on the light. Soft light. She took a steadying breath.

Should she start stripping? Maybe she should touch him the way he had been touching her. Should she wait for him to make the next move? She really didn't know the protocol. Instead she focused on the room.

Unlike her room, everything seemed neat and tidy. He didn't have any pictures on the wall or any decoration unless you included the guitar and guitar case beside the window. It barely looked lived in.

"I haven't heard you play the guitar." She gestured toward the instrument.

"I don't play much anymore."

She wanted to ask why, but since he didn't volunteer, she let it go. Somehow, it felt more intimate than what they'd been doing on the couch.

"Do you have more things in storage?" She sat on the end of the bed. Talking was easier than trying to figure out how to keep the sex going. The comforter was dark blue with white stars on it. She traced her fingers around a couple of stars.

"No." He pulled off his shirt and dropped it next to the hamper. Her mouth watered at his chest and abs. She didn't think she'd ever not react to them. He slipped off his pants and underwear until he stood naked before her. Maybe she should have stripped.

She swallowed, still not used to seeing all of Jonah. He was almost too much for her to take in. His body was beautiful. She focused on what she wanted to ask.

"Where's your stuff?" She couldn't imagine only having a suitcase full of clothes and a guitar. Her closet was a disaster area of memories and things that at one point had served a purpose.

He paused. "Stuff?"

"Pictures, old textbooks, books, the lamp your mother gave you that doesn't actually go with anything but you still use it. The blanket your nana quilted you so you wouldn't get cold on winter nights. The stuff you gather by living your life."

He shrugged and moved to kneel before her. "When you don't have anywhere to land, why collect stuff you'd have to carry on your back?"

He started unbuttoning her shirt, but she was still caught up in their conversation. Her pulse kicked up a notch with every loosened button. She liked the idea of minimalism, but even then there was stuff she'd keep because of sentimental value.

"Are you going to get an apartment of your own when Brenda returns?" She didn't even know why she was asking this. They weren't permanent. She and Jonah weren't a couple, but he did work with her and that wouldn't change.

After this.

"If I decide to stay here." He slipped her shirt down her arms.

She hadn't bothered to put on a bra. His eyes darkened as he focused on her breasts. He leaned in and kissed her. Thoughts of his nomadic lifestyle slipped from her mind. His warm chest rubbed against her breasts and her thoughts focused in on Jonah again. He tipped her back on the bed and pulled her pants and underwear off.

He continued to kiss down her neck, spending some time sucking and kissing her breasts until her breath came out in small hitches. Her hands tangled in his hair. Just when she thought she couldn't take anymore, he continued to trail his kisses down her stomach. He tugged her down to the edge of the bed and put her legs over his shoulders before his lips found her sex.

Tensing against the bed, she held her breath. When his tongue swiped over her, she cried out at the flood of desire that spiraled through her. His lips, tongue, and teeth did wicked things to her folds while his finger delved into her core. Her heart pounded like she had run miles. Her thighs squeezed against his shoulders. Just when she thought she'd tip over the edge, he'd change the tempo or ease up on the pressure, making her ride an endless roller coaster of need.

"Jonah!" Her fingers clenched into the comforter. A fine sheen of sweat covered her body as he kept her from release once again. How much more could she take?

He chuckled darkly against her folds, the vibration making everything more sensitive. He sucked and tongued her bundle of nerves, this time not releasing until she saw stars as she crested the peak and stayed there as his fingers kept up their torment.

Suddenly Jonah replaced his fingers with his cock and she hit a new level of awareness. She arched into him as her climax released. He thrust in and out of her, drawing her right back to the edge. She never knew it could be like this. His mouth crashed down on hers. She could taste herself in his kiss. Her body was so primed when he found his release, she came again.

He collapsed on the bed next to her, throwing away the condom in a trash basket near his nightstand, and pulled her into his arms.

She took deep breaths to try to steady her shaking limbs.

"You okay?" He pressed his lips against her forehead.

She tried to laugh at him as she lifted her head from his chest. "Were you trying to kill me? Because I'm pretty sure if I were a cat, I lost one of my lives."

"Good thing you have more than one then." His hand trailed down her spine. The gesture warmed her as her body grew heavy.

"I'm definitely going to need another shower." She started to sit up, but he pulled her down on top of him.

"Later." His dark blue eyes entranced her as he lifted her to kiss her lips.

CHAPTER 15

"We are definitely watching a movie this time." Lacy held out the remote control at Jonah like it was a weapon. His feisty little bird.

"Sure." He chuckled and held up his hands in surrender. "Last time wasn't my fault."

Lacy blushed fiercely. They had stayed in bed for a while and then showered and ate lunch. Lacy had once again offered a movie and been the one to drag him to his own bedroom that time. Not that he wasn't at fault, and he hadn't complained. At all.

"Even so. Movie. This one I haven't seen so. . . ." She pointed the controller at the corner of the couch. "Stay over there."

He smiled, shook his head, and took the spot she indicated with his hands still held up.

"Good." She relaxed into the opposite corner of the couch, still in her kissing frog pajamas. He loved those frog pajamas.

The movie was some cheesy teen rom com. Not that he expected anything else. Lacy was as predictable as she was unpredictable. Wonderfully unpredictable when it came to sex. He'd wanted to believe there was a sex kitten waiting inside her and he hadn't been disappointed all day.

"Stop thinking about sex," Lacy said in a gruff voice. She didn't look away from the TV.

"I'm not."

She gave him a side glare before returning her focus to the show. Honestly, he'd never been like this with anyone. Yes, it was all new and fascinating to Lacy, but somehow being with her made sex feel new and fascinating to him.

They hadn't finished discussing time frames. He worried about Lacy. He didn't want to be her new Chet. She hadn't had a just-sex relationship before, and a set time limit should help ensure they didn't get their emotions tangled into it. Hurting her wasn't an option.

But he didn't want to bring up a finish date again yet. What if he wasn't ready to be done when they reached the date?

The thought startled him, but then again, nothing about Lacy had been normal for him.

Both of their phones chimed on the coffee table. He leaned forward and snatched them both before Lacy could grab hers.

"Hey." She pushed forward to his side of the couch like he knew she would.

Hiding his smirk, he glanced at her phone. Text from Logan. *Hey, want to come and hang with Claire and me at Legend's Sports Bar? I can teach you about football.*

Something twisted in his gut. Fucking Wolverine. Jonah was willing to bet he hadn't gotten a similar invite.

"Would you stop reading my text?" Lacy reached her arms around him, but it was easy to keep the phone away from her short arms.

His text was from his recruiter who had placed him at Taylor and King. *Got a new job offer to present to you.*

Lacy had managed to look over his shoulder as she practically climbed on his back. "New job offer? Are you still looking?"

He turned and pressed her down on the couch, holding her with his body.

"Logan wants to know if you want to come out to play." He tossed both phones on the coffee table and grabbed her hands to stretch them above her head.

The startled look left her eyes and soon they were the dark abysses he adored.

"I'm not dressed to go out." She wrapped her legs around his waist and pulled him into her. He settled between her welcoming thighs. He began to wonder if he'd ever get enough of her.

"Did you want to go put on a sexy outfit and watch a football game with Wolverine?" He lowered his head to her neck and found the spot that wound her up.

"I already have on my sexy outfit." She glanced down at her pajamas with a grin.

"Kissing frogs are hot," he whispered against her ear.

She giggled as his lips found hers.

Keys rattled in the door. Lacy squeaked and suddenly Jonah found himself on the floor next to the couch instead of on top of her. Lacy sat up and stared at the TV as the front door opened.

It happened so quickly Jonah still didn't know how he ended up on the floor, but he did manage to move to lean against the couch so it looked like he was watching the movie too before Sophie burst in.

Sophie dropped her keys on the console table and let the door shut. "Hey, Lacy."

"Hi, Sophie." Lacy waved at Sophie without turning

around. Lacy's face was probably bright red. He tried to suppress his smile.

Sophie's eyes narrowed on him. "Hey. Jonah."

"Hey." Apparently they were trying to pretend nothing had happened. Jonah felt like he was in high school, trying to make out with his girlfriend and not get caught by his mom. If Sophie had come in fifteen minutes later, there would have been a whole lot happening. He did a quick mental checklist of the apartment and what they had gotten up to all day. They'd definitely picked up out here. That was good. Lunch would have covered any evidence in the trash can.

"Be right back." He rose and headed to the bathroom where he made sure he had stashed the extra condoms in his bag and the ones in the trash were adequately buried. He took an extra moment before flushing the toilet and heading back in.

He resumed his seat on the floor.

"I guess you guys are getting along fine then?" Sophie had wheeled her bag closer to the hallway but she still stood there with her arms crossed over her chest.

"Ends up we work at the same company." Lacy paused the movie and looked over at Sophie. "It's been an interesting week."

Jonah struggled to keep his gaze on the paused teens on the TV and managed to keep the smirk off his face. "Interesting" was one way to put it.

"Weird. Why didn't Brenda tell us you worked at the same company?" Sophie raised her eyebrow at Jonah and he swore she would start tapping her foot any moment.

"She didn't know." Jonah finally met Sophie's eyes.

She narrowed her eyes at him.

"Anyway," Lacy said. "Jonah is fine. I'm fine. We're all fine."

Jonah closed his eyes but didn't wince. *Too many fines, Lacy.*

"What are you doing home?" Lacy asked.

He finally turned to look at Lacy, but she seemed to have it all together. Her cheeks had only a slight tinge of pink. The color deepened slightly at his gaze, but she didn't look at him.

Sophie sighed. "I'm here this week. They cancelled the travel scheduled so here I am." She shrugged. "I don't have to go in until late, so you can have the bathroom to yourself, Lacy."

"Great." Lacy pointed the remote at the TV. "We were just watching this new rom com on Netflix so. . . ."

"Yeah, sure, go ahead. I'm going to unpack and probably take a shower." Sophie started toward her room. "Have you guys had dinner?"

They both shook their heads.

"Wanna get something delivered? I'm starving and could use a nice greasy pizza. All the meats."

"I can order a couple." Jonah picked up his phone and dismissed the text notification before finding the app for the pizza place.

"Great." Sophie disappeared into her room.

Lacy pressed play on the movie and turned up the volume. She released a huge breath. "Sorry about the toss."

"It's fine." He reached over and traced the tops of her toes peeking out from her pajamas.

"Can we not tell anyone?" Lacy leaned close to him. Her words soft and almost breathless.

"Is this the end?" He turned to face her. His heart clattered to a stop, waiting for her answer. Their mouths so close he could kiss her.

"Do you. . . want it to be?"

He lifted his hand to brush her hair behind her ear. "Hell no."

Her eyebrow went up and she smiled. "Me either."

"It just got complicated." He ran his thumb over her lower lip. He wanted to trace it with his tongue, but he wouldn't. He wouldn't be doing much with Sophie here.

"Very."

LACY KEPT GLANCING over at Sophie. Sophie had decided after dinner to join Lacy for a movie. Jonah had excused himself and disappeared into his bedroom. God, she wanted to be in there with him, even if she was a bit sore. They had gone from zero to sixty in one day.

She couldn't even text Beth about what had happened with Sophie sitting here. Sophie wouldn't understand. She'd think Jonah coerced Lacy into it. She wasn't sure Beth would understand either. Lacy didn't fully understand and she was involved.

"Do I have something on my face?" Sophie finally asked.

"What? No." Lacy refocused on the movie. "I am just still surprised you're here."

"This is still my apartment too, right?" Sophie smiled at Lacy, her tone teasing. "What's gotten into you?"

"Nothing." She bit her lip. Except Jonah. Multiple times today. And she'd been hoping for more. It was almost embarrassing to think of how insatiable she felt around him.

"Did something happen with Logan?" Sophie hit pause on the movie and turned on the couch to face Lacy. She tossed the remote between them. "Is he dating someone else? Did he say something to you?"

"Actually, we went out as a group to a club on Saturday." Maybe that would satisfy Sophie on her Lacy-is-acting-weird radar. Besides it had happened, even if it felt like eons ago. So much had happened since. "We even danced together."

Sophie raised her eyebrow and pursed her lips. "Actually?"

"Yes." Lacy rolled her eyes and hit play on the movie. "We drank. We danced. He went home with some other girl. He even texted me tonight to join him and Claire at a bar."

Lacy almost smacked her head. She never answered the text. He would probably never invite her out again. Crap. Where was her phone anyway?

"Wait." Sophie snatched the remote and pressed pause. "He went home with some other girl when you were out with him? That's not cool, Lacy."

Oops. She'd kind of skimmed over that part. Lacy took a breath and turned toward Sophie. "We went out as a group. I wasn't planning on going home with Logan. I don't want to be one of his one night stands. It wasn't a big deal."

"Still. He has to be blind to not know how you feel about him." Sophie punched the pillow for effect. "To flaunt that in your face. What an ass."

Lacy could feel the heat spreading through her cheeks. She couldn't tell Sophie Jonah had been there for her. That he had brought her home and kissed her fucking senseless. Or about falling asleep with him on the couch and every-thing that happened when they woke up.

Besides Sophie was focused on Logan, and Lacy wanted to keep her focus there. "I don't think Logan knows I like him."

"Seriously?" Sophie's mouth dropped open dramatically. "Then he's too stupid for you anyway, Lacy."

Lacy laughed. "Thanks, but you know me, I still like him. He's been my crush for months."

It felt off to say that about Logan. Especially after everything she'd done today with Jonah, but if it kept Sophie off their trail. . . .

"Oof. Those guys you like have no idea what they are passing up on." Sophie held out the remote to her. "You've practically saved all your love for your crushes and they can't even see that. God save us from the men in this world."

The refrigerator opened. Lacy spun around on the couch. Jonah's back was to them. He closed the fridge and turned with a bottle of water. Her eyes caught his and her heart skipped. Had he heard all that? Did it matter if he did? After all, her infatuation with Logan was common knowledge. Jonah had even said something about it after they got home last night.

Was it weird Logan was still her crush when she'd been in bed and out of bed all day with Jonah? She'd done things with Jonah she'd never even imagined doing with Logan. And there was still so much more to explore. She didn't even know if she wanted to do those things with Logan, but with Jonah, yes, please.

"Oh, Jonah, just the man whose opinion we need." Sophie had spun around on the couch and rested her arms on the back.

"Great," Jonah said with no amount of enthusiasm at all. His eyes flicked between the two of them.

"You know Logan from work, yeah?" Sophie glanced toward Lacy and winked. What the hell was she up to?

"Sure." Jonah started toward his bedroom.

Before he could get to the hallway, Sophie said, "Do you think Lacy has a shot with him?"

Jonah froze. His blue eyes captured Lacy's as he leaned against the wall casually. Heat glinted in them and she hoped Sophie wouldn't notice. But the storm inside her grew more chaotic.

What would be the harm in Sophie knowing she and

Jonah had sex? Of course, Sophie had always been protective of Lacy. She'd steered quite a few guys away from Lacy over the years. Thankfully. But Lacy didn't want her to do that with Jonah.

"I think Logan could realize Lacy isn't someone you let slip through your fingers." Jonah's voice rushed through her like lightning.

Lacy bit her lip as Sophie said, "Interesting."

"But," Jonah said as he turned toward his door, "I don't think he's good enough for her."

He closed his door behind him. What the hell was that supposed to mean? Not good enough for her? Then who was?

"Hmph." Sophie turned to Lacy. "He hasn't been putting the moves on you, has he?"

Lacy's eyes widened and she shook her head. "No, of course not. Why would you even think that? He doesn't like me that way."

Sophie's eyes narrowed on her. Lacy swallowed and kept her wide-eyed look. Was that too much? Would Sophie guess what they'd done here, there, and everywhere? Lacy looked down at the remote.

"I probably wouldn't recognize moves if he did put them on me." Lacy hit play and pretended to be into the movie again. "Now can we watch the movie? We both have work in the morning."

"He's right though. Logan isn't good enough for you if he's going home with other girls while you are around." Sophie sank into the couch. After a few minutes, she said, "I bet he has a micropenis."

Lacy snorted and covered her mouth with her hands. Sophie raised her eyebrow and chuckled softly.

"I missed you," Lacy said softly.

"My cell still works outside of this apartment, Lacy."

Sophie pulled the blanket down from the back of the couch and spread it over her legs. "You know you can tell me anything."

Lacy nodded and kept herself from glancing toward Jonah's room.

~

JONAH TENSED as Lacy's fingers bumped into his side. Just like clockwork. He turned off the blender.

"Coffee." Her hair fell in a tangled mess over her eyes and her hands stayed on his T-shirt.

He pressed the full mug into her hands.

Her lips tipped into a smile. "Thank you."

She wandered to her spot on the couch. Jonah turned to look at Sophie's door to see if she'd come out too, but she didn't appear. He filled his glass and went over to the chair next to Lacy's spot.

"How did you sleep?" He kept his voice quiet.

Lacy grunted in response and continued to drink her coffee.

He reclined in his chair and watched her try to wake up. "Want to share the shower?"

She sputtered on her coffee and lifted her hair out of her eyes to glare at him.

He leaned closer to her. "It would be time efficient."

She scoffed.

"You wash me and I'll wash you," he cajoled, tracing one of her frogs on her pajama pants.

She stood up with her mug and stared down the hallway. Sophie's door was at the end but to one side. Jonah trailed his hand up her thigh to trace another frog. Lacy looked down at him while she sipped her coffee.

He was so hard if she gave any sign, he'd drag her to his

bedroom where she should have stayed the night. Instead, he'd laid awake thinking about her across the hall, wondering if she ached for him as much as he ached for her.

After a moment, she straddled his lap with her knees on either side of his hips. He swallowed and set his smoothie on the end table. He grabbed her hips and drew her closer to him.

She finished her coffee and set it next to his smoothie. She leaned in and instead of kissing him, her mouth touched his earlobe. Desire spread like a white-hot fire through his veins.

"Sophie's a fairly sound sleeper." She brought her face in front of his. Her dark brown eyes were so fucking blown with desire, reminding him of all the things they hadn't done yet. She tilted her head like she was going in for a kiss.

Fuck, he didn't care if Sophie beat him up because he'd "taken advantage" of Lacy. He'd let her punch him every day if it meant being able to slide deep within Lacy and making her come so hard she fucking saw stars.

"But. . . ." She traced her index finger over his lower lip. Her eyes twinkled mischievously. "I don't think we should be late for work."

She kissed the tip of his nose and grinned at him as she started to move off him. His little bird thought she could get away with teasing him.

"Not so fast." He tightened his hold on her hips and rocked his erection against the spot where he knew she throbbed for him. She gasped at the contact. Taking advantage, he leaned in and crushed her lips beneath his. His hand wrapped behind her neck to hold her there when she would have pulled away.

Instead, her fingers threaded into his hair and she returned his ravishing kiss with her own. After yesterday, his jets should have cooled some for her, but instead he just wanted her more. When they broke apart, they were both breathing heavily, staring into each other's eyes.

She cleared her throat. "I need to. . . um. . . take a shower and get. . . ready for work."

She moved her hands to his shoulders to push herself up. He released her this time. When he started to stand too, she held up her hands to ward him off.

"Alone." She smirked at him.

He adjusted his cock, drawing her eyes down. He loved she saw what she did to him. He'd really love to show her how much he'd missed her last night, but he grabbed his glass and her cup and moved to the kitchen.

"Better hurry," he said when she stood there watching him. "I'm more than willing to come in if you take too long."

For a moment she stood there in indecision. But then she spun on her heel and disappeared into the bathroom. Today would be painful.

AFTER DANCING around each other in the apartment and riding to work together, Lacy needed more coffee. Leaving Jonah behind, she waved at Emily as she passed her and went into the breakroom. Her body was entirely keyed up for Jonah and there wouldn't be an outlet for it with Sophie around. The temptation to drag him into the shower with her had almost overwhelmed her. But she managed to stop herself.

She was kind of done with people this morning.

Fortunately, the breakroom was empty. Unfortunately, all the mugs were on one of the tall shelves. She started to drag over a chair as Logan and Claire walked in.

"Let me get that for you, Lace." Logan reached up and grabbed a mug.

"Thanks." She flushed red, remembering she'd never answered his text on Sunday. As she poured her coffee, she couldn't help the twinge of guilt that flooded her because of what, or rather who she'd been doing instead. At least before Sophie came home.

It wasn't like she'd cheated on Logan. He definitely wouldn't care. They weren't anything to each other besides coworkers. Sure, she had feelings for him. Logan was still her crush, but the reality was he didn't want her. Not for now or for the long haul. At least not in the foreseeable future. She'd get over it, just like she had the other guys.

But Jonah wanted her now.

"We missed you at the bar last night. Did you get the text Logan sent?" Claire asked as she waited for Logan to finish with the coffee.

"I didn't see the message until late. Sorry." Lacy sipped her coffee. "It sounded like fun."

"The game was great." Logan sat at the table. "It would have been more fun if you'd been there."

Lacy smiled. Surely, he was just being nice. Nothing to get her panties in a twist over. Logan obviously didn't feel the same way about her as she felt about him. At least right now. Lacy pulled her hair back and over her shoulder.

"Is that a love bite, Hatcher?" Claire said with surprise.

Dammit. Lacy reached up and touched her neck. She'd forgotten about Saturday night's mementos. "Uh. . . ."

"Nice, Lace. Guess I wasn't the only one who got lucky this weekend." Logan congratulated her? Ouch. Guess he really didn't have any feelings for her besides coworkers.

"Hey, I got digits." Claire smacked his arm as she took the seat next to him.

Jonah walked in at that particular moment. His presence raised the hairs on the back of Lacy's neck. They hadn't gone over what to say at work. He'd been too busy driving her out of her mind. There wasn't really supposed to be actual evidence of them fooling around.

"Who's the lucky guy, Hatcher?" Claire asked.

Before they even started anything, Jonah had been clear whatever was between them was only about sex. No need to complicate work over it by admitting Jonah had blown her mind this weekend.

"A guy at the club," Lacy rushed out, definitely not a lie.

She couldn't look at Jonah. If she did, it would be all over her face. His mouth, his hands, what he did to her yesterday. And that kiss this morning. The temptation to drag him to her bed and forget about work entirely had been strong. She wanted more. More kissing, more touching, more of him.

"Must have happened after we got separated." Logan scratched the side of his neck. Yes, when Logan went and danced with a much easier girl. Lacy could feel the heat bubbling under her skin. She'd met Jonah a little over a week ago. Did that mean she was easy?

"I left her with Jonah." Claire held up her hands and brought Lacy back into the conversation. She almost interrupted when Logan turned to Jonah.

"Did you see the guy that marked Lacy?" Logan asked. Everyone assumed it wasn't Jonah.

Marked? Lacy's face couldn't get any redder. This was the first time anyone had discussed *her* love life in years. It was pretty much the first time she'd *had* a love life to discuss.

Jonah poured himself coffee. He glanced at her neck. His gaze felt like a physical caress and she had to stop herself from shivering. Maybe he'd forgotten about the hickeys too. His gaze met Lacy's for a sec before he shrugged. "It was pretty crowded in the club."

And he'd never let her out of his sight the whole night. Always within an arm's reach of her. She caught herself before she smiled at him like an idiot.

"Are you going to see this guy again?" Claire drank her coffee. She looked genuinely interested.

"I hope so," Lacy said, careful not to look Jonah's way. If Sophie hadn't come home, would they have slept together? Or would they have had sex and gone to their separate beds? She didn't know the protocol for just-sex relationships. Was there cuddling involved or just orgasms?

"Apparently we should all go out more often." Logan looked at Jonah. "Except Jonah hasn't said anything. What about it, Jonah? Did everyone get lucky this weekend?"

"A gentleman never tells." His lips quirked up a little. Her insides twisted in a good way.

Claire laughed. "What a load of shit. Just saying that means you did. Otherwise, you would just say no."

A gentleman did very naughty things with his mouth, with his hands, with his body. She'd lost count of the times he'd taken her over the edge. She was still a little miffed they'd been cut short because of Sophie's arrival. Last night, she'd laid in bed and thought about crossing the hall to his room. Would he have left it unlocked for her? Was he waiting for her? She couldn't build up the courage to make the move though. It was too fresh and she was too uncertain.

"Must have been good, if you're not saying anything." Logan leaned back in his chair, considering Jonah.

Jonah turned his back on the others, heading toward the door. His eyes met hers. "The best."

Her breath caught at the heat in his eyes. She didn't dare maintain eye contact for longer than a second, but it was almost painful to look away. Logan smirked at Jonah's back.

Jonah walked by her and she could feel his heat even though he didn't touch her. Her insides trembled in response. Damn. She didn't move, afraid she'd give everything away as the door opened behind her and Jonah left. She released the breath she'd been holding.

"There you go. Everyone got lucky." Logan tapped his mug against Claire's. Claire glared at him playfully.

"And that's my cue to get to work," Lacy said.

Logan gave her a speculative look. "You definitely have to come out with us more."

"We'll see." Lacy's insides warmed slightly. Not as hot as the inferno Jonah unleashed, but it was nice. Maybe Logan was warming up to her after all.

CHAPTER 16

JONAH TAPPED his pen against his desk. Lacy kept biting the end of her pen while she worked. She bit it and then brushed it over her lower lip as she stared at her screen. She didn't seem to be aware of him watching her. He should be doing his own work, but with his desk pointed toward hers, concentrating on photoshopping a dog food ad really wasn't possible.

She'd worn her dark hair down today. Most likely to hide the trail of hickeys he'd left on her neck Saturday night. Not to mention the few he'd given her Sunday. Her hair wasn't that effective. He could see them and remembered her moans as he gave them to her. The memories and that damned pen made him so damn hard, which kept him from leaving his desk.

"What do you think of this picture for the Berrington ad?" Logan rolled his chair over next to Lacy with his tablet.

Jonah set his pen aside. From his vantage point, he couldn't see what Logan tried to show her. Her cheeks brightened a little as she finished whatever she worked on. Jonah should look at his computer screen and actually do some work too, but he was far more interested in what was happening at Lacy's desk. She finally glanced down at the image.

"Oh." Lacy's gaze flitted up to Logan's and then to Jonah's. She held Jonah's gaze for a moment as if surprised to catch him watching her. He gave her a small smirk. The color in her cheeks deepened and she returned her gaze to the tablet.

"If I crop it here?" Logan drew his finger across the tablet, still focused on the work.

"Maybe. But it still seems a little. . . risqué?" Lacy swiped her tongue across her bottom lip. "We don't want to push the envelope too much given the ad space."

Logan smirked and nudged her with his elbow. "Come on. Everyone likes looking at a beautiful body. Part of our whole deal here at Taylor and King is giving the client something unexpected, but traditional."

Lacy pursed her lips and contemplated the image again.

Logan's gaze flicked up to watch her face. He seemed to be studying her.

"Maybe if you crop a little more like this." She drew her finger along the screen.

Staring at the image, Logan grinned. He held out his fist to Lacy. "Excellent."

She bumped her fist against his and shook her head as he wheeled away.

"You're awesome, Lacy." Logan attached his tablet to his keyboard.

"Thanks," she said, still a little flustered apparently.

Was Logan paying attention to Lacy more because of how she looked on Saturday night? Or because of the trail of hickeys Jonah had left? Or was this normal? Jonah had only a week to compare this behavior to and that week he'd spent in lust with his coworker/roommate.

Maybe he'd been right; Logan would have to be a fool to

not know Lacy was into him. Maybe proof someone else wanted Lacy was enough to make Logan want her. Fuck.

"Monday meeting, folks." Drew came out of his office and set his laptop on the conference table.

Fortunately thinking about Logan had diminished Jonah's previous state enough he could move comfortably to the table to join the meeting. Everyone brought their tablets to the table and took their seats. Claire and Logan chose to sit on the far side. Lacy took a seat toward the end of the table. Jonah sat next to her, enjoying the blush that tinged her cheeks.

Phoebe sauntered in at that particular moment, drawing everyone's attention.

"Another meeting? Is this going to be an every week thing?" Phoebe put her purse on her desk and crossed her arms, looking at Drew. Morgan came out of their office.

"It's probably why we decided to call it the Monday meeting," Morgan said, raising her eyebrow at Phoebe.

"Yes, but does it have to be every Monday?" Phoebe sipped from her Starbucks' coffee cup.

"Kind of the point." Morgan sat next to Drew and stared pointedly at Phoebe.

"Fine." Phoebe strolled over to the conference table and sat next to Morgan. "Weren't we hiring another person?"

Drew reclined in his chair. "We're still negotiating. We want someone who can work the sales angle more. That way Morgan and I can focus on working the creative side."

"I thought I was your sales team?" Phoebe pouted at Morgan.

"Once there are two of you, there will be a team." Morgan placed her hands on the table and gave Phoebe a pointed look. "Can we get on with the meeting?"

"Go ahead." Phoebe waved her hand, dismissively.

"Thank you, Phoebe." Drew's voice was heavy with

sarcasm as he shook his head. "We have a few new clients to look over and a few deadlines approaching. Unfortunately, that means some of you will need to work late this week."

"We may need all hands for a night, if the meeting we have this afternoon goes the way we want it to." Morgan glanced at Drew. "We've avoided all-nighters as much as possible. But this client would solidify us as a competitive ad agency. Their deadline is tight."

"We'll talk more about them after our meeting," Drew said. "Assignments—"

"Wait. Assignments?" Claire looked around. "I thought we all worked on everything."

Drew's lips pressed into a thin line. "Not this week. We have too many pieces to let any one thing fall through the cracks because we didn't have time to work on it."

Even though it went against the culture of the new company, that made a lot of sense. Jonah was glad they could be fluid to work through problem situations. The corporation he worked at before hadn't been flexible at all.

"Who gets to pick the assignments?" Logan asked.

Drew rubbed his neck. "Morgan, Phoebe, and I will be working the sales angle and we will all be working on the major project for the week. We have two smaller projects we would like you guys to divide and conquer. One is the seasonal campaign for Olly's Dog Food."

Morgan pressed on her tablet. "Olly's wants to try to get a push for their organic premium puppy food for the spring. It will be a sixty second video for internet and television with a cut ad for shorter time slots. The other campaign is Violett Industries' new perfume, Timeless."

Drew took over. "This will be a multi-layered project. They want a short thirty second ad for the internet and a comprehensive layout for multiple placements, print and internet."

Logan looked smug as he glanced around the table. "We all know Lacy loves puppies, and Claire and I bring the sexy."

Wolverine was being extra irritating today. Just because Lacy hadn't brought the sexy before didn't mean she should automatically get the puppy campaign. Lacy just had a different brand of sexy those two weren't used to.

Morgan's eyes narrowed at Logan. "That may be the case, Logan, but that's not how this company works."

Logan retreated in his chair and nodded.

"We need to mix things up and not let things get stagnant." Drew set his tablet down. "Phoebe, since you aren't involved, why don't you sort out assignments."

Phoebe grinned wickedly and touched the tip of her red fingernail against her lips as she contemplated all of them. "I'll assign team leads and then let the lead pick their team. Because who didn't love doing that in gym class."

Everyone groaned at the table.

Phoebe just smiled. "Logan and Jonah will be the team leads. Jonah, you can pick first. Which campaign and which partner?"

Phoebe leaned back with her hands clasped over her stomach like some evil genius. Jonah looked at Logan and Claire and then at Lacy. If they really want to mix things up, he had a plan.

"I'll take the Timeless campaign," Jonah said.

Logan glanced at Claire and shrugged. Then he smiled as his eyes landed on Lacy, who flushed at his attention and gave him a smile in return. She probably wanted to work on the cute puppy campaign. If Jonah picked Claire, it would give Lacy time to be with her crush. Even though Logan had gone home with someone else, Jonah wasn't surprised Lacy still liked the guy. She had a blind spot for the guys she was love drunk on apparently.

Claire gave Jonah a huge smile like everyone knew

already what he would do. Claire hadn't been very subtle about her attraction to Jonah at the club, but when she hadn't made any headway with him, she'd wandered off. He wouldn't be surprised if she suspected Jonah was into Lacy. Claire wouldn't have been far off if she did.

Perfume ads tended to be sexy which was why everyone expected him to pick Claire. She dressed sexy and oozed sex out her pores, even if she did come across as one of the guys.

But Lacy. . . there was a whole other side of her that rarely showed itself. He wanted to expose that part of her. Besides if he had to spend a late night with anyone, he'd want it to be Lacy.

"So Lacy or Claire, Jonah?" Phoebe leaned forward and arched her eyebrow at him.

"Lacy."

Lacy's eyes flew to him and her lips parted slightly. Pink crept up her cheeks.

"Great, that leaves Logan and Claire working on the Olly campaign." Phoebe turned to Drew. "Easy peasy."

"These campaigns need to be wrapped up by tomorrow so we can focus on finishing the proposal for Rutledge Jewelry. Get the mockups to Morgan and me by noon. Feel free to stay as late as you need to. The rest of the week, we'll be working on. . . ." Drew gestured to Morgan to continue talking about the week they had in front of them. Jonah zoned out slightly.

Lacy focused her attention on Morgan, but Jonah kept a close eye on the others at the table. Logan wasn't fuming, more disappointed. He probably thought he'd get to spend some time alone with Lacy.

Was he actually interested in her? When Jonah had first met him, the guy didn't really have any feeling one way or the other about Lacy. But Logan had definitely taken notice of her at the club and the way she leaned into Jonah.

Maybe Logan was just disappointed he had to work on the dog food campaign. Claire seemed miffed at Jonah for not picking her.

Logan and Claire would work together just fine though. Who cares if they had to play cute instead of sexy for a day or two. It would be good for them.

Lacy flushed but didn't look at him when his gaze settled on her. These people kept pigeonholing her and she let them. Sure, Lacy had a lock on cute with her silly pajamas and just by being herself, but she also had a sensual side that, like a hibernating bear, had just woken up. He wanted to see if poking it would unleash her inner wild child.

Besides, he enjoyed riling up his little bird and couldn't wait to get her alone.

As the meeting ended, Lacy headed into the breakroom. Apparently, there wasn't enough coffee in the world to face a day like today. She wished she'd slept better last night. She filled her mug and stared at the wall while she took a few needed sips.

Logan was acting odd today. First the picture for the ad. It was a sexy pic of a man and a woman kissing. The odd part was he'd asked her opinion. Usually Claire was his go-to gal for that kind of thing. Sure, she'd been in the copy room at the time, but usually he'd just wait for her to return instead of asking Lacy's opinion.

When Jonah picked the perfume, Lacy was sure he'd pick Claire to work with him. After all, everyone in the office knew Lacy loved working on the puppy campaigns. And Claire breathed sex. Logan had even said it to everyone.

But Jonah had chosen her. Her whole body tingled in anticipation of being near him. Alone. Working. God, she needed to focus. This campaign was big and needed a delicate touch. An opportunity to show the rest of them she was more than just cute.

"You okay?" Claire's voice caused Lacy to jump and almost spill her coffee.

She turned. Claire stood at the coffee pot with a full mug. Lacy hadn't even heard her come in.

"You seemed a little lost there." Claire gestured vaguely toward the wall.

Lacy nodded. "Just lost in thought. Clearly not enough caffeine."

"My sentiments exactly." Claire chuckled and held her cup up in a salute before taking a drink. "At least Logan and I should be able to get out of here somewhat early. The Timeless campaign seems like a lot to do in a short span of time."

"I don't know. With the Olly's campaign, I would have gotten lost in puppy pictures for hours." Lacy smiled. "Maybe it's better I'm not on that one."

"Probably." Her smile slipped as Claire's lips pressed together for a second. "You're okay with this, right? If you want, I can go to Jonah and tell him you'd rather work on the puppy campaign."

Lacy frowned. "What do you mean?"

Claire glanced at the door and moved closer. "I know you might not be comfortable with the sexy campaigns. You always let Logan and me deal with them. If you need me to step in—"

"Whoa." Lacy held her palm up at Claire. "I was a copy writer before I came here and worked on plenty of sexy campaigns. It's part of my job whether I like them or not. I'm perfectly capable."

It was Claire's turn to frown. "I know you are capable, but I just wanted to make sure you would be comfortable being alone with Jonah."

"You mean, my coworker *and* roommate? The guy who got me home when I was drunk on Friday and who you guys left me with on Saturday? Why would I be uncomfortable with him?"

Claire backed up a step and held up her palm in surrender. "You're right. We just tend to be protective of you."

Protective, like a little sister. Grrr. that might not be all that was going through Claire's head. The image of Claire and Jonah standing at the bar with Claire's hand on his chest burned in Lacy's mind. Her stomach hardened. Did Claire want time with Jonah? Alone time? Was she hoping late tonight Jonah might slip up and kiss her? Was that what this was about?

Her heart sped up. What the hell was Lacy thinking? It didn't matter what Claire thought. Jonah had promised to only be with Lacy for now. Even if he wanted to, he wouldn't go after Claire. At least not while they were doing what they were doing. And it most definitely wasn't over yet. Just waylaid by the arrival of their roommate. That kiss this morning proved that.

Lacy took a deep breath and calmed down. Jonah wasn't hers for the long term, but he was right now. Besides, maybe Claire was just being considerate. No need to get her panties all in a bunch. "I'll be fine, Claire. Thank you for your concern."

Claire nodded. "I think one of us should have been a lead. Then we could have gone for boys versus girls. You and I would have rocked the perfume ad."

"That would have been fun." A smile lit Lacy's face. It would have been too.

"If you need anything, let me know." Claire reached out and touched Lacy's arm. "Us girls need to stick together."

Her hand dropped as the door opened. Logan strolled in. "Hello, ladies."

Claire rolled her eyes at Lacy before turning to face Logan. "Puppy chow, huh?"

"Seems like. Bring on the puppies." Logan's gaze roamed over Lacy. Almost aggressively. Definitely not with brotherly intent.

The urge to cover herself up and hide from his gaze flowed through her.

"Getting your caffeine in for the long haul, Lace?"

"It probably won't take that long." Lacy almost flushed, thinking of Jonah and what they had gotten up to all day yesterday. What they would have done last night. What Sophie had basically stuck a pin in.

"Maybe not, but it won't be as fun as puppies." Logan grinned. "If I'd had the option, I would have picked you, Lace. I know how much you like puppies. You always bring the playful to puppy ads."

Something stirred in her heart. See, he did know her. Of course, pretty much everyone in the office knew that about her, but it showed Logan paid attention to her. And he'd wanted to work with her. At least on the puppy campaign. Which had cute written all over it. The light dimmed in her heart. If he had first choice, would he have picked Claire and the perfume? She shook off the feeling.

"Thanks." She sipped on her coffee, unsure of what else she could say.

"Let's get busy, Claire. There's a game on tonight and I don't want to miss it." Logan headed toward the door and held it open.

"I'm sure we'll have plenty of time." Claire walked through the door but winked at Lacy.

Tossing a smile Claire's way, Lacy headed out to her desk. Before she could take her seat, Jonah stood and stepped closer. Not too close but close enough her insides melted.

"Let's talk about the campaign over lunch. My treat." He pushed his chair under his desk.

"Sounds good." Taking a large gulp of her coffee, Lacy didn't look at the other people in the office. She grabbed her purse and slid her work tablet in it, just in case they needed to take notes. She followed Jonah out with a quick wave to Emily and into the elevator.

"How's your day going?" he said, nonchalantly, and leaned toward her in the back of the elevator.

"Good. You?" She turned her face toward him and got lost in the blue of his eyes. Her insides stirred up, whipping quickly into a storm. If she moved an inch or two up, she could press her lips against his and get swept away.

His gaze dropped to her lips for a second before returning to her eyes. "We have a lot of work ahead of us. I downloaded all the specs. We may be here late tonight."

Right, work. "Shouldn't be a problem."

The elevator stopped and more people crowded on. Jonah stepped closer to her and the backs of his fingers brushed hers. His ocean scent filled her nose. Her knees weakened and she was thankful for the wall behind her, holding her up. Especially when his fingers loosely tangled with her own. Her heartbeat quickened. She glanced up at him, but he watched the numbers counting down above the door. A hint of a smile tugged at his lips.

They reached the lobby and his hand slipped from hers as they followed the crowd out.

"You like fish and chips?" Jonah headed toward the side door.

"Sure." She'd follow him anywhere if he kept looking at her like she was the only woman in the world. Her heart felt too large for her chest as he took her hand in his and led her along the crowded sidewalk.

The air had a slight chill to it, but it was a sunny day for the fall. Jonah stopped at a street vendor and got two fish and chips wrapped in newspaper cones. He handed her one as he grabbed napkins. They walked together across the street and into a small park the size of a city block.

A fountain sat at the center with people everywhere enjoying the gorgeous day for their lunch break. Jonah found them a seat on the fountain on the far side away from the office and pulled her down next to him. From hip to thigh, they were connected.

Tingles filled her as her insides pulsed at his proximity. If they were going to work together all evening, she definitely needed to pull it together. Yes, Jonah was a very attractive man and yes, what he did to her made her want more, but they needed to focus on getting the job done.

"You ready to bring the sexy?" Jonah asked as he took a bite of fish and stared at a clown making balloon animals for a crowd of children.

"That would be perfect for a puppy commercial." She sighed. Cute was her main focus.

"Mad I chose you?" He didn't look at her, but she glanced up at him.

"No," she said softly.

He tipped his face toward hers. His blue eyes shined with banked heat. "Good."

She picked at her fries, aka chips. "I just don't know how much I'll have to contribute for a sexy perfume campaign."

"Sexy is a lot of things. Confidence can be sexier than anything else. Whatever we land on will be sexy if we let it be." Jonah pointed toward the clown and the kids swarming around them. "That's definitely under the category of cute. But if you look around, the couple over there is romantic."

A young couple in their early twenties had a blanket spread out under a tree. The woman sat cross-legged, leaning against the tree with the man's head in her lap. She held a book in one hand and the other hand played with the man's long dark hair. His eyes were closed, but a smile lit his face.

"Romantic but cute," Lacy pointed out.

"What would make it sexy?" Jonah leaned in closer to her and whispered in her ear. "If the woman had on more revealing clothes? Maybe a skirt and a low-cut blouse. If the man's chest were showing? Does showing skin make something sexier? What if her hand trailed not in his hair, but up and down his chest?"

The images he painted were definitely sexy to Lacy's mind. "Is it the lack of clothing or the intimacy you suggested that makes it sexy?"

"Mmmm." Jonah finished the bite he'd taken and crumped up the newspaper. "Exactly."

She turned to him as she finished her own lunch. "When we went shopping, you said sexy wasn't just about showing more skin."

"It doesn't matter how much skin is shown as long as the intimacy is there." Jonah pulled a couple of peppermint candies from his pocket and handed one to her. He must have grabbed them at the vendor too.

She popped the candy in her mouth. He took their trash and threw it in the garbage before returning to sit at her side.

"A kiss is sexy, right?" Jonah turned and put one of his knees up on the fountain between them.

Lacy's gaze fell to his lips. Her fingers tingled, wanting to reach out and feel the softness of them. Yesterday, she'd been able to give into those impulses. "Mmmhmm."

"Eye contact, eye to lip. Even lips close enough to almost kiss are sexy." Jonah's eyes lit up as she started to follow his thoughts.

"So, if that couple were staring into each other's eyes, even that might make the scene sexier?"

"Potentially. I think for this particular ad campaign we

don't want sex that hits you over the head with a hammer, drags you into the bushes and has its way with you." Jonah brushed a stray strand of hair off her cheek and behind her ear. His fingers lingered behind her ear, ratcheting up her pulse. "We want something soft and intimate that pulls at that desire within everyone to feel close."

She swallowed. A kiss would be enough. Just Jonah's lips against hers would satisfy her until they could find time to be together again. For a moment, she thought he might lean in and give her what she wanted, but instead he glanced down at his phone. She blew out a frustrated breath.

"We should get back." He stood and held out his hand to her.

After he helped her to her feet, he kept her hand in his as they strolled through the park to their office building. His thumb brushed over her wrist and she hoped he couldn't feel the crazy beat of her pulse under it.

Maybe Sophie would be home late tonight. Maybe Lacy could find the courage to ask Jonah to sneak into her room or find her own courage and sneak into his. Either way, she wanted to be with him again tonight. Maybe Sunday was a fluke. A one-off, and now that the initial desire was out of their systems, things would cool down.

Jonah tugged her into the corner of the elevator and smiled down at her as he tucked her against him. Her whole body lit up from the contact, like he was a live wire electrifying her being. Maybe it wasn't a fluke.

CHAPTER 17

"Here." Lacy held out the sample of the perfume sent by the client. It was a small vial with a screw-on lid.

Jonah took it from her, letting his fingers slide against hers. She glanced up at him, trying to figure out if he purposely tried to drive her crazy. They'd decided to work in one of the extra offices since the puppy talk from Logan and Claire had begun to distract Lacy. Now they were in a room all by themselves and Lacy tried not to let Jonah distract her from their job.

Which proved more difficult than ignoring the puppy talk. She occupied herself with setting up her laptop with the interactive whiteboard in the room. Trying to get the Bluetooth to talk to each other wasn't cooperating today.

"Notes of peach and hyacinth flowers." Jonah's voice close to her ear drew her attention.

She straightened. His heat engulfed her as he closed in on her from behind. Apparently the setup had been very distracting. She hadn't even heard him move.

"Peaches is a good scent on you." His words were low and

almost menacing, at least to keeping her mind on work. The urge to lean into him nearly overwhelmed her.

"Jonah?" she said softly, trying to remind him they were at work. Her heart throbbed in time with the rest of her as his hand slid down her arm to circle her wrist. She desperately wanted to forget where they were and what they should be doing.

She glanced at the closed door and then over her shoulder. He gave her a smirk she felt all the way through her bones.

"Would you help me?" His words were soft enough anyone outside of the room wouldn't hear. He held the vial up with his other hand. "Unscrew the cap?"

She narrowed her eyes at him. What the hell was he up to? Using her free hand, she removed the lid from the vial.

"Thank you." He held the vial between his thumb and forefinger and tipped it upside down on his finger. "You can replace the lid."

She did as he asked and set the vial on the desk. Trying to be professional, she asked, "Are we ready to work then?"

"Almost." His arms came from behind to either side of her. He held her wrist in front of her and dragged his perfume-laden finger across her wrist. "Perfume should be smelled as intended."

His touch sent bolts of desire threading through her. Her breath caught as he brought her wrist up to his nose.

"Perfect." His breath was hot on her ear.

Surely she would burst into flames with as hot as he made her. He slipped away and she nearly sagged against the desk. She brought her gaze up to his innocent smiling face. Then she glanced down and noticed the bulge in his pants. He was just as affected.

"Enjoying the torture?" She brushed her hand down her shirt and caught the scent of the perfume. It was light for having floral notes. Just a touch of peach and a dash of flow-ers. "The scent is quite nice."

"I agree." He settled into a chair and readjusted himself before clearing his throat.

Ignoring the flood of desire he'd created in her wasn't easy, but when a sharp burst of laughter right outside the door rang out, she remembered exactly where they were. She sighed.

Time to focus on work. Her brain had already started to work with the scent of the perfume.

"The backdrop should be a garden. Flowers all around, but also lush greenery. Maybe a peach tree," she said. She sat at her computer and started typing in notes. Focus on getting the work done. That was the most important thing right now.

"I think we should go with a picnic like in the park." His blue eyes darkened as he rubbed his finger and thumb together.

A shiver worked its way slowly down her spine. "The romantic or the half-naked style?"

"Somewhere in between." His gravelly voice sparked along her skin.

Unable to just sit there, she stood up and slipped off her flats. She paced her side of the table. Jonah's gaze followed her, adding to her keyed-up state. She needed to focus on the job at hand. Not on Jonah's hands. Definitely not on Jonah's hands. And especially not Jonah's erection.

"Picnic." She stopped and covered her eyes with her hands, trying to block out Jonah. The perfume wafted down from her wrist, filling her nose. She could almost feel the memory of his arms around her. His front pressed against her back. His breath on her neck.

She opened her eyes to the blank wall and shook the desire out of her head. "Garden. Peaches. Maybe a small pile of peaches on the blanket. Or the woman feeding one to the man?"

Spinning, her eyes locked with Jonah's. Her lips parted. If she could capture that look from Jonah, they'd make millions off the perfume. But his eyes were so horribly distracting to her. All she could think about was what he could do to her body. How he'd owned it yesterday. How Sophie had effectively cockblocked them. How much Lacy wanted him to own her body again and again and again.

"I'm not sure I can work with you." The words left her mouth before she could stop them.

He cocked an eyebrow at her. "Why not?"

She slumped down in the chair.

"Everything. I just want to. . . ." Her eyes widened and she shut her mouth. She couldn't tell him what she wanted. Not here. Not at work. They were outside the bubble of their apartment. Any moment someone could come in to talk to them.

It wasn't Jonah's fault she couldn't control herself better. She'd never felt this way in her life. Her infatuations had nothing on how consuming her obsession with Jonah hounded her. He'd engraved himself on her very being. Her mind knew to focus on work, but with him close, everything shut down and all she wanted was his hands on her. His mouth exploring hers. His body between her legs.

"What do you want, little bird?" His low, quiet voice was like satin sheets against her naked skin. Could she come from just his voice? She wasn't willing to sit around to find out.

Hitting print on the open file on her desktop, she stood abruptly and went the long way to the door to avoid passing close to him. "I'm. . . ."

He stood.

She held her hand up to ward him off. She needed to

breathe air without his ocean scent in it. "I need to get something off the printer."

~

Lacy slipped out of the room and Jonah took a deep breath. Her scent lingered in the air, mixed with the perfume. He tipped his head and stared up at the ceiling. An edge of suppressed desire hung between them. It prevented them from doing their job effectively.

Maybe he just needed an excuse to relieve the ache being near her caused. He glanced over and saw Lacy's shoes beside her chair. He couldn't help smiling at his little bird being so worked up she crossed the office without her shoes on. Her little toes curling into the carpet with each step.

Fuck. He rubbed his neck as he turned his helpless stare at the door. He should give her time to get her mind back onto work. He should be doing the same.

Unfortunately, the only thing he could think about was Lacy's lips slightly parted. The surprised ecstatic look that crept over her face as she hurled into an orgasm. The warm snugness of her wrapped around his cock when she exploded all around him.

Fuck it. He opened the office door and took note of where everyone was. Emily sat at her desk on the phone. Drew, Morgan, and Phoebe had left to give the new client a presentation at their office and wouldn't return for at least an hour. Logan and Claire headed toward the breakroom. If he and Lacy were quick. . . .

He didn't let himself finish his thought as he entered the copy room. Because if he was smart, he wouldn't do anything with Lacy at work. Lacy stood at the copier staring down at the papers in her hands. The room easily could have been an office so it had a lock on it. Before he could talk himself out of it, he snicked the lock in place.

Setting the papers down, Lacy glanced behind her toward him. "What—"

He closed the distance between them as she turned to face him. His lips crashed down over hers like he hadn't kissed her in weeks. Her arms wrapped around his neck without hesitation. At her sigh of surrender, he gentled the kiss, lightly coaxing her to open to him.

She whimpered slightly before she pressed up on her toes to meet his demanding lips. His chest rumbled in approval as he lifted her up against the copier to get closer. She wrapped her legs around his waist and they both gasped as his erection settled against her intimately.

He leaned his forehead against hers as they tried to catch their breath.

"What are we doing?" she said softly. Her fingers whispered over the tight skin of his neck. Her dark eyes locked on him with so much trust he knew deep down he didn't deserve this woman or what she let him do with her. But he also knew he wasn't strong enough to walk away right now.

"Releasing the tension." He nipped at her luscious bottom lip. His hand slipped beneath her shirt to tease her nipple.

"Here?" She gasped and didn't try to pull away.

"You know somewhere better?" He grinned against her lips, before teasing them with his tongue and teeth. His fingers slipped beneath the cup of her bra to circle her nipple.

She shook her head and met his gaze with her desire-laden eyes. "Now."

The copier beeped as she leaned against it slightly.

He lifted her off it and whispered against her lips, "If we break the copier, they might figure it out."

"True." Her eyes glowed with mischief.

He let her legs slip down from his hips. "You should wear more skirts."

"I'll try to remember." She smiled as her hands went to work on her pants.

Undoing the buttons on her shirt, he leaned down to kiss the exposed flesh of her breasts. He flipped the cup of her bra out of the way and latched onto her nipple. A growl rumbled in his chest at the feel of her tight nipple against his tongue. Her breath was short and quick near his ear. She kicked her pants off to the side and grabbed his belt.

When she had him unzipped, he lifted his head from her breast and claimed her mouth again. He backed her up until the wall stopped them. Reaching into his pocket, he pulled out a condom. Their foreheads touched as he put the condom on.

"We're really doing this. Here?" Lacy leaned her head on the wall to meet his eyes.

He slid his hand between her legs and caressed her wetness. Her breath came out in pants as he stroked her faster. Her eyes slipped shut and she bit her bottom lip. He closed the distance between them until their mouths almost touched and whispered, "Do you want me to stop?"

Her eyes opened, so far gone, and she shook her head.

"Good." He lifted her against the wall and surged into her. She wrapped her legs around his waist. He stilled at the perfection of this moment. She felt so good wrapped around him, like coming home.

"Jonah," she moaned his name softly. His cock twitched inside her.

"So fucking good." He withdrew almost all the way out before fully seating himself in her again.

Her hands held the sides of his face and pulled his mouth to hers. They moved together slowly at first. But as the tension built within them, their pace quickened.

"So close," she whispered into his mouth.

He reached between them and rubbed her bundle of nerves roughly. He swallowed her sounds as she came hard against him, drawing him into his own orgasm. He slowed down the kiss, gently nipping at her lips as they came down together.

The copier started spitting out a print job. Jonah covered Lacy's mouth before she had a chance to squeak. Someone tried the door to the copy room. They quickly untangled themselves. Jonah did up his pants while Lacy struggled into hers.

"The door's locked," came a feminine voice through the door.

"Must have accidentally hit the button," Jonah said loudly toward the door. "Give me a second."

He glanced at Lacy. She buttoned her pants and started looking around.

"What?" he mouthed at her.

She held up her bare foot. She mouthed, "Shoes?"

He grinned and whispered, "You left them in the other office."

She blushed and held her arms out for him to double check her. He smiled softly at her slightly rumpled appearance. He smoothed her shirt, dragged his thumb along her lips to clean off her smeared lipstick, and gave her a quick kiss before heading to the door. They probably both looked like they just had a quickie in the copy room, but they didn't have time to cool down.

As soon as he opened the door, Claire came through and scanned them both. Her eyebrow went up. Lacy kept her face averted as she grabbed the papers she'd abandoned and hurried out into the office.

"Accidentally?" Claire gave him a knowing smile.

Jonah shrugged and took a few random office supplies.

"Don't know how it happened. Didn't even realize it had locked."

Claire grabbed her papers off the printer and preceded him out of the room. He ignored her as he headed toward the bathroom to clean up.

"Everything all right in there?" Logan asked no one in particular.

Claire shrugged. "The door 'accidentally' locked apparently. Be careful next time you're in there."

Logan glanced over at Jonah and his eyes went to the office where Lacy had disappeared. Jonah could almost see the wheels turning in Logan's head, before Logan said, "Weird."

CHAPTER 18

LACY LIFTED her head off her arms and wiped away the little bit of drool from the corner of her mouth. "What time is it?"

Jonah worked on his laptop. They had moved out to the main office area after everyone else had left around six o'clock. Jonah and Lacy had shared some take-out dinner and started finishing their idea of the garden picnic with the couple, who were both fully clothed. Well, mostly clothed. The woman wore a white satin crop top and tea length satin ball gown skirt with a floral motif, and the man wore a white suit with the peach tie undone and his collar opened, showing a nice amount of chest. Both were barefoot.

Jonah had added that part.

"Almost ten." Jonah leaned back in his chair and stretched.

Lacy had only meant to rest her eyes, but apparently she'd been asleep for almost a half hour. "Why didn't you wake me?"

"You looked like you needed the sleep." He half smiled at her and those funny trills of happiness floated through her chest, wrapping around her heart. The quickie in the copy room had been unexpected but had gone a long way in relieving the tension between them.

"I didn't sleep well last night," she confessed. The office seemed more empty with just the two of them in here. "I haven't been here this late before."

Jonah glanced around before returning his gaze to his screen. "We're almost done and then we can head back to the apartment."

The apartment, never "home" for Jonah. She'd noticed it before but it just struck her funny tonight. Did he even consider any place home?

"What can I do to help?" She pushed away from her desk and strolled around behind him.

A bunch of different images filled the screen. Jonah had taken the photos they'd found an hour ago and put them together in a seamless presentation. She couldn't find anything she'd tweak to make the image better.

"Did you finish the script for the ad?" He spun his chair around to face her. Before she could answer, he grabbed her hips and pulled her down across his lap. Heat flushed through her.

"Hey," she said and made an attempt to stand.

Instead, he spun them to his desk and trapped her in as his hands returned to the keyboard.

"Is this really helping?" She grabbed his beard and gave it a gentle tug. He playfully nipped the air near her hand.

"Definitely." He continued to work on the remaining few slides of the presentation. This side of Jonah made her feel light and warm inside.

"If you say so." Her fingers went into his hair and played with the silky strands. He had to move his head a little to be able to see his screen around her arms. Fighting a grin, she slid her fingers down to his ears and followed the swirls of them.

"What time does Sophie get home?" Jonah's chest rumbled pleasantly against her side.

"She texted about an hour ago wondering where I was." Her fingers followed the sides of his beard down to his lips. "I told her we are working late and not to wait up."

She stroked her finger across his soft lower lip. Part of her couldn't get over the fact she could touch him like this and he wanted her to be close to him. The other part wondered if they could get away with another quickie at work. At least no one was around to rattle the doorknob.

"Do you think we can sneak you into my room tonight?" Jonah didn't look up from his work.

An even better idea.

Butterflies danced in her stomach at the thought of sleeping with Jonah. Sure, she'd slept with him on the couch and they'd been naked in his bed multiple times yesterday, but she hadn't literally slept with him in his bed.

"We might be able to risk it."

He grabbed her hand and kissed her fingertips. "Good."

Had it really only been a little over a week since they met. Of course, things had escalated quickly between them. The free sex show. Him caring for her when she got drunk. Shopping for something sexy together. Going out. Sex in the kitchen. In the shower. In his bed. In the copy room.

"What's got you all red?" Jonah said, his hands still on his mouse and keyboard.

"You. Me. This thing." She sighed and rested her head on his shoulder. "I feel like I'm on a runaway train and I should want to get off, but I don't want to stop."

"Do you want to slow down?" His voice rumbled low and stirred up all sorts of sparks within her.

"No." She fiddled with his shirt button. She couldn't talk about this to anyone except him right now. She hadn't even texted Beth about it. Too afraid Beth would pop up as a

Jonah intervention. "I just don't know what's going to happen when the train eventually crashes."

She didn't know how she would feel when this ended. She'd never had anything like this before.

Jonah pushed back from his desk and wrapped his arms around her. He pressed a kiss to her forehead and breathed in deep. She never wanted to move from this spot. Safe and warm. Cared for. She felt it all.

"Little bird, I promise to always listen and try to help settle your worries. I don't know how this ends yet, but I hope we can remain friends afterwards."

She flattened her palm against his chest and the steady beat of his heart comforted her. She raised her head to meet his eyes. "I'd like that."

He leaned in and pressed his lips gently and way too briefly against hers. The kiss had been so gentle she wanted to sigh in happiness. That hint of tenderness made her chest ache for something more. She couldn't handle the warmth in his eyes much longer though. This wasn't anything more than sex. If she forgot that, she could end up falling for Jonah and that would be a mess.

"Are we done?" She turned to look at his computer screen, but she couldn't quite make herself leave his lap.

"With the campaign, yes." Jonah shut his computer.

With his help, Lacy stood. She went to her desk to close her computer and grab her stuff.

"Car will be here in ten." Jonah turned off the lights in the copy room and breakroom while Lacy stood near the front door. Her breath caught and held as he walked through the office toward her. Everything about him was gorgeous and took her breath away.

He stopped in front of her and lowered his face until they were on the same level. His blue eyes sparkled with mischief. "Ready to go?"

Her grin widened and she nodded. Her obsession with him couldn't be healthier than her crushes, but the rush was so much more. Jonah took her hand in his and hit the lights for the office. For now, she was all his.

~

"Where's home for you?" Lacy laid on top of Jonah, naked and slightly sweaty. He trailed his fingers over her spine. Her head rested over his pounding heart. The lamp on the nightstand barely cast a dim light over them.

They had managed to sneak into the apartment and into his bedroom without waking Sophie or alerting her at least. Even though it was late, they had taken their time reexploring each other. His heart hadn't had a chance to slow down before she asked her question.

"What?" Jonah hadn't misheard her, but he didn't understand the intent behind her question. He stroked his hand down her back and over the curve of her ass. He couldn't get enough of touching her, tasting her, fucking her. Even though he had just come, he wanted her again.

She drew a little circle over his heart and then looked up at him with her dark eyes. He wasn't sure how much sleep they would manage tonight if she kept looking at him like she couldn't get enough either. "You don't have stuff. Everyone has a place they consider home. Whether it's where they grew up or where their heart is. Where's home for you?"

Jonah chuckled, warily, trying to make light. "I don't think I've ever had a home."

Lacy propped her elbows on his chest and rested her head on her hands to look down at him with astonishment and a hint of pity. "You've never had a home?"

"Growing up, we moved around a lot for my dad's job." He put his hands behind his head. Her body rested comfortably over his, her softness covering his hard muscles. Just being close to her turned him on. But with both of them naked and touching, it wouldn't be long before he rolled her over and sank inside her. He exhaled, knowing she expected more words than that. "Just when we would get settled, it would be time to move. You get used to not accumulating stuff or people. You can't keep anything or anybody. It's just you and the next thing. You learn to let go and move on. To never have a home."

Lacy stared at him intently like she wanted to delve inside him. Wanting something more than physical intimacy. He didn't really have anything to hide from her. He'd been honest from the start. He wanted her, but he couldn't keep her. He wasn't the guy who stayed. He didn't form meaningful attachments.

It was easier that way. If you didn't have stuff, then it didn't matter when it got broken or lost. If you didn't bond with people, it wouldn't hurt when one of you failed to keep in touch. His mother had always tried to keep them together, but when she passed a couple years ago, even their family had fallen apart. Jonah hadn't been enough to keep them together.

That was why he knew he could never be what Lacy needed. Something inside him was broken like his family was. He didn't know how to keep anyone anymore.

"Was this an experiment?" she asked.

He raised his eyebrow at her in question.

"Not us." She tapped her finger over his heart. "The job, moving here. You said you never stayed anywhere long. But you took this job knowing it didn't involve travel. Just one office and a bunch of coworkers. Are you here just to see if you can stay?"

He took a deep breath and looked up at the ceiling. "You don't ask the easy questions."

She grinned. "I can be complicated."

He studied her eyes. The dark brown had flecks of almost gold in them. He wanted to explain to her. He wanted her to understand his frustration. "Yes and no. Something needed to change in my life. I didn't even have a real place in L.A., only a hotel I frequented and a P.O. box I checked when I happened to be in town. My whole life filled a suitcase. I was sick of living in hotels. Not having real friends or anything lasting."

Lacy rested her head against his heart. "Tired of change?"

"Maybe." Jonah couldn't resist running the palm of his hand over her soft hair. "I had a classmate that went to work for Hart Association after graduation. He told me about these two powerhouse assistant creative directors who put together an amazing ad campaign for Bradbury Industries and ended up leaving to start their own firm. Did you ever see the Foxx Vodka ad?"

She nodded against his chest. "It was amazing."

"I did a little more research on some of the projects they worked on and honestly I was impressed. All the clients I had wanted the same exact thing as always. Nothing new, just churn out the same trite campaign that worked last year. It became less about creativity and more about producing the same thing over and over."

Lacy shivered and he rubbed his hands over her back to warm her up.

"I was bored. Bored of my job. Bored of the same hotel rooms. Bored of the same woman in different cities," he said. She stiffened against him, but he just ran his hand against her naked skin. Lacy wasn't the same at all. "Everything was the same. Just different shades of gray."

"Is everything still gray?" Her words were soft against his chest.

He rolled with her and settled her against the pillows

beneath him. Lacy's hair spread around her head like a dark halo and her dark eyes shone up at him. No woman had ever made him feel this content before, yet excited him at the same time.

"How could it be?" he said, tucking a strand of hair behind her ear. "There's browns and golds and berry pink lips."

She tilted her head as if she would kiss him but stopped. "Are you still bored with everything?"

He lowered his lips to just above hers.

"Never," he said against her lips. He kissed her slowly like they had all the time in the world to just kiss. Just be in this moment. Him and her. Her hands stroked down his chest and pulled his waist down until his body half rested on hers. He didn't know if he'd ever get enough of her and that scared him.

He wasn't the guy for a woman like Lacy. Not for the long haul. He needed change in his life to thrive. Maybe this was an experiment. Maybe he'd fail, but until then. . . .

He relinquished her lips and trailed kisses down her jaw and onto her neck. She gasped as he sucked on the spot between her neck and shoulder. He took his time and tortured the spot with his teeth and tongue and lips until her hips pressed up against his.

He rose up over her and captured her mouth at the same time his hand slipped down over her stomach and between her legs. Her hands curled around his shoulders. He swallowed her moan as his fingers discovered all the hidden secrets she kept from everyone but him. He lifted his head and waited for her eyes to open. Dark pools of brown and gold, filled with lust, stared up at him.

"You could never be boring, Lacy." His fingers sank into her core and her lips parted as her eyes slid shut. He kissed her. "Open your eyes, little bird. Let me see you fly."

Her eyes opened and held his. His fingers moved over her and in her. Her hips followed his motions, but she kept her eyes opened and locked on his. She gave herself to him completely every time. No hesitation, no artifice. Just pure, unadulterated Lacy.

Each little gasp and moan made his cock harder and spurred him on. Her hands slipped up to cradle his face. Half frenzied, she searched his eyes. He hoped she saw what she did to him. Her eyes darkened and she arched against him, pressing every inch of her to every inch of him.

"Jonah. Please. I need you."

The need to claim her as his own swelled within him. To keep this one thing always. To be the one who drove her over the edge and held her while she crashed down to Earth every fucking time. He circled her bundle of nerves. It was the final push she needed. She tightened all around him. Her eyes widened as her mouth opened in a silent scream as she went over the edge.

Her fingers slid into his hair and stroked over his neck. He slowed his movements to help her come down before he reached over for a condom. His lips dropped to hers and he teased her mouth with his tongue before he eased inside her.

She moaned against his lips. He held still for a moment, completely immersed in her. This was what he wanted. This moment when she welcomed him in with her arms open. He broke off the kiss and looked down into her eyes when she opened them. Her eyes were like staring into her soul. She never shut him out. Everything good and right stared back at him as she cradled him between her legs.

"I need you, Lacy." The words tore out of him from deep inside. If anyone felt like home to him, it was her. "I need you."

"You have me." She traced his cheekbone with the gentlest

of touches, almost as if she were afraid to break him. "Always."

His heart lurched in his chest, not knowing if he could be enough for her, but he couldn't give her up. Not yet. He slowly thrust within her, dragging almost all the way out before sliding in completely. They moved together, eyes locked on each other. The pressure built between them, but he wanted to hold back, to stay in this moment, to feel the way he felt when he was with her forever.

She increased the pace until they both strained for the edge. His name slipped out of her lips on a moan as she came. Her body arched into his like the distance between them was too much. He couldn't hold back his own release as she dragged him with her. He collapsed over her body, careful not to put all his weight on her. Her arms and legs cradled him, holding him like a lifeline.

"Is it always like this?" She sighed and trailed a hand down his back.

He wanted to tell her yes, that it was always like this, but he knew it would be a lie. He'd never felt like this with any of the other women he'd slept with. Even after he'd been with Lacy, he wanted her again. Needed her again. Couldn't seem to stop himself from wanting her.

"Sometimes." He lifted his head and brought his forehead to hers. How could he ever let someone else have her? "But you and me" —he placed his hand over her heart— "always."

CHAPTER 19

LACY DIDN'T WANT to think of how this thing with Jonah would end as they rode the elevator to work the next day. Waking up in Jonah's arms had been an experience she wanted always. Especially how he'd woken her up, slowly tormenting her until she shattered all around him. Even her shower hadn't managed to tone down the permanent blush on her cheeks.

For now, she decided to let herself stay in fantasy land where everything Jonah said meant more than it did. And pretend she wasn't falling in love with him and letting him go wouldn't break her heart into a thousand pieces.

Even knowing the end was inevitable, she wanted to give Jonah something he'd never had before, but she wasn't sure how you gave someone a home. Obviously it wasn't just a place, but a feeling. Her mind turned it over while they walked into the office.

"Hey, guys," Emily's bright voice greeted them.

Lacy smiled. She had to remember to people today. "Morning. How are you today?"

"Couldn't be better." Emily shifted her attention to Jonah. "How about you?"

"Never better."

Lacy managed to catch a glimpse of the smile Jonah gave with that statement. Then his blue eyes collided with hers and the smile turned softer. Her heart filled her chest like an inflated balloon.

Warning bells should be going off in her head. She should really talk to Beth. She needed to be talked down before her heart did something stupid and fell off the really high ledge and hoped to land in Jonah's hands. Though she knew it would just shatter on the concrete. She smiled back at Jonah and headed for the breakroom, not even stopping at her desk to drop off her purse.

Coffee would help her think. Coffee would return her rationality.

The breakroom was empty, but of course, all the coffee mugs were on the upper shelf again. Lacy dropped her purse on the table and tugged a chair over to the counter. She was standing on the counter when the breakroom door opened.

"Lace?" Logan's voice made her turn a little too quickly.

She swayed to get her balance, but she couldn't quite get it. Hands grabbed her thighs under her skirt, which she wore because of Jonah, but those weren't Jonah's hands.

"I've got you," Logan said.

Her face was warm as she realized Logan's hands were under her skirt and all she could think was how they didn't feel a thing like Jonah's hands on her thighs. No tingling or thoughts of sex at all. Only white-hot embarrassment.

"I think I'm balanced now." She needed his hands off her. They felt wrong. She reached down a hand to him.

Logan removed one of his hands but left the other one in place and grabbed her hand to help her step down. "You could have just asked for a mug."

When she stepped onto the chair, he pulled his hand off her other thigh but kept her hand to help her to the floor. She wanted to say maybe whoever put the mugs up in the morning could leave a few down for those who can't reach, but instead she simply said, "Thank you."

"That would have been quite the fall for a cup of coffee." He released her hand and got down two coffee mugs.

"That's me. Willing to die for coffee." She tried to smile, but her crush had had his hands on her thighs and she'd felt nothing. Not even a microscopic jolt of what she felt when Jonah touched her. Maybe being with Jonah was messing with her head.

"Sorry about grabbing you inappropriately, but in my defense, I was pretty sure I was saving your life." Logan held out the coffee pot to fill hers before he moved to fill his own. "Do we need to fill out HR forms? Or watch a sexual harassment video?"

"No harm done, and you definitely saved me from a nasty fall." She shrugged and sipped the warm coffee. "My hero."

"You're welcome to call me Superman whenever you want." He gave her a wink.

Not even a little thrill at the wink. She still gave him a small smile. "Don't you mean Wolverine?"

"Ugh, please not you too. It's not often, but occasionally a woman will ask if she can call me that." He ran a hand over his hair and his dark eyes met hers with a smirk. "As long as you only do it when no one else is around, you can call me Wolverine."

She shook her head. "I was only teasing you."

She didn't add the only one who called him Wolverine was Jonah.

"Did you guys finish the Timeless campaign last night?" Logan leaned against the wall opposite of where she leaned against the counter.

Lacy nodded. "How about Olly's?"

"All finished." Logan rubbed his cleanshaven jaw. "It would have been better with you on it. You always manage to come up with the cutest puppies and situations."

"I enjoyed working on the perfume. Jonah and I work well together." She tried to not let heat creep into her cheeks. They worked real well in bed.

"Personally, I think you and I would make a great team." Logan's voice seemed lower in tone. "You know, I've been thinking since Saturday—"

The door to the breakroom opened and Jonah stepped through. Her heart did a jig as he met her eyes.

"We can talk later, Lace." Logan walked out of the breakroom.

Jonah glanced at the closing door. "What was that about?"

"I almost fell getting a coffee mug and Logan came to my rescue."

"Are you okay?" Jonah closed the distance between them and his gaze searched her head to toe and back again. He hadn't even touched her and he lit a fire that had been absent when Logan had touched her.

"Except for a bruised pride, I think I'll be fine." She returned the chair to the table.

"I'm glad you aren't hurt." His voice low and gravelly wrapped around her. Jonah closed the remaining distance between them and for a brief second, she thought he might kiss her, but the door swung open.

Jonah stepped away as if he'd never been close.

"Logan just told me what happened," Claire said as she rushed in. She touched Lacy's arm. "Are you okay? I promise to leave a few coffee mugs on the counter for you from now on."

"I'm good. That would be great. Thanks." Lacy glanced at

Jonah briefly before sighing. She was so screwed. "I think I'll go get to work now."

~

Logan's rescue had been the topic of the day. Even after they'd given both presentations and Drew and Morgan accepted them, it was "thank God Logan had been there to catch Lacy."

Fucking Wolverine.

Jonah had hoped Lacy would receive some more recognition for their perfume ad. They'd received praise for the combination of innocence and sexy, but he couldn't help but wonder if their coworkers thought he'd been the one to bring the sexy.

Morgan announced the client they had been courting was Bradbury, which in Jonah's opinion seemed like too big of a client for the boutique agency. But Drew had assured them it would be on a project-by-project basis, not the whole account.

"Bradbury just wants to see what we come up with as opposed to the big guys." Drew sat at the head of the conference table where they had gathered. "They haven't been happy with some of what Hart Association has presented them with. We have a non-compete clause with Hart Association for clients we worked with. Both Morgan and I will be heading over to a meeting with Thomas today to discuss an amendment."

"Smack Robin when you see her and tell her it's from me," Phoebe said with a smirk.

"No one is smacking Robin." Morgan gave Phoebe a chastising look, though she also had a hint of a smile. "Today we need you guys to prepare for tomorrow, because if Hart Association agrees to our amendment, then we're going to be hauling ass to work on a new cologne ad for Bradbury Industries. The turnaround is quick because we're being called in late in the game."

Jonah nodded along with everyone else. There were always other projects to work on in the meantime. Nothing as urgent as the two they just completed though. But the jewelry ad needed work. As they broke up to head to their desks, Jonah grabbed Lacy's arm.

She stopped and looked up at him. The temptation to lean in and kiss her had been pressing on him since the elevator. Fuck, this was hard. He said, under his breath, "Have lunch with me?"

Her eyes widened and she nodded briefly. He drew in her peaches and cream scent and released her arm. Her fingers brushed the backs of his as she headed to her desk. As soon as she sat down, Logan hovered over her. Jonah couldn't hear what Logan said but he felt Lacy's laugh like a punch to the gut.

Fucking Wolverine. He seemed much more interested in Lacy this week, which only pissed Jonah off. If Logan couldn't see how attractive Lacy was prior to this weekend, he didn't deserve her. Besides, right now, she was Jonah's. He wasn't about to give her up just because her stupid crush finally screwed his head on right.

Logan's interest was likely temporary. It would run its course before Jonah and Lacy stopped fucking.

Everyone returned to their respective seats to work. It was much more quiet today than it had been for the past week. Even the phones didn't ring as much. Midmorning, Lacy headed into the breakroom with her coffee mug. He tried to resist for a moment.

Grabbing his coffee mug, he followed her.

Lacy waited for the coffee to brew. The door shut behind him and they were alone for a second.

She smiled up at him. "I didn't get much sleep last night. Can't afford to go into zombie mode."

A flash of desire struck through him, thinking about last night and this morning. She'd been tucked against him and he couldn't resist her warmth. He set his mug on the table and sat to wait. "A shame about your sleep."

Her cheeks flushed as she dropped into the chair next to him, resting her arms on the table. "It's bad enough my roommate wakes me too early with a blender most days."

"That's a bad roommate. Why do you put up with him?" He traced his finger around the rim of his coffee cup while holding her gaze.

Her chest rose and fell rapidly and she crossed her legs, drawing his attention to them and her skirt. He never should have suggested she wear a skirt. If this room had a lock. . . .

"He does have some things going for him," she said.

His attention returned to her face. "Such as?"

"Well, he's tall and can reach the top shelf."

"Very important for a roommate."

"That, and he's so strong, he can open pretty much every jar."

"Amazing. How did you ever get by without him?"

"There still is the blender though." She gave him a fake sad face.

He shook his head slowly. "That is a shame."

"Oh, but. . . ." She stood and went to the coffee pot. "He always has coffee ready for me in the morning."

He walked to the counter and closed the distance between them until he could feel the heat of her body. He held his cup out for her to fill it "Always?"

She turned those bright eyes up at him and said simply, "Always."

The door handle turned and Jonah took a step back before Claire came in.

"Fresh coffee?" Claire asked, practically holding her mug out. Her gaze glanced between the two of them and a wrinkle appeared between her eyebrows.

Lacy nodded and poured Claire a cup as Jonah went out into the office.

～

INSTEAD OF EATING in the breakroom as always, Lacy sat across from Jonah in a booth, looking at a pub house menu. He'd found a million ways to touch her discreetly all morning. Borrowing something so their fingers would brush. Leaning down to look at the screen of her computer, he'd stroked her shoulder. Passing by so he could graze her skirt. On the way here, he'd held her hand with their fingers intertwined.

She needed the water the waitress brought over to help cool her down. She wasn't really reading the menu, but she needed a break from his eyes. She wanted to lose herself in them but that would serve no purpose. Her heart wasn't exactly listening to reason anymore.

"What can I get for you two?" The waitress smiled at both of them, though her eyes lingered a little longer on Jonah. Lacy couldn't really blame the woman. Jonah was a good-looking man, but she did feel a slight pinch in her heart when he smiled at the woman.

"I'll take the pub veggie burger with a salad." Jonah turned his smile to Lacy and her heart started again.

"Um. . . ." Lacy glanced at the menu for a second. "Grilled chicken sandwich with fries, please."

"Great." The waitress took the menus and disappeared.

"Tell me more about Lacy." Jonah's legs slid against hers under the table, trapping her in. Her heart fluttered.

"What do you want to know?" She shrugged. Honestly,

what didn't Jonah know about her at this point. "You know about my hopeless crushes and about my horrible college experience."

His eyes pinned her to her seat. "That doesn't define who you are. Those are things that happen. You fall for guys. Okay. Sure, most girls wait to be in a relationship, but at least you fall. Some people never take the time to make anything theirs."

She wanted to ask if that's what he did. Never make anything his. Not anywhere or anyone. She wanted to know everything about him, but it really wasn't her place to ask.

She cleared her throat. "Okay, how about the basics. I have three older brothers. As their baby sister, they used to look out for me. Of course that meant they also discouraged guys from asking me out. Not that I'm the type of girl who attracted much attention, but what little I did, they made sure no one thought twice about me. By high school, I had my crushes. Guys who it would have never happen with, but I could sit and fantasize about a day when we'd be together."

The server stopped at their table and put their orders down. They both declined needing anything else right now.

"You know what's messed up." Lacy held up a fry and pointed it at Jonah. "I didn't even care if my crush had girlfriends. Even if a part of me held out hope someday he'd notice me, I didn't really expect him to. Ergo, my lack of experience when it comes to guys. But honestly, I'm not sure I wanted them to shatter the illusion of who I thought they were."

"I have a kid sister." Jonah straightened to eat his food.

She lifted her head to look in his eyes. She honestly didn't know much about Jonah. Last night had been the first time he'd actually answered her questions. She never expected him to, but now he volunteered information. She wanted more, greedy for anything more from him.

After finishing a bite, Jonah continued, "I probably wasn't as protective as your brothers, but we pretty much only had each other sometimes. What with moving around all the time with my father's job. You may not have dated, but as soon as I'd start to date someone, I'd have to leave. Long distance never worked out, especially in high school. It didn't make sense to hold onto a girlfriend or even try to keep in touch with a guy friend. At some point, I just stopped trying."

Her heart broke a little for young Jonah. Never having a home was one thing, but giving up on love because it just became too hard? That hurt deep in her chest.

Lacy cleared the lump from her throat. "I could see that. I should have stopped trying when Chet used me, but there was always another guy to obsess over. I did okay after college ended before I started at Taylor and King. It was easy to focus on work and not worry about guys, but my friends all seemed to have someone or some ones. And how was I to meet a guy when I never liked going out."

"Then Wolverine walked into your life," Jonah said with a crooked smile.

She returned his smile. "I don't know why, but Logan just checked off a lot of what I thought I wanted in a guy. Even though I found out pretty quick he was a player. But he comes from a solid family and he's good looking. He's a nice guy."

She thought she caught a glimpse of pain on Jonah's face, but it vanished so fast she probably imagined it.

Jonah's phone rang. He glanced at the screen.

"You can answer it." Lacy picked up her sandwich. "I don't mind."

He nodded and picked up the call. "Dalton, what can I do for you?"

Lacy made a big show out of eating so he wouldn't think

she listened to every word he said, even though she was. And he probably knew it.

"Yeah, I got the email." He listened to whoever was on the other end. "I could be convinced."

Jonah's gaze flicked to her briefly before he turned a little away. "Up the salary and benefits, but it would have to be pretty impressive to have another move make sense right now. I'm just settling into Taylor and King."

She swallowed her chicken and felt it sink like lead in her stomach. Was Jonah looking for another job? He just got here.

His eyes found hers and she forced a smile, while taking another bite of her sandwich.

"Yes, let me know. Thanks, Dalton."

He set his phone down and started eating. Lacy swallowed her bite and took a drink. How did she even approach this?

"Are you looking for another job?" The words slipped out before she could finish thinking it through.

"I like to keep my options open." Jonah shrugged. "I'm hoping Taylor and King works out, but it's always good to have feelers in the industry. Just in case."

Did Jonah do that with everything? Was he even now scoping out the next woman to conquer? The only limit on what their situation was they wouldn't do it with anyone else while they were doing it with each other. Maybe when women like the waitress gave him their number, he kept a stack next to his bed so when he finally got bored of Lacy, he had options.

She set down the last bit of her sandwich, no longer hungry, and took a drink. The waitress moved through the tables efficiently. Lacy figured the waitress would be more than willing to enter into a Candy-type relationship with Jonah. No strings, just amazing sex. She probably wouldn't even make him settle on just one woman at a time.

The back of Lacy's throat stung.

"Hey," Jonah's rough voice was soft.

She couldn't resist looking at him. He reached out and tucked a strand of her hair behind her ear.

"Where'd you go, little bird?"

Her heart pulsed, and in that instant, she realized it was too late. Her heart had done what it always did. It fell hard and fully for the guy who was unavailable and out of her league. She just hadn't noticed it happening because she'd been so wrapped up in trying to get Logan to notice her.

"Lacy?" His finger tipped up her chin. "Everything okay?"

She forced herself to smile. Not that it was hard when he looked at her like that. Like she was the only person in the room. He made her feel special and cared for, but he hadn't really offered himself to her. Just his talented body to show her what sex should feel like.

"I'm good, just thinking about possibly having to work late tomorrow."

He didn't look convinced, but what could she say? *I've realized I love you and that goes against everything we talked about when this thing started. Not that you'd believe me if I told you because I thought I knew what love was before, but I didn't.*

Jonah didn't feel like a crush. He was real and flawed and everything she'd never thought she'd want. But he made her laugh and took care of her and made her feel things no one had ever made her feel before. Getting over him would take her a long time, but until he left her, she'd enjoy what she could and take anything he would give her.

"I'm subletting Brenda's room for a few more months before getting a place of my own," Jonah said. "I really do want to make this work."

She nodded, knowing he was talking about his job and

not about the two of them, but it didn't stop the little part of her that hoped. The hopeless romantic. "But you are keeping your options open?"

Jonah stroked his beard. "It's always good to know what your skills are worth in the marketplace."

She shrugged and looked down at the cloth napkin that would be in shreds if it were paper. "I like Taylor and King. The people are good and the work is challenging, but doable. I don't think I could leave even for more money."

"It's not just an experiment, Lacy. I want this to work. I'm not leaving."

You and *yet*. Those words floated in the air unsaid, but not needing to be vocalized to be felt. She didn't want to spoil what they had by mourning him before she even lost him.

She took a deep breath and looked up into his beautiful blue eyes.

"You know I like teenage rom-coms. Young love seems so much easier and less. . . complicated than being a grown up. But I have no idea what you like to watch on TV."

She gave him a full smile and let the worries float to the back of her mind. She would have all the time to get over him when he ended things.

CHAPTER 20

"Sex."

Jonah's eyes met Lacy's while a fierce blush rose on her cheeks. A small smile tugged at his lips.

Lacy had spent another night in his bed last night and the sex had been amazing. Jonah should have been satiated, but he just wanted more. But tonight they needed to focus on work.

Morgan had multiple ads up on the whiteboard. Half eaten pizzas and almost empty two-liter bottles of soda littered the conference table.

"That's what Bradbury says they want. But what Bradbury says they want and what they actually want usually are two different things." Morgan pointed at the ads she and Drew created for Bradbury before they got fired from Hart Associates. "They say they want sex that smacks you upside your head."

"But when another firm gave them a full-scale orgy, the product didn't do well and they came back to us." Drew opened the ad for Désir perfume. The ad played at a low volume as it was just music. "A missed connection story won out over a torrid office affair ad. They say they want sex, but what they are really looking for is a story and intimacy."

Lacy's eyes returned to Jonah. She was probably thinking about the ad they put together two days ago. And not about last night when they'd once again fallen asleep in each other's arms after he'd exhausted her. A few times he'd had to cover her mouth to keep her noises from alerting Sophie. While Sophie hadn't seemed to catch on yet, Jonah wasn't sure she didn't suspect something. Though with their work schedules, they hadn't actually seen Sophie the last few days.

Lacy wore another skirt today, and sitting next to her at the conference table tempted him to the point of distraction. He hadn't taken advantage of her skirt yesterday until they were safely ensconced in his bedroom. No one would notice if he slid his hand beneath her skirt, but they'd all notice Lacy's reaction. Because her reactions to him were natural, disarming, captivating, and so fucking addictive.

But not for public consumption. His gaze flicked to Logan and Claire across the table.

"For the cologne print ad they had us work on, we gave them two options." Drew pulled up two images. "One after a formal night out, a man relaxes in a chair with a woman leaning over him. The other image though was much more evocative."

"We went with the feel of the name of the cologne: Censured. The scent had deep sandalwood notes which helped conjure the image. Our ad had two lovers beneath sheets in a darkened room. Hints of skin. Playing with light and shadow." Morgan pointed at the second picture. "This is what they went with. The sheets in the dark. No nudity, just hints of skin peeking beneath. Again the main theme of this ad was sex. One hundred percent."

Everyone laughed.

"But it's the intimacy that drew people into the image."

Morgan leaned back in her chair and looked around the table. "We have tonight to nail down a concept for their new cologne, Sinful. This is for a thirty second video ad."

"They came to us for something new and intimate. Yes, they said sex, but what they really want is intimacy." Drew put his hand over Morgan's and squeezed. "We have a bottle of Sinful. Pass it around while we clean up from dinner. The sooner we get a concept, the sooner we all go home."

Everyone stood and started cleaning up. Jonah remained in his seat while Lacy stood up next to him. He didn't know if he could wait to touch her until he got her home tonight. Whatever time that ended up being. The copy room had been perfect to release the tension the other day. Of course, fewer people were around then too.

Honestly, he'd been surprised she hadn't protested more. But Lacy constantly surprised him. In very good ways.

Lacy took the bottle of cologne and sprayed some in the air in front of her. Her eyes closed as she leaned in and sniffed delicately. "Hmmm."

"Do you like it?" Jonah said, glancing around to see who was nearby and who might be listening. Everyone either talked in a small group or headed to the breakroom.

"It smells like warm wood and patchouli." She handed him the bottle. "It's nice."

He held her hand captive as he took the bottle. Looking up at her dark eyes, he sprayed the cologne on her arm.

"Really?" she squeaked and tried to pull her wrist away. "I'm not a man."

"But I'd still prefer to smell it on you rather than on Logan." He smiled up at her and drew her wrist to his nose.

"You could have sprayed it on yourself." She almost rolled her eyes, but she couldn't hide the heat in them. Not from him.

"It works on you," he said softly. The smell combined

with her peaches scent perfectly. Not releasing her arm, he stood next to her and she tipped her face to look up at him. Her eyes darkened and her tongue darted out to lick her lips. Would she ever be able to hide her reaction to him?

God, he hoped not. Her lips tempted him so damn much. When he got her alone, he could kiss her whenever he liked. It was intoxicating.

They were playing a dangerous game. The lines had begun to blur. If someone happened to look at them, that person would likely realize they were more than just room-mates. Not that it posed a problem with work. A rule didn't exist against them being together. Not like some companies.

But he didn't want to put thoughts into someone like Logan's head that Lacy would be open to sex without strings. Of course, no one would know their agreement unless him or Lacy said something.

Honestly, he didn't want Logan anywhere near Lacy, but that wasn't his call to make. That was totally up to Lacy. Jonah had only claimed her body, not all of her. Definitely not her heart. He couldn't hurt her like that.

Lacy bit her lip and stepped back. He fought the urge to step with her. Her eyes held his captive for a moment. She picked up a pizza box from the table and headed into the breakroom.

Jonah turned to watch her and met Phoebe's brown eyes, watching him speculatively. He held out the cologne to her.

"Careful." Phoebe took the bottle and spritzed some in the air before smelling it. "The games we play aren't for everyone."

He nodded. "What do you think of the cologne?"

Phoebe smirked. "It smells like good sex. A little rough around the edges but hits all the right notes."

Jonah started to move away, but Phoebe caught his sleeve. She closed the distance between them and she became serious. "Dragging her out of her shell could make others notice what they've missed before."

He followed Phoebe's gaze to Logan and Lacy coming out of the breakroom. They were both smiling and talking. Jonah returned his gaze to Phoebe who just smiled.

"Might want to lock that down if that's what you want." She shrugged and placed the cologne on the table before grabbing some of the trash.

The only thing Jonah knew he wanted right now was Lacy. But would he ever be enough for her?

Could he even stay? For her? For himself?

Did he want to have Lacy as more than a friend and a behind-the-scenes lover?

Could he watch her move on with someone else?

He couldn't begin to answer his own questions. He shook his head and got busy cleaning up.

LACY SLID the pizza into the refrigerator and sighed. That look on Jonah's face shouldn't still key her up, but she wished they could go home, snuggle on the couch until the temptation to tear his clothes off became too much. Then spend hours in his bed. She really liked being in his bed. Waking up in his arms.

She sighed. Instead they had to work.

"Hey, Lace."

She turned to see Logan standing with a box of pizza. Her body blocked the refrigerator.

"Sorry, my mind drifted." She reached out and took the leftovers from him to add to the fridge.

"Not surprised. It's going to be a long night." Logan leaned against the sink. "Did you get a chance to smell the cologne?"

"Not only smell it but wear it." She held up her wrist.

Logan surprised her when he took her hand and pulled her wrist to his nose. Just surprise, no tingles. It seemed like her crush had faded into nothing. "Have to admit it smells better on you than on me."

He held out his wrist under her nose and she obligingly took a whiff.

"Not bad." She shrugged. She liked Jonah's smell better. Ocean air.

"But not good either." He laughed. "When I walked in, I half expected to find you climbing the walls again. Needing a rescue."

Heat rushed to her cheeks as she remembered his hands on her thighs when she almost fell. When Jonah had put his hands on her thighs last night, she'd practically come unglued. "I've given up my climbing ways."

"Probably for the best." Logan started toward the door but waited for her.

"I'm sure you and Claire already have a pitch in mind for the cologne." She walked with him.

He pulled the door open and gave her a nod to go first. He'd been a lot more attentive to her this week. Two weeks ago, she would have been over the moon and reading so much into it, but now, she couldn't help but wonder *why* now.

"Thank you." She slipped through the door.

"Not a single idea. I'm pretty sure we're going to end up spending the night here." Logan chuckled. "I feel like we are at one of those YMCA overnight things for kids. Except instead of playing basketball and walking around the track, we have to dig deep for a super sexy ad campaign."

Lacy laughed. "Yeah, not exactly the same thing."

"You never know, maybe I'll make you a friendship bracelet." Logan winked at her.

She just shook her head and smiled. "I'd wear it forever."

Logan stopped and grinned. "Good to know. Now I just have to find a YouTube video on friendship bracelet making. Unless you want to show me how it's done."

"I think you're on your own for that one." Lacy's gaze fell on Jonah. His lips were tight as he made his way into the breakroom with some trash. She hadn't seen him grouchy for a while. She almost turned to follow him.

"We can sit and doodle our crush's names in hearts." Logan's words drew her attention.

Her heart stuttered to a stop. Did Logan know he was her crush? Or was he still playing his silly game? Or did he think she had a crush on Jonah? She forced herself to laugh.

"Let me guess." Lacy pretended to think for a moment. "You are going to put Jonah in your hearts."

Logan laughed out loud. "You know me so well."

"What's so funny?" Claire joined them next to the table.

"Lacy says I have a crush on Jonah." Logan grinned.

"She's not wrong. You do seem to seek him out. I'm thinking it won't be long before the two of you are wearing those necklaces with best friends forever split across them." Claire took a seat at the table.

Lacy couldn't stop the chuckle that found its way out.

Logan shrugged. "What can I say, I have a man crush."

The hairs on the nape of Lacy's neck stood on end before heat engulfed her back.

"You have a man crush?" Jonah's gravelly voice right beside Lacy's ear made a shiver flow over her. She desperately wanted to lean against him and soak up his scent, his warmth, his touch. But she couldn't at work.

"It's a secret." Logan winked at Lacy and Claire.

"You mean your crush on Jonah?" Phoebe lowered herself into her chair. "Everyone knows about that crush."

"Shit, the secret's out." Logan dropped into the chair next

to Claire and put his arm around her shoulders. His grin had a silly quirk to it.

"Didn't know it was a secret," Jonah said. His sleeve grazed hers as he walked to his chair and sat down. "You aren't exactly shy about it."

Claire laughed. "Yeah, Logan doesn't have a shy bone in his body."

"I'm hurt." Logan looked at Claire like she'd stolen his last M&M.

"No, you're not." Claire rolled her eyes.

"You're right. What do you say, Jonah? Wanna get matching BFF necklaces?" Logan batted his eyelashes like a schoolgirl at Jonah.

"I think we should get to know each other better first." While everyone laughed, Jonah pushed out the chair next to him with his foot and looked at Lacy expectantly.

She wished she had the balls to sit somewhere else. To not want to be as close as possible to him while this thing lasted. But she didn't want to be strong. She just wanted to be close to Jonah. She wondered if that feeling would disappear when he left her in his dust. Or if she'd continue to moon after him like a pathetic loser.

As she sat, Drew and Morgan came out of their office. Morgan straightened her skirt while Drew rolled up his sleeves. Phoebe let out a low whistle and Morgan's face turned red.

"All right, anyone got an idea or should we start spitballing?" Drew sat in his chair and pulled Morgan into hers next to him. The look Drew gave her was perfection.

Lacy sighed. #relationshipgoals

"There was this one ad that just showed pictures of the notes of the fragrance a while ago," Claire said. "I found it really original."

"We can't copy it per se, but I'll add it to the idea board."

Morgan wrote it on the whiteboard. "The more ideas we have, the easier it will be to find something."

"Fantasies obviously work." Phoebe scribbled in the air at Morgan. "Those are always fun to come up with. Forbidden works too."

Morgan added them to the board.

"We want to tell a story." Drew touched his lips with his fingertips. "But we can also go for the absurd."

"What about taking a cue from your original proposal? It's a great visual." Jonah leaned forward. His knee brushed against Lacy's under the table. "A couple coming home after a night out. Elegantly dressed. Him collapsing in a chair and her coming onto him."

"Not a bad idea," Drew said.

Morgan added it to the board.

"Okay," Logan leaned forward on the table. "I saw this one perfume ad from Gucci that was just beyond weird. Like crazy trippy hippy dippy with Angelica Houston in it. Why don't we embrace the weird?"

Lacy glanced around the table. Everyone had varying looks of doubt.

"Let's hear what you've got." Drew gestured for Logan to continue.

Logan's dark eyes met Lacy's for a moment with a smile. It would have set off butterflies last week. Maybe. Her leg brushed against the backs of Jonah's fingers where they rested on his own leg. It wasn't just butterflies, but the whole damn zoo set off within her.

Out of the corner of her eye, she saw Jonah's lip quirk up on one side as his fingers flared out against her bare leg, sending the zoo into a stampede.

"What if there was this old timey wooden stage. Kind of like a burlesque style stage with huge velvet curtains drawn back but stay in frame." Logan drew everyone's attention. "It feels like one of those really old films. You know the kind with the skips and scratches over it. And this gorgeous practically naked wood nymph with golden wings descends from the top of the stage on obvious ropes."

"Obvious?" Claire gave him a look that said she wasn't quite following his train of thought.

Logan smiled. "Just wait. It should look like an old-timey production. You have this golden-winged nymph in the center of the stage. The music starts out like Mozart, all flowy and shit. And then changes to hip hop and that's when the burly guys run out. Bare chested with flannel shirts hanging open with the sleeves torn off. Maybe short shorts on."

"Of course," Phoebe said, grinning.

"And they circle around the nymph. They are all barefoot. And they circle kind of like Ring Around the Rosie, but more like Nutcracker Ring Around the Rosie. Oh, and they have big bushy beards. And the nymph covers them with gold glitter."

Lacy had to cover her mouth to stop herself from laughing out loud. Morgan apparently had no problem laughing though.

"I will give it you that's really weird and out there." Morgan wrote *Wood nymph lumber jack pixie dream* on the board. "Hey, stranger things have made it to commercial. I'm just saying ideas can spark new ideas. Some of our best ideas came from something absurd."

The scent wafted up to Lacy from her arm. It wasn't a bad scent, not at all. The backs of Jonah's fingers moved slightly against her leg, causing a riot inside her. The scent reminded her of incense Sophie used to burn in college. It would float over Lacy and calm her but also make her long for something more. She never knew what that something was until Jonah.

"I'm always good with hot model guy," Claire started,

"half naked in some body of water, looking all broody with a sexy song playing over it."

"Hot broody water-soaked dude," Morgan said as she wrote it on the board.

"I'm on board with that one. I'm willing to look for the model too." Phoebe raised her hand and looked at Lacy. "How about it, Lacy? How does hot broody guy sound to you?"

The attention focused in on her and she forgot to breathe for a moment. Normally they just skipped over her in these kinds of meetings or she'd say pass. Maybe Jonah had inspired her. Maybe the call-out put her on the spot. Maybe the scent had messed with her head.

"I do like the idea of a hot guy. I mean who doesn't." Lacy tapped her finger against her lip. "The scent makes me think more primal than water though. Not that I don't like the idea of a water-soaked hot guy."

"Amen to that," Claire said with a smile.

"I like what everyone else has offered. We've all seen the cologne and perfume ads where the guy chases the girl."

Everyone nodded and Lacy tucked her hair behind her ear. Jonah gave her an encouraging smile.

"What if we flip the script. Instead of the guy chasing the girl, have the girl chase the guy. The fragrance is called Sinful and with the wood scent, I think the setting should be at night in the woods. Maybe have them dressed formally. Barefoot." She nodded at Logan and he returned her acknowledgment. "Basically playing hide and seek in the forest with a beautiful full moon over head. He can leave a trail of clothes for her to find him. When she catches him, they kiss."

Lacy knew her cheeks were rosy after explaining her idea, but at least she was contributing. Jonah's hand clasped over her thigh under the table and warmth flooded her. It wasn't a sensual touch. He was proud of her and wanted her to know it. Her insides trilled in happiness.

"I love it." Morgan sat at her laptop and wrote down everything Lacy had said. "They could even start at a party backing to the woods. Almost like a regency era party with a stone patio. The music could drift out from the party."

"The music is going to make this commercial. It should have a chase feeling to it, enough for the execs to get the feel, but we may end up hiring out to a composer for the final product." Drew pulled over his sketch pad. "Let's divide and conquer, folks. Logan, Claire, find a suitable venue and outfits for our characters. Phoebe, make sure this hasn't been done before. Lacy, Jonah, do the honors of finding the right song to go with this ad. Morgan and I will work on script and art."

"Maybe we won't have to stay all night after all," Logan said, catching Lacy's attention. He gave her a smile and a wink. He didn't even make her nervous inside anymore.

Jonah leaned close to her and said, "Come on, let's find somewhere private to listen to music."

CHAPTER 21

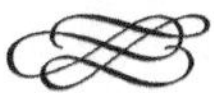

JONAH AND LACY had been in the separate office listening to music for almost an hour, trying to find the right vibe for Lacy's commercial. He couldn't help the burst of pride in his chest. His little bird finally showed everyone what she was made of. He also managed to keep things professional even though they were alone.

The sooner they finished tonight, the sooner she'd be all his.

Lacy put her headphones on the table and leaned into a stretch. "I need a break."

Jonah nodded and looked at her cup. "Do you want me to get you more soda or would you like coffee?"

A soft smile tugged at Lacy's lips. "Coffee please."

"I'm on it."

Lacy made a beeline for the bathroom while he stopped at her desk to grab her coffee mug before going to the break-room. He emptied the pot from earlier and started a new one. It had just started to drip when Logan walked in.

"Hey, man." Logan set his cup on the table and sat down. "How's the music going?"

"Good. How's your part going?" Jonah leaned against the sink and watched the coffee slowly drip.

"Can't complain about looking at gorgeous people and gorgeous places." Logan chuckled slightly before he glanced at the door quickly. "Hey, I've been meaning to ask you. . . ."

Jonah tensed up, wondering what Logan wanted this time. More clubbing? Talk about the girl he scored with last weekend? Whatever it was, Jonah probably wasn't going to like it. "Yeah?"

"Is Lacy still seeing that guy from the club?" Logan rubbed at the scruff on his jaw. "You know the guy that gave her the hickeys?"

"Why?" Jonah had already been suspicious of the sudden attention Wolverine had shown Lacy this week. Especially since the week before he barely noticed her as more than a coworker. She stopped trying so hard and suddenly he's interested?

"To be honest, I don't know. There's just something different about her. You know?" Logan narrowed his eyes at Jonah and sighed. "Maybe you don't know since you're new. But Lacy seems different, more confident."

The coffee finished and Jonah filled Lacy's mug without saying anything. His back was to Logan. Of course, Jonah knew all about Lacy's awakening. He'd enjoyed every second of it.

"That day she almost fell. . . ." Logan made a noise like he was biting his knuckle. "Those legs. Damn, man. Have you seen those skirts she's been wearing and those legs? I thought Lacy was cute before, but something has definitely changed."

Jonah's fingers flexed on the mug. A muscle ticked in his jaw. Those skirts were for him, not Logan.

"Dude, I know you see it too." Logan moved up next to Jonah to pour himself some coffee.

Fuck. The compulsion to hit Logan swirled within Jonah.

His control was fraying, listening to Logan talk about Lacy like *he* knew her. He didn't know a goddamn thing about her. Jonah knew the fragile bird inside of her and the fierce little bird that came out when she was challenged. He also knew she was way too good for either of them. But at least Jonah wouldn't hurt her. Logan could tear her heart apart without even trying.

"Anyway, I hope that guy is out of the picture so I can get my hands back on those thighs." Logan chuckled.

A burning sensation coursed through Jonah's chest. He clenched his jaw to keep from releasing the low growl that formed at Logan's words. Logan didn't say get his hands *on*, but get his hands *back* on Lacy's thighs. Lacy hadn't told Jonah Logan had touched her inappropriately. It better have been when she'd almost fallen.

Fucking Wolverine.

Jonah took a deep breath, trying to steady himself. He couldn't tell Logan to back the fuck off because she was Jonah's. She wasn't his, technically. She was for now though. But he did have an out here.

"I don't monitor Lacy's dating. But I did notice a new hickey, she must be seeing someone." Jonah's voice was rough, but he coughed once to try to disguise it. And if the love bites had faded, he would make damn sure there would be fresh ones by tomorrow.

"Damn, where does she find the time? Between the extra assignments and tonight, this week has been hellish to get out. Even some of my usuals have been busy." Logan leaned against the wall and drank some of his coffee.

Jonah pretended to relax against the sink. He had to figure out what Logan's end game was. "You plan on adding Lacy to your usuals?"

"Nah, man. I don't think Lacy is the type of girl to be cool with hooking up with other girls while you're seeing her. If you know what I mean." Logan shrugged. "I don't normally dip in the company ink, but she's got me thinking."

Fucking fantastic.

Claire walked in and looked between Logan and Jonah. "What's up, my dudes?"

The tension must have been thick, at least on Jonah's part.

Lacy followed behind and hesitated, giving a quick look at everyone. When Jonah held out the mug of coffee, her eyes lit up and Lacy walked to him to take it.

"Thanks," she said. She took a sip and looked at Claire and Logan. "What?"

Claire shrugged. "I don't know. It felt tense when I walked in. Maybe too much testosterone."

"We should get back to work," Jonah said, low to Lacy. Her eyes flashed up at him, but she nodded. She loved his gravelly voice and he knew it.

"When's the next get-together to see where we are?" Lacy asked Claire.

"Probably on the hour." Claire got down a mug and filled it. "Seems like everything is going smoothly though. We shouldn't be at it much longer. By the way, great idea, Lacy."

Lacy blushed. "It's nothing."

"Glad to see you can do more than cute puppies, Lace." Logan winked at her.

Jonah resisted growling at the guy, but that damned nickname and what Logan had said before the women arrived ate at his insides. Maybe Logan really wanted to date Lacy. Maybe he just wanted to fuck her. Either way, who was Jonah to stand in the way?

The guy currently fucking her?

"We need to find that song before we all meet again." Jonah started toward the door and was happy to see Lacy fall in line behind him. Something eased inside his chest.

As they entered the small office, Lacy set her coffee mug

next to her laptop. "I actually think I have a good song. I thought of it when I was heading to the breakroom. Want to hear it?"

He nodded, not trusting his voice right now.

She unplugged her headphones and pressed on her mouse. A piano with strings accompaniment rang out. The driving beat gradually grew louder until the violins began chasing each other. The piano layer added a dark tone to the piece. Perfect for a chase scene in the woods.

"It's a start. Whether we can license it or if we'll have to find a composer to do something similar, we'll have to see." Lacy tucked a strand of hair behind her ear and turned to him with her guileless smile. "What do you think?"

Jonah swallowed. He wasn't sure what he was thinking. Not about the song, but about Lacy. "It's perfect."

"Are you okay? What happened between you and Logan?" Lacy's brows pinched together as she stepped toward him with her hand outstretched like she was about to touch him. Everything slowed down for a second as his mind raced.

Logan's voice echoed in his head. Logan wanted what Jonah had. He wanted Lacy. If Jonah told her, would she go running off to Logan? Her infatuation. The guy she professed to love almost two weeks ago.

Her hand touched his arm and triggered his reaction and returned the flow of time. He pressed her against the wall and kissed her. He needed to claim her. Remind her she was his. *His* little bird. That he could make her fly so high.

She moaned against his lips and gave in. Every fucking time, she gave in to him. Melting and becoming part of him. Seeping into the center of him until he couldn't imagine him without her. They were on the wall next to the door. He reached over and locked it.

The music played on as he lifted his lips from hers and looked down into her darkened eyes. She searched his eyes for a moment, her chest pressing into his with every stuttering breath. He brushed a stray hair behind her ear and she shivered against him.

"Jonah?"

His name brought his attention to her lips. They parted on her exhale. Taking a deep breath, he should wait until they were at their apartment. He needed to step back. They shouldn't be much longer at work.

"Please." She brought her hands to his belt.

He would never be strong enough to say no to Lacy. He captured her lips as she worked on loosening his belt. His hands drew her skirt up and cupped between her legs, feeling her warmth through her panties. She made an impatient noise and he smiled against her lips. He drew her underwear down her thighs until they fluttered to the floor.

She had moved on to the button and zipper of his pants. When she reached her hand into his boxers and stroked over him, he slid his fingers through her wetness and into the heat of her. She gasped against his lips and stroked him faster.

They didn't have a lot of time. Keeping his mouth on hers, he grabbed a condom from his pocket and pushed his pants down. Her hand left his cock and she braced herself on his shoulders. A smile played on his lips at her actions. This wasn't the first time they'd done this. As soon as the condom was in place, he lifted her and buried himself deep within her, swallowing her cry with his mouth.

He couldn't get enough of her. He'd never had sex at work before her. It had never been an issue to wait but being near her drove him almost insane. Knowing someone else wanted to take her away, he began to thrust, quickening his pace with each stroke. Claiming her as his. Any minute they could be asked to rejoin the team. Lacy must have felt the urgency too as she kept up with him stroke for stroke. Her tongue caressed his and he bit back his own groan.

He buried himself deep within her and stopped. Supporting her with the wall and one hand on her ass, he brought his other hand around to stoke the fire brighter within her by circling her bundle of nerves. Her head tipped back as her mouth opened in ecstasy.

He loved watching her tip over the edge. Even now after they had been together so many times, it never failed to amaze him. Her eyes widened in surprise and then softened into a haze as she came down. He could spend a lifetime exploring her body and giving her orgasms and never tire of her.

As her dark eyes focused on him, he had this urge to stay. With her. Not just for now, but always.

"Take me, Jonah." Her hand cupped his cheek and she leaned forward to press her mouth to his. As her tongue touched his, he forgot about everything. Nothing mattered in this moment but Lacy.

He rocked into her. The whole office could beat down the door and it wouldn't make a difference. He wanted her to come again. He wanted to make sure she would never forget him and what he did for her. He wanted to plant himself so deep in her psyche no man would ever measure up to him, as a friend or as a lover.

Her lips opened against his as she came undone again. He swallowed any sound she made and followed her over the edge. Air filling his lungs. His heart slowing. He kissed her soundly before resting his head on her shoulder. He didn't want to move. He didn't want to leave her. But he had to.

He pulled away, gently lowering her to her feet. She grinned up at him and his heart melted. They quickly fixed their clothing. The song had been playing on repeat in the background. He reached up and cupped her face, staring into her dark eyes and wanting so badly to say words he never thought he could.

He fucking loved this woman.

"We should get back to work," she whispered.

How could she not see it on him? How could she not know how much he worshipped her? How much he loved her.

He blew out his breath. He had to leave. He could never be what she needed. Someone solid and dependable. Someone who knew how to love someone like her and protect her from guys like him. He couldn't even admit to her that he loved her.

He couldn't stay here and watch Lacy find happiness with someone else. Someone who deserved her.

Even if he tried to keep her for himself, his love would never be enough. He didn't know how to love someone. He'd never stayed around until things got bad. She deserved someone better.

Lacy had never been the broken one, but she would be if he stayed. He would break her, because that was what he did. He couldn't do that to her. Right now, the only one broken was him and he meant to keep it that way.

SOMETHING HAD HAPPENED. Lacy didn't know what, but Jonah acted strange. They cleaned up and joined the rest of the team to finish working on the presentation. After almost an hour of sitting at the conference table, they decided to take another quick break to wake up.

Jonah walked off with his cell phone in his hand. He'd been texting every now and then during their work. She couldn't help being curious. What drew his attention away from work?

She pulled out her own phone and texted Beth. *Sorry so late. Work is taking forever. We should talk soon. Stuff happening.*

The three little dots appeared almost immediately. *Work has me up at all hours too. If you want to call me, I'll be working for another hour or so before heading to bed.*

We are on a quick break. I'm not sure how much longer this is going to take. Lacy glanced around the office at the others all in their own little worlds. *It may not be tonight.*

The dots appeared. *Okay. Soon though. I miss you.*

Miss you too.

Lacy slid her phone into her purse. She stood at her desk looking out to the hallway where Jonah had disappeared. Everyone else was either in the breakroom or standing around the conference table.

After she and Jonah had sex, at work, again, his eyes had been filled with an almost tenderness. Which of course, made her heart jump to all sorts of conclusions that definitely wouldn't stand up to any litmus test. Yes, Jonah liked her. He liked having sex with her and she loved having sex with him. They were friends with benefits.

That should be it. Except half of them had fallen in love with the other half.

"Hey, Lacy." Logan leaned against her desk next to her. "You staying awake?"

"Barely." She smiled to wipe off the frown that had probably formed on her face. "How about you?"

"I'm hanging in there." Logan's gaze flowed over her and she worried something was out of place from her time with Jonah. But she'd double checked her outfit in the bathroom. Everything had been how it should be and he didn't leave any new marks or beard burn on her neck.

Logan blew out a breath and she tightened her lips. And that was about the extent of what Logan and she had to say to each other. Lacy was too tired to try to come up with something new so she just looked down at the carpet.

"The football game on Sunday should be good." Logan

shifted on his feet. "Claire has to go spend time with her family. I was probably just going to watch it at home, but if you want to learn about the game, we could go to the bar and catch it. Unless you have other plans?"

Her brows furrowed as she tried to understand what exactly Logan wanted to accomplish. Was he asking because he wanted company? Was he planning on asking Jonah too? Or to see if she already had plans? Or was this supposed to be like a date?

The hairs on the back of her neck stood on end just as she was about to tell Logan she wasn't interested. She turned to find Jonah at his desk with his lips in a thin line. He wasn't looking at them, but she had no idea how much he'd heard.

"You can let me know later," Logan said with an easy smile. Probably not a date? He walked into the breakroom.

"What was that?" Jonah asked with a nod towards where Logan disappeared.

"Logan asked me to watch the game with him on Sunday." She shrugged. She had no desire to go.

He grunted and she turned fully to face him.

"Unless I already have plans?" She couldn't keep the hopeful tone from her voice. She would much rather spend time with Jonah than Logan.

Jonah finally lifted his gaze to hers. "I'm flying out Saturday morning."

What? Her mouth dropped open as a million questions flooded her mind.

"All right, everyone. Let's wrap this up." Drew's voice barely registered in her brain.

Jonah was leaving? For how long? Would he be coming back? Was this about that other job?

She couldn't ask him right now. They were at work. But she wanted to know.

Her heart raced and her palms grew sweaty. She trailed

behind him as they returned to the conference table. His leg didn't brush against hers at all.

Did she do something wrong? What did any of this mean?

He said she could ask him anything and he would tell her. She'd just have to wait until they got back home.

CHAPTER 22

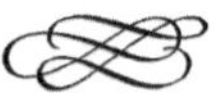

JONAH HAD to prepare for the inevitable. Even if the hurt in Lacy's eyes hit him like a bullet through his heart. They'd finished the presentation and had been given permission to come in a few hours late in the morning so they could get sleep. Jonah didn't want to waste any time he had left with Lacy sleeping.

Lacy smiled softly as she opened the apartment door. She held her finger to her lips as they waited to see if Sophie was up. After a couple of seconds, they slipped their shoes off near the door and moved through the apartment. Lacy opened her bedroom door. He grabbed her hand and spun her to the other side of him. His back was in her open doorway.

She looked up at him and he gestured with his head toward his room. She shook her head and whispered, "We need sleep."

He leaned closer to her. "We'll get sleep."

She grinned at him. "Liar."

A door opened. Lacy put her hands on his chest and shoved him through her door and closed it. It was so damned quick, just like the sofa. Maybe Lacy should have been a ninja.

"Hey, Lacy." Sophie's voice was muffled through the door. "Both you and Jonah got home?"

"Yeah, I was just going to use the bathroom and then go to bed." Lacy's voice was slightly higher in pitch. He imagined her practically dancing on her toes as she made that statement, making him smile.

"I just needed a drink. My throat has been scratchy lately." Sophie's voice trailed away.

"Hope you aren't coming down with something." Lacy's voice grew louder to follow Sophie. "I'm going to do my thing. Good night."

"Night."

The door to the bathroom closed. Fortunately, Lacy had already turned on her light in the bedroom because his little bird was messy. Her room wasn't a complete disaster, but he definitely had to watch his step as he stepped over a pair of black lace panties. Clothes were tossed near the hamper. Her folded clothes still sat in a laundry basket. Stacks of paperbacks covered her nightstand and spilled onto the floor.

Her bed wasn't close to being made. The sheet and comforter were wadded into a pile in the center of the bed. Given how she looked like she'd wrestled a raccoon all night long when she woke up, he wasn't surprised.

Of course, it had been a couple of days since she last slept in here. She wasn't quite as messed up when she slept with him or, more to the point, on him.

She had a bunch of framed pictures of friends on a wall. He examined teenage Lacy in the photos. She had been cute and young looking in high school. The girl next to her looked like she was already in her twenties and gorgeous. He assumed that was Beth, the friend she talked to all the time.

Compared to her best friend, Lacy looked like a child.

Another photo had her surrounded by three guys who looked like masculine versions of Lacy. Her older brothers? There were photos of her in college with Sophie and more recent photos of Sophie, Brenda, and Lacy. Again, next to the sexual sophistication of those two, Lacy appeared much younger and innocent. A recent picture of the staff at Taylor and King hung next to the others. Her eyes in the picture were focused on Logan, and the way she looked at him tore at Jonah's heart.

She'd claimed to love Logan.

A door shut in the apartment somewhere. Probably Sophie's. Then another door opened and closed, closer, the bathroom. Finally, the door opened and Lacy's gaze met his before falling to her floor. Her cheeks burned red as she quickly shut the door behind her.

She waited until she was away from the door before whispering, "I'm not really prepared for company."

"I don't care." He took a step toward her.

She fidgeted with her hands and dropped down to pick up the panties before tossing them in the hamper. "We can go to your room now. The coast is clear."

He stopped in front of her and tipped her chin up with his finger. "I don't care if your room isn't neat or your bed isn't made. I'm fascinated to see this side of you."

"I could fix the blankets at least." Her gaze went to her bed, but she didn't move away from him.

"Who needs sheets?" He lowered his head until their lips almost touched. Waiting there for a moment, memorizing the look of anticipation on her face.

She pressed up until their lips met. He wrapped his arms around her waist and pulled her in tight against him. When he started to trail his lips down her jawline, Lacy cleared her throat.

"Where are you going to this weekend?" she whispered.

"L.A." He kept kissing his way down her throat.

Her breath hitched when his hand touched the bare skin of her waist under her shirt. "What for?"

Shit, he knew she would ask about that. He lifted his head from her throat and went to work on the buttons on her shirt. "I need to go check in with my dad. He lives out there."

"Oh." She visibly relaxed in his arms.

He didn't want to tell her the other reason was an interview he'd lined up on Monday. He slipped her shirt off and let it fall to the floor. "What about you?"

She looked up at him with a question in her eyes as she untucked his shirt.

"You going to go hang out with Logan this weekend?" He tried to ask it like a friend and not like the jealous lover he was.

"It's going to be a busy weekend with errands. I didn't do laundry last week. Or grocery shop." She started unbuttoning his shirt. "I haven't talked to Beth either."

"Those won't take all weekend." He shrugged off his shirt as she helped push it off.

Her hands settled on his abs while his settled on her hips. Her eyes stayed down.

"Do you think I should go?" Her voice was soft.

He wanted to say no. He wanted to stay and spend all weekend making love to her, but that wasn't his reality. "If you want to go."

She looked up at him like he kicked her puppy. Was she hoping he'd say no?

"You might have fun," he suggested, wanting to kick himself even as the words came out of his mouth. Why was he pressing this? Logan wasn't right for her either.

Her gaze fell to her finger slowly drawing the outline of his muscles. "I'll think about it."

It shouldn't have hurt, but it did. More reason to find a

job away from Logan and Lacy. If he had to see them come out from the copy room like Lacy and Jonah had, it would kill him.

If he could even give her up.

She needed someone better than them both.

If she got with Logan, he couldn't be here to see that.

"I wish you didn't have to leave." She pressed her cheek against his chest over his heart and her arms wrapped around his neck.

He slid his hands up to the clasp of her bra. "I'm here now."

That was all he had to offer her. One night to show her the love he could never say out loud.

LACY SHIFTED as she started to wake up. Tingles coursed through her restless body. She was warm all over and her breathing was erratic. Lips caressed across her abdomen, leaving sparks in their wake, and hands held her hips still as she tried to wiggle free. The morning light barely showed through the curtains.

"It's too early," she complained. Jonah's deep chuckle rumbled next to her stomach, bringing a smile to Lacy's lips. His touch was unrelenting. She relaxed into the sheets and enjoyed the morning wakeup.

Last night had been amazing. Even though it'd been late, Jonah had taken his time. It had almost been painful, knowing she loved him and he would be leaving soon. At least it was only for a weekend. She tried to push those thoughts away and just enjoy what he had to offer her.

However, given how late they were up and they didn't have to be in the office until later this morning, she'd really hoped to sleep in. But if she had to be up and the wakeup choice was between the blender or this, this was definitely a better way to wake up, slow and easy.

Jonah settled lower and his tongue caressed her sex. He thrust his finger into her and she caught her breath as he took her higher again. She arched her back. So much for slow and easy. Her body was already primed and ready to go as she slipped over the edge into freefall.

As she caught her breath, Jonah moved up over her. His mouth claimed hers as he slid inside her. Still coming down from her orgasm, she barely even noticed him grabbing a condom.

His hips moved slowly and methodically. Heat built up within her as they found a rhythm together. She could feel herself getting closer as he trailed his mouth down her neck and sucked on the spot he'd already marked with a hickey last night. It was all she needed to tip right over the edge.

At her release, his lips curved into a smile against her neck, but he never slowed. He rose above her, hovering, as he continued to thrust. She held his gaze and cupped his cheek with her hand. Her legs wrapped around him as she stared up into his eyes. She loved this man. The words burned in her chest, longing to come out. He thrust in one last time and held still as he came. Ecstasy in his expression.

She wanted to cling onto him and never leave this moment. The two of them intimately connected and satiated. But she let him go as he rolled to her side. After taking care of the condom, he turned onto his side and looked down at her.

"Good morning," he said as his hand trailed down her body.

She didn't have enough energy to pull the covers over herself. She could feel the heat in her cheeks as she smiled up at him. "Good morning."

"Want me to make you some coffee?" He dropped his lips to hers, lingering as if they had all day.

She sighed and nodded. She'd been right about him being the type to wake up without anything to encourage him. While that was a particularly nice way to start the day, she still needed her caffeine. "Yes, please."

He leaned down and kissed the tip of her nose. A warmth rushed through her. He left the bed and put on his clothes from yesterday while she rolled over and grabbed her phone. It was actually later than she thought.

Jonah opened the door at the same time another door opened.

"Morning, Lac—" Sophie's voice cut off.

Jonah stood there in the door frame. Oh, shit. Heart racing, Lacy couldn't see Sophie, but she quickly slipped on a pair of pajamas.

"What—"

Lacy could almost imagine Sophie standing there trying to figure out what to say. A man had never come out of Lacy's bedroom before. The other two bedrooms. . . yeah. Lacy had to greet at least a few guys before coffee because they were sneaking out of either Brenda's or Sophie's room.

Lacy hurried to the door and slid beside Jonah. Oh, crap, now she had to say something to diffuse this situation. But her mind went completely blank. Jonah just stood there. Sophie's wide eyes darted between Jonah and Lacy, while she held her robe together with both hands like she was the prude of the group.

"Umm," Lacy said, almost smacking herself in the head. Smooth. Totally what was needed in this situation.

Sophie's eyes returned to their normal size and softened. "I'm going to go finish getting ready for work."

She narrowed her eyes at Jonah for a second before going around them to get to her door.

Lacy released a breath and finally looked up at Jonah. His expression was blank. She reached for his hand and held onto it for a moment.

"Jonah?"

As soon as she said his name, he turned and drew her into his arms. "I should have made sure the coast was clear."

"It's not a big deal." She smiled as she rested her head against his chest.

He released her and tipped her face up to his. "You wanted to keep this secret."

"At least we won't have to sneak around anymore." She shrugged, feeling calmer. "Here."

His lips thinned for a moment before he nodded. He kissed her and grabbed the tag sticking out of her shirt in the front. He said softly, "You're a little turned inside out and backwards this morning, little bird."

A grin tugged at her cheeks. "I was in a hurry and haven't had coffee."

"Let me get on that." Jonah released her and walked away to the kitchen. She closed the bedroom door and fixed her clothes before heading to the bathroom to clean up a little.

It shouldn't be a big deal for Sophie to know about her and Jonah. After all, Sophie really didn't have any room to chastise Lacy for sleeping with someone. Sure, their roommate might not have been the best choice, but she and Jonah weren't hurting anyone.

She finally finished and went into the hallway, more awake than usual without her morning coffee. Morning sex followed by Sophie discovering Jonah coming out of her room would do that to a person. She shrugged it off as she followed the scent of coffee.

Jonah sat at the table with two mugs. He pushed her chair out with his foot and she dropped into it.

"Thank you."

He nodded at her as he sipped his coffee.

Sophie's door opened and the tension returned to Lacy's spine. She knew Sophie well enough to know she needed to process what she saw before she had her say. When Sophie walked into the kitchen and poured herself a mug without looking at Jonah and Lacy, Lacy knew they were in for it.

Lacy held her breath as Sophie put creamer and sugar into her coffee before she headed to the table and sat across from them. She positioned her coffee mug directly in front of her and raised her eyes to Lacy.

"You good?" Sophie asked.

"Yeah." Lacy glanced over at Jonah, but he'd returned to his blank expression.

Sophie lifted the coffee mug and took a sip. When she set it down, she said, "So what is this? Because Lacy isn't the type of girl to just give it up to a hot guy. No matter how hot he is, And I know for damn sure, you aren't her crush because regardless of how stupid her choices in that category may be, they never overlap."

Lacy swallowed. Here was her chance to prove she was an adult and not someone that needed protection. But her insides churned and she took a drink of her coffee. Jonah remained quiet, but he was paying attention. She drew in a breath.

"We're friends, coworkers, and roommates." She glanced down at her fingernails. "We had an attraction and I wanted to take advantage of it since my only time was with someone who had no regard for my feelings."

"And he does?" Sophie lifted her eyebrow but didn't look at Jonah.

"He does," Jonah said.

His voice drew her eyes to him. Even in yesterday's clothes, he looked good. He did care about her. Everything he'd done showed he did, but it wasn't love. Even if it was on her part.

"It's not like we're going to fall in love, Sophie." The words pierced Lacy's heart even as she said them, but she had to say them. Not only to Sophie, but so Jonah wouldn't worry she had fallen madly in love with him. "I'm twenty-six years old and it was past time for me to take control of my life."

Even if it seemed like everything spun slowly out of control. That train she had jumped definitely was going to crash and probably career off a bridge.

"What about your crush on Logan?" This time Sophie's eyes did flick over to Jonah for an instant, probably to gauge his reaction.

For her, the crush was completely and utterly gone, but she couldn't say that in front of Jonah. Lacy having a crush on someone else was supposed to keep her from falling in love with him. She was sure that was the only reason he was still having sex with her.

"What about it?" Lacy shrugged her shoulders nonchalantly.

"You still trying to start a relationship with that asshat while screwing this asshat?" Sophie didn't break a smile or anything.

"I know you're worried about me, Sophie, but honestly, I'm fine." Lacy wrapped her hands around her mug and gave Sophie a sincere look. "I'm not looking to start a relationship. I'm enjoying the single life like you do."

"Hmph," Sophie breathed out and lifted her coffee to her lips. She drank the rest before standing up. "I have to get to work."

She met Lacy's eyes again and her narrowed. "You and me are going to have a talk later."

CHAPTER 23

Jonah finished getting dressed before heading to the kitchen to make breakfast for him and Lacy. Sophie finding out was bad timing. But like Lacy said they weren't supposed to fall in love, even if he had. It was time to end it before he couldn't anymore.

Tonight would be happy hour at the bar and tomorrow he flew to L.A. They had a few hours before work started and he knew it was time to have a talk. He shouldn't put it off until he returned.

He had just put the pan on the burner when Lacy walked barefoot and still damp from her shower into the kitchen. She wore a flowy skirt and a button-down top. She wrapped her arms around his waist and rested her cheek against his back. He savored this contact even if he knew he should be pushing her away.

"You okay?" he asked.

"With Sophie?" She stepped away and leaned against the sink. "I'm surprised she didn't find out before now. We've been stealthy, but still. . . ."

He dumped the cut-up veggies into the pan to give them a little time to cook before he added the eggs for the omelet.

"That wasn't the real talk though, so I do have that to look forward to." Lacy winced. "Sometimes I think my friends forget I have needs like everyone else does. I just choose not to go up to strangers in bars and bring them home."

Jonah's lips tilted up. No, his little bird definitely wouldn't be good at one-night stands.

"Though now that I know what I'm missing out on. . . ." She looked up at him through her lashes.

Fuck, he wanted to be strong, but when she looked at him like that, his cock took over the thinking function. He didn't want to imagine Lacy being with anyone but him. Which was why he couldn't screw up this interview. He had to leave before that happened.

He added some cheese to the omelet and flipped half over. "Can you grab a plate?"

She stepped over and reached up to do so. Her shirt lifted out of her skirt and flashed some skin at her waist. His insides were combusting and he tried to hold himself back.

Leaning against the sink, she handed him the plate. "I'll let Sophie know she has nothing to worry about. We're being safe, responsible adults. Who don't have to be to work for another hour and a half and Sophie is at work."

He plated the omelet and caught her molten dark eyes. "We should eat this before it gets cold."

"Only one?" She grabbed two forks.

"It'll be enough." He didn't think he could wait while cooking another, which was why he'd put everything together and had planned to split it in half. With Lacy looking at him like she was hungry for something else, he figured he'd improvise.

He went to the table and set the plate down and before she could sit in her chair, he tugged her onto his lap.

"Is this your thing?" She squirmed to get more settled but didn't try to get off his lap.

Good. "My thing?"

She cut into the omelet and held out a bite for him with her hand positioned under the fork. "You know, some people are into feet. Others are into spanking. Is me sitting on your lap your thing?"

"I do like it." He took the bite into his mouth and chewed while she took a bite for herself. "But I think it's because I like you."

She grinned at him like she'd won a prize.

His fingers started to slowly gather her skirt to her lap while she was occupied cutting another bite for him. They finished over half of the omelet like that.

When her skirt was gathered at her thighs, he took the bite from the fork and skimmed his hand up the inside of her thighs. She parted her thighs and her lips at his touch. His pulse throbbed as his cock hardened even more.

He had to have her. Just one more time. Knowing it would never be enough.

He kissed her neck near where it joined her shoulder. She shuddered against him and then took a bite of omelet.

"This is a really good omelet." Her voice was shaky and her breathing quickened. She held out a bite for him and he took it.

He glided his fingers against her silken thighs higher and higher. Instead of panties, he met her warm flesh. He growled against her neck.

"I knew I forgot something this morning," she said, smugly as she took a bite.

After she swallowed her bite, he slid his two fingers along her slit and right into her core. She hissed at the suddenness, but she was more than wet enough for him.

"Do you want more omelet?" He lifted his gaze to her eyes and she shook her head. "Put the fork down."

She complied quickly. Removing his hand, he stood her up and she started to walk away. He grabbed her hand and tugged her back.

"Where are you going, little bird?"

"I was—" She pointed with her finger toward the bedrooms with a small frown.

He pulled her down on his lap, this time straddling his legs. "I think we should stay right here."

She leaned against the table, giving him the room to open his pants and release his cock. He gathered her skirt at her waist and let the rest of it flow down his pant legs.

"What if Sophie comes home?" Lacy glanced over her shoulder, but she didn't seem too concerned about it.

"Then she'll get a show." He dragged her closer to devour her mouth. Her wetness pressed against his cock and they both moaned. He would never get tired of Lacy or her body. He would always want her. The more he had her, the more he wanted her.

"I want you inside me," she whispered against his lips and almost made him come right there.

He grabbed a condom from his pocket and moved her back a little on his lap so he could sheath himself. As soon as he finished, she lifted up and sank down on his cock with a gasp. He groaned and rested his forehead against hers. Her hands squeezed his shoulders.

"I could stay like this forever." The words came out of his mouth before he could stop them. He should be letting Lacy go; instead he was fucking her again.

Her feet must have found the spindle under the chair, because she lifted up and sank back down on him. She gave him a cheeky grin and said, "I like it better with movement."

His hands slipped to her ass and next time she lifted, he

helped. And when she came down, he thrust up at the same time.

"I don't know how long I can do that," she panted after a couple more times.

"Move how it feels good then, little bird." He rocked his hips under hers and soon she found a rhythm. Every inch of him was buried inside her and her movements drove him deeper.

His lips found hers. She gasped into the kiss every time she hit a good spot. He could tell she was close. She was going to come. He let her lead, happy to follow, knowing once she got hers, he'd be free to find his way over the edge too.

She froze over him as her orgasm took over. He continued to rock against her, drawing it out, making her feel every second of her climax.

She dropped her head to his shoulder. Her whole being wrapped around him in that instant. He stroked his hands up and down her back, waiting for her to recover. His cock pulsed inside her. Reaching behind her, he shoved the omelet plate out of the way on the table.

He stood with her still attached to him, still inside her and lowered her onto the table. She drew his mouth down to hers for a kiss he wanted to remember forever. Sweet and soft just like his little bird. He lifted his mouth from hers and stood up straight.

Thrusting his hips more freely while standing, he also had better access to her clit in this position. He found her tiny bud and tormented it while he drove into her.

"Jonah." Biting her lip, she arched against the table as she peaked again.

"Fuck, Lacy." This time he followed her over the edge. Time stood still for a moment as her core pulsed around him. A part of him longed to stay like this. To keep Lacy as his for as long as she'd let him, but he knew it wouldn't last. He hadn't even made it two weeks at his new job before he made an interview with a traveling job. He withdrew and tugged her to standing with him. He wrapped his arms around her and hugged her tight.

She snuggled against him with her head against his heart. This right here was why he loved his little bird. And also why he had to let her go.

He wouldn't be strong enough if he kept coming back for more. The more he took, the more he needed from her. They separated to take care of the mess they'd made. He went into his bedroom to change his pants while Lacy slipped into the bathroom.

When he came out, she sat on the couch, doing something on her phone. He took a deep breath and walked over. She smiled up at him as he sat down in the chair next to her. Her smile was so soft and tender it nearly broke his heart.

"Just when I think I know everything, you show me another secret." She set her phone on the coffee table.

His chest hurt more than he expected it to. "We should stop this."

"What?" She turned her head slightly like she didn't hear him well. The smile slipped from her lips and he longed to put it back there.

"I'm going to be gone this weekend. It's a good time to end. . . us for lack of a better word." He leaned his arms on his knees and stared at Lacy's eyes. Her cheeks were red and her eyes swam with unshed tears.

"You don't want to have sex with me anymore?" She took a deep breath and blinked away the tears.

"I'll always want to have sex with you, Lacy, but it's not fair to you. It won't let you find someone who will keep you."

Her eyes narrowed on him. "Shouldn't I be the one to decide that?"

"We shouldn't get attached. I may not stay here, but if I do, it could get awkward. I don't want to end up hurting you." He rubbed the back of his neck while looking down at the floor. He was hurting her, he knew it. But it was better now than when he actually left.

"What about hooking up while looking for this mythical beast of a man?" Lacy pulled her knees up, wrapping her arms around them. "Like Candy?"

"You were never like Candy."

"Of course, I'm not like Candy. She's gorgeous and I'm just me."

Jonah reached out and touched her cheek. "You are so much more than Candy. I need to stop doing this and if I don't stop now, I don't think I'll ever be able to stop."

Lacy's mouth opened and closed. She looked down at her knee and then up at the ceiling before she turned those beautiful eyes to him. "What about tonight?"

"With the happy hour and my early morning flight, I don't think we'll have the time." Everything inside him wanted to scream yes. Sleep wasn't necessary. He could spend the whole night making love to Lacy one final night. But he couldn't slip. He had to be strong.

She nodded and stood, straightening her skirt. "Okay then."

He felt like he'd been punched in the gut, but he stood up next to her.

"Still friends?" She looked up at him.

He nodded his head, even if it fucking killed him. "Still friends."

"We want to thank you all for your hard work on the Bradbury campaign." Drew stood next to Morgan at the end of the bar table. He practically shouted to be heard over the din of the bar on a Friday night.

When Logan had steered Lacy to sit near him, she hadn't protested. Sitting next to Jonah wasn't an option because he'd basically broken up with her. Not that they had ever really been a couple. He'd been nice during the ride to work and then at work, but it wasn't the same.

"Lacy!"

Her attention returned to Drew at the end of the table. Everyone turned to look at her and she could feel the heat in her cheeks. What did she miss?

"While it was a team effort, your idea put us over the top."

She flushed with pride as Logan slung his arm around her shoulders and pulled her against him. She'd contributed before but nothing like this. This campaign was huge for their company.

"We'll be buying tonight so don't go crazy. Also make sure you have a designated person to help you home."

Lacy's gaze couldn't help finding Jonah. He'd made sure to get her home before, but he'd given her so much more. He gave her a nod to let her know he'd see her home tonight. She sighed. She didn't want just his protection. She wanted more. But they were still friends, so protection would be all she could get.

She swirled her straw in her glass, not really in the mood to drink.

Drew and Morgan sat and everyone started talking and passing the pitchers around the table.

"Still seeing that guy?" Logan said, drawing her attention.

"What?" Lacy bit her lip. No one knew about her and Jonah.

"Looks like you have a fresh love bite." Logan nodded toward her neck and took a drink of his beer. "I'm just surprised you can find the time. I might need some pointers."

"No, that guy isn't in the picture anymore." Lacy glanced at Jonah, who talked with Claire and Phoebe. He wasn't close enough to brush his legs against hers and she missed it. Of course she was the one stupid enough to fall in love with the guy who offered her no strings sex.

"That's a shame. If you need someone to talk to, I'm here."

She turned to look into Logan's dark eyes. He seemed sincere. She still didn't understand why he'd suddenly become attentive when she'd stopped wanting to be with him, but it was interesting.

"Thanks, Logan. You're a good friend." She used that term specifically to discourage him. She really wasn't into him anymore. At least Jonah had cured her of her crush. She didn't think she'd ever feel a crush on anyone else again. Or feel what she did for Jonah with anyone else.

Logan nudged her with his elbow. "I'll be whatever you need."

She smiled at him but really didn't have anything else to add. She turned to Emily. "I'm glad you could make it out tonight."

"I need to get out more. Grandma says it isn't good to only spend time with her." Emily shrugged and smiled as she tucked some of her blond hair behind her ear. "I just know she won't be here forever, so I want to make the most of my time with her."

Lacy thought that was the most Emily had ever said at one time to her. "I get that, but finding friends is important too."

Emily nodded and took a sip of water. "This is such an amazing accomplishment for you."

"Thank you." Lacy smiled and that tinge of heat flooded her face again.

"I also loved what you did with the Timeless perfume campaign." Emily leaned in and glanced up at the others. "I like that you went for subtle rather than outright sex. It actually seems sexier that way."

"Jonah helped a lot on that one." Lacy forced herself to not look over at him. He didn't want to be with her anymore.

"I'm taking a few classes to up my marketing knowledge." Emily played with her straw. "It's slow going because I can only do so much between work and grandma."

"I didn't know you were taking classes."

"I want to be able to contribute more." Emily smiled. "Morgan has mentioned pulling me in on some of the team projects."

"That's good." Lacy noticed Jonah's attention shift to someone not at the table. Her heart started thudding in her chest as she recognized the woman coming in for a hug from Jonah.

Candy.

CHAPTER 24

LACY COULDN'T SEEM to catch her breath as Jonah and Candy stood smiling and talking together. Was this why he wanted to call things off with her?

He'd promised to not sleep with anyone else while sleeping with her. Now he'd be free to be with someone more experienced like Candy. Who he wouldn't have to help figure out how to move with him. Who just knew more and probably had tricks that made men into her love slaves.

Lacy downed about half of her margarita, the liquid burning like acid sliding down her throat. When Candy kept her hand on Jonah's arm, Lacy finished the rest of her margarita to try to cool the flame inside her stomach. Instead her stomach clenched painfully.

She needed to be mature about this. She agreed to no strings. She just didn't count on falling in love with Jonah. It was probably for the best he ended things before she got too attached. Still, he could have waited at least a few days to hook up with someone else.

"Who's the chick with Jonah?" Logan leaned forward with his eyes practically devouring Candy.

"I only know her name is Candy." Lacy reached for the pitcher and refilled her empty glass. Of course, she'd gotten an eyeful of Candy the night she saw her.

"I wouldn't mind some Candy," Logan said under his breath.

"You should go meet her." Lacy brightened at the thought. Yeah, Logan could distract her from Jonah. "I'm sure Jonah would be happy to introduce you to her."

Logan's eyebrows drew together as he looked at Lacy. "You're not a normal girl, are you, Lace?"

She pressed her lips together and shook her head. "Probably not."

His hand closed over her shoulder when he got up. She looked up at him. His eyes were kind and curious.

"We should talk more," he said. He squeezed her shoulder.

"Sure." She would have laughed, but his expression was actually serious. If he'd said that to her last month, she would have been floating on air. But now, she just wanted him to break up the Jonah and Candy show so the tight knot in her chest would loosen.

Rubbing her hand absently over the ache in her chest, she tried not to watch as Logan walked over and started talking with Candy and Jonah. Jonah glanced her way, checking in on her. Probably because he thought she still loved Logan, she just shrugged and took a drink before trying to focus on the conversation happening around her.

Candy grabbed Jonah's arm and whispered something in his ear. He nodded and she grinned. Lacy drew on her straw, surprised when nothing come out. She must be hella thirsty.

"Plans for the weekend, Lacy?" Phoebe's voice drew her back to the table and her coworkers. Crying her eyes out probably wouldn't be an acceptable answer.

"The usual. Laundry, reading, errands." She glanced

toward Jonah, but only he and Logan stood there, talking. Where the fuck did Candy go?

"Hello, kitty." Candy slipped into Logan's seat next to her.

Oh, fuck. Lacy closed her eyes and took a breath. She could not hiss at the woman. She needed to shake the jealousy off herself right now. She opened her eyes to Candy's green ones. Not sure why Candy was even over here. They didn't really know each other. "Hi?"

"Last time we met you didn't say a word." Candy picked up Logan's beer and finished it. "Jonah really won't say anything about you, so I figured I'd come over and see how you like living with Jonah."

"It's fine," Lacy bit out and refilled her glass with the pitcher to keep her hands from around this woman's neck. Her insides burned. She'd never wanted to do physical harm to another person before. Not even Chet. But Candy brought out that side of her.

"All I can imagine is that beautiful body on display twenty-four seven." Candy pursed her lips as she raked her gaze over Jonah.

Lacy nodded and drank down her margarita. His body was beautiful and so fucking tempting. She didn't know how she would manage to be around him now that they weren't having sex.

Candy laughed. "I was hoping to convince him to invite me over tonight, but he said he's flying out. Isn't that the way with him. One day he's there and the next gone. But his body is worth the wait."

Lacy was intimately familiar with Jonah's body. All the dips and curves and the hardness. . . . God, the hardness. Her cheeks flushed, but she couldn't tell if it was from the three margaritas she'd just pounded or from thinking about Jonah's hardness.

"I hope he doesn't get that job though. I'd love it if he stayed here." Candy pulled Lacy out of her reminiscence.

"What?" What job? Jonah had a job with her.

"Having access to that man every weekend would be awesome." Candy refilled Logan's mug and drank more. "Can you imagine?"

Imagining Jonah and Candy having sex every weekend turned Lacy's stomach so suddenly she almost puked right there. All over Candy and her barely-there outfit. Lacy bolted from the table toward the bathroom.

"You okay, kitty?" Candy's voice followed her, but no one else did.

Lacy burst into the bathroom and clung to the sink. Her stomach settled a little, but then she thought of Candy bent over the counter with Jonah thrusting behind her. It was burned into Lacy's memory. Before it had intrigued her, now it gouged at her insides like a beast. The mirror reflected her pale face, and she leaned her forehead down onto the cool sink.

She couldn't do this. She wasn't mature enough for this. To watch the man she loved fuck another woman. To watch him bring another into his bed, knowing exactly what he'd do. How he'd touch her.

Her heart felt like a piece of paper, crumpled hard in his fist and lit on fire. She couldn't breathe. The air wouldn't come to her.

Pulling out her phone, she texted Beth. *I am so fucked.*

She wet a napkin and held it to her neck. She couldn't go out there. She couldn't be around Candy and not break down. Sure he wasn't bringing Candy home *tonight,* but how long before he had an "itch" and called her.

Claws shredded her insides until she could barely stand.

What happened? Beth texted.

So much. Lacy choked on a sob but refused to cry.

I messed up. Lacy pushed send and then continued. *I had sex with Jonah. A lot. No strings. And we ended it, but I can't think about him sleeping with someone else without feeling like someone is stabbing me in the gut.*

Three dots showed up. Lacy cooled the napkin again in the water and held it to her neck.

I'm coming.

Her stomach settled. Beth would help her through this. It had only been a fucking week after all. She'd never felt this twisting pain before though. Not even when her crushes made out with a girl right in front of her. She couldn't go out there. She couldn't face the possibility of Candy draped all over Jonah.

But she had to. Maybe Candy was right where Lacy left her, just waiting to rub Lacy's face in her torrid affair with Jonah. Lacy shook her head and stared at herself in the mirror. *Get yourself together.* She could do this. She could go out there and pretend her heart wasn't a pile of ash.

She stayed in the bathroom for a few more minutes until she didn't look like she'd seen a ghost. Taking deep breaths, she held her own gaze in the mirror. As long as she didn't have to see Candy and Jonah *together* together, she'd be fine. She could do this.

Just pretend he was like every other guy she had a crush on. Who he was with didn't matter because eventually he'd be with her. A tear slipped from her eye, but she fought back the rest. She could breakdown in bed later. All alone with the scent of ocean and Jonah all over her sheets.

She drew in several deep breaths and blew them out through her mouth. She could do this.

She pushed out of the bathroom and headed to the table. Everyone, including Jonah, was in their seats and Candy was nowhere to be seen. Her chest loosened slightly as she dropped into the seat next to Logan. Maybe Candy wouldn't be an issue tonight. After all, he'd turned Lacy down for tonight and she was convenient.

"You just missed Candy." Logan leaned on the table.

Couldn't say that she missed her. "Oh, that's too bad."

"Apparently she's going to a club. I'm thinking of hitting it up after this. You want to go?" Logan took a drink of his beer.

Seriously? He wanted her to go to a club so he can try to hookup with Jonah's ex hookup who might become his current hookup again because he dumped Lacy? Nah.

"I'm kind of tired. I'm going to call it a night after this." Lacy tried to give him a tired smile. "But thanks for asking."

"Anytime." Logan seemed happily clueless as always. He leaned across the table to talk with Claire.

Lacy tried her hardest not to look at Jonah. She didn't want to think about him and Candy picking back up where they left off. Lacy must have just been an anomaly. An attraction he had to get out of his system, and apparently, he did. Now he would be free to leave and find other women to fuck.

Oh, God, what if the reason he wanted to end things was because he had a woman out in L.A.? She was spiraling again so she filled her glass again and downed the cool margarita. Maybe once the tequila hit, she wouldn't think anymore. Especially about Jonah.

"Maybe you should slow down?" Emily's soft voice came from beside her.

Lacy turned a little too fast and the room spun around her. She grabbed onto the edge of the table to keep herself upright.

Once the room stopped, she said, "I'm fine."

Sure, it was a little slurred, but the man she loved was leaving her. She deserved a little libation to make the pain go away. At least she no longer felt like crying or throwing up.

Now if the room would stop spinning, everything would be sweet.

She stared at the bottom of the glass in her hand. How many did she have? Margaritas from a pitcher had to be less potent than actual margaritas, right?

The party went on around her. Drew teased Morgan. Phoebe teased Morgan. Jonah talked with everyone but Lacy. Logan tried to involve her in a few conversations but she lost track of what they were talking about.

Everyone was talking again, but they swayed back and forth. Were they on a boat? Was she on a boat? She glanced down under the table.

"Come on, Lacy."

Lacy's head turned to Claire, standing behind her. "What?"

"We need to go to the bathroom." Claire grabbed her arm and gave her a tug.

Lacy frowned and looked at Claire's hand on her arm before glancing at the table. Drew and Morgan were gone. When did they leave? How did they get off the boat? Did she want off the boat?

She tried to reach for the pitcher to fill up her glass, but Claire's hold wouldn't let her. She glanced up at Claire.

"What?"

"Lacy, stand up." Claire tugged her again, practically lifting her from the chair.

Lacy staggered to her feet and Claire dragged her through the crowded bar, past the restrooms and to a side door that was propped open. The cold air caressed Lacy's face and she sighed.

"You can't hold your drink." Claire propped Lacy against the wall before leaning next to her.

"Nope." Lacy popped the p and snickered. The cold air slowly lifted a little of the fog in her brain.

The crowded bar hid their table from their view.

"What's with the alcohol binge?" Claire looked at her fingernails and then stretched her arms over her head. "Usually you sip, not chug."

Lacy tapped her fingers against her lips. Her lips felt funny. Maybe they looked funny too. She couldn't see them from this angle.

"Please tell me this does not have to do with Logan?"

Lacy's head whipped toward Claire and her eyesight took a second to catch up, causing the room to lurch. "What?"

"You have a thing for Logan. Now he's acting all nice like he wants to get into your pants and you are probably freaking out." Claire shrugged. "It makes sense."

"What?" Words were coming out of Claire's mouth, but Lacy couldn't see where she was going with those words. Logan was being nice? Yeah, so. He wasn't Jonah.

"Don't sleep with Logan." Claire pressed a finger to Lacy's forehead.

She almost went cross-eyed trying to see it.

"He's not the kind of guy to settle down. No matter how much he thinks he might want to." Claire removed her finger and blew a stray hair out of her face. "I love the guy, but he's got the worst sense of timing. It's obvious Jonah has a thing for you. I think that's the only reason Logan wants to make a move."

"What?" Lacy felt like she was stuck on that one word, but Claire wasn't making sense to her alcohol-soaked brain. Why were they talking about Logan?

"Logan only wants you because Jonah wants you."

"Jonah doesn't want me." The ashes of Lacy's heart tossed like confetti in her chest. Worst party ever.

"The guy can't take his eyes off you." Claire shook her head. "He's been so fucking worried about you all night he finally asked me to check in with you to make sure you are all right. That boy has it bad."

Tears sprang forward and Lacy blinked them away. "He's just a friend."

"That's not the way friends look at each other. Trust me." Claire leaned her head against the wall.

Lacy mimicked her and inhaled the cold air. The air did help a little with the swaying. She released her breath and turned her head toward Claire. "He's leaving."

"Jonah?" Claire turned her head to Lacy for confirmation, then turned it back and shrugged. "It won't stick. He may think he has to leave, but he has something to come back for now."

"What?" Lacy asked softly.

"You."

CHAPTER 25

JONAH BREATHED EASIER when Claire brought Lacy back and swapped places with her. Claire took the seat next to Logan and Lacy took Claire's seat next to him. Lacy sat quietly with a napkin, slowly tearing it into tiny pieces. She didn't seem out of it now, at least.

The pitchers of alcohol were farther away and a glass of water sat in front of Lacy.

When he shifted his leg toward hers, she moved out of the way. She still wouldn't look at him. He should leave it alone. It should be better this way.

But he wanted to still be Lacy's friend. Even if it shredded his heart like her napkin.

"I've got to go if I'm going to make it to Grams before ten." Emily stood, gathering her stuff. "Anyone want a ride?"

Lacy started to raise her hand, but Jonah captured it before she had it high enough for Emily to see. Lacy stared at his fingers wrapped around hers. She'd had way too much to drink tonight.

"Can you drop Claire and me off at Fire?" Logan spoke up.

"Yeah, sure, it's on the way to the bridge." Emily shrugged. "Anyone else?"

"I've got an early morning. We'll Uber it." Jonah nudged Lacy's shoulder to bring her eyes up from their hands.

"I'm up for Fire." Phoebe grabbed her purse and downed the rest of her margarita. She eyed Lacy. "You want to go dancing, wild child?"

Lacy's eyes were huge as they danced around trying to follow Phoebe, even though Phoebe stood still. "I'm good."

"Hit me up if you want to catch the game on Sunday, Lace." Logan leaned across the table and held his fist out to Lacy.

She stared at it like he had handed her something rare and unique. She grabbed his fist and shook it.

"Better text her that one." Claire chuckled. Her eyes met Jonah's. "Take care of our little lightweight. Hopefully she won't be worshipping the porcelain gods tonight."

Jonah nodded and finished ordering the car on his phone as everyone said their goodnights.

Lacy sighed. "Guess you're stuck with me."

"Not stuck." He slid his phone into his pocket and stood, bringing her upright with him.

He held an arm around her waist to get her out to the curb. She didn't snuggle into him like before, just wrapped her arms around herself and stared into the distance.

He was an ass. Everything in him warned him to stay away. She wasn't the girl for him, but he couldn't seem to help himself. Even now, he just wanted to wrap his arms around her and hold her tight against him. But he wouldn't be that kind of ass.

Sending mix messages would only hurt Lacy more.

Fortunately, the car was close.

When they took off, Lacy picked at her skirt. Images of her in the kitchen with that skirt, her mischievous smile, and no panties had him hard in an instant. Add in her peaches and cream scent surrounding him in the back seat and he wasn't sure he could resist tasting those decadent lips.

He needed to leave. Tomorrow morning wasn't soon enough.

"Are you going to be with someone in L.A.?" Her voice was so soft he almost didn't hear her.

"What?"

She lifted her dark eyes to his and he forgot how to breathe.

"Are you going to fuck someone in L.A.?" She winced at using the word fuck. "Is that why you broke things off?"

Her words were harsh like she'd been chewing on them all night and couldn't help but spit the bitterness out.

"No." He wouldn't lie to her. He couldn't. He might not be able to tell her about his stupid feelings, but he wouldn't lie to her face. Not even if it would be easier for her.

"Oh." She fell back into herself for the rest of the ride to their place.

They were silent as they reached their apartment elevator. She huddled into the corner of the elevator while he pressed the button to their floor.

"You just don't want me anymore?" She didn't seem sad or angry, just accepting.

Thinking about what that fucker Chet had done and all those things she'd taken in stride with her crushes and what they had done to her self-esteem, he couldn't let her think he didn't want her anymore. Especially when that was the furthest thing from the truth. He didn't want to push her back down.

"I don't want to hurt you." He kept his gaze on the floor numbers.

When she didn't respond, he glanced over at her. She looked down at her shoes. Fuck.

"I wanted you to find your way out of that box you hide yourself in." He shook his head, closed his eyes and pinched the bridge of his nose. "You are so determined to be in love, you don't even look twice before falling. These guys you crush on were never the guys who lived in your imagination."

She made a scoffing noise and he turned to her. Her eyes widened as he moved closer.

"You don't love Logan because you don't see Logan."

Her lips pressed into a thin line.

"Logan isn't someone who's going to settle down with a girlfriend. He couldn't even keep it in his pants at the club last week for one night to hang out with his coworkers. And tonight he practically drooled all over Candy."

Fire danced in her eyes when she looked up at him, but she kept those stubborn lips closed.

"You want the guy you see on paper and who you imagine he should be, but when he actually shows you his true colors, you run away." He closed in until he could almost feel her warmth against him. "Logan never looked twice at you. He was safe. Safe to fantasize about and hide away from all the real guys who would give anything to have a shot with you."

Her lips parted as if she would deny what he said, but he pressed his thumb over her lips. His fingertips stroked down her jawline. His tone softened when he continued.

"You let guys like Chet keep you from experiencing life and what real love could feel like." He wanted to kiss her right now, but he shouldn't. He had to be strong. "How am I your fantasy, little bird? I never promised you more than my warm body. I never promised to stay."

The elevator doors dinged. She slipped by him and down the hallway. She fumbled with her keys, dropping them. He scooped them up and held them out to her.

"Did you think I'd be your prince charming? Did you

imagine I would be like one of those guys from your movies? Make some fucking big gesture at the end to show you how much I really love you? That we'd live happily ever after?"

She didn't lift her eyes to his as she opened the apartment door. He closed the door and locked it. She didn't look at him as she slipped off her shoes.

"Lacy?" He caught her hand as she tried to walk away. He tugged her to him and lifted her chin with his finger.

Tears streamed down her face. They made his chest ache. He brushed them away with his thumbs and rested his forehead against hers. She took in a shuddering breath.

"I didn't want to hurt you, little bird." He wanted to take away the pain he saw in her eyes. Erase all the pain and leave only the pleasure, but he didn't know how. Not without hurting her more.

"No." She shoved him away from her. Though he could have held onto her, he released her.

She glared at him and he almost smiled at seeing his fierce little bird ready to do battle.

"You have never and will never be a prince charming." She flicked her tears away. "You are flawed and imperfect. You think it's easier to leave than to feel something real? Well, fuck you, Jonah. You had a screwed-up childhood. Welcome to the fucking world. Everyone had a screwed-up childhood or something that hurt them and made them into the person they are today. You're not fucking special."

She paced away and came back. "You cared about me. You took care of me when I needed it. You called me sexy when no one in their right mind would do so. You made me feel something I'd never felt before and you don't get to take that away with your stupid words."

She covered her mouth and looked up. He could only watch her, knowing this was the breaking point. He'd pushed her to this because he couldn't leave well enough alone. He should have let her grab a ride with Emily, but he hadn't wanted Lacy out of his sight. Couldn't stand to be parted from her for one goddamn second.

"You know what?" She smiled but it wasn't a good smile. Her eyes were watery, but no tears fell. "Fuck this. I don't fucking want Logan. I never did. You're right about my crushes. They shield me from feeling anything real. I never got jealous seeing those guys with anyone else. I definitely never cried over them leaving me."

She stepped up to him until they were toe to toe and her finger poked him in the chest. "You can leave. You can go find a job that will keep you from settling in one place long enough to feel like you have a home. But stop pretending you are saving me from getting hurt because fuck you, I'm hurt. I've felt things I never expected to in the last couple of weeks. With you."

Her hand flattened over his heart. "Just because you are a coward doesn't mean I didn't fall in love, and before you say I don't know what love is, a week ago you would have been right."

She stepped back and her hand dropped to her side. "All those times I claimed to love my crushes meant absolutely nothing. I was obsessed and crazed over them, but I never really knew what love was. I didn't know them. I didn't know love until you."

She laughed and tears rolled down her cheeks. "Beth was right. When I fall, I fall fast and absolutely. But don't stand there and tell me it meant nothing. We might have tried to claim no strings attached, but every time we came together those strings wrapped tighter and tighter around us. So go off to whatever job you have in L.A., but you *do not* get to tell me what I feel."

He couldn't respond. He couldn't move. He couldn't breathe.

"I love you, Jonah. So fuck you." She brushed past him and he heard the bathroom door close.

His little bird had torn him to shreds. He was lucky to remain standing after her brutal takedown. Maybe he didn't give her enough credit, but he couldn't back down now. He wasn't the right one for Lacy. He knew that from the start, so he'd do what he always did.

He'd leave.

CHAPTER 26

BETH BURST into Lacy's room at ten the next morning. Lacy had been awake since six when she heard Jonah leaving. His footsteps had lingered outside her door for what seemed like an eternity while she held herself from running to open it.

She didn't want to move from her bed because as soon as she left this room, reality would smack her in the face again. Jonah had left. Her chest ached where her heart used to be.

Beth dropped her suitcase and closed the door behind her. Her shoes must have been out by the door. She climbed up on the bed and laid down facing Lacy. She mirrored Lacy's pose: hands beneath her face, laying on her side.

"Want to talk about it?" Beth's voice opened up a fresh wave of tears.

Beth drew Lacy into her arms and rubbed her back. She made shushing noises, not for Lacy to be quiet, but comforting her. Lacy released the tension in her body and let Beth hold her. This wasn't the first time one of them had to be the support for the other and it probably wouldn't be the last.

"I told him I loved him and then I told him fuck you,"

Lacy said through her tears. She'd been sober enough to remember everything from when they headed home. But not sober enough to stop from spilling her heart onto the floor at Jonah's feet while he stared at her helplessly. "I'm thinking of taking up day drinking."

Beth chuckled. "Maybe just for today, but let's not make it a habit. Is the coast clear?"

"Do you mean has Jonah left?" Lacy peeked up at Beth. The hollow feeling in her chest widened.

Beth nodded, looking at the door like a fierce mama bear ready to take down a lion to keep Lacy safe.

"He left hours ago." Lacy dropped her head down on her pillow. "Thank you for coming."

"Of course, I'd come. This is huge for you and I want all the details. But first, what stage are we at?"

Lacy blinked up at Beth. "Stage?"

"I'm assuming the crying stage, but have we gotten to the angry crying stage yet?" Beth settled into the bed more. She made faces to go along with her speech. "Are we to the play break up songs that make us cry or break up songs that make us swear at the guy? Do we need alcohol, chocolate, or ice cream?"

"I have to chose?" Lacy smiled as the tears started to dry up.

"Nah, no choosing. You want it all? I make a mean mud slide as long as you have a blender." Beth's smile slipped as tears started to flow more. "Crap, what did I say?"

"Blender," Lacy said into her pillow. This was ridiculous, but she couldn't help it. Every piece of her was broken right now. She shouldn't cry because Jonah woke her up with the blender and made her coffee every morning. She definitely shouldn't be crying because Jonah wasn't here to run the blender and wake her up. But she was.

"Okay, this is going to be a long day." Beth blew out a

breath. "I'm going to check to see if Sophie wants to hang out with us today."

Beth pressed a kiss to Lacy's forehead and shoved a handful of tissues at her before heading out the door. When the door shut, Lacy could hear the murmur of their voices outside it. She rolled onto her back and blew her nose. Last night she'd tugged on some pajamas, not really caring what they were. She'd discovered earlier they were the kitten pajamas she'd met Jonah in. And yes, earlier she'd cried about that. Gah, ridiculous.

Jonah was probably still on a plane. She picked up her phone and saw a notification that multiple text messages had come in. She opened it and saw messages from Logan, Claire, even Emily, and then Jonah. Her heart stopped for a moment.

Beth came in and stopped cold. "Why do you look like you saw a ghost?"

Lacy held out her phone to Beth. She couldn't deal with this. Beth scrolled down.

"Emily wanted to check to make sure you are feeling okay. Claire says fuck guys. They're all assholes." Beth glanced up. "I like Claire. Logan wants to know if you wanna go watch a game on Sunday.

"Why is Logan texting you?" Beth again looked at Lacy. "I definitely need to be caught up to speed."

She clicked on the final text and Lacy held her breath. Beth's face gave nothing away.

"Just tell me." Lacy hugged the pillow that still smelled like Jonah to her chest and braced herself for something truly awful. After all, she'd been mean last night. She hadn't wanted to tell him she loved him because it would ruin everything. But everything had already been ruined.

"It doesn't even make sense." Beth shrugged and held the phone out for Lacy to look at it.

Stay fierce, little bird.

~

"Hey, Dad," Jonah yelled as he entered his father's condo. He set his bag inside the door and tossed the keys to his rental car onto the console table. Leaving this morning had been more difficult than he'd expected. Especially not saying goodbye to Lacy, knowing she was pissed at him.

Even after quitting years ago, Howard Sinclair's apartment smelled like pipe tobacco with a hint of mint. It was familiar and almost soothing to Jonah's tattered heart.

"What are you doing here?" His dad poked his head out of the living room and looked Jonah up and down.

"I was in L.A. for an interview and thought I'd stop in to see you." Jonah took a step in and said, "That all right with you?"

Howard grunted and disappeared into the living room. Jonah followed. He'd planned this week off just in case things didn't work out at Taylor and King. He wanted to keep his options open. The intention was always to come out here and check in on his father.

The chairs were all the same, except the dent in his father's recliner was deeper as he sank into it. Jonah sat on the couch. The television was on golf but muted.

"Got an interview?" Howard questioned as he reclined his recliner and picked up a glass of iced tea.

"Boyer Grant is hiring. Pay is high. Loads of travel though." Jonah leaned his elbows on his knees as he stared at the moving pictures, not really focusing on the actual golf game happening.

"More travel. Thought you were trying to get away from that." It wasn't a question.

Jonah nodded. "Just considering. The pay is worth the look."

"What do you need money for?" His dad scoffed and

picked up his bowl of shelled walnuts. "Without a house or a family, you should have tons of money by now."

Jonah grunted in response. Money wasn't the issue. His bank account was why he could afford to work at a startup. All those years not buying anything or even paying rent had lined his bank accounts nicely. He could even take a few years off and not have to worry. But he needed work. Work would keep him sane.

"You've been at this new job, what, three weeks?"

"Two," Jonah replied. Images of Lacy filled his mind. She'd become an integral part of his life. Always there whether at work or at home.

"Always figured your sister would be the one with the wanderlust," his father said.

"What do you mean?"

"You hated leaving places growing up." Howard tossed a few walnuts in his mouth and chewed for a moment. "If it weren't for my job, your mom would have had us settle down somewhere, but she always tried to make wherever we landed home."

Jonah looked at his hands. His mom had been a great mother. Even though a few years had passed since she died, it still hit his heart funny when they talked about her. "You still have the bowl?"

Howard chuckled. "On the table. Couldn't part with it if I wanted to. Before Roxie died, she swore to me to keep that bowl until the day I died and make sure one of you kids got it."

The bowl. It had a prominent place on the dining room table in every house or apartment they had lived in. Once when he and his sister Allison had been teenagers, they had moved to a new place. They had been bickering the whole way. Angering their father and annoying their mother. Neither of them wanted to leave their school behind.

For once, Jonah had a girlfriend and Allison had gotten involved in several clubs and had finally made a few friends. They had settled in a place long enough they had become part of the community. Then dad's job had moved them again.

Unpacking was a ritual for Roxie and she made both of them help. He and Allison had argued over a box and who should carry it when it fell. The box held one item: the bowl.

When they opened the box, the bowl had broken in half. Mom had cried because her mother had given her that bowl for her wedding. With their nomadic lifestyle, Roxie had to give up on keeping everything. Things broke or got lost all the time, but she never wanted to part with that bowl.

Allison and Jonah had spent the next hours running to get superglue and restoring the bowl. It still had a crack down the center you could see but it was together at least. Their mother had hugged them both and placed the bowl in the center of the table. Jonah smiled at the memory.

"Did it bother you that we didn't have a home?" Jonah couldn't help asking. Lacy's words bubbled up within him.

His father laughed. "What are you talking about? We always had a home."

"Not a place to live but home."

Howard leaned toward Jonah. "Where we landed or lived never mattered. As long as your mother was with me, I was home. Roxie was home for me. She was home for all of us."

Maybe that was why Jonah had been feeling so lost lately. His mother's death had weighed on his mind for the past year. She'd wanted to see them all settled, but Jonah's job had kept him moving.

He took a deep breath in and even now, looking around his father's living room, he could see every little touch his mother had left behind. Her grandmother's quilt draped over a rocking chair in the corner. An old picture Roxie had found at a thrift store for ten dollars hung behind the couch. The few bits and pieces of her life were scattered everywhere.

This morning he'd packed up his suitcase and walked out his door, ready to leave everything behind. He hadn't taken everything, but knew it wouldn't take much to get what little he had. But he'd stopped in front of Lacy's door.

He broke her heart yesterday.

Two weeks ago, he would have laughed off her declaration of love. How could anyone fall in love in such a short amount of time? It didn't seem possible. But as he stood there this morning, he wanted nothing more than to go in and beg her forgiveness. Tell her how stupid he'd been. Tell her the words he couldn't find the night before or had been too scared to say out loud.

"As long as I had Roxie and you kids, the place didn't matter." His father held out the remote and changed to a football game. "The stuff never mattered to me, but it did to your mom. That made it matter to me."

Jonah rubbed the back of his neck and almost said fuck, but his father didn't like swearing.

Lacy had become the one thing he couldn't leave behind. He'd thought he'd eventually leave her because that was what he'd always done, but this morning he could barely leave without her. He might not be the right guy for her, but he couldn't let her go. Not until she knew how he felt about her. Not without trying.

But it wasn't just her—granted it was mostly her, but he also liked working at Taylor and King. Tossing ideas around with Phoebe. Emily's welcoming smile every morning. Claire and Logan's weird friendship. The confidence both Drew and Morgan projected to every one of their employees.

Working with his little bird. Watching her spread her wings at work and in bed.

He hadn't been gone even twenty-four hours and he

already missed Lacy. He'd missed her last night in his bed. Holding her while her breath deepened and she slipped into sleep against his heart.

Jonah lifted his head and looked at his father. "I think I screwed up, Dad."

CHAPTER 27

Lacy spun in her office chair on Friday afternoon. Apparently, this week had been a negotiated week of vacation time for Jonah. Not that Jonah had told her, but when he hadn't come home by Monday afternoon, Lacy had asked. She'd been afraid he'd quit and taken whatever job he'd run off to interview for. Even though she was sad, she was glad Jonah hadn't just quit.

This week had dragged without Jonah. Over the weekend, Beth had been there with her and Sophie, and they'd both kept Lacy's spirits up. They'd eaten way too much ice cream and watched romantic comedies.

Jonah never completely left her mind, but she'd had moments where her heart didn't feel completely obliterated.

"I swear." Claire's voice made Lacy stop her random spinning.

Logan and Claire stopped on their way to their desks and stared at her. Yeah, she'd been spinning like a kid instead of working on the art sheet for the Patterson ad, so what.

"What do you swear?" Lacy asked. It wasn't like they knew she and Jonah had had a thing. Or that Lacy loved

Jonah. Or her heart had been broken. But they still walked on eggshells around her. Even she admitted she'd been less than enthusiastic for work this week. But at least she'd shown up, which is more than she could say about Jonah.

A gleam hit Logan's eyes as he smiled. "There's this new place we want to check out. You wanna come with us tonight? The whole gang will be there."

Sophie had left Tuesday for parts unknown, leaving Lacy all alone in the apartment with only her memories of Jonah. Last night she'd snuck into his room and slept in his bed because the pillow of hers had stopped smelling like him.

Maybe instead of crushing on someone, she'd start stalking. Move up the food chain a notch.

"It's a new place everyone is anxious to try," Logan said. Claire elbowed him in the side.

Lacy's brows drew together. She didn't have anything better to do but he was pushing really hard. What was going on?

Claire held up her hands. "He's obviously not selling this place well."

Lacy sighed. It didn't really matter where they went. Anywhere was better than home. "Ok."

Logan and Claire seemed super excited about this new place; besides it kept Lacy from going home to an empty apartment for at least one night. Hopefully it would wear her out and she'd pass out as soon as she got home.

She barely noticed when Logan and Claire disappeared again. Today had been like that. The only one Lacy saw most of the day was Emily. Everyone else seemed occupied. She stopped her spinning and pulled up to her desk. Her gaze fell on Jonah's desk and the remnants of her heart pulsed in her chest.

Melodrama 101, Beth would say if she were here.

Lacy glanced around and since no one was here, she

picked up her phone and looked at the last text Jonah had sent her. *Stay fierce, little bird.*

She never did ask him why he called her that. Maybe he called all his women that. She couldn't even get mad anymore. All she wanted was to see him. She'd settle for being friends again, but she couldn't text him about it. She'd have to wait until he showed up, which should be Sunday at the latest. After all, he still had work on Monday.

"Let's get this show on the road." Phoebe clapped as she came out of Drew and Morgan's office.

"What are we doing?" Lacy could pretend to work. After all it was only four in the afternoon. They had an hour before quitting time.

"Grab your things, wild child. We're hitting a new place tonight." Phoebe blew Lacy a kiss.

"Isn't it too early?" Not that Lacy had been getting much done. But still she should probably work the rest of the day because her whole week hadn't been very inspiring. Her body had been at work, but her mind and heart had been elsewhere.

"Not tonight." Drew came out of his office followed by Morgan. "Since we worked extra hard last week, we deserve to cut out a little early."

Everyone gathered in the front lobby, even Emily seemed excited for this "new place."

"Do you know where we're going?" Lacy asked Emily covertly.

Emily shook her head.

"Multiple cars will be needed. I've got an Uber minivan and an Uber MINI Cooper." Phoebe looked up from her phone.

"Lacy and I will take the MINI Cooper." Logan threw his arm around her shoulder and tugged her into him.

Lacy shrugged. It didn't matter to her.

"Great, let's go."

~

"I NEED to stop by my buddy's place first. Do you mind, Lace?" Logan turned around from the front seat to ask her. Obviously he wasn't still into her because he didn't even hesitate to sit up front instead of in the back seat with her. Not that she wanted Logan to like her, but it left her alone with her thoughts. Thoughts about Jonah.

How would it be until he returned?

"That's fine." She gave Logan a small smile to placate him. She didn't have anywhere else pressing to be.

Logan's smile was almost mischievous. He talked to the driver, but with the music and the fan blowing, Lacy couldn't make out a word they said. She pulled out her phone.

How's it going? Beth had texted. Lacy hadn't answered her yet because she knew just saying "good" would start an inquest she wasn't prepared to deal with. Last weekend had been her weeping and sorting out her emotions. She had to be done with that by Sunday if Jonah returned. She had to be strong.

Lacy blew her hair out of her eyes. *Fine. Planning on drinking heavily tonight. Haven't decided if it will be a whole binge weekend thing yet.*

After she sent that, she continued, *Not really. Going to hang out with the gang from work.*

Beth sent the eyeroll emoji. *You're too much of a light weight to start drinking. Glad you will be with friends tonight.*

He's gotta come home at some point, right? Lacy tried to ignore the flutters that went off throughout her at the thought of Jonah coming home. Not that he would call it home.

He didn't take everything last week, so yeah.

Lacy set the phone down. He'd taken almost everything except his guitar and some clothes. Or was the guitar just another thing he would leave behind? Like her. She rubbed the dull ache in her chest.

"We're here." Logan caught her attention as he got out of the vehicle.

"I can wait here." Lacy barely registered the apartment building they'd stopped in front of.

"You should come with. It might be a minute. We'll order another Uber after." Logan opened her door and held his hand out to her.

She shrugged and climbed out, ignoring his hand. She didn't want to lead him on if he thought she might be available again. That would be really awkward.

"Okay, follow me." He led her into the apartment building and into the elevator. "My friend is new in town and hasn't had a chance to get furniture yet, so don't be alarmed."

"I'm sure if you wanted to murder me, you had plenty of chances before now." Lacy gave him a half smile. It was about all she could muster. It would take a while, but eventually she'd get over Jonah. Of course, seeing him everyday would delay it, but she'd rather see him than not see him at all.

As the elevator climbed, Logan turned to her. "You okay, Lace? You seemed pretty distant this week."

Lacy closed her eyes and rubbed her forehead with her fingers. "I'm good, just tired."

"Did you know that Candy chick is a bartender? Claire and I went to the bar she works at on Saturday." Logan leaned against the back wall of the elevator.

"Hmmm." Lacy didn't want to think about Candy or what might happen once Jonah returned. Maybe he'd start up with Candy again. Maybe he'd be more discreet after what Lacy and he shared. Maybe he would take that job in L.A. and leave.

The elevator doors opened and Lacy followed Logan down a hallway. It was a nice building. Logan stopped at a door and looked at her, expectantly.

"What?" she asked.

Logan shrugged with a half smile on his lips. "Just hoping tonight lifts your spirits."

Lacy narrowed her eyes at him. What was that supposed to mean? Her gut churned as if to warn her.

Before she could ask, he opened the door without knocking and went in. She looked down the hallway and thought about leaving, but to go do what? Spend the night binging ice cream and watching Netflix, wondering if Jonah would actually return or if she'd ever see him again. Pulling up his text and not texting him back because she didn't want to sound needy.

But she was. She wanted to see Jonah. Hear his weird-ass, gravelly voice and have him growl at her. Feel his heat as he stood too close to her. Touch him and know he was as much hers as she was his.

"You coming, Lace?" Logan's voice came from inside the apartment.

She wiped away the stray tear that had managed to escape and sorted herself. Taking a deep breath, she stepped into the apartment. Logan was right. No furniture in the living room or what must be a dining area. It felt really weird, hollow like her chest.

"In here." Logan's voice came from the door off the dining room.

Maybe he really was going to kill her. Man, she had awful taste in crushes.

Walking through the living room, she stopped at the entryway to the kitchen. Logan stood at the far end of the island.

"What do you think?" Logan gestured to the kitchen.

The kitchen was big for an apartment and seemed nice enough. Lacy shrugged. "Don't we need to get going? Where's your friend?"

Logan smiled and gestured with his head toward her.

"I was hoping we could talk."

She shut her eyes at the wave of pleasure hearing that gravelly voice brought her. His warmth closed in on her from behind. The lure of his ocean scent surrounded her. She wanted to lean into Jonah, feel his arms wrap around her, but she couldn't. That wasn't what they were anymore and never had been in front of anyone else.

She wished Logan wasn't here because she'd have to pretend for him. Pretend Jonah hadn't ripped out her heart and left it in ashes. As far as he knew, Jonah and she were coworkers, friends, and roommates.

Taking a deep breath, she opened her eyes.

"I'm going to use the bathroom." Logan gestured toward a hallway. He patted his stomach and winked. "I might be a while."

Lacy shifted to the side before turning to look at Jonah. Her heart caught in her throat. His blue eyes focused on her. He appeared tired but also happy. The dumper always had it easier than the dumpee.

Butterflies flew rampant in her stomach and her insides whipped into a hurricane to blow around the dust of her heart.

"What is this?" Lacy moved into the kitchen, needing space from him to clear her head.

"It's my new apartment." He stopped on the other side of the island and leaned against the counter.

"Moving out?" she said, softly.

"Thought it was time." His fingers twitched by his side.

She thought her heart couldn't hurt anymore, but she'd

been wrong. She managed to force a smile onto her face. "That's great."

Her stupid heart wanted her to move closer to Jonah, while everything else screamed at her to leave. He didn't want her anymore, even as a roommate. Her chest ached.

She glanced at where Logan disappeared to. "Are you coming with us tonight?"

Jonah drew his hand over his beard. "I need to talk to you."

He lifted his gaze to her. Her pulse was chaotic. She couldn't say anything. She shrugged, but she couldn't tear her gaze from his eyes.

"You asked me once if I had a home." He seemed to want her to confirm this.

She swallowed and nodded.

"I got to see my dad while I was in L.A. wrapping up some things." His gaze didn't waver. "He reminded me while we moved a lot, we always had a home, because we had our family. When my mom died, our family didn't seem as cohesive as it used to."

Her heart stopped for a second at the thought of Jonah losing his mother. He didn't pause though.

"As a kid, I didn't like moving around, liked it even less as a teenager, but then fell into a job that kept me moving. Never letting me settle."

Lacy shifted nervously. What if Logan came back in? What if he realized Jonah and Lacy had been more than just roommates and coworkers? "You don't have to—"

Jonah stepped closer. "Something has always been missing. Even more so after my mom passed. It wasn't just boredom that made me take a job that would keep me in one place."

Lacy looked down at her feet. He had this apartment so he

didn't have to live with her anymore. Tears choked the back of her throat. Maybe he just wanted to explain why he didn't want to be with her anymore, but she didn't want to hear the words.

Suddenly Jonah stood in front of her, tipping her chin until she looked at him. His touch sent a shiver of longing down her spine. "I wasn't just looking for a new job. I was looking for a home. Some place I could stay and finally have all the stuff you collect over a lifetime. And I found that in you, Lacy."

She couldn't pull away from him. The dust in her chest pulsed back to life.

"You are my home. The only reason I'd ever leave here would be to follow you. I know I fucked up. I know I hurt you. I hurt myself too, thinking I was doing right by you. I don't want to sneak around anymore. I love you, little bird."

A tear slipped out of her eye to trail down her cheek. He reached up and captured it with his fingertip. She could barely breathe. He reached into his pocket.

"We aren't to the point of marriage yet, but you are still all three choices for me, Lacy."

Warmth filled her cheeks when she remembered kiss, marry, fuck. He opened his hand and she looked down at it. In it was a single brass key.

His blue eyes sparkled with a hint of fear but also love. "I signed a year lease. It's a one bedroom, one bath apartment close to work. If you are willing to share, I want you to be my roommate, my friend, my lover."

She covered her mouth as her heart swelled against her ribs.

"Hang your bras in my bathroom. Clutter my room with all your memories. Watch your teen romances. Pick off the veggies on your pizza. Be my little bird day and night."

She couldn't speak. This was too much. He'd left her, but

he came back. Tears ran down unchecked over her cheeks. He came back.

"What do you say?" Jonah's eyes glistened slightly. "We could also wait a few months and see how things go. Do the normal dating thing. But I really love living with you."

He called her his home and said he loved her. What the hell was happening?

"This doesn't happen to me." Lacy shook her head and ignored the rush of tears down her face. "I fantasized about guys who would never notice me. I'm the girl no one wants."

"I want you, Lacy." Jonah closed the distance between them. He lifted his hand to brush her hair behind her ear. His blue eyes captured hers, holding her. "I have from the moment I met you. I love you."

She swiped at her tears. Her heart pounded so loud he had to hear it. "I love you."

He swept her into his arms and his mouth caught hers. Jonah pressed tight against her. His kiss was tender and perfect. When he lifted his head, she stared into his eyes, dazed. He loved her.

"So," Logan's voice dragged out the sound, "should I let the others know it's okay to come up now?"

Lacy buried her face in Jonah's shirt as her cheeks flushed with heat. How much had Logan heard? Jonah stroked his hand over her hair and pressed a kiss to her head.

"I wanted the office to be here for you." Jonah tipped her chin up. He grinned down at her. "Just in case you told me to go fuck myself again."

She chuckled as he brushed away her tears with his thumbs. "They can come up."

Logan smirked. "I'll be right back."

When the door closed, Lacy sighed. "You don't want to live at our apartment anymore?"

"I wanted to put down roots. I wanted to prove to you

that I was fully committed. To you. To the job. To making this work. I'll still pay for the sublease." Jonah stroked her cheek. He leaned down and his lips pressed against her ear as he said, "I want to be able to fuck you on the kitchen island without worrying about Sophie coming home."

Her cheeks flushed with heat. Her eyes strayed to the island and that storm whipped around inside her. "We should probably try actually dating before I move in."

"Anything you want, little bird. I'm all in." Jonah's smile went straight to her heart as he leaned in and kissed her again. "Since I don't have any furniture yet, I'll be coming home with you tonight."

She grinned. "Sophie is out of town if you want to—"

"So, I'm guessing the copy room door didn't accidentally lock." Claire's voice pulled them apart.

Everyone laughed. Lacy could feel her face growing even warmer, but her heart felt too big for her chest. Jonah still had his arms around her and didn't seem to want to let her go. Not that she wanted to leave his arms ever again.

She pressed her cheek to his heart as she looked at her coworkers smiling at them. Jonah rested his chin against the top of her head. Her arms locked around him. She wished they could try out the new island, but the peninsula at home should work later. She'd even wear her heels.

Phoebe moved into the space and started working on drinks and passing them out. Everyone filled in around the island.

Lacy pulled back and looked up at him. "Very important question."

Jonah kissed her and looked at her with love in his eyes.

"When I move in with you, will you make me coffee in the mornings?"

His thumb traced over her lower lip. "Always."

CHAPTER 28

"You're sure about this?" Beth's voice echoed in the empty room, grabbing Jonah's attention from the hallway. He stopped outside the door. "It's a huge move. You don't think it's too soon?"

"It's not too soon. I love him, Beth." Lacy's voice filled his chest.

He moved into the room and came up behind Lacy, wrapping his arms around her waist and hugging her to him.

"Hello, Beth."

She waved to him on the screen. "Just checking in with my girl."

"She's only moving a few blocks and you already know the reception is good there." He kissed Lacy's neck as he pulled away.

"I should go. Bye, Beth." Lacy disconnected the call and turned to face him with her cheeks glowing pink.

"This is it, right?" Jonah went over to the only box left in the room and picked it up, looking over Lacy's empty room.

A tear slid down her cheek. Jonah set down the box and crossed the room to her.

"What's wrong, little bird?" He caught the tear with his thumb and then wrapped his arms around her waist.

"I can't believe I'm leaving this apartment." She dropped her forehead onto his chest.

It had been two months since Jonah asked her to move in with him. She didn't want to leave Sophie in a lurch. Even though Jonah had offered every day of it to pay her share of the rent here until they could find another roommate, Lacy had insisted on staying in her apartment. To make sure this really was what Lacy and Jonah wanted.

She'd spent almost every night over at his place or he'd spent the night here. And every night, he reminded her how much he loved her and how much he wanted her. And every morning, he made her coffee.

"Your friends can come over anytime and we have a standing dinner date with both Sophie and Brenda," he assured her.

Now that it was official she was actually moving, he couldn't wait to get her home.

"You two better not be having sex in there." Sophie's voice travelled closer until she appeared in the doorway. She smiled softly as she caught the tears on Lacy's face. "Oh, Lacy."

Brenda popped up behind her. "What's going on?"

Lacy looked up and tears trailed down her cheeks. "I'm going to miss you guys."

She slipped out of his arms and went into her friends' arms. They hugged each other tight.

"The only way I saw you guys was because I was here." Lacy's voice was muffled. "Now I won't see you at all."

"Nonsense." Sophie stroked her hand over Lacy's hair. "We have texting and of course watching any love-related reality TV Netflix show."

"Yeah, they come out with a new one like every few

months." Brenda looked over at Jonah and winked at him. They had gone to college together and she'd been his friend's girlfriend. When she'd broken up with his friend, Jonah had stayed friends with Brenda and not the guy. Best decision of his life.

Lacy finally unclenched her friends and walked over to him with a smile as she wiped her eyes. He opened his arms and she stepped into them. God, he never wanted this feeling to end. Every time he held her it was like coming home.

"Do you mind if the girls come hang out tonight?" Lacy played with the ends of his T-shirt and gave him a sly smile.

He smiled down at her. He'd been hoping to break in the new furniture they'd bought. It had been one of the last things Lacy had been waiting for before moving in.

"An early dinner?" he suggested and then leaned down until his mouth touched her ear, whispering, "But dessert alone."

She gasped as he took her earlobe in his mouth and gently sucked on it. When he lifted his head, her eyes were dark and fathomless. She nodded, not breaking eye contact.

"I love you, Jonah." She reached up and cupped his face.

"I love you, little bird." He lowered his mouth to hover over hers. "Always."

THE END

ACKNOWLEDGMENTS

Not Quite Roommates was both easy and hard to write. There were so many directions I could take Lacy's and Jonah's story that I went the wrong way a few too many times, which means bonus content for the reader.

Thank you to Bria Quinlan for editing this book and making it the best possible book it can be. Your encouragement means a lot to me. MK Book Editing for providing copy edits and keeping me on track with my characters. Amanda Bonilla for proofreading and catching the things my eyes just can't find at this stage. Amy Halter for your excellent beta reading skills. And for the wonderful covers, thank you Sarah Kil Creative Studio.

My writing life wouldn't happen without Jeannie, Shawntelle, and Sela. We've been together since the start of this crazy journey for all of us. The encouragement and help we provide each other is necessary to keep me sane in this career.

To the Hermits! Our beach retreat helped me get back on task and a lot of the words in this series were made during our time together.

To the friends I've made during the pandemic and who kept me accountable for every word written. Who knew video sprints were what I was always looking for? To Carrie, Sarah, Holly, Selena, Danielle, Ivy, and a whole host of others: Thank you for being my daily push I need to stop procrastinating and do!

ABOUT THE AUTHOR

Amy Lark is a contemporary romance author. A Midwest girl stuck in the swamps of the South, she lives with her husband, her dog, and two cats. When not writing steamy romance, she's doling out advice to her children and bowing to her pets many demands. Find out more about upcoming books at amylark.com.

ALSO BY AMY LARK

Just Ad Love Series

Not Quite Enemies

Not Quite the Boss

Not Quite Faking It

Also by Amanda Berry

L.A. Cinderella

PUBLISHED BY HARLEQUIN

Fox Creek Series

Yours at Last

One Night with the Best Man

PUBLISHED BY HARLEQUIN

More Than Friends

* 9 7 8 1 9 5 7 6 5 7 0 3 5 *